Under Western Stars

UNDER WESTERN STARS

STORIES BY THE WESTERN FICTIONEERS

EDITED BY
RICHARD PROSCH

THORNDIKE PRESS
A part of Gale, a Cengage Company

Copyright © 2020 by Western Fictioneers.
Thorndike Press, a part of Gale, a Cengage Company.

ALL RIGHTS RESERVED
These stories are works of fiction. Places and incidents are the product of the author's imagination or in the case of actual locations, are used fictitiously. Any similarity to any persons, living or dead, past, present or future is coincidental.
Thorndike Press® Large Print Hardcover Western.
The text of this Large Print edition is unabridged.
Other aspects of the book may vary from the original edition.
Set in 16 pt. Plantin.

**LIBRARY OF CONGRESS CIP DATA ON FILE.
CATALOGUING IN PUBLICATION FOR THIS BOOK
IS AVAILABLE FROM THE LIBRARY OF CONGRESS.**

ISBN-13: 979-8-88579-649-1 (hardcover alk. paper)

Published in 2024 by arrangement with Western Fictioneers, an imprint of Livia J. Reasoner.

Printed in Mexico
Printed Number: 1   Print Year: 2024

CONTENTS

INTRODUCTION 7

Blood Epiphany 11
    Easy Jackson
The Night the Stars Fell 39
    Jackson Lowry
West of Noah 62
    Richard Prosch
Double Trouble 87
    Meg Mims
Gilbert Hopkins is Going to Die . . . 111
    Angela Raines
Foresight 136
    Clay More
The Gunsmith of Elk Creek 163
    Big Jim Williams
French Cooking and Fibs 195
    Susan Murrie Macdonald
Incident at Mission de San Miguel . . 230
    James J. Griffin

Special Occasions. 244
    J. L. Guin
Joe the Bartender Saves the Day . . . 264
    Ben Goheen
Blood Money 279
    Barbara Shepherd
The Miner and the Greenhorn . . . 289
    Charlie Steel
A Little Night Action 308
    J.E.S. Hays
The Midnight Train 342
    Jeffrey J. Mariotte
Cybil 367
    Edward Massey
Hanging Tree Bounty 376
    Benjamin Thomas
Night Trail 419
    G. Wayne Tilman
Taking Bliss Home 454
    Terry Alexander

INTRODUCTION

I started writing stories when I was nine years old. One of the first was about a cowboy whose horse got stuck in the mud. I don't remember a lot about the character or how he wound up in the predicament he did. What I do know is I had a lot of fun describing that mud. It sloshed and splooshed and stunk like cowpies in July. I used words like *muck* and *mire,* and when I ran out, I cracked the old thesaurus on the shelf for more.

My mud *oozed* and *trickled* and even *percolated* in the sun. More than half the story was about that darned mud. My fifth-grade teacher gave me an A, said the tale had great depth, but with a side note she asked, "What happened to the cowboy?" Oh, yeah. I got so busy describing the mud, I forgot about him and his trusty horse.

As an adult writer that memory haunts me. Not so much when I'm putting pen to paper, but instead, when I'm not.

Depth of setting is important, in the written story, and in life. But sometimes I get so busy thinking and talking about the writing environment, the blogs, the podcasts, the social media feeds, the Kindle boards, the signings, the conventions, the organizations . . . I forget about actually writing the stories.

What happened to the cowboy?

Western Fictioneers is first and foremost, an organization of writers — *fiction* writers. Storytellers. That's what we do. There's an over-abundance of groups in today's world that will tell you how to design a book cover or market yourself. At Western Fictioneers, we write stories. We help each other write stories. We encourage each other. We learn from each other.

We get each other unstuck from the mud.

In this, our 10th Anniversary year, I can honestly say without the membership and support of Western Fictioneers, I never would have continued to write fiction in a serious way. I always dabbled, probably would have continued dabbling. But without the early support of this group through blogs, personal emails, and the anthology collections, I never would have made an honest go at it.

So, what happened to the cowboy?

After more than 40 years, I'm gonna tell you. With the help of his friends, he got unstuck. With his trusty horse by his side, he went on to help others get unstuck. At the end of the day, the mud dried up, and everybody had a party.

Under Western stars.

That's how I'd like to think of the collection of stories you hold in your hands.

As the sun goes down behind the long, low western horizon, imagine a gathering of friends who write stories, share stories, encourage new stories, and visit about the craft of fiction. Young, old, new to writing, or an old hand, we're all here, and we all have new things to learn and new stories to tell.

As a reader, you'll find stories about family, lost and found. Tales of Civil War and reconciliation. Gunfighters.

Bounty hunters. Small towns and cemeteries. You'll find ghosts, real and imagined. Adventure and romance. You'll make new friends and rekindle old flames. You'll live under western stars, with a harvest moon overhead and laughter and suspense all around.

Pull up a stump and join us around the

campfire.

Richard Prosch
President, Western Fictioneers
West of the Missouri
August 2020

Blood Epiphany
Easy Jackson

Dudford Washburn rolled over, hoping to blot out the snoring of his cell mate. The blanket underneath him smelled of stale sweat and vomit. Dud closed one eye tighter — the other eye was already swollen shut. Aching all over, he tried to recall the events of the night before. Running his thickened tongue over his teeth, it relieved him to find them all there. Twenty-five years old and he felt like fifty.

"Get up, Washburn!"

Dud opened his good eye and rolled over. The sheriff stood on the other side of the bars, looking none too happy with him. He got up on one elbow, but had to pause before rising because all the blood seemed to be whirling in his head instead of his legs.

"Hurry it up. I ain't got all day."

Dud stood up while the sheriff unlocked the door and motioned him to get out. With a pounding head and shaky legs, Dud did as he was told.

"Your uncle paid your fine."

Dud nodded and followed the sheriff into his office. The sheriff went around to his desk, taking out Dud's holster and gun from a drawer. The door opened, and the sheriff's young daughter entered carrying a basket. Dud removed his hat and nodded his head.

"Ma'am."

A look of horror came over her face. "Oh, Mr. Washburn, you've been hurt!" she cried.

"Daughter! Leave my supper on the desk and get on home. You leave Mr. Washburn alone. He's a married man."

"Not any more I'm not," Dud said under his breath.

Dud put on his gun belt and checked to make sure his Colt revolver was loaded before putting it back in its holster. The sheriff's daughter left with obvious reluctance. Her father watched her go out the door before turning to glare at Dud.

"You ain't much to look at Washburn, especially since you come back from the war. I don't know what it is women see in you. Skinny bag of bones with mousy brown hair is all I see."

"Oh, yeah. They are all in love with me," Dud replied. Except his wife. Or rather, his ex-wife. "Where's Ponder?"

"Outside waiting for you. Git."

Dud walked out, shutting the door behind him as softly as he could. If he slammed it, his head might blow off. Ponder stood leaning his tall, lanky frame against a post, looking out over the street, his big hat pushed back and to one side, showing his thinning dark hair. He turned, running his eyes up and down over Dud, his great dark mustache silent and still in disapproval.

"Thanks for paying my fine," Dud said, rubbing the right side of his face and eye. "I'm surprised you left the poker table long enough to find out I was in jail."

"Poker is what paid your fine," Ponder said, standing upright and pulling his hat down. "What the hell is the matter with you, Dud? Tearing up the best saloon in San Antonio. Couldn't you have picked a less expensive dump to start throwing punches?"

Dud sighed. "Come on, I'm going back to the ranch with you. And don't talk so loud."

They began to walk down the Main Plaza, dodging pigs roaming the streets, stepping over lazy dogs. Poor looking mules with destitute ex-Confederates rode by, while Union officers escorted their ladies in fine carriages and buggies, staring with disdain and curiosity at Dud and the Mexicans and Germans mingling around them. They had only walked a short distance when Ponder spoke.

"I've got to get some bait first. What about your job?"

"Forget that. And I can't eat nothing. I'd probably throw up on the table looking at food."

"I don't care. You can sit and watch me eat, and if you think you are going to throw up, you can go outside."

Dud stopped. "Uncle Ponder, can't you get it through your thick head I want to leave this town right now?"

"Well, get it through your dunderhead I'm going to eat first."

Dud shook his head. "Why did Pa have to die at Palmito?"

He had gotten along so well with his pappy, but he and his uncle crossed swords at every turn. He didn't wait for Ponder to answer, but began walking again. Ponder kept in step with him and spoke his mind fast enough.

"Why did Rayford have to die at Gettysburg? Why did Milford and Bradford have to die at Shiloh? Hell, I don't know the answer. I just know I'm stuck with you, and you're stuck with me cause we are the only two Washburns left."

Dud said nothing, knowing they were

headed for Ponder's favorite dive that sold beans and heaven only knew what else wrapped in tortillas. Mad that Ponder insisted on eating first, Dud nevertheless didn't object as strenuously as he might have, knowing it would be unlikely they would meet anybody they knew except a few Mexicans who would not ask questions.

The little café was crowded, but they found a table in the center, next to a wall. They were the only white men in the place, but in due time, a pretty little señorita came to take Ponder's order. She looked knowingly at Dud and smiled at Ponder before walking away to yell to the cook in Spanish what was wanted of him.

"What about Beatrice? She ain't going back to the ranch with us?" Ponder asked.

"She doesn't want to be known as Bee-at-trice anymore; she wants to be Bee-ah-trice. She says it's more refined. And no, she's not going back." She hardly ever did, but Dud understood Ponder was just hoping this would not be one of the rare occasions she decided to leave the city.

"My things are waiting for me at the stage office. She was getting ready to ship them to me. I returned faster than she thought I would."

The waitress brought Ponder his food.

Dud looked at it and decided he might could eat a little something after all. "Bring me some of that, please, ma'am."

She nodded and walked away, shrugging her shoulders at the *caprichos* of white men.

"What brought this on?" Ponder said, digging into his food.

Dud shrugged. "She doesn't want to be married to a rancher or a mule skinner. I don't make enough money for her."

He had to admit it had been hard on her, being the daughter of a pastor to a wealthy church, where all the patrons wore fancy clothes and lived in fine homes. She was drinking coffee adulterated with ground okra seeds and eating pork belly while everyone around her was feasting on champagne and oysters. Since the war, ninety-five percent of the people in Texas were too poor to pay attention, but there was always that five percent who managed to live high on the hog.

"I told you and told you not to marry that woman, that she was too high-toned for you. But you had to do it anyway."

Dud rubbed his forehead. How many times had Ponder said that? He was not being entirely truthful. "Aw, she was tired of me being jumpy all the time since I came back. I'd wake in the middle of night, thrashing around in the bed, thinking somebody was after me."

The war had affected them in different ways. He had nightmares. His brother-in-law hardly spoke and spent hours alone. When Ponder was not working cattle or around the ranch, he would be in a saloon or the back room of a store, compulsively playing one card game after another until he dropped with exhaustion or ran out of money.

"What does her pa think about this, him being a man of the cloth?"

"It doesn't matter what he thinks; you know that, Uncle Ponder. It's whatever Beatrice and her mother tell him to do. And they told him to get her the quickest and quietest divorce he could."

The waitress brought Dud's food. As he nodded his thanks, she gave him a sly wink before leaving. Conversation swirled at the tables around them, all of it in Spanish. He was a fair hand at Spanish, and Ponder spoke it better than some Mexicans did, but he wasn't interested in what they were saying. He sat for a minute before blurting, "She told me not to be coming back to San Antonio, and if I did, to pretend I didn't know who she was. They are going to tell people her husband died. She said it was better for her reputation."

"You gonna take that lying down?"

"Yeah, Uncle Ponder, I am," Dud said, his voice getting loud. He strove to lower it. "What difference does it make? It's not likely I will to be moving in her circle of friends no how."

Ponder stared at him while chewing on his food. He swallowed and spoke. "There's more to it than what you're telling me."

Dud did not know if he should keep it to himself or not. He decided to admit part of it.

"She wants to have children, and she thinks she ain't gonna get any out of me."

Her exact words were, "Let's face it, Dud, you're shooting blanks just like Ponder." Ponder had been married two or three times, and none of those women had missed so much as one monthly cycle. But they had not left him because of it. Fever and disease killed them, not childbirth or lack of it.

That painful confession stopped all conversation, and the two men ate in silence. Dud ruminated in his own world. Maybe if he had made plenty of money, she would have overlooked not having children and stayed with him.

The men behind him were loud and boisterous, and it irritated him that he could not eat in peace when his world was crumbling. He could feel his heart pounding, and his blood getting hotter and hotter as they kept on talking and boasting.

He looked up to see Ponder staring at him.

"I ain't got no more money to get you out of jail."

Dud nodded and felt his anger draining away. It was not anybody else's fault his wife did not want him. He bent his head down and took another bite.

He had just started to chew when a fat man one table over jumped up and began screaming, running the words together so fast, Dud could not at first catch what he was saying.

The irate man was hollering toward the kitchen, and picking up something from his plate, he threw it at the cook. He spouted a lot of Mexican cuss words, and something about the cattle roaming the outskirts of town being as thick as fleas, so why did they have to serve him a cat's jaw?

As soon as Dud heard *mandíbula de gato,* he spit his food out, he and Ponder leaping from the table at the same time. Throwing money down, they escaped in a hurry, before chairs started being thrown and knives were drawn.

Dud took one last look through the doorway at the melee beginning inside before striding away, keeping up with Ponder and his long legs.

"That's the last time you are taking me into that place."

"Quit bellyaching, Dud. You know you've had to eat worse. Come on, let's go to the station and pick up your things."

Dusk began to fall on their way to the stagecoach station, and they argued back and forth. Dud wanted to go leave San Antonio immediately and lick his wounds in the privacy of darkness. Ponder wanted to sleep in the stables and head out just before daylight.

Approaching an itinerate preacher standing on a chair and exhorting a crowd in the fading light, they stopped cussing one another long enough to get past the preacher.

"For God has tested us; He has tried us as silver is tried. He has laid a crushing burden on our backs," the preacher cried in a loud voice. "We have gone through fire and through water, yet God has brought us to a place of abundance, brothers and sisters."

Someone picked up a rock and threw it at the preacher, narrowly missing his head. "You lie, preacher! There ain't no abundance here!"

He stooped to pick up another rock, but before he could, Ponder lifted one of his boots and kicked him firmly in the back. The man fell face down and rolled over on his side. Ponder kicked him again in the stomach.

"Show some manners. That ain't no way to speak to a man of God."

All he did was groan and vomit. Dud pulled on Ponder's arm.

"I ain't got no money to get you out of jail either, old man."

They walked in silence along the darkening street, Dud again inwardly lamenting his lack of funds. If he just had a big enough wad of money to buy her a fine house, maybe she would come back to him.

The stagecoach station operated out of one of the finer hotels. Always a busy spot, the sidewalks hummed with activity despite the fading light. The stagecoach had been late coming in, and people jockeyed around it, reaching for their baggage or greeting the folks waiting for them. Dud and Ponder pushed their way through toward the hotel doors. The flickering street lanterns above their heads lit the face of a severe looking woman with a harsh New England accent who had just alighted. She upbraided her husband with little care that anyone around them could hear every word spoken. Dud forced himself to shove down the anger that always rose when he saw people of the North flocking to Texas to take advantage of a broken and defeated people. They had asked for the trouble they had, but that did not make it any easier to swallow.

". . . bring me to this godforsaken place," the woman was saying. "Those cattle with those beastly long horns, blocking the road, making travel impossible . . . ."

Dud looked at the husband — nodding, trying to calm his wife while he felt completely out of place and unsure of what to do — and he suddenly felt better. Men in the North had just as many marital troubles as men in the South. He felt like patting him on the back and saying, "I understand, brother."

He and Ponder went inside, making their way through the bustling crowd to the ticket counter. Polished wood and shining brass were everywhere, gleaming in the glow from overhead lamps that managed to hold on to the illusion of genteel prosperity in a state now raw with upheaval. Just as Dud was about to introduce himself to the clerk, a tall man in a well-cut suit cut in front of him.

"I need two tickets for Corpus Christi and get with it. I'm in a hurry."

Dud glared at him — he was one of those men who had stayed home from war "to take care of business" and somehow managed to amass a personal fortune while everyone around him went hungry. He had a beak of a nose that made him look like a parrot, and Dud was getting ready to rare back and hit it when Ponder strode on his boot.

Dud scowled at Ponder but let go of his anger. All he wanted to do was get out of San Antonio as soon as possible.

"That will be twenty-five dollars," the ticket clerk said.

He threw money on the counter, grabbed the tickets and left. Dud and Ponder in their cowboy attire were invisible to him. Dud stepped forward and gave the clerk his name.

"I'm here to pick up some crates that were addressed to me in Goliad."

The clerk in his visor and gartered sleeves gave him a keen look. "There's only one package here with your name on it, Mr. Washburn."

He reached under the counter and brought out a lump wrapped in brown paper, throwing it on the counter in front of Dud.

Dud took it, like a man in a dream. It was soft and pliable, and he knew inside would be the few clothes he owned. All the tools he had collected, his books, the rifle that had belonged to his father — all of them gone.

He turned around, looking at Ponder with unbelieving eyes. He swallowed hard and made his way out of the hotel with Ponder at his heels. At the stable, they saddled their horses in the dark and left San Antonio with barely three or four sentences spoken between them.

"At least she left me the ranch."

"You better check at the courthouse when we get home and make sure."

After that, conversation bit the dust, and all that could be heard was the sound of horses' hooves pounding on the parallel dirt trails that served as a road. Keeping a steady pace, it would take them four days to get to the Washburn ranch. Despite the blackness of the night, they knew the way well, and late into that first evening, they stopped at the home of a longtime friend.

"I got nothing, Dud," he said as they sat outside with only an occasional star peeking through the clouds for light. "The Confederate Army swept through here and took every animal on the place. It took me a year to raise enough money for a horse and one old mule that I got to guard ever night like they was gold."

With a shotgun across his lap, he talked about a mutual acquaintance who was making a little cash rounding up wild mustangs on the prairie and selling them.

"He rides with them for miles, never letting them stop for food or water, until he can work them to getting into a pen he made around an old watering hole."

They talked far into the night, discussing horses, cattle, politics, and naturally, women. Dud gave their host a brief account of his divorce. While sympathetic to Dud's troubles, he and Ponder mercifully did not press him for more details. Not that there were that many to tell.

They left the next morning, refreshed and feeling better, with their friend standing on the veranda waving goodbye and calling, "Y'all come see me now and then."

They intended on spending the following night in the next town. Because they had stayed later at their friend's ranch than they had planned, it was dusk when they finally rode into town, stopping to stable their horses before heading for a saloon where they hoped to meet an old acquaintance or two who might invite them home for the night. Otherwise, they would go back to the stable and sleep with the horses.

As they made their way to the saloon, Dud looked up and down the empty streets. "Where the hell is everybody?"

"Danged if I know," Ponder answered.

The saloon, however, was crowded. Ponder immediately found a poker game to join while Dud stood at the bar. He was not much of a drinker and could nurse a beer for half the night if he had someone to talk to, and thankfully, several men he knew came in and joined him. They answered his question readily enough.

"The Union Army has taken up residence. You know we're under martial law. Don't go anywhere at night by yourself, Dud. It ain't safe."

Dud looked around. "Then why the hell aren't they in here? I never knew a career army soldier that couldn't drink his weight in whiskey in one night."

"They will be. Their money is welcome, but they ain't. If they settle in for too long, the place will slowly empty until they ain't nobody left but them, so old Joe there," he said, motioning his head to the bartender, "makes sure they don't overstay their welcome."

Dud glanced at the bartender with his striped shirt, bowtie, and dark hair parted and slicked down with bear grease. "How does he do that?" he asked, turning back to his companion.

The man took a long drink and turned, placing his elbows on the bar as he surveyed the room.

"Varnish solvent," he said, not looking at Dud. "It gets stronger as the night goes on, until their bellies begin to feel afire."

Dud grimaced into his glass and took another sip. Outside, a lamplighter was going up and down the street, lighting coal oil lanterns that gave the night a soft glow. The lanterns in the saloon had already been lit in readiness for nightfall.

Shadows were flickering on the wall when the soldiers came in about an hour later, six of them. As soon as they entered, men stopped talking, and the saloon became as quiet as a church house on a Friday night. Knowing better than to stare openly and invite trouble, Dud gave discreet looks into the mirror behind the bar. He counted five enlisted men led by a big, burly sergeant who looked like he chewed glass for supper.

They sat at a table behind him, boisterous

and noisy at first, pretending they were not the cause of the unnatural silence in the room.

Dud glanced in the mirror at the table where Ponder sat playing poker. It was as if they were playing in some kind of sign language, because no lips moved.

After a while, when the soldiers had started in on their second and third bottles of whiskey, they began to complain and speak disparaging remarks about Texas in general, hoping to get a rise.

"If New Mexico Territory was the devil's playground, then this place is hell's kitchen."

"Fort Sumner with its starving Indians was a picnic compared to this."

"The only thing that smells worse than an Indian is a Texan."

When no one responded, they started in on Confederate soldiers. Still, the room remained silent.

"And you know who were the worst cowards of them all?" the sergeant blared. "The Eighth Texas Cavalry, that's who."

Dud did not think he let his back stiffen, but they must have picked up on some vibration from him. He had been one of Terry's Rangers.

They continued their verbal assault on the

Eighth Texas, mocking their reputation, calling them yellow cur dogs and the like. Men who had been standing by Dud at the bar silently drifted away, until he was left standing alone. Two nights before, he had been looking for a bar fight, now that one was offered to him, he did not necessarily want it.

He looked in the mirror at Ponder. When Ponder was ready for a brawl, he would spit out his wad of chewing tobacco so he did not accidentally swallow it. But Ponder's lower lip still had a telltale bulge, and he concentrated heavily on his cards. Ponder, who never backed down from a fight, for some reason did not want Dud to start one in this barroom.

As Dud looked into his beer glass, and the soldiers behind him continued a rant against his fallen comrades that ordinarily would have had his fists flying, he realized why. All of Texas was under martial law. The newspapers reported Major General Phillip Sheridan, the military commander of Texas and Louisiana as saying, "Texas has not yet suffered from the war and will require some intimidation." And he intended to see that they got it.

If the army wanted to, they could arrest every man in the saloon and keep them in jail so long, they would not be able to feed their family and could possibly lose everything they owned. Instead of fighting, they had to sit in silent hatred, and they were asking Dud not to make them join him in a public fight that could cost them their livelihood.

So, he said nothing, believing the soldiers would approach him any minute and start one on their own. To his surprise, they did not, and glancing in the mirror, he saw the sergeant put his hand out to stop someone in midsentence. He looked at Dud and motioned to his men to leave.

They rose from the table and departed, the sergeant the last one out the door.

The noise level did not rise immediately. It took some time before the saloon returned to normal. In the meantime, Dud remained at the bar, starting his second beer as his companions drifted back to him. All of them, himself included, began to talk about horses, cattle, and women again as if they had never been interrupted.

After a while, Dud grew restless. He walked over to Ponder's game to stand and watch for a while. But Ponder's pile of money stayed more or less the same, and Dud knew he would continue to play as long as he had money and someone to keep dealing the cards to him.

Dud left him and went to the door, looking over the batwings at the dimly lit street.

A young woman appeared, walking timidly, looking over her shoulder as if she was afraid. Dud glanced back at the poker players. Ponder's pile had grown larger, not smaller. He turned to look outside again at the woman who seemed so all alone and scared.

Without hesitation, he pushed open the swinging doors and walked across the street.

The wind blew in little gusts, picking up bits of trash, lifting them up to swirl and depositing them farther down the street. Dud looked right and left, but the streets remained deserted. He removed his hat as he approached the woman.

When she saw him, she put a hand to her breast. "Oh, you frightened me!"

"I'm sorry, ma'am. You look a little scared out here. May I escort you somewhere?"

In the light of the lantern, she looked older than he had first thought and a lot harder. But he did not retract his offer. She gave him an unsure glance, and said, "I guess so. I stayed at my friend's house longer than I intended."

Dud held out his arm, and she put her hand on it. They began walking together on the wooden sidewalk.

"My name's Dud Washburn, from down Goliad way," Dud stated.

"Oh, yes, I know exactly where that's at," she said, her eyes glancing anxiously up the street.

As they walked by an alley, she paused, moving her hand up his sleeve. She raised her lips, and before he knew what was happening, she was kissing his lips and groping him all over. At the heels of the first shock came a tremendous rush of pleasure, and just as the warning bells were beginning to make themselves heard, she removed her hands and melted into the darkness.

His hand went to his holster, but the pistol was gone. Before he could chase after her, the six soldiers from the saloon stepped out of the alley, casting long shadows and blocking his way. One of them held an ax handle in one hand that he used to pound rhythmically in the palm of the other. The big burly sergeant was rolling up his sleeves with a look of glee on his face.

Dud knew he was in for it; nevertheless, he took the offensive and charged in. He managed to knock two of them down before the others grabbed his arms and held him. The sergeant took a sadistic swing at his abdomen, and Dud bent over, his mouth filling with vomit. While they laughed, Dud shot out a foot, kicking one of them in the groin. Dud used their surprise to escape, but they rallied, catching him in one vicious pounce.

They dragged him into the alley where the blackness was like dark ink painting every surface. Making himself dead weight, Dud managed to slip their grasp long enough to fall into a ball on the ground. As they kicked him and swung at him with the ax handle, he did what he could to keep the blows away from his head and kidneys.

Wave after wave of pain came over him, and he tried to block it out while at the same time protecting his body the best he could. With blood spurting from his wounds, the voices of people in San Antonio and the saloon played over and over in his mind. "I'm tired of being married to a freight hauler." "A place of abundance." "Cattle as thick as fleas." "Starving Indians on the reservation."

A roar of gunfire blotted out everything. The alley lit up with fire belching from pistols, and the smell of gun smoke burned in his nostrils. The soldiers no longer beat him. Instead, they fell beside him in pools of blood.

Dud could barely open his eyes. He saw Ponder with a smoking pistol in his hand,

and the men from the saloon behind him, holding guns that reeked of gunpowder.

"Get him on a horse if you can, Ponder," one of them was saying. "Ride out of here and don't say nothing about tonight. We'll handle it from here."

Ponder walked to him and looked him over. "Can you ride, Dud?"

Dud felt his head nod.

Later on, he could barely remember what he did. Somehow Ponder got him on his horse, and somehow, he managed to stay on until Ponder found an abandoned shack far from town. Dud remembered Ponder making him a pallet on a dirt floor and helping him to lie down. How many hours or days he slept; he was not sure. He only remembered awakening and seeing Ponder bending over him.

"You gonna be all right, boy?"

Dud struggled to raise up on one elbow. All he could think about was getting to his brother-in-law.

"We got to go to Fitz's, Uncle Ponder. I've got to talk him."

Ponder nodded, placing his hand on Dud's shoulder and gently pushing it down. "We'll go. Just rest for a while first."

The next day, Dud kept assuring Ponder he was well enough to travel. That evening,

Ponder helped him on his horse and handed him a new army issue Colt Navy revolver stolen from one of the dead soldiers to replace the one the kiss had cost him. The kiss had been delightful, and the pistol was of a much better make than the one it replaced, so perhaps it was worth all the hide that had been extracted for it.

To avoid any militia that might be looking for them, they traveled by night, taking it easy and stopping at daylight to visit at the ranches of people they knew. News traveled slow, but it did travel, and no one said a word about any army soldiers being murdered. Neither did they ask Dud where or how he received his bruises. Instead, they welcomed them, eager for company, and shared what little food they had. Dud felt guilty for taking their grub, but since he was a poor cook and Ponder an even worse one, he couldn't help but feel grateful. He and Ponder brought in squirrels or rabbits, even a possum if nothing else, to every house they stopped at.

Nevertheless, Dud rode on, every bounce of the horse causing shocks of pain. He could not complain, because now that Ponder knew he was not going to die, he would just say he was paying for his sins. All he could think about was getting to his sister and brother-in-law's ranch.

"How come you so all fired in a rush to see Fitz?" Ponder asked.

"I'll tell you when we get to Fitz's." He didn't want to argue with Ponder while on the road.

There were no signs of anyone following them, but still they traveled by night. The weather had turned sharp, and they clutched at thin jackets, trying to stay warm while the horses seemed to enjoy the cold air and walking through darkness.

"I'll bet you they stripped them soldiers of anything that could identify them and buried them miles out of town," Ponder said. "I know just where, too. There's a swampy spot near the creek, and I bet you anything that's where they buried those bodies so deep, won't nobody find them excepting maybe somebody a hundred years from now, and they still won't figure out it was them army fellers."

"What's the army going to do when they finally figure out them soldiers are missing?"

"I bet nothing. Everything is in such an uproar right now, it will take them forever to realize they is missing. And when they do, they'll think they deserted, and that will be that."

Dud hoped so. He had fought against the

Union Army for four years, and he did not want to fight them anymore. The war was over; the South lost, and that was it. But there were always people on both sides who kept hanging on to hatred.

That part of Dud's life had finished. He would meet with Fitz and explain the plan that had come to him as he was being beaten. He would send Fitz and Ponder to round up every longhorn they could find that wasn't branded, while he went mustanging for the necessary horses. They were cut off from driving cattle north or east because of Texas tick fever, but they could drive them west to the Indians on the reservation at Fort Sumner and sell everything they could to the army they had once fought so bitterly. Ponder would argue that it was too dangerous going through lands Indians still raided, and then he would insist on coming along.

Dud raised his head to look at the stars, reassured that even though his world had shattered, there was still enough hope left in the universe to go on. And he would, even if it meant fussing and fighting with Ponder every step of the way. He shut his eyes and gave a silent prayer of thanks for his Uncle Ponder.

Easy Jackson is a pseudonym for author Vicky J. Rose, who also writes under the name of V. J. Rose. Born in a small Texas town with a wild and woolly past, Rose grew up listening to enthralling stories of killings, lynchings, and vigilantes — excitement she tries to add to her writing so the reader, too, can experience the thrill of the Old West. In addition to short stories, Jackson's novels are available online, in Walmart, and fine bookstores everywhere. She has written and is working on producing "Lost Pines," a Christmas Western set for filming in 2021. Her web site is: www.vickyjrose.com

The Night the Stars Fell

JACKSON LOWRY

Amos Bell watched the sky fall, one shooting star after another. The sight of so many fiery trails held his attention more than the sleeping cattle surrounding him. The beeves were boring. He clung to his saddle horn, muttering choice words for having to ride night herd. This wasn't his job. He was a wrangler. Well, not a wrangler. An assistant wrangler. He loved horses and didn't mind tending them, but the Circle P ranch was so short handed he had to work double duty. Not only did he tend the horses for the other cowboys on the drive, but now he had to keep the herd quiet at night because Jimmy Thomas had taken it into his head to up and leave without so much as a fare-thee-well.

The shooting stars were diverting. Then stark panic seized him when the earth quivered and shook like it had a bad fever.

His horse reared and pawed at the air.

Amos kept his seat and finally realized why the earth was dancing all over the place.

"Stampede!" He yelled at the top of his lungs. It took a few seconds to realize nobody heard him. The thunder of hooves as the herd began its frantic run drowned out any warning. He drew his pistol and fired in the air a couple times. Hearing this warning over the earthquake caused by thousands of crashing hooves wasn't likely. The other cowboys had to know by now, no matter what he did.

What he had to do was ride for his life because the herd turned in his direction. The moon hadn't risen yet, but the stars — even the falling ones — gave him enough light to pick a better trail than the cattle. They ran wildly, without any thought. Amos hoped he chose better. He avoided the arroyos and rocky patches so his horse wouldn't stumble and fall.

If Old Glory ever stepped in a prairie dog hole as she lengthened her stride he was a goner. The herd would stomp him into the ground and leave nothing but bloody hoofprints for a mile or two. That would be all she wrote. He fired a couple more times. In the distance he heard return gunfire. The camp had twigged to the danger. In a trice all the cowboys would be saddled and out to turn the herd.

Amos glanced over his shoulder and saw the leading steer. Its eyes were wild and it snorted and its vicious horns, though polled, were long enough to gut Old Glory. And him. He started to fire into the air, then lowered his aim. The final two rounds in his six-shooter hit the steer smack dab in the center of its head. The thick bone kept the lead from sinking into its brain and killing the charging behemoth, but he got its attention. It veered, cut across the leading edge of the stampede and as suddenly as the danger had presented itself, it went away.

Within a hundred yards the cattle had lost their fright and settled down, milling about aimlessly. Amos rode around to the north, applied his lariat to bovine rumps and formed up a herd again. By the time the ramrod, Big Sid Leslie, came riding up, there didn't seem to be any trouble.

Except for the stars still falling out of the sky.

"Go on back to camp, Amos. I saw how you turned the herd. Not bad for somebody who's not a cowpuncher."

"Thank you kindly." Amos looked up as two flaming trails crossed the sky. One ended in a bright green burst. "You think that started the stampede?"

Leslie looked up, then at Amos. "What are you talking about? There's no telling what spooked the cattle. They're dumb critters, but they got to know they're heading to the railhead to get shipped to a slaughterhouse."

"You don't think the stars coming down like they are tonight scared 'em?"

"Go get some of Pete's coffee and try to sleep for an hour or two before we head out." Leslie added, "You sure you didn't hit your head?" He glanced up into the sky. No shooting stars. "Git." Then he started his patrol.

Amos wanted to argue what he had seen. The earthquake had been the herd beginning its run, but maybe that steer he'd shot had looked up and seen the flaming sky trail and tried to run away. Maybe. All the way back to camp, Amos kept one eye on the heavens but didn't see any more shooting stars when there had been a dozen or more all coming down at once. And the one that blew up all green and bright and —

"You, Amos. Amos Bell. Get over here." The voice was deep and just a tad cracked from old age. It belonged to Mr. Pickering, and from the razors in his voice, he was righteously angry over something.

He directed Old Glory toward the chuck

wagon where the Circle P owner alternately bellowed at Pete, the cook, and gestured wildly toward the hills to the west. Amos dismounted and stood, reins in hand, waiting for his turn to get chewed out. It came mighty fast.

"You're the wrangler, aren't you?" Mr. Pickering knew he was. Pretending he didn't put Amos on guard.

"Yes, sir, I am. Well, assistant wrangler. Billy's the head wrangler."

"Bartholemew rode out at sunset. That's two men I lost in two days."

"Jimmy Thomas took off 'cuz he ain't got paid in a month, he said," Pete spoke up. Angering the boss further didn't bother him much. He was a decent trail cook, part-time sawbones, careful dispenser of whiskey, confidante and indispensable. And he knew it. "He knew pay was waitin' at the end of the trail, so quittin' is all on him, but Billy 'Bejesus' said he got a calling. He's off to be a preacher man."

"He traded a herd for a flock?" Amos shook his head in dismay. "I never knew he was a religious sort."

"Don't you go gettin' any ideas, Amos," Pete said. "You might be sweet on that li'l filly at the mercantile, but don't expect Billy 'Bejesus' to marry you anytime soon. She don't even know you exist."

"You be careful talking about Miss Emily." Amos felt his hackles rising. He had been through too much that night to let Pete rag on a girl he was sweet on.

"Quiet!" Mr. Pickering roared. "I don't want to hear about your love life, Bartholemew's conversion or how Thomas left this drive without his services when I needed him most."

"I turned the herd when they —" Amos shut up when Mr. Pickering spun on him, face florid with anger. The heavy wrinkles crossing his forehead looked like red furrows dancing in the firelight, his eyes blazed from the bottom of dark, deadly pits and his lips were pulled back like a wolf's, showing vicious yellowed fangs. Amos had no idea why his boss was so mad. A few head always got trampled in any stampede, but he had done his job — had done Jimmy Thomas' job better than the cowboy would have — and deserved praise, not such towering anger.

"You're head wrangler now. Find my horse!"

"Your horse? What's happened to Black Diamond?" His heart came up into his throat. Mr. Pickering's horse was a purebred and the most beautiful animal he'd ever seen. Amos tugged on Old Glory's reins. His mare was a sturdy horse and dependable. She'd shown that tonight, racing through the darkness and never once putting him in danger. Well, not much. But Black Diamond was worth a young fortune. He'd even heard another rancher offer Mr. Pickering a thousand dollars for the stallion. Mr. Pickering had laughed at such a lowball price.

"He's not in the corral. He got loose during the stampede. Find him, Bell. You find him or know the reason!" Mr. Pickering stalked away, cursing sulphurously.

Amos stared after his boss, then turned to the cook. Pete kept his head down, pretending not to have overheard a word of the tirade.

"You got any notion what happened?"

Pete silently handed Amos a cup of his bitter coffee. Amos knew it was bad when the cook offered him some of the sugar he kept in a bitters jar. Pete guarded that sugar with his life, as if it were more valuable than mere money. And out on the trail it was.

Amos took a pinch, put it into the coffee and stirred with his grimy finger. The coffee was always so bad that dissolved dirt could only help its taste. He sipped, liked what he tasted, then downed the cup in a single gulp. It burned at his lips and seared his tongue, but it brought him fully awake. Doing two men's jobs had left him shy on sleep. He handed the tin cup back to Pete and shuffled away from the chuck wagon. Pete let out a gusty sigh, then began rattling pots and pans, preparing biscuits for the cowboys' breakfast in a few hours.

Rather than go directly to the rope corral he had built, Amos stopped by his tack and rummaged around until he found a box of shells for his six-shooter. He took the time to reload, then plodded over to the corral. A feeling grew that he'd be out on the trail for quite a spell. Black Diamond was a powerful animal. If he'd taken off at a run, frightened by the cattle, he could be cropping prairie flowers miles off.

"No, no!" Amos ran his hand along the rope, skipping over the tethers of the cowboys' spare horses, until he came to where he remembered Black Diamond being hitched. The halter hadn't come loose. It had been cut with a sharp knife. The boss' horse had been stolen.

Amos sagged, then patted Old Glory on the neck and said, "We're in for a long ride, I'm afeared. It must have been Jimmy Thomas that took Mr. Pickering's mount. I never pegged him for a horse thief, but then

I never thought he'd leave the drive the way he did." Amos began studying the chopped up ground. "Might be he thought Black Diamond was his due for all the work he'd done. To earn that much, he'd have to work a hundred years. More."

He circled the area, then found hoofprints leading away that had to be Black Diamond's. The horse was large, and the boss always told the farrier to put on special shoes. Amos wasn't an expert tracker, but the tracks looked different. He walked beside the suspect hoofprints cut into the prairie and then stopped and stared. Dropping to his knees, he lightly traced a footprint of whoever led Black Diamond.

"Oh, no, no, no," he sobbed out. "I apologize what I was thinking about you Jimmy. You wore boots. The horse thief had on moccasins."

An Indian had stolen the horse. Considering where they had bedded down the herd for the night, the thief was likely a Cheyenne. Amos kept walking, leading his mare, until the footprints disappeared and Black Diamond started cantering. The thief had mounted and now rode his prize. Amos swung up into the saddle and stared into the night. The tracks led away from camp as straight as an arrow for a ridge a few miles distant. While he didn't know much about the Cheyenne, that low mountain festooned with pines and maybe an aspen or two looked to be where Indians would camp.

He gave Old Glory her head and kept the dark mountain directly in front. Now and then he caught sight of Black Diamond's tracks, then the ground got too rocky. He rode ahead on faith. And as he rode, he looked up at the night sky. A glow at the far horizon hinted at moonrise. That would help him tracking, but he was more curious about the occasional shooting stars. Nobody had ever told him why the stars fell out of the sky this way. The bright green ball had been the most unusual, but the number had to be something to spin tales about around the campfire for years to come.

Not that he'd be the one telling the stories. Only a few of the cowboys had the knack of keeping everyone entertained. He had tried his hand a few times, telling stories his pa and uncle had told him when he was a youngster, but the others had never listened for long. Not like when Pete began his tall tales. They were outrageous and funny and everyone laughed and begged for another when he finished. The whole time Amos had ridden with the Circle P, he had never heard Pete repeat himself. The cook had a knack. He wasn't as good a cook as he was at telling his stories. That might be why Mr. Pickering kept him on year after year. Keeping the hands from getting bored meant they weren't as likely to get into fights.

Amos wished he had Pete's skill. He heaved a sigh, then looked up fast to see another shooting star. This wasn't as spectacular as the green fireball, but it left spinning sparks like a Fourth of July rocket halfway across the night sky.

"I wish I wasn't so boring," Amos said. "That's the wish I'm making on that star, even if it isn't the first one of the evening." Then he wondered if it was allowed for him to change the wish. Not being so tongue tied around Miss Emily was a better wish. If he wasn't such a dullard she might take notice of him. If he had the gumption to even talk to her. If, if, if . . . .

His hand flashed to his six-gun when a loud whinny came from the darkness ahead. One horse sounded like another to him, but if he had been a betting man, his whole stake would have been shoved onto the table with the declaration that he had found Black Diamond. He tapped his heels against Old Glory's flanks, and he picked up the pace. From what spoor he had seen along the trail, and that trail had remained as straight as an arrow for this mountain, he only had one Indian to deal with. He wasn't much of a sharpshooter, but if he got the drop on the horse thief, he'd have Black Diamond back in the corral before sunrise.

A worn trail presented itself in the sharp starlight. Amos saw a pile of still hot horse flop. Black Diamond marked the trail for him. His mare began climbing with a will now. She scented her stable mate ahead. Trying to keep alert became harder when the starlight faded and eventually disappeared entirely. Clouds built, heavy and bellies laden with rain. He worried he might lose the trail if it rained, then realized the trail led one way only. Up. Losing the trail was less a worry than running into the horse thief and the rest of his clan camped above.

The scent of a fire drifted down to make his nostrils flare. If the Cheyenne stopped to cook a meal it made the job of recovering the stolen horse easier. All he had to do was waltz in, wave his gun around and take back Black Diamond. As he worked out his plan, Amos began to worry. He'd never shot anyone before, even a horse thief. If the need arose, could he pull the trigger? Never in his wildest dreams had he ever thought of himself as a gun sharp. Truth to tell, he had seldom fired his six-shooter. Tonight was the first time in almost a year when he had shot a rattler. And it hadn't even been a full-grown snake. There had been three rattles shaking at the tip of the tail. Billy Bartholemew had joshed him about letting it go until it grew up and came back with a real stack of rattles.

Amos jerked out of his reverie. Everything happened too fast. He blundered into a clearing at the summit. Black Diamond reared and pawed at the air the best he could since his reins had been looped around a low limb. A quick pull filled Amos' hand with his six-gun. He pointed it at the Indian sitting cross-legged at a small fire. The war-painted Cheyenne brave chanted, raised his hands to the cloudy sky and ignored Amos entirely.

"Don't you move an inch. I got the drop on you, you horse thief!"

The Indian kept his hands raised. He opened his eyes and pivoted slightly toward Amos. He finished his chant, lowered his heavens-imploring hands, then fell silent.

Amos didn't know what to do. He rode around to Black Diamond but couldn't reach the tether if he stayed astride his mare. With a quick move, he slipped off and went to the purebred. He tried to gentle the stallion, but the high-strung horse wasn't having any of it.

"You'd better get used to me, boy," Amos said. "I'll be tending you. I'm the new head wrangler."

The horse ignored him and tried to rear. He held onto the reins and kept it down. Letting those massive hooves lash out would do him in. Keeping at it, he calmed the horse enough to go to the fire and accost the Indian. Amos raised his gun again. The brave had gotten to his feet and started a slow dance around the fire. From the way he hobbled and lurched, he had a bad foot.

"Just because you got a gimpy leg's no reason to steal a horse." Amos wasn't sure if he wanted to chastise the Indian or — what? "I'm taking the horse you stole, but I'm not taking you back to stand trial." He sucked in his breath. Mr. Pickering was so angry that he'd sooner string up the Indian than turn him over to the marshal in whatever the next town they came to.

The Cheyenne didn't look to be all that much of a threat, not hopping and hobbling around like he did. There was a bone-handled knife sheathed at his waist, but Amos didn't see a rifle or even bow and arrow anywhere around the simple camp.

"If you apologize for taking the horse, I'll let you be. It'd be good if you promised not to steal any more horses, but I know your word's not likely to be good on that account." Amos kept his six-shooter levelled as he stepped closer to the fire.

"You shoot me?" The Indian continued to dance as he spoke.

"You make it sound like you want me to. That's plumb loco." Amos' hand shook just a little from strain. He was only a trigger pull away from gunning the man down.

"I came to this sacred grove to die."

Amos looked around. There wasn't anything to tell him this was a sacred place. There wasn't a cross or Bible to be seen, but the Cheyenne had other ideas.

"Seems you're in good enough shape to steal what doesn't belong to you." Amos glanced over his shoulder. Black Diamond jerked and pulled at his tether. Old Glory stood by peaceably enough, hunting for a patch of grass to nibble.

The Indian hobbled around the fire one last time, then sank to the ground. Amos circled to keep the fire between them. He wasn't taking any chances. He studied the brave and saw a decrepit man who might not be fibbing about being at Heaven's Gate.

"I had to come here. To die." The Indian coughed up a bloody gob and spat into the fire. The sizzle caused Amos to jerk back, even though he should have expected it. He watched steam twist up into the sky. The moon was finally creeping higher, but the clouds kept it from shining too brightly.

"You do sound to be in a bad way," Amos said. He slid his six-shooter back into its holster. "Can I do something for you? I'm not much of a doctor. Truth is, I'm not much of anything." He laughed harshly. "I work as head wrangler, but I got the position because nobody else wanted it. That's the way my whole life's been."

The Indian nodded sagely, wiped his lips and then said in a small voice, "We are alike. You and I. Broken Foot was never a brave warrior. Often, I robbed the bodies of fallen enemies like a squaw."

"That's your name? Broken Foot?" Amos lowered himself to a seat on the cold ground. "You couldn't fight because of your foot? What happened?"

"A horse stepped on me. I never healed."

"It sorta took away your confidence? Well now, from my point of view, that might have been for the best. If you couldn't kill any of my people, I see that as a good thing."

"I never spoke in council. When I tried,

others ignored me because I failed to count coup, to take scalps or horses."

Amos nodded knowingly. Nobody paid him or his opinions any heed.

"I never took a scalp, either. I'm just speaking figuratively since none of my people scalp their enemies. Leastwise, not any more. They have other ways of defeating them."

"Better to die than to live in shame." Broken Foot thrust out his leg and warmed the injured foot closer to the fire.

"It's not so bad, not being noticed. I don't get into trouble that way." Amos clamped his lips shut and stared into the fire. The sparks danced about and occasionally escaped to rise rapidly. If only he could escape the prison wrapped around him like a blanket.

"What is her name?"

Amos jerked upright and stared across the fire at Broken Foot. The Cheyenne fixed him with a piercing stare.

"What are you talking about? My mare? Her name's Old Glory."

"Not the horse. You have a woman?" Broken Foot spat into the fire again, watched the rising steam and then again stared hard at Amos.

As much as he wanted to keep quiet about

Miss Emily, he found himself going on and on about her. None of the cowboys he rode with would have listened more than a few seconds without making a lewd comment, but Broken Foot listened. Occasionally he nodded in agreement or shook his head slowly, sympathizing. Amos forgot he was opening his soul to a horse thief. When he finally ran down, the Cheyenne spoke softly, "She wants you as much as you do her."

"I don't know."

"You have not spoken to her. How can you know her spirit?"

This made Amos uncomfortable. Even an Indian who didn't know him from Adam saw straight to the heart of the matter. Amos was a failure. All he wanted to do was change the subject and not feel so worthless.

"Why'd you come up here? You said it was a sacred spot."

"I have come to die," Broken Foot said. "The Sky Chief summons me. Beside him I will be a brave warrior." He looked up at the roiling clouds. The silver moon poked through here and there.

"How'd this Sky Chief fellow call you? I know some folks who hear voices. They're mostly loco in the cabeza, as the Mexicans'd say."

"He called to me by throwing rocks at the earth." Broken Foot reached into a pouch and took out a small black pebble. "From the sky he sent this stone to give me strength."

"How's it work?" Amos peered at the rock. It was smoother than most he'd seen that hadn't been plucked from the bottom of a stream, but tiny holes made it look like a mouse had nibbled away at a hunk of cheese.

"It is a spirit stone. I looked up and saw many of them falling. This landed at my feet."

"Do tell."

"It was cold when I picked it up. That is how I knew the Sky Chief sent it to me alone. I will join him as he crosses the happy hunting ground."

Amos fell silent when Broken Foot closed his hand around the stone. It seemed incredible that a rock could fall out of the sky, but he had seen dozens of shooting stars that very night. There wasn't any reason for them and who was he to tell Broken Foot he was wrong?

"I better take my boss' horse and get back to camp. Will you be all right, staying up here all by your lonesome?" Amos waited for a reply. Broken Foot didn't stir. "You listening? Are you? Dang." Angry, Amos shot to his feet and started to leave. He'd gotten used to having someone listen to him and understanding what was went on in his head.

And now Broken Foot was just like the cowboys, ignoring him.

He reversed course and went to the seated Indian. "You can at least thank me for not turning you over to the law." He grabbed the brave's shoulder.

Broken Foot slumped over.

"You passed out? You been drinking firewater?" Amos dropped to his knees and poked and shoved the inert body until Broken Foot lay stretched out, his face turned upward to the moon. Amos held his forefinger under the Indian's nose. No breath. He rocked back and stared. "Reckon I wish you had been on a bender and passed out from too much popskull."

He got to his feet and backed off, not sure what to do. Halfway to the horses, he stopped. His shoulders sagged. He knew what he had to do, but giving Broken Foot a Christian burial was all wrong. The Indian had gone on and on about a Sky Chief and joining him.

It took Amos the better part of an hour to build a raised platform and lay a decent amount of dried wood under it. Wrestling Broken Foot onto the pyre proved to be more of a chore than he expected, but some of it came from distaste at lugging a corpse around. More than once he almost left Broken Foot where he lay so he could ride off. But he finally heaved the body atop the pyre.

Amos stood back and wiped sweat from his forehead. "I swear, I didn't know you, but you could have been a friend. A good one, too. You listened to me." He grabbed a burning piece of wood from the campfire and tossed it under the pyre. The dried brush caught immediately and began igniting the bigger limbs laid crisscross. As the flames surrounded Broken Foot, Amos said in a voice too low for anyone to hear, "And I listened to you."

He backed away as the fire grew more intense. Smoke from the wood and body rose skyward. He smiled just a little as the clouds parted to allow the moon to shine down and accept Broken Foot's essence. Amos wasn't sure and would never swear on a Bible but he thought the clouds formed the outline of a giant man.

"Do right by him, Sky Chief. Take care of my friend."

Amos turned to go again, then stopped.

He had no reason to watch the cremation but he did. As the body turned to ash, something fell from the top of the pyre into the ashes. He used a green stick to bat it out.

He gingerly touched the stone, then picked it up.

"Broken Foot was right. It does feel cold." Amos turned the black rock over and over in his hand. He started to throw it back into the fire. Instead, he tucked it away in his vest pocket.

Only then did he mount Old Glory, snag Black Diamond's bridle and tug gently to get the horse to follow him down the mountainside. As he rode, he thought of all that had happened.

"Miss Emily," he said. Amos warmed to the speech. "Would you do me the honor of accompanying me to church this Sunday? I hear there's a new preacher man by the name of Reverend Bartholemew. He's surely looking for good folks to marry in his new church."

Amos Bell would never have dared say such a thing to Miss Emily. But that was before. His fingers traced the outline of the sky stone in his pocket. Now he could. After all he was the head wrangler on a big ranch and deserved respect — and love. The Sky Chief said so.

Jackson Lowry is the pen name (among many) of Robert E. Vardeman, the author of almost 200 westerns, many in series such as Jake Logan, Trailsman, West of the Big River, and Blaze!. He has garnered award nominations for novels *Drifter, Sonora Noose, China Jack* and was honored with the Western Fictioneers Life Achievement Award in 2017. Current titles written for the Ralph Compton series include *Tin Star, Never Bet Against the Bullet, The Lost Banshee Mine* and forthcoming, in 2021, *Shot to Hell* and *Flames of Silver*. He can be found online at his web site: www.jacksonlowry.cenotaphroad.com

WEST OF NOAH
RICHARD PROSCH

According to the Indians, Coyote is the trickster.

He can change shapes, appear in two places at once, and sometimes — when the stars align just right — become invisible.

When Hobnail Higgins found scat on a trail west of Noah, he forgot all the wild stories. He only had one thing in mind.

He was hellbent to blast a brush wolf.

That anything other than an honest-to-St. Pete coyote had dropped the drying turds never crossed his mind.

Thirteen years-old, Hob had never been hoodwinked before.

He turned his back on the scat, and the great hunter was off for the far reaches of the trail.

Hob wanted a coyote more than anything in the world. Not for the pelt or because the dogs had become a nuisance to the community, but just to show Dowd Dempsey and Stick McCain and the Kempker boys that he was good as any of 'em when it came to guns, guts, and gumption.

West of Noah, the vast pan of Wyoming grass was still and the morning sky a lid of gray dark clouds, and Hob had marched away from Ma's one-room cabin in the Laramie foothills without bothering to bring along lunch or a jug full of water.

He lugged his pa's Henry .44 up against his shoulder, like a soldier, proud and erect. After a while, he got tired and cradled it in his arms, tender — like a newborn calf. The durned thing wasn't so much heavy as awkward, and since sunrise he'd come a good four miles from home.

He'd been looking forward to this day — his thirteenth birthday — for a long time.

Ever since Ma laid down the date he could go out and hunt alone — all by himself.

He'd been waiting ever since his pa died in bed, shriveled up in the parlor room, a few last words of instruction on his lips. "Hobnail, make good now," he said. "You make good."

I will, Papa.

From somewhere up ahead there came a mournful wail. Wiping each hand in turn on the slick worn thighs of his loose corduroy britches, Hob reclaimed his manly grip on the rifle's hard steel barrel.

Hobnail Higgins surged forward.

The first week of October had accommodated Hob with an opening volley of overcast days and afternoon rain that caught the local aspens dropping their leaves like tongues of dying embers to the cold grass.

Days where the air was wet and perfectly attuned to the coyote's frenzied cries.

Hob listened to them from his bedroom window each night before sleep, anticipating his big hunt. On the eve of his birthday, he'd gone to bed with the daylight, and sirens of the brush wolf pack called to him from the dark with a scurrilous nature that made two or three seem like ten.

Coyote — the trickster.

Far enough across the range for Hob to feel brave.

In his imagination there were dozens of the ornery devils, maybe hundreds, and he saw himself standing triumphant on a pile of bloody pelts, the head of the biggest king coyote held high in both hands. Dowd, and Stick, and the Kempker boys crouching far below.

Surrounding him on all sides of the mountain, the girls from school looked up to him with admiration.

The cowboys and church ladies smiled

with respect.

In the morning, Hob left a hasty note for his ma, and set out along Japheth Crick for the open range past Ketchum's place.

Ketchum trapped all sorts of game — coyote included — but the crazy old coot never showed himself in Noah. Some folks said he hadn't been to town in forty years. Sniffing the sage October air, Hob felt a drop of water hit his nose even as his stomach complained for the twentieth time.

Hob told his stomach to pipe down.

He could always pop a squirrel or rabbit later on.

Ketchum's land was stuffed with game.

First would come the brush wolf.

To his left was Japheth creek, running high with brown water and rimmed with a scarf of cedar trees and chaff bent low and covered in mud from recent floods. The land to his right was an open swale — a vast expanse of gamma grass, bowing away from him, stunted and yellow all the way to the horizon. He imagined the coyote bounding out over the prairie, haughty and full of vinegar, the animal's tarnished dark coat ruffled by its passage, its ears pricked high, nose twitching, eyes sharp as a hawk.

It would be completely ignorant of Hob and the Henry firm against his shoulder.

Hob pulled the rifle up and, not wanting to waste a cartridge, pretended to lob a round at the imaginary beast without pulling the trigger.

The iron sites were clear under his lashes. His breath came easy as he turned in harmony with his make believe target.

Hob imagined squeezing the trigger, oh so gentle now . . . slowly letting out his breath . . .

There would be a loud explosion.

A blanket of starlings would lift high above the creek from their nests.

Under the weight of Hob's bullet, the brush wolf would roll and twist, kicking up a cloud of dirt. Hob would have to fire once, twice, maybe three more times to take down such a monster.

"Ker-schpooooow," whispered Hob.

It was going to be glorious.

A few hundred yards off the trail, blocking off the fields beyond, the tall rocky butte that King Ketchum used as a property line and fence reared up like an ancient castle fortress. Hob followed its black granite rim for half a mile along the horizon, wondering how much property Ketchum owned. Off in the distance, he heard the strained howl he'd heard before, and his fingers tightened on the rifle stock.

It could have been a coyote. It *must* have been.

A hedge of multiflora rose bush stood up from the crick bank and covered the base of the imposing rocky butte like a thorny apron — the perfect place for a critter to nest. A safe place for a coyote's den of pups.

Maybe?

Fueled by fantasy, Hob left the path and trudged toward the tall rock outcropping, his tongue rough against dry lips, his stomach scraping his backbone.

As soon as he bagged the coyote, he'd find some game. Maybe build a fire.

The air smelled heavy with rain from the north and . . . a wild odor Hob's couldn't place.

He lifted his chin and his toe hit something hard and he wind milled forward, almost losing the rifle, almost eating the dirt. What the heck had he tripped over?

Buried in a soft red clay, the old sign came loose in two pieces, a knobby cedar pole and a roughhewn plank with words sun-faded and barely legible. Hobs picked up the sign and read it.

No trespassing.

Hob let the board fall back at his feet and carried on.

If King Ketchum had a problem with him being there, then old King Ketchum could just come down from his high palace on the other side of the bluff and stop him.

Hob bit his lip and screwed up his nerve. "Just let him try to stop me," he said.

Tossing the Henry back on his shoulder, he marched ahead, full of defiance. The clouds played along, grumbling under their breath with thunder.

More sprinkles. And then the rain came down, reluctant spatters at first, dollops of cold water slapping at Hob's thin linsey shirt. Then an even, steady fall.

Hob mopped water from his eyes.

How long, he thought, before he turned around? How long until he gave up?

After all, he had plenty of time to make it back home before supper. He imagined Ma's table with a blue gingham cloth lousy with taters and gravy and a platter stacked with ham. Bowls of bread stuffing and a hot pie cooling on the stove. Hot lemon tea.

This time the howl came with a warning growl after, and Hob knew it was a coyote.

He was sure of it.

There, shadowed against the wall of the butte, where the flat grass was washed away and the range was speckled with a few prickly pears, an animal swayed back and forth on four legs. Hob picked out the shape against the background rock.

The beast gave off a series of staccato yips punctuated by enraged yowls.

It didn't look like a coyote.

Transfixed, Hob walked toward the creature.

Too big to be a coyote. A wolf? For a wild split-second Hob imagined it was a moose.

Impossible, thought Hob. There hadn't been a moose around Noah for a coon's age. At least, that's what Ma said.

The rain came hard and the sweep of it soaked down Hob's clothes and blurred his vision.

He hunched over the gun with an impossible idea of keeping it dry. But he kept moving forward, confident because of his weapon, lured toward the curious figure at the bluff, a dark shape now pacing in a tight circle.

He walked from a clear space of mud into a patch of grass less than a hundred yards away and the curtains of rain parted. Hob held the rifle up, muzzle pointed at the sky with one hand while he knuckled water from his vision.

In front of him, the creature growled low in its throat, with an odd whistle, like a dying steam engine.

69

Or one just getting started.

Hob's loose, rolling stomach pulled tight with a near-painful tug. His feet were iron weights sinking into the clay.

He was closer than he'd imagined. Less than thirty feet.

The black bear curled back his top lip and bared his yellow-brown fangs.

It was a healthy young male, not yet fully grown, but rippling with life. This was no mangy, rail-thin scavenger.

No, this was a trophy, a sleek monarch with thick black fur who reared up on two legs shoulder high and weighed twice as much as Hob, and maybe then some again.

With pitched ears and clear eyes, the beast rocked up and down, seemingly set to pounce.

Hob felt a flutter in his chest travel up both arms like an electric shock and his hands fumbled around with the rifle.

He dropped it just as the bear made its move.

Hob toppled backwards onto his behind, rolled, made a sprawling grab for the rifle —

Felt a thud vibrate through his wrist, then saw only red as a searing jolt of agony tore through his arm. For an instant, that's all there was to Hob's world — pain and sheets of red followed by an all-enveloping darkness.

Hob couldn't move, could only scream out loud, the noise pouring out of him like a torrent.

Then he jerked open his eyes and saw the horrible truth.

His wrist was broken, crushed in the horrible steel jaws of a fur-trader's trap, the iron vice staked with a chain to a patch of bare earth.

Hob struggled to catch up to the pain. Struggled to control his breathing.

King Ketchum had stopped him after all.

Then the bear wailed — like an eerie mix of a heavy dog's bark and a Tom cat's squealing cry. But not exactly like either, and Hob flipped over to his back, tearing at the skin of his mangled wrist, enduring the torment to kick with his heels away from the lunging, snapping jaws of the creature.

"Grawrf, rarf, raaaar!"

The bear kept its distance.

Hob rolled back, frantically circling the stake in the ground, dragging out the attached chain with his captured wrist at the end to its farthest possible length. He saw the Henry .44 resting in the saturated grass and stretched out his good arm.

A foot too short.

He cried with frustration and pain, pounding the ground, the bear's insistent growls punctuating a rolling squall of thunder overhead, his hulking shadow lunging . . .

But it never reached Hob.

At the last second, the bear yelped and shied away, and the clouds cut loose with an ocean.

Hob rolled onto his stomach and struggled to slow down his breathing.

The bear was gone.

Why? How?

Madly, Hob decided maybe it had seen the gun. Maybe somebody had taken a few shots at it once or twice before and it had learned to fear the firestick.

Firestick — like the Indians in books called a rifle.

Indians called coyote the trickster.

Was that it?

Hob had ventured out to hunt a coyote. Was this him — the trickster, the shape-changer in the form of a bear?

Or was bear a trickster as well?

Was this momentary reprieve a prank? Was the bear waiting for him to open his eyes? To sit up? Would it come for him at any second with wild eyes and gaping jaws?

Hob listened to the roar of the rain, felt it trickling down his face.

The iron bite of Ketchum's trap was excruciating but he thought he could move without crying.

Slowly, he lifted himself up on his left arm and then into a sitting position before his heart stopped once again.

The bear also sat. Six feet away.

Staring at him with bare teeth.

Drenched, miserable in the storm, the bear lips twitched and the slow growl from his chest continued, like the rumble of an interior grindstone spinning . . . ever spinning.

Hob sat stock still, let his eyes play over the scene.

It had to be a trick. Maybe the bear was sick with rabies. Playing with him before racing forward to tear out his throat.

The bear didn't look sick. His eyes were clear.

He looked scared.

Probably the same way Hobnail looked to the bear.

"Hey, boy . . . ," he ventured. "Hey —"

The beast lurched forward with a mad yapping and Hob flinched. But this time he kept his eyes open and watched with amazement as — mid-leap — the attack was cut short. The bear fell backwards. Once again it cried out with pained frustration.

Then Hob saw it, the bloody bare spot where the iron clamp had rubbed away the fur, heard the rattle of the chain as the animal fell back to nip at his right back leg.

Another one of King Ketchum's traps.

The two of them were in the same pickle then.

Trapped by a set of iron jaws affixed at the hinge to a chain two feet-long, the chain in turned attached to a steel stake driven into the ground. Hob was caught at the wrist. The bear, in his trap, was held by his back leg. Each of them claimed a circle of territory around his central stake.

The circles intersected, but as long as Hob stayed on the far side of his stake from the bear, chain stretched to its full length, he was out of reach.

The bear couldn't hurt him.

As long as Hob's stake held, he couldn't reach the rifle.

He was no threat to the bear.

"I won't hurt you, boy," said Hob, trying to block out his morning's dreams of doing far more than that to a coyote or dinner-time rabbit. Even now, soaked to the skin, with a broken wrist, he couldn't help but think what a prize the bear's hide would make.

For his part, the bear turned away from

Hob. He was complacent now, sitting at the far edge of his circle, panting, letting the rain pour over his broad forehead without blinking, occasionally lashing his narrow snout with a long pink tongue.

But there was no way to know how long Sam was going to behave.

Sam. As good a name as any for a bear.

Hob's wrist was throbbing and purple but the bleeding had stopped. Any attempt to pry open the trap with his free hand resulted in shards of pain that made his head swim.

Instead of getting free, he tried capturing the gun — two tasks equally impossible.

Even stretched out flat in the mud, he couldn't reach it — not even with the toe of his boot.

At one point, Sam wandered over into Hob's territory. Inside the circumference of the trap's circle, the bear swatted at the stake that held Hob's chain.

"You trying to help me, boy?" Hob marveled at the look of curiosity on the bear's face. "Or are you asking for help?"

Sam peeled back his jowls, snuffed and wheezed a halfhearted answer before backing away into his own place.

Another wave of rain came, and when Sam finally settled down again, Hob used

75

his good hand to dig at the trap's deeply embedded stake. It must've been at least two feet long, driven to the earth tight with a hammer.

Hob sat back, the nails of his fingers caked with loam.

He wished he had the bear's claws. He jerked his head to the right and, spying the other trap's stake saw that yes — Sam had been digging at his anchor too. For all the good it had done him. The bear's stake was just as firm as Hob's.

Maybe he had been asking Hob for help after all.

Fatigue washed over him with the storm, and this time the rain didn't stop.

Late in the afternoon, Sam acted out again, scuffled around, dug some more at his stake with his forepaws, then thrust his claws through the hinged steel locked around his back foot. He whimpered and cajoled, roared with rage and shook himself into a frenzy.

Hob stayed at the far end of his leash, wondering what would happen if Sam got free. Would the bear rend Hob from chin to chuckwagon?

Or would he run loose in the opposite direction?

Hob didn't want to find out, so he stayed as vigilante as he could against the increasing cold.

Unable to control the trembling.

The day wore on and the rain didn't end. Puddles appeared on the open range. Puddles that became ponds.

Ponds threatening to grow into lakes.

Hob's empty stomach was a chronic ache, his arm a numb, dead weight. Before long, he couldn't keep his eyes open.

When he woke up, it was dusk. He had to relieve himself something awful, but was ashamed to wet his pants.

Laying in a shallow pool of rain slop, soaked to the skin like a sponge in a hog wallow, he couldn't help but wonder what difference more water could make?

Afterwards, he felt better and rolled onto his back with mouth agape, slurping at the fresh water from the sky. As long as the clouds kept giving, he wouldn't die of thirst.

He stomached cramped into an agonizing ball — like an interior fist that squeezed itself red.

He looked across the darkening ground at the black shafts of grass and wished he could cram his mouth full of hay.

Nearby, Sam let out a long sigh and whined quietly to himself.

"You're hungry too, ain'tcha?" said Hob.

Sam cried softly as if in answer.

A wave of anger crashed over Hob then, momentarily washing away the despair.

"Darn you, King Ketchum," he said. "Darn you and your stupid traps to hell."

When fear came again, it came with a gnawing, relentless delirium.

The day had washed away the hunter. Now Hob was just like the bear. Just like the coyote. Hob was the prey, and he was as lost to himself as to the world.

He was going to die here.

He was sure of it.

Would Ma ever know what became of him?

Would King Ketchum find him? Long after the rains and the field dried to a crusty clay mud, would Hobnail Higgins' bones be half interred therein with the remains of a bear?

While Hob slipped in and out of consciousness, the day turned to night and the rain didn't stop.

He woke up, and he couldn't breathe.

The thundering roar in his ears came from behind and below and all around, and he tried to get his bearings, but couldn't.

Hob gagged on the sour stink of creek

water in his nose and choked as it clogged his throat. His stomach spasmed and he retched up a stream of bile and his arm screamed as his body was pulled parallel with the rushing current.

He struggled through a cave of darkness and was blinded by bolts of bright lightning.

During the night, the creek had overflowed, the swale was flooded nearly two feet deep, and the rush of water across the open field was trying to wrench Hob free of his trap. He flailed in the water, the oncoming waves breaking against his shoulder and rib cage, a battered knee jammed tight against the mud below the surface, his other leg trailing out and away.

Hob tilted his head back and around, water smashing into this forehead, eyes, nose.

He couldn't see Sam anywhere.

The creek washed over him, gray and cold. The agony of his ensnared wrist pounded him back to the fuzzy border between waking and nightmare and he fought to stay aware.

Then Sam was there, right beside him, rolling, barking, panic in his eyes, his massive forelegs thrashing up out of the water.

Hobs was too close. The current had washed him to Sam's side of his own circle.

He tried to push against the floor of the newly created river channel, but his feet washed out from under. He kicked against the mud and the tug of his arm in the trap.

Sam's iron-tough nails raked down through the water and caught Hob on the knee, slicing open the skin like a pocket knife through the red of an apple.

Compared to the pain in his arm, it was nothing.

Filled with terror, he pushed back against the current as hard as he could.

How long he struggled, he had no idea.

In and out of darkness, tossed and turned and twisted by the water.

Half-way in water, he turned his face sideways and in a blast of lightning saw the rifle coming toward him. Rocking up and down, pounding down on him along the surface of the water.

But of course it wasn't the rifle. That had been washed away hours ago.

The long shape barreling toward him, growing longer and larger by the seconds, was a twisted, broke tree branch. And then Hob saw there were other branches lurching through the water as well.

If one of them should smash into his skull . . .

But how would he see them in the dark?

He flipped over into the onrush of water and tried to gauge where the branch was. If only the clouds would light up again. And when they did, if they did — maybe he could —

The branch careened into his back, sending him across the streams toward Sam — wherever he was — whirling — gasping — swallowing too much water.

He was hit again, but this time the branch only scraped his arm.

The next floater was bigger — man-sized. It slammed into his sore arm, but Hob managed to put his weight onto the bow and tip it down.

It spun out of control and bobbed up, knocking him in the chin before it hurried along its way, following the mad torrent.

The water was nearly three feet deep. With his arm stuck in the trap, there was nothing he could do but drown.

Hob rolled over, stopped fighting, and the water pulled him out as far as the chain would allow.

He rode the top of the current that way, floating on his back, avoiding the blunt impact of death by some divine providence.

As the early gray of dawn crawled across the sky, Hob realized he'd survived the night.

To his left, a fat black ball lolled this way and that — half submerged in the water.

Sam!

The rain was coming down more evenly now, in little more than a mist, and Hob watched the bear bob this way and that in the flood water. Not dead, surely? But not alive?

How strangely unreasonable that he, a wastrel of a boy (as Dowd and Stick and the Kempker boys called him) should survive such an ordeal, but a big, strong, denizen of nature be taken away.

It couldn't be true.

The water rushed on as it had all through the night and Hob tried to rouse the bear from his slumber. "S-sam?"

His voice was little more than a mouse's squeak.

"Sam?"

He bent one knee and was able to dip down and touch the slimy ground with a toe.

In spite of the current's tug, or maybe because of its numbing cold, his arm didn't hurt anymore, and Hob was able to navigate toward the bear.

When he got within the radius of Sam's sweeping claws, he hesitated. But there was no motion from the bear.

Hob was near the stake that held Sam's trap in the ground, could thrust his head under water and make out the wavering black shape. It swayed with the river water, loose, but still making a claim in the ground.

"If I could get behind it," thought Hob, "add my weight to the flow of the current . . ."

But of course, the idea wasn't so logically articulated.

Battered, starved, exhausted . . . Hob didn't truly think at all.

Sam was the coyote. The trickster.

This was all some kind of test, wasn't it? Hob narrowed his eyes and grinned.

Of course it was. A trick. A prank. A coyote test.

He pushed himself under and, reaching Sam's anchor, wrapped his good arm around it.

And pushed in the direction of the current.

If one of them should survive, it would be Sam.

Wouldn't that show coyote a thing or two? Hobnail Higgins wasn't so easily fooled.

Hobnail Higgins persevered.

There was great wrenching of the earth then, and another torrent of water hit, and spinning back toward his own circle of terror, Hob fell back into the dark.

The sun stabbed Hob's eyes with light.
Angry, he rolled over and pushed his face into the sloppy wet clay and growled.
"G'way . . ." he said. But the light wouldn't go away.
And something nudged him.
When he tried to move again, the hot pain in his arm forced his eyes open.
Sam's hot breath blew across his forehead from two inches away.
His long pink tongue shot out, dragged through Hob's hairline, reeled itself back in.
The bear's breath smelled like a latrine.
"H-hey . . . S-am."
Hob swallowed hard, realized he was still caught fast . . . but Sam was free.
The clouds had gone and the sky above was a shocking blue.
A gunshot in the distance pushed Sam to his hindlegs. The bear turned away to look up toward the rocky bluff. His nose twitched and the snuffing was as loud as the birdsong coming from the region of the creek.
Hob saw the water was slipping back into its border.
Sam lumbered a few steps back, dragging the chain and iron stake from the clamp on

his paw. He looked over his shoulder at Sam, then back toward the bluff as another gunshot rippled through the air.

"Get away there," said a cranky loud voice. "Get on with you." The gunshot again.

Sam gave Hob one last look, a parting glance after all they'd been through together.

Then the bear trundled across the open expanse of the field.

Hob watched him recede back up the trail he'd traveled down the morning before.

Even as King Ketchum hurried toward him, cursing under his breath, asking him if he was okay, Hob kept his eye on Sam's dark shape.

And at the very last, when there was nothing left but a speck and Ketchum knelt down beside him, Hob saw the bear turn into a coyote. He saw the trap slip away from the suddenly narrow hind leg and watched the trickster lope into the tall grass and disappear.

After growing up on a Nebraska farm, Spur Award and Amazon best-selling author **Richard Prosch** worked as a professional writer, artist, and teacher in Wyoming, South Carolina, and Missouri. His western crime fiction captures the fleeting history and lonely frontier stories of his youth where characters aren't always what they seem, and the windburned landscapes are filled with swift, deadly danger. Visit him online at www.RichardProsch.com.

DOUBLE TROUBLE
MEG MIMS

Ace Diamond checked the tough prairie grass for a clear spot to make a campfire. "This is as good a spot as any, I suppose."

His brother Layne stabbed a finger at him. "Just don't go burnin' the coffee tomorrow morning, like you did the other day."

Ace grunted. "Make it yourself then."

"I been doin' it near every time. I'm only asking for one day when I can get a little more shut-eye before we start out."

Layne swiped his sweaty forehead with his bandanna. His brown hair had been coated with prairie dust, cotton shirt and trousers, too, and his boots remained mud-caked from the last shallow river they'd crossed. Layne, younger by only eleven months and as near a twin in looks if not manner, had several inches on him — standing closer to six feet than Ace ever would. Layne slapped dust from his hat, almost futile given the dry summer weather.

"Whoo-whee. Hotter than those whiptail lizards roasted on a stick."

"Find something better for supper tonight." Ace walked back to his sorrel gelding. "I sure hope you figger out what you want to do soon."

"I know what I want. I'm just takin' my time getting there." Layne grinned. "You, on the other hand — well, Pa would say you're a tumbleweed."

"Better than endin' up a dead Army scout."

"I make good money. And you came close to bein' skinned alive by that sore loser, last poker game you played."

"Some people think good luck is the same as cheating."

"Well, I'm off. How about a chicken?" Layne slid his shotgun free from its scabbard and pocketed a dozen shells of ammunition. "Or a brace of jack rabbits."

"At this point I'd be happy with a snake. No more lizards, though."

Layne saluted him, mounted up, and rode west toward the taller grass. "I still say you're too picky, Ace."

He squinted one eye and stared at the relentless browned land around them. Ace had no idea if they'd crossed from northern Kansas into Nebraska Territory by now.

He'd ridden from Texas to meet up with Layne near Wichita, south of Fort Riley, early in the spring. To him, they'd wasted enough time wandering. Time to decide before autumn settled in, harboring colder weather. And Ace didn't cotton to shivering through a prairie winter.

Low bushes and a stunted cottonwood blocked their way east. That could mark a creek. He relieved his faithful horse of the saddle, then led Old Reb down slope toward a slow trickle that meandered west. Not much to drink their fill, but Ace slurped a few handfuls and splashed his dirt-streaked face and neck. Then he brushed his horse and checked each hoof. All this rolling prairie grass, the same view north, east, west, and south, didn't satisfy him.

He was tired of sitting in the saddle all day, too.

Ace had had his fill driving cattle last year, riding drag or back with the remuda, eating dust. What did he want? To stay alive, mainly, not taking hellish risks like his brother. He needed to find something fresh. Something new he could learn. Anything. Ace heard about the new railroad that snaked its way from Omaha across to Wyoming, across the mountains, and down to California. It sounded . . . too far. A thousand miles might as well be to the moon.

Then again, maybe he could win a stake and buy a train ticket west.

After hobbling Old Reb, Ace set about cutting the tough prairie grass with his knife. He widened the circle, took the coffeepot to fill it at the stream, then set it aside while he poured beans from their dwindling supply of Arbuckle's into the grinder.

Ace and his brother had moseyed around since they met. Layne had been on the lookout for a younger horse; they checked out small settlements and lonely farms until he succeeded. Checked out the few saloons, too. Luck was with them from the start, avoiding a party of outlaws — a mix of hard-nosed rustlers and horse thieves north of Fort Riley. Close call, that. And they'd barely survived the altercation with the gambler.

Now Layne had a week to reach Sherman Barracks a bit north of Omaha, to quit for good or sign on for a third term. The hot late July sun beating down wasn't their friend. Not enough water, too many gnats and horseflies. Once the beans were ground, Ace dumped them into the coffeepot. Maybe he did want to see the western mountains.

Not as an Army scout, though. Ace had

heard too many stories of violent run-ins with Indians for his taste. Taken too many orders from the trail boss or other hands. Spent too many nights on the hard ground with only a blanket. Not that he was soft, or wanted to settle in a town, but his own ranch? Maybe so. Breeding horses. That would suit him.

He'd had enough of wandering. Being his own boss was a long-held dream. Ace wasn't about to march under the broiling sun for hours on end, whenever Lieutenant Colonel Custer had a burr up his britches. The son of a gun treated his dogs better than his men, from what Layne told him. And he related a hair-raising tale of the Washita River battle, when they'd raided Black Kettle's Cheyenne camp. Ace had listened in silence.

Layne's hands had shaken in regret. "Custer is plum loco. He's not long for this world, the way his ego pushes him."

"Never thought you'd be party to such killing women and children."

"I ain't proud of it. But those Cheyenne raided and killed settlers."

"You could've snuck off without anyone noticing."

"And get shot in the back? What do you know about — oh, go to the devil!"

Layne had jumped him at that point, madder than a bronc busting loose. Ace got his fill in of punches while waiting for his brother's temper to cool. That cleared the air between them. They'd lost so much during the war — three older brothers had died at Shiloh. Layne and Ace had served under Rip Ford in Texas, then survived a few lean years after tracking ornery mossy horns in Texas. And Ace had long ago witnessed a cousin commit cold-blooded murder.

Who was he to judge his brother?

Layne had split off and chosen his path. Ace had done the same, but he wasn't sure if he could stomach knowing his brother wanted another term as a scout or soldier.

Ace found some dried dung and gathered some dead brushwood, then twisted some long buffalo grass to start the fire. His belly grumbled. That lizard last night hadn't taken the edge off the hunger pains that plagued him all day. He eyed grass all around, pistol ready, ready to bring down anything that moved. But only insects whirred around him as dusk deepened.

A short time later, Layne's low whistle signaled him from afar. That meant two things — trouble or a warning of it. Ace checked his pistol again. Each chamber full. Bowie knife at his hip, within reach. The handle of another knife tucked inside his boot. Ready for anything.

"Lookee what I found," Layne sang out, emerging on foot with his horse's reins in hand. "We got some company tonight."

Ace squinted against the setting sun. A female — a girl, probably sixteen or so by her wide pale eyes and fresh face, plus long black braids pinned over her head — perched atop his brother's saddle. Ace noted her brown dress, worn at the hem and mended badly on one side, hitched to show a dirty petticoat. Her slim ankles were encased in torn stockings, plus a pair of shoes with a cracked sole. A broken down nag followed his brother, its head down, and stumbled to a halt.

Along with an older man, white hair uncombed, beard flowing over his chest, who held a riding crop in one hand, a leather-bound Bible, and a chain with a wooden cross in the other.

"Preacher Willis at your service. Me and my daughter lost our way. We're lucky Mr. Diamond here came across us. We've got provisions to share, if you're willing."

"Not my call to make," Ace said, his voice low, and grabbed the dry brush and a thick chunk of wood his brother handed him. "No meat?"

"Nary a chicken in sight." Layne stared him down. "The girl's hurt. Knife cut, pretty deep. Might be infected."

"You a sawbones all of a sudden?"

"Shut up."

His brother reached up to circle her small waist and helped ease her from the saddle. The girl whimpered, favoring a leg, and slumped to the ground with a sob. She stared at Ace, which made him uncomfortable. The girl lifted a finger at him.

"Your eyes. They're different colors."

Her voice was raspy and high-pitched. His brother answered for him, though. "Ace was hit smack in one eye as a young'un. Both would be blue otherwise," Layne added. "Not his fault. But he's not as handsome as me, of course."

The girl smiled at that, which made his brother laugh. The preacher scowled. Ace ignored them all, busy building up the campfire. They were in for it, good or bad. Layne had a weakness for skirts. Once he caught sight of a female, nothing would hold him back except a wedding ring. Ace liked a pretty girl, no question of that, but not one who looked half-wild and scared. Out in the middle of nowhere, when females preferred civilized towns.

A dirty strip of muslin wrapped one of

her hands. Who could say how the girl got cut? And by who . . . given the old man's riding crop. Ace didn't like this. Not one bit.

Preacher Willis unpacked a fry pan from his saddle bag. "We got a tin or two of beans, at least, if there ain't no meat. Sorry we scared off the grouse, Mr. Diamond. We seen a blackbird, a ways back, but couldn't bring it down. Too bad. They make good eatin' in a pinch."

"Takes four and twenty for a pie," Layne said cheerfully. "From what my mama used to sing to us when we were young'uns. Ain't that right, Ace?"

"What an unusual moniker. The ace in a deck of cards, I presume." The old man shook a finger. "Gambling is one of the devil's games. You heard that, surely?"

"My brother is one of the luckiest players around."

"Luck is a myth. Only God's blessings are real."

"Well, me and my brothers started calling him that since he beat us all with three aces and a pair of queens. And cleaned out all the boys we served with during the war, too." Layne hunched down near the girl, as if expecting her to hold out her hand. "Even won a pot of gold and a fine watch from a real card shark. Everyone in the saloon was suspicious when he pulled out a fifth king from his sleeve! They all supported Ace."

The preacher clamped a hand on the girl's shoulder. "Let the man look at your wound, Hannah, for heaven's sake. 'Money gained by cheating is soon gone,' as the good book says. Cheating is a sin, and so is gambling, but that must have been an unwelcome surprise."

Ace wondered what the preacher meant — a surprise for the card shark, or him. He also didn't like the implication of being a sinner by gambling, but kept his focus on getting a spark from his flint. The grass finally caught, curled with a tiny flume of smoke, and flamed toward the brush wood. He didn't like Willis, who sat the cans of beans on the ground and settled on his haunches. Couldn't say why. His gut told him something was off.

Ace glanced at the silent girl. That bothered him, too.

When she gazed his way, he caught a slyness in her eyes that quickly vanished. She seemed skilled at using a mask of indifference. Or was it watchfulness? Hmm. Willis's gnarled hands showed his age as well past fifty. Even sixty. Had he fathered the girl? Or picked her up on his preaching circuit?

They didn't resemble each other in the least. Not like him and his brother. The girl's injuries rankled Ace as well.

"Where are you boys heading?" Preacher Willis asked. "We're shootin' for Dodge City. Heard there's ornery fellas in need of being wakened to the Spirit."

"Nowhere special." Ace flashed his brother a warning look, but Layne missed it.

"Reckon I'll rejoin the Army as a scout," he said. "We're heading north of Omaha, to Sherman Barracks."

"Fighting the Injuns, then?"

"Whatever we're assigned to do, we do."

The preacher nodded, although Ace caught a glint in his eye before he turned back to his horse. What the devil did these two want? And why would Layne trust them so easy? He took out the last of the cornmeal, added a little oil and salt to their skillet, and fried up four cakes. Layne stuck his knife in the tin cans, pried them open, and dumped them into Preacher Willis's pan. Too bad his brother hadn't brought back a real supper instead of strangers.

Their guests ate in silence, using bits of their corncakes to spoon up the beans. The girl kept one pale eye on Layne, although one stray hunk of dark hair hid most of her face. The old man slurped coffee from a tin cup and then yanked the empty plate from his daughter.

"Quit moonin', Hannah," he growled, "and wash up the dishes."

"No need." Ace spooned the last of his beans. "I'll take care of it."

"Well, we're obliged for sharin' supper with us."

"Same here. Now I'd better take a look see at that cut." Layne squatted beside Hannah. Once he stripped off the bandage, he winced. "Don't look good. I'll have to wash it out, and then see if I can sew it up."

"No needle or thread on us," Preacher Willis said. "Clumsy girl hurt her leg. It's her fault she sliced her hand open, too."

Ace noticed an old bruise on the girl's temple before Hannah used her stray hair to hide her face again. He figured she had other hurts and scars beneath her dress. The old man probably knocked her around. He glanced at his brother, who slowly poured water from his canteen over Hannah's cut, then sloshed a bit of whiskey over it. She yelped, snatching her arm away, and fell backwards on the ground. Scuttled away like a scared rabbit and cowered near Willis.

"Go on, girl. He's trying to help. You can't do a lick of work unless that heals up."

The preacher shoved her toward Layne.

Ace jumped to his feet, his anger simmering. He didn't take to seeing women or girls mistreated, but Layne plucked his sleeve. Shouldered him aside, and fetched something from his saddlebag.

"You're in luck, Miss Hannah." He shook out his spare kerchief and showed a handful of greenery. "I picked these yesterday when we headed out from camp. Yarrow."

"What the hell is that?"

Willis sounded surly, as if he'd turned suspicious. He didn't sound preacher-like now, to Ace's ears. He itched to call the man out as a liar, and find out what he really wanted from them, but Layne held up a hand.

"This will heal her cut. See that line of red, going up to her wrist? That's a bad sign."

"Am I gonna die?" she whispered, her high voice trembling.

"Nah. This will help draw the poison out. You'll be good as new soon."

Hannah inched forward, and bit her lip to keep from crying out when Layne dabbed more whiskey over the palm with a clean cloth. Then he placed the young leaves along the cut and bound up the wound. Layne flashed his broad, friendly smile when she settled back in relief. Willis laid out a blanket on the ground and set his horse's saddle to use as a pillow. He didn't bother giving his blanket to the girl.

If Hannah really was the old man's daughter, Ace would eat his hat.

Uneasy, he sat on a rise, loosened his spurs, and set them aside with reluctance. Pulled off his boots, then poured a fine red powder and gravel from them. "I'll be. To think I been walkin' on Texas dirt all this time."

"We always carry burdens, every one of us," Willis said, shaking a finger. "We are all sinners. We deserve fire and brimstone according to the good book —"

"Leave the good book closed, Preacher," Layne interrupted. "It ain't Sunday."

"The Bible is not only a guide for the Lord's day. One should read the Word every day, and follow it." He glared at Hannah. "Some children have fallen far, and cannot see the way it leads to redemption. Sinners will be punished!"

"Is that right." Ace pushed his hat back on his head and squinted at Willis. "That how she got cut? Wasn't from a knife, but a whip. Like the one you carry."

"You lie, and your eyes are the devil's own," Willis roared. "I never seen a man before with mismatched eyes! And one green — that's the mark of Satan."

"Easy now, preacher." Layne had his pistol in hand, although he didn't cock it. "You can mosey off right now, you and your daughter, or apologize to my brother. Like I said, it wasn't his fault gettin' hit as a boy. And there ain't no devil's work here unless you brought it."

Willis calmed down at that, but remained grim. "You'd turn us out in the darkness? That is callow, sir. My daughter is injured, she cannot walk half a mile or more. And my horse is nearly lame."

"Apologize or head out."

The old man glared at Ace and muttered a 'sorry' under his breath. Layne grinned. "You know, I heard enough about sin whenever a new missionary came around the barracks, hoping to save lost souls of the Injuns. Promise you'll leave off the preaching."

"Hannah?" The old man glanced at the girl, who had rummaged in her father's saddlebag and brought out a tattered shawl. Now she hunched on the fire's other side and nodded. "Then it's settled. I will leave off preaching — although you both look like you could use several Scripture verses from Proverbs. Surely you wouldn't object to wise sayings?"

Ace snorted. "Depends on who's doing

the saying."

Willis glared at him. " 'The fear of the Lord is the beginning of wisdom —' "

"You promised," Hannah whispered. "Hush."

"We shall sleep now." The old man stretched out on his side, facing the fire.

"All right then." Layne slid the pistol into his holster with a nod. "I'll fetch more wood. We'll keep the fire going all night, keep the coyotes at bay."

Once his brother returned with an armful of dead branches, Ace joined him in breaking them up and setting them near the crackling campfire. "What have you gotten us into," he said in a hissed whisper. "Custer sure fried your brain, but good."

"No harm in a little girl. And either one of us can take that old man." Layne glanced at Willis, already snoring. "You'll see. And you're right about that cut. He lashed her but good with that quirt. Old nag has scars, too. We oughter thrash him with it, see how he likes it. I don't cotton to any coward takin' out his anger on animals or kids."

"We'll take turns then, keeping watch."

His brother sighed. "You first. I'm bushed."

Darkness had fallen, although the moon hadn't risen yet. Ace pulled his boots back on, rolled his blanket tight, and used it as a pillow when he stretched out flat on his back. Willis snored loud, head resting sideways on his saddle bags. Layne curled on the ground. He snored within minutes. His brother could sleep in a wink of an eye. Ace remained wary, though. He'd slept deep the night before. He didn't mind watching the sky overhead, wondering what the next few days would bring. The next week. A month from now.

He had no real plans. Maybe he ought to come up with one.

The constant chirr-chirr of crickets mingled with an occasional pop from the wood in their dancing campfire. Ace scratched his chest and perked up at a coyote's distant howl. The horses didn't notice. Reb swished his tail when someone sighed deep and shifted. He stared upward, the tiny white pinpricks wheeling side to side. When the fire's light dimmed, Ace set a few more pieces of wood cross-wise over the charred pieces in the dirt.

Settled back down, shifted his pillow, and checked his gun. Loaded and ready. He wasn't gonna get caught off-guard. Not with strangers sharing their campfire.

So Layne decided to sign up again as an Army Scout. Ace could think of a dozen things far better. His brother had ridden part of the way from Wyoming east on the new transcontinental railroad. Ace figured he'd head in the opposite direction. There was bound to be men eager to play a hand or two of poker, whiling away the long journey to California. But how could he earn fast money for a ticket? Only by gambling, and that meant heading to Omaha.

Ace wasn't sure he ought to risk another face-off with a professional gambler. They sure hated to lose. But he hadn't cheated back in Wolf Creek. Ace managed to avoid the law, given what happened, but had to pay off the saloon owner for the damages. Layne had borrowed Ace's last few dollars when his horse went lame, and found a decent bay, not too old. That meant his brother planned to rejoin the Army long before he announced it today.

The sliver of a moon slowly moved while he pondered his future. Ace figured midnight must have come and gone, but Layne slept on. He didn't have the heart to let him take over the watch. Serving in the Army didn't seem much better than chasing cattle.

He sighed, closing his eyes for a moment.

Ace startled awake at Reb's restless snort. A shadow hovered over him. He twisted aside on instinct at Layne's yelp of warning, scrabbled for his pistol. Gone. He snatched up something close at hand, though, and swung it in a high arc sideways with all his might. Willis screamed in agony and fell with a thump.

"Hold it right there, mister. I dunno what you just did to the preacher, but I'm the one in charge." Hannah's high voice crackled. Ace could barely see her, his own pistol in her hand, beside the dying fire. She cocked it, too. "Don't try anything funny."

"Try what?" Ace inched a hand closer to his boot. "Layne? You all right?"

"I'm here—"

Ace heard a pistol shot, which ricocheted off a tree in his brother's direction. "Stop, stop! You'll shoot one of the horses," Layne shouted. "Looks like she's got the drop on us, Ace. Better do as she says."

"Smart man." Hannah sounded hardened, so different from the timid girl who'd cowered earlier. "Willis said you might not be worth the trouble, but I disagreed. We killed the last two who didn't cooperate. Now hand over the gold, or I'll shoot you in the head."

"Gold?" Layne snorted. "We don't have any gold."

"You told us your brother won a pot of

gold. Must be in your saddle bags. I ain't stupid. He's been guarding those bags like they're chock full. Hand over the watch, too. I can sell it, if it fetches a good price. Come on, do as I say."

"We don't have a pot to piss in, except the one we use for coffee." Layne cursed when she fired another shot from the pistol, and all three horses shied in terror. "We're flat broke, Hannah. I swear it."

Ace rose slowly onto one knee, crouching low. How the hell would they get out of this predicament in one piece? He'd known these two were trouble. Layne had gone soft in the head, and now they were paying for it.

"Don't lie to me about the gold," Hannah cried out. "One last chance, mister."

Preacher Willis moaned and rolled aside. He didn't raise his head or body, however. Ace wondered how badly the man was wounded. Layne sucked in a deep breath.

"Girl, you got us dead wrong."

"You got the dead part right —"

Ace had reached into his boot, however, and flung his knife at the girl. Hannah gurgled in her throat at the same time as a third deafening pistol shot rang out. Layne grabbed the weapon she dropped before she fell to her knees. Ace rushed over, saw his stiletto sticking out the side of her neck, and barely avoided the blood spraying forth. Talk about pure luck. He'd only guessed the direction of where she stood by the sound of her voice.

He wiped sweaty palms on his trousers. "Layne? You all right?"

"Yeah." His brother sighed. "You?"

"I'm good."

"So what the hell happened to Willis? First let's see to the girl."

Layne dragged Hannah closer to the fire's light. Her pale eyes widened, and her body went limp. Her bound hand slid from the knife's handle. Guilt washed over Ace. He'd never killed a woman before, and his stomach roiled. He turned away and walked to check on the old man lying on his side. Ace crouched beside him. Was he a goner, too? Willis moaned aloud.

Layne clapped Ace on the back, startling him, and so hard he almost lost his balance. "Guess he ain't dead yet, but not far from it," his brother said. "Sure packed a wallop with that spur of yours. Cracked his head open, and he's bleedin' like a stuck pig."

Ace glanced at the blood streaming from the preacher's head, drenching his face, coat, shirt, and collar. One of his spurs was also stained red, and he realized he'd swung it so hard in anger and frustration at being taken by surprise.

"What should we do?"

"Nothing much to do." Layne dragged Willis next toward the fire's embers, beside the dead girl. "Old man, can you hear me?"

"My head's on fire." The preacher breathed heavy. "That girl roped me into thievery. For that I am sorry. I have sinned, and now am paying for it."

Ace peered at the wide open gash on Willis's skull. He wasn't sure, but thought he saw white bone. "Can't you bind this up for him, Layne?"

"I doubt it would help. Lost too much blood, for sure."

"Leave me be," Willis whispered. "I'm dyin'. No promised land for me, boys."

His breathing slowed. Willis refused a drink of water, so Layne sat back on his heels. Ace and his brother waited until they heard the death rattle a short time later. Ace shook his head in regret at two deaths on his head.

"Damnation."

Layne stuck the pistol in his belt. "Would have been us, you know. Sure as shootin', they'd have gutted us and stolen our horses. They admitted to murder before. And for what? They wouldn't have gotten any pot of gold from us."

"You shouldn't have been bragging on me."

"Maybe so, but these two deserved their fate. Without a shovel, we can't bury either 'em. This will have to do." Layne fetched the blankets and covered both bodies. "Well, Ace. We're even. I saved your hide down at Palmito Ranch. You saved mine tonight."

"Don't even remind me of Palmito. And I'm waiting till full light," Ace said. "I ain't gonna risk my Reb breaking a leg in the dark. No way can I get me a better horse. And I hope you learned your lesson. Quit bein' a sucker, even for a ripped and dirty skirt."

Layne wiped his sweaty face with a sleeve. "You been suspicious your whole life of everyone and everything."

"Comes from havin' older brothers. Couldn't trust any of them."

Ace couldn't sleep much, dozing off and on for several hours until dawn. Then they kicked dirt over what was left of the burned wood and ashes, saddled up, and didn't look back at the blanketed forms under the splintered cottonwood. Nature would take its course.

Ace eyed the eastern sky, tippling yellow and rose against the purple horizon, while

Layne bit off a plug of tobacco. "You decide where you're going, Ace?"

"Omaha. Gonna head out to California, if I can make it that far."

Layne nodded. "You will, somehow. Just keep a spur handy."

Award-winning mystery author **Meg Mims** earned a Spur Award for Best First Novel, *Double Crossing* in 2012 from the Western Writers of America, and a Laramie Award for the sequel, *Double or Nothing*. Both feature the character of Ace Diamond and are available from Prairie Rose Publications. Meg has also written several western romance novellas, plus several short stories in the Wolf Creek series by Western Fictioneers. Meg lives in Southeastern Michigan, loves reading historical and contemporary mysteries, gardening, and watercolor painting.

Gilbert Hopkins is Going to Die
Angela Raines

"You're going to die, Gilbert Hopkins, everyone does. But not today." Gilbert said every morning upon arising, and every evening after his meal. "You have yet to make your mark on the world." He also would remind himself at odd times during the day.

The day was like so many others in his life. At the start of the day, Gilbert would put on the coffee, take care of his ablutions, then sit and prepare the list of his daily tasks. Day after day he followed this routine. At night he would review his list and add anything he felt should be included. In his mind, this was the perfect way to achieve his goal of making his mark in the world. Gilbert knew he was going to die, everyone did. However, he wanted to be remembered.

From an early age, Gilbert always believed he would make a huge difference in the world. He'd pondered how he'd accomplish this goal and decided being a newspaperman was the way to achieve it. He'd studied important reporters and newspaper owners trying to learn their secrets. He made sure he went to school every single day soaking in all the teacher offered. When he decided he was ready, although only thirteen, he got a job with the local paper. He believed starting at the bottom was the best way to learn the business, even if it meant working in the evenings after school.

After about six months, Gilbert started hinting to his boss that he should let him report on what was happening in the town around them.

"Mr. Harper, I'm out and about a great deal and you would be surprised at how people talk when they think it's only a youngster standing nearby."

Mr. Harper would stand there, hand smoothing his beard as if he were contemplating letting Gilbert try his hand at reporting. In the end, however, he would shake his head in the negative saying, "You may have a point, but I don't think you're ready."

These setbacks only incited Gilbert to try again and again and again until finally, one evening when the two of them were closing up, Mr. Harper gave his assent.

Gilbert smiled at himself in the mirror

remembering that first story. It was about how the local mill owner was shortchanging his customers by a few ounces each. Gilbert cringed at the memory of Mr. Harper's response to his story.

"Gilbert, you have the makings of a reporter, but you have to remember papers run on revenue from advertisements. Mr. Grassland spends a great deal on advertising in this paper. Do you understand what I'm saying?"

"But Mr. Harper I thought reporting was just that, telling the truth?"

It had been ten years since that day. Ten years to the day Gilbert realized. He'd learned his lesson but it was not one he'd enjoyed. Now as the owner of the prairie town of Travers only newspaper he realized that Mr. Harper had been correct. It still rankled that money was more important than telling the whole truth. Still, a person had to eat. "At least you can tell the truth most of the time," he told his reflection.

Washing the dishes from this morning's and evening meals, Gilbert put on his coat and headed to the newspaper office to finish the copy for the upcoming issue.

Walking down that dusty street his eyes took in the weathered storefronts, worn hitch rails, and the periodic busted slats of the boardwalk. They didn't look so old and forlorn in the rosy glow of the setting sun he thought with a smile.

At the end of the short street, where it met the main thoroughfare sat his small newspaper office. With a smile on his face and a lift of his shoulders, Gilbert unlocked the door and stepped inside. The smell of oil, ink, and he had to admit sweat, greeted him.

He turned right and walked to his desk removing his coat and hanging it on the hat tree. He lit the lamp and pulling out his chair Gilbert reread the notes he'd made for his upcoming editorial beginning the process of editing before setting the type for tomorrow's paper.

When he'd arrived in this small town it had been his goal to grow the paper to a daily publication. But weather, crop failures, lowered cattle prices, and the recession squashed that dream. Still, he was not ready to give up.

"You will make a difference in this world, Gilbert Hopkins, you will," he said to the four walls surrounding him. "You are still young and have plenty of time."

He was almost finished with the edits when he heard the door open. Glancing up Gilbert saw a young child about the age of eight, the small frame back-lit by the setting sun.

" 'Scuse me, sir," the child said. "Are ya the one I talk to 'bout puttin' a ad in the paper?"

"Yes, I am," Gilbert replied. The little imp of a child made him wonder what kind of advertisement they were thinking of. He asked the first questions that popped into his head. "How old are you? And what type of advertisement were you thinking of?"

"I'm twelve, an' I'm hopin' ta find my mother."

Of all the things Gilbert would have expected, the words startled him. Still, he felt his reputation as one of seeking the truth was worth finding out more. It was an attitude, a badge of honor so to speak.

At the same time, Gilbert wanted to know what happened and why someone so young would want to advertise for their mother?

As he thought about it, Gilbert knew he had a story, if the child were willing to share what happened with him. Gently and professionally as possible he asked a general question, "Do you think your mother lives here, or somewhere in the area?"

The child, who looked nowhere near twelve with big brown eyes and short auburn hair, looked first right then left, then softly answered, "Don't know. Father has, had, a place 'bout twenty miles north o' here. A'for he died he told me ta' try and find my mother."

"Did you walk all the way here?" Gilbert asked, wondering at the constitution of the child if they'd walked the whole way. Then he realized the child said the father had died. He frowned, his brow furrowing.

"I 'ave money ta pay," the child interjected quickly having seen the frown. Then as if anticipating a rejection added, "Father said mother left when I was 'bout a year old. I 'ave a picture if'n that'll help."

Reaching out Gilbert took the photograph, smiling at how quickly the child had driven the point home. Looking down at the young face he could see the resemblance. He wondered what would have caused the woman to leave, to leave her child. What kind of woman or what circumstances led to her actions?

Looking up Gilbert saw the hope in the child's eyes. He didn't want to disappoint yet he didn't want to give false hope. "I know most of the people around here, and I've not seen anyone who looks like this woman. If you would like we can send her description to the papers in addition to this one and see if anyone might know of her whereabouts. Would that be okay?"

"If'n it'll help me find my mother," the child answered, an attitude of hope straightening the tired shoulders and bringing a smile to brown eyes. "Mother's name, accordin' to father, was Esther, Esther Giddens. My name is Zoe Giddens."

So, the child was a girl. Gilbert chastised himself for not realizing or asking earlier. Smiling to hide his misstep, Gilbert said, "Well Zoe Giddens, let's see if we can find your mother. It would help if you could tell me your father's name."

"Micah, why?"

"Well, sometimes when you are looking for people, they may have the same name. If you know the other family names, it helps to find the right one."

"Oh, never, thought o' that."

"You said your father was dead?"

"Yes, sir."

"When? What happened?"

Zoe cast her eyes downward. "Last week. The horse fell on him an' I couldn't get it off'en him."

Gilbert came from around the desk. Had this child tried to move a horse from on top of her father? What an ordeal that must have been, he thought. "I'm sorry. Is that why you are looking for your mother?"

At a nod from Zoe, Gilbert suggested, "What say we start by seeing if anyone recognizes this photograph? It's not so late that some folks are still around. Then later, if you feel like it, you can tell me more of what happened."

Gilbert hoped by giving the child time and the chance to feel a bit more comfortable with him, he would get a more complete and truthful story.

Zoe smiled and taking Gilbert's hand they walked from the office. Crossing the street, they turned left heading toward the General Store. Old man Clemens, a skinflint, but Gilbert's best customer, had been in the area almost since the beginning. In some ways, he was the reason Gilbert's plans hadn't happened as quickly as possible. He'd hoped to bring news and culture to the area, but when the biggest customer fought you at every step, it made things difficult. Still, he hadn't given up hope, yet.

As the two walked into the store Clemens looked up. Frowning, he groused, "Oh it's you, I done put my ad in this week."

"And I appreciate it," Gilbert smiled at the old goat out of habit. "What I came in for is to see if you remember this woman?"

The old man reached for the photo Gilbert held. Pulling his spectacles down to the end of his nose he studied the photo. "Nope, who is she?"

"This young lady's mother, Esther Giddens, this young lady is Zoe Giddens."

Zoe held back, hiding behind Gilbert's legs. She flinched when Clemens looked at her as he queried, "Giddens, you any relation to Micah Giddens?"

"She's his daughter," Gilbert answered.

Gilbert watched Clemens' eyes take on a hard look. His stomach tensed as he asked, "You look like you know, ah, knew him?"

"What you mean knew?" Clemens asked. "That no account bum owes me twenty dollars and it's been almost a year."

Zoe stared at the old man, tears forming in her eyes. She cautiously stepped backward, moving even further behind Gilbert.

"This young lady said he's dead," Gilbert said, glaring at the callousness of the old man.

"Well then, I suppose the young lady can work his debt off," Clemens stated.

"Work his debt off, what are you talking about?" Gilbert demanded. He was having problems trying to comprehend how someone could be so callous as to ask a twelve-year-old girl to work off her father's debt.

"I can't run a store with no money," Clemens justified, "an' since she's his next

119

of kin she owes his money."

Reaching into his pocket, Gilbert snarled, "Here's your twenty. Zoe, I think it's time we left, we'll get no help here."

Out on the walk, Gilbert looked at the child in the fast-fading light. Her eyes were moist as she brushed the back of her hand against them. "We'll head over to the livery. Phin's also been around these parts for some time, he may know something."

Striding down the street, Gilbert's mind was jumping ahead to the editorial he would be writing for the next issue of the paper. He'd overlooked many things over the years, especially in this town he'd made his home, but now was the time to take a stand. He would make Clemens wish he had never been born. Gilbert's anger cooled with the evening wind. His common sense and the need to pay his bills intruded in on his thoughts of righteousness. Still, he felt Clemens's behavior was beyond acceptable, he just didn't know how he could deal with the issue.

Gilbert was brought up short by a mournful cry from behind him.

"Wait, wait."

Looking back Gilbert realized in his anger at the recent incident and his long strides he'd left Zoe far behind. Releasing clenched fist, Gilbert stopped, taking in a deep breath.

Watching Zoe hurrying forward, Gilbert caught a glimpse of her mother's beauty beneath the ragged clothes and dirty feet.

Soon, the two were standing in front of the livery. Phineas was nowhere to be seen. Peering into the dark interior Gilbert could just make out movement at the back of the building just beyond the lamplight. "Hey, is that you back there, Phineas?"

Hearing no answer, Gilbert asked again, louder this time. Whoever was there turned, and Gilbert felt a bullet fly by his ear as the shot sounded. He could barely make out someone running out the back. Turning to Zoe, and seeing she hadn't been hurt, Gilbert ordered, "You stay here."

Gilbert took off after the shooter. Just before the backdoor Gilbert tripped. Leaning down Gilbert saw Phineas lying on his side blood matting his hair near the temple. Seeing that the old man was still breathing he called to Zoe, "Go get the doctor, Zoe, his house is about five down from my newspaper office."

Gilbert took off after the fleeing shooter. He didn't know if he would catch them, but without any law, in their small town, he felt that his civic duty to do his best. He didn't think, with the poor light, that he was in any danger of being shot. It seemed the person was more interested in getting away.

Shooting out of the back door of the livery, Gilbert quickly looked left then right. He didn't think the person would've gone straight for the corral was that way. He was wrong. Gilbert caught a movement on the backside of the corral just as another shot rang out.

Gilbert saw the shooter run off into the dark. With a burst of speed, Gilbert took off after them. He'd almost caught up to what he saw was a young man when he tripped over a log. It probably saved his life as another bullet flew by. Jumping up he continued after the fleeing man, chanting to himself, "You're going to die, Gilbert Hopkins, everyone does."

Five minutes later the runner looked to be struggling to keep going. Gilbert despite his sedentary job was feeling good. No further shots rang out for which Gilbert was grateful. His chanting seemed to keep his feet moving steadily. With a final burst of speed, Gilbert tackled the man to the ground. His captive swung the gun toward Gilbert. Gilbert ducked rolling over and up while retaining a hand on the man's shirt. With a triumphant shout, Gilbert finished, "But not today."

"What?" his captive asked.

"Never mind. Why did you hit Phineas?"

"Phineas? Don't know what you're talking about," the man snarled.

"Phineas is the man in the livery, the one who's lying there, his hair matted with blood where you," Gilbert was unable to finish as the man began struggling, trying to bring the empty gun to bear.

"I didn't do it, I didn't do it," the man began once Gilbert had wrenched the gun away. "He was that way when I walked in and I was checking on him when I heard you holler. I got scared and took off."

"Well, we'll just have to go back and check your story out. Of course, you shooting at me doesn't help your story. You better hope Phineas will be okay," Gilbert said, then added, "because if he dies,"

"Because if he dies, you'll blame me," the man finished.

"So, you better hope Phineas doesn't die," Gilbert replied, tightening his grip. "Now, let's head back and find out, shall we."

The man stopped struggling, but Gilbert didn't let up his grip as they walked back. At the rear of the livery, Gilbert saw Zoe's big eyes staring at him in the lantern light, then at the man with her. She backed up, as the two entered the building. "The doctor is lookin' at the man who was hurt," she told him.

"Thank you, Zoe. I couldn't have done it without you."

Zoe shook her head as if to deny what Gilbert said, but her eyes told a different story. Gilbert found himself feeling good about what he'd done but wasn't sure what to do with his captive.

"Take him over to the storage shed behind Clemens' store. He should be secure enough until we can get the marshal over here," the doctor said, looking up at Gilbert's question.

"What about Phineas?" Gilbert asked.

"He'll have a headache, but nothing else seems to be wrong."

Gilbert thanked the doctor, relieved the old man was going to be okay. Then steering the attacker out the door, Gilbert marched the man over to the shed, Zoe following along. Clemens, seeing them coming started to complain when Gilbert cut the man off. "Get the keys to the shed. We're holding this man for assaulting Phineas."

Clemens went inside, returning with the keys. Once the man was secure, Gilbert took Zoe by the hand, ignoring Clemens' demand for details. "You can read about it in the paper," then to Zoe, he added, "let's see if we can get you cleaned up and a place to stay while we look for your mother."

The next morning Gilbert, after sending out the papers, went to the livery to rent a horse for a trip to Zoe's home. Phineas insisted he ride along.

"Are you sure you're up to it, Phin?"

"Son, if what you've said is true, you're gonna' need help."

They arrived mid-afternoon to a barren piece of land with a dilapidated cabin. Gilbert gagged at the smell when they located the dead horse along with the man under him in the field not too far from the house.

"Pretty young to die," Phineas commented as the two walked up to the scavenged corpses.

Gilbert thought of what Phineas said. It hit him that Zoe's father was about the same age as himself. "Yeah, he was."

"Still, he left a mighty fine young daughter," Phineas added as they moved the horse from atop Micah Giddens. They buried him under a tree near the house.

By the time they'd finished, it was dark, so the two stayed in the cabin.

"Seems somehow wrong to stay here," Gilbert said as they made their beds near the door.

"Perhaps, but it's better than bein' caught out in the rain."

"But . . ."

"Son, if there's shelter, take it. 'Sides, you can take back the girl's things."

"What few she may have," Gilbert said, as he lit another lantern and started searching the place.

"What you doin'?"

"I'd rather look tonight and get an early start in the morning."

"Just don't take too long," Phineas groused the white bandage on his head bobbing as he lay down, his head resting on his saddle.

"I won't," Gilbert answered grinning at the old man's advice.

Three weeks later Gilbert was in a fine mood. After writing the modified editorial about the selfishness of some people he felt satisfied, although Clemens was none too happy. The story of the trial of Phineas' attacker and subsequent jail time had helped paper sales too.

Gilbert was amazed at how Zoe had flourished, quickly learning her letters. She was also working her way through learning to read. He'd brought back some papers he'd found that the young girl might want when older, but little else was worth anything at her former home.

Gilbert had sent wires of the story to the large cities around the country having failed to learn anything close by. Three days ago he received an answer. Zoe's aunt was arriving today. Gilbert also learned that Zoe's mother had died of consumption in Colorado. Her aunt had lost track of her brother in law and was looking forward to seeing her niece.

Gilbert hurried through his day. He wanted to have a chance to speak with Zoe about what she might expect. He had to admit to himself that he'd become very fond of the young girl, almost as if she were his child.

Hurrying down the street to the Widow Harkins place, Gilbert hoped he would be in time to join Zoe and the widow, who had taken her in, for the evening meal.

Knocking on the door Gilbert smoothed his hair after removing his hat. He was in the act of replacing it just as the door opened. Quickly removing it again, Gilbert smiled, "Good evening Mrs. Harkins, I've come to speak with Zoe if she's available."

Mrs. Harkins smiled, the edge of her gray eyes crinkling in her aged face as she replied, "Yes she is. She's been excited all day. I've had my hands full keeping her occupied," the lady smiled even wider, "and you are just in time for dinner."

Gilbert knew that he should dissemble but somehow that didn't fit his mood. "Now how did you know I'd not eaten?"

Mrs. Harkins laughed, "I know you young man, homemade bread, jam, and beef stew are a sure thing with you."

"You know me so well Mrs. Harkins, I never could pass up a slice of freshly baked bread, and you make the best."

"I swear Gilbert, your enthusiasm for my cooking makes me wonder if you ever get a decent meal," Mrs. Harkins said stepping aside to let Gilbert in.

Gilbert placed his hat on the hat rack, following Mrs. Harkins as she entered the kitchen. Zoe sat at the table her hair shining and wearing a new dress. If Gilbert had been so inclined, he would be jealous of this relative that was coming to take Zoe away. What started as a scary, tenuous journey had blossomed into a community's love for the young orphan. Once they heard her story they were all eager to do what they could to make her stay in town as enjoyable as possible.

Seating himself at the table Gilbert turned toward Zoe asking, "Are you excited about meeting your aunt?"

"How do we know it's my aunt? To tell you the truth Mr. Gilbert, I'm scared."

Mrs. Harkins walked in as Zoe answered Gilbert's question. Setting the stew along with the jam and bread on the table she placed a hand on the young girl's shoulder. "You know Zoe, chances are your aunt is anxious to meet you, but if you need more time the two of you can stay with me as you get to know each other. How does that sound to you?"

"Could I really do that?" Zoe asked in a shy voice.

Gilbert smiled at Mrs. Harkins, pleased she'd found the right way to answer Zoe's question. He turned to Mrs. Harkins and then Zoe. "Mrs. Harkins is right, but we will be right here with you until the matter is settled. Now, how about we eat," Gilbert added as he reached for a slice of bread at the same time Zoe did. The two of them set off in a fit of giggles and Mrs. Harkins smiled widely.

The three set about making inroads on the food. Glancing at his watch Gilbert said," I need to get down to the paper, but I will be back in plenty of time to go with you to meet your aunt."

"And I will go with you," Mrs. Harkins added.

"I wish I could stay here with both of you," Zoe said, "but sometimes we don't get to do what we want to do we?"

"Zoe, you have a long life ahead of you, don't be afraid of setbacks, or worrying about what your life might be. You are going to do something great, I just know," Gilbert said as he rose and patted her on the shoulder.

Gilbert started to walk away then remembering returned to the kitchen, "Shall I bring some flowers to give to your aunt?"

Mrs. Harkins looked at Zoe, a question in her eyes. At a nod, Mrs. Harkins replied, "I think that might be a good idea." If experience had taught her anything, Mrs. Harkins knew based on her history how sometimes something so simple as a gift of flowers could ease a tough situation.

Gilbert nodded and grabbing his hat walked out the door. First, he headed to the newspaper office and there Mr. Clemens greeted him with a scowl on his face. "I thought it over and suggest you retract what you said, or I'll pull all my advertising from your paper."

Gilbert knew this might happen, but he was unwilling to be flexible on this subject.

It was time Mr. Clemens was held accountable for his behavior. "I understand your need for people to pay their bills, but to be rude to a child who just lost her parent is unacceptable. If you choose to pull your advertising, I understand but I stand by what I wrote."

Clemens's face turned red, his eyes flashing, "Very well, consider my business at an end with you."

Gilbert watched the man walk away. He realized he might be slitting his own throat, but his principles would not allow him to back down again.

After Clemens left, he walked over to the stage stop where he learned the stage would probably be on time. Gilbert thought he might be able to check with Miss Winters about placing an ad for her sewing. He was crossing the street when he heard a shout from Clemens store.

"Stop that thief!"

After the way Clemens had acted Gilbert was tempted to turn the other way, but seeing the young man run past, an apple in his hand, Gilbert reached out to halt the fleeing thief. Somehow the young man twisted away dashing across the street. With a glance at Clemens, who was standing and shouting, the setting sun at his back, Gilbert took off after the culprit. The young man had just cleared the street, Gilbert close behind, when the stage came around the corner. Gilbert tried to dodge out of the way, but the lead horse clipped him across the back then as he was trying to regain his balance the stage wheel hit him. His mind screamed *I can't die; I've not made a difference. No, no . . . ,* as the world faded to black.

The stage stopped. The driver jumped down, as a passenger alighted from inside. Both rushed to the unconscious man. From down the street, a high sharp cry sounded as Zoe rushed up to where Gilbert lay.

"Mr. Gilbert, Mr. Gilbert," Zoe cried as she lay her small body across her friend.

Mrs. Harkins following close behind reached down to lift Zoe, but the child refused to let go. "Zoe, you need to step back so we can see,"

"I can't let him go, I need to take care of him," the young girl interrupted, tears streaming down her face.

The passenger, a well-dressed young woman, reached over, and placing a hand on Gilbert's neck, turned toward the young child. "He's still alive, but we need to get him to a doctor. Is there one in town?"

"Yes, there is," Mrs. Harkins answered. "If

you wouldn't mind staying here, I'll go get him?"

"I don't mind," the woman said, then turning to Zoe added, "young lady, I know he means a lot to you. It would help if you stepped back so the driver and I can take a look."

Zoe stared at the woman, then wiping the tears from her eyes with the back of her hand she nodded and moved back about two steps.

Gilbert groaned as they gently turned him over. His eyes fluttered open, "You look just like,"

Whatever he was going to say remained unsaid as he passed out again.

Zoe started crying, large tears of fear and pain flowing down her cheeks.

"Young lady, everybody dies, but Mr. Gilbert is not going to die today!" The young woman stated as she reached for the young girl's hand.

Two hours later Mrs. Harkins, Zoe, and the stagecoach passenger were there when Gilbert opened his eyes. "I seem to remember being hit by a horse, but I must be okay or in heaven."

"You're not in heaven," said the young woman, "and I am glad. Allow me to formally introduce myself to you and my niece,

I am Ruth Banks, sister to Zoe's mother."

"Nice to meet you, Mrs. Banks," Gilbert said, his eyes taking in the chestnut hair, a glow like a halo surrounding the woman. He knew it was just the lamplight, but he sensed she was an angel.

"You're my aunt?" Zoe asked.

Kneeling, Ruth looked Zoe in the eyes. "Yes, I am. You know you look a lot like your mother."

"That's what my father," Zoe began, then she rushed to her aunt, hugging her close.

Rising, Zoe's hand in hers she turned to Gilbert saying, "And it's Miss Banks."

Gilbert looked at Zoe and her aunt. Their faces were shadowed, halos surrounding their heads from the lamplight behind them. His head hurt and his body ached, but he felt lucky to be alive, especially with the ladies looking down at him. He thought *You are going to die Gilbert Hopkins, everyone does. But not today.*

Angela Raines is the pen name for Doris McCraw. Doris is an author, historian, poet and actor/musician. She moved from the historically rich region of West Central Illinois to the equally history rich Colorado. The author of three novels and numerous short stories, most inspired by the history the author researches. As Doris McCraw she has published articles and blogs on the history of her adopted state of Colorado. Make sure to visit her website: www.angelaraines.net

Foresight

CLAY MORE

The light of the waning moon made Doctor Wes Farris more than a little cautious as he drove his horse and buggy along the undulating trail back to Dirtville. It wasn't that he was concerned about ambushers, it was more that he was dog-tired and felt that he needed to lie down and sleep.

"You're a damned fool, Wes Farris," he chided himself. "Why did I let that old Scotsman talk me into drinking a whole mug of coffee laced with that rot-gut whiskey he makes?" Then he chuckled and said out loud to his horse, "Damn it, Jethro, but it was strong stuff. A good thing all I have to do when we get back is bed you down before I fall into my own bed."

The Dirtville town doctor had barely slept the night before and had been working all day. In all that time the only food he had was the meager breakfast he had allowed himself that morning. A confirmed bachelor a couple of years shy of fifty he was still in good condition and full of vigor. He had set his shingle up in Dirtville ten years before and enjoyed the respect of his fellow citizens and a reasonable lifestyle on account of being an able surgeon and physician, always ready to be called upon in an emergency.

That morning he had opened up his office and settled down at his big roll-top desk and pitched straight into work. As usual he saw around twenty patients with coughs and splutters, sore throats, assorted bowel problems and the usual mix of bruises, sprains and cuts. Once he had finished he made up potions, dispensed various pills and ointments and neatly labelled each one. As usual he left them on the old table in the waiting room to be collected while he went out on his walking round of town. Then, after a cup of strong coffee and his first pipe of the day he hitched up his horse Jethro and headed out of town to visit the ranches and homesteads where there were patients in need of his care.

First he saw Tom Seaton's wife at the Twisted T ranch who he had delivered of twins four days previously. She had lost around two pints of blood after the birth of the boy, the second of the pair and he had made up a tonic of iron, made from the quench water he obtained from the town blacksmith.

"We're going to call our daughter Mirabelle, after my mother," Esther Seaton told him.

"And we're calling our son Wesley after you, Doctor," added her husband. "Assuming that's OK with you?"

"I feel honored and I thank you both. Just make sure he doesn't get a hankering to study medicine. It tends to mean you don't get a lot of shut-eye."

As he completed his examination of the twins he noted the yellow tinge in the whites of both their eyes. "They both have a little jaundice," he told them.

"Is it dangerous, Doctor Farris?" Martha asked, anxiety written across her face.

"No, it's normal with most babies for about a week, and more so with twins. Just put their cribs close to the window so they get plenty of sun, but not so much that they get sunburned."

Often Wes did not receive actual money from his home visits, but he never went away empty handed. When he mounted his buggy he found a sack of potatoes by his feet.

From there he had gone over to their neighbor at the Rocking Z to remove Ben

Zemlik's ten-year-old son's tonsils. He would have liked them to have scrubbed the kitchen table with more vigor, but he had sprinkled the surface with surgical spirit before lighting his spirit burner to prepare his instruments. Getting Ben to hold a shaving mirror at the right angle to reflect the afternoon sun down the boy's throat while Helen his wife held her son's mouth open, he was able to use his tonsil guillotine to encircle each of young Bob's offending tonsils, each as big as a prickly pear fruit and detach it from its anatomical bed and remove them with minimal blood loss.

Fortified by coffee, the Zemlik's thanks and payment of a dozen eggs and a huge hunk of cheese to take home, Wes drove out to the way station to check on and resplint Chuck Jeffries busted left leg before making his way to see the O'Donohue family at their homestead. There were eleven kids in the family and as Wes had predicted they had each one developed chickenpox. Nine of the youngsters had been affected mildly, but the two oldest had been ill enough for Wes to keep them on his visiting list, treating them with a zinc ointment of his own devising and copious bottles of tonic and cough medicine.

He left with two sourdough loaves and a

jar of pickles.

It was late afternoon and the light was already fading before he set off to see Finlay McPherson at his one-man silver mine.

In the gloomy light of the single candle that illuminated the old ridge cabin Wes looked straight into the bloodshot eyes of the old Scottish miner as he lay back against the sack stuffed with rags that he used as a pillow on top of the crude bunk bed. Despite the pain and obvious distress that every breath caused, a twinkle of humor still lurked in them.

"If I was a gambling man . . ." he rasped, his prominent Adam's apple moving tremulously up and down to emphasize the effort each breath took. "I would bet you a silver nugget . . . that I won't see the week out, Doc?"

Wes removed his stethoscope and folded it before dropping it in his bag. He ran a finger over his well-trimmed mustache and smiled, reciprocating his patient's good humor and using his well-practiced bedside manner to boost his morale. "I practice medicine not soothsaying, Finlay. Your lungs have sure seen better days, but they've still got years of work left in them."

"Well that's good . . . to know, Doc. I reckon it's all that dust I've breathed in . . .

over the years. It musta . . . clogged them up."

"That's exactly the case," Wes agreed. "You've got what we call emphysema, which means that the dust has eroded cavities in your lungs, so you've got less lung tissue than you need to get air into your body."

"Och, that's the price . . . I've paid in my search to get rich. It sounds like this . . . *empfi-whatever-you call* . . . is like mining. It digs holes . . . . and shafts inside me."

"That's part of it, Finlay. You can live with it, but it makes you prone to get infections, like the pneumonia you have now."

He picked up the damp cloth from the overturned box that Finlay used as a bedside table and mopped the old man's brow. "If you'd just let me take you back to town with me I could treat you better. We could trim that bush of a beard of yours, get some good food inside you and some fresh air."

Finlay McPherson grinned, revealing his paucity of teeth. "I canna do that, Doc. My mine . . . it needs me. My animals . . . need me. I'm grateful for the medicine you bring me." He winked and took a few more breaths before continuing. "That and my *peatreek* will keep me going. If I live out the week . . . and when I'm better I'll come into town."

"Are you sure, Finlay? You've barely got the strength to fix food."

"I've plenty of beans," the old miner replied. "I can open tins . . . cook them on my old pot belly stove. And coffee is . . . always on the stove."

Wes rose to his feet. "Mind if I have a mug? It smells good."

"Aye, help yourself and . . . pour one for me. Just half a mug each."

Wes poured the coffee into two tin mugs and returned to the bedside in time to see the old Scotsman sitting up, having produced a bottle of pale amber liquid from under his bed.

"This will put hairs . . . on your chest, Doc," he said as he pulled the cork stopper and topped up each mug. He pointed over to a rough deal table on which were two more bottles, one with a string tied round its neck. "I had them ready for you . . . one of each, as usual."

Wes crossed and placed the two bottles into his open bag. "Thanks, Finlay. I had just about used up all of my surgical spirit on my round today. That's good to have a replenishment."

"Don't mix them up, Doc. The one with the —"

"— string is for burning and rubbing, I

know," Wes anticipated. He raised his mug and took a hefty swig of the coffee laced with Finlay's moonshine whiskey. It hit his empty stomach and made him inhale a sharp breath of air. "Wow! That's stronger than ever, Finlay."

The miner chuckled and followed suit, taking a deep breath as well. "Good old peatreek, just like I made back in Old Scotland."

Wes had often seen the illicit still with its copper drum and the twisted metal worm in the old lean-to, where Finlay made his hooch. "I guess it is just as illegal back there as it is here?"

"Aye, we have excise men there. Thank your President Lincoln and . . . his lasted Revenue Act for this. There is no way I'll pay . . . his blamed excise for whiskey that is'na half as good as this."

Wes laughed. "Well, I'll certainly enjoy the good stuff and as you know, I'll make good use of the other."

They chinked mugs and drank again.

Half an hour later Wes took his leave of the old miner, arranging to visit again the next day. He set off down the old trail, passing the coral where Finlay kept his old horse and the mule he used to drive the *arrastra* rock-crushing machine. Water trickled down through a series of rocker cradles that the old miner used to wash the rocks to find his silver.

He liked Finlay MacPherson and hoped he'd get well.

On the way back to Dirtville Wes succumbed to the temptation of the bottle and had another hefty swig to try to assuage the hunger that had begun to gnaw away at him. It worked well, but at the cost of making him feel drowsy as well as more inebriated than he liked people to see him.

He was soon sobered when he entered Dirtville for Deputy Clem Brooks came running from the sheriff's office as he drove up the main street towards the livery. Lights still shone in the Lucky Strike Saloon and as he drove his buggy up the street the batwing doors opened and several men spilled out, immediately calling to others to follow. Several ran out and joined a small gathering about the sheriff's office.

"Doc Farris, thank the Lord! Where you been, Doc? We need you — Sheriff Lennox has been shot and I'm scared he's going to die."

"What happened, Clem?" Wes asked as turned his buggy, dismounted and hitched Jethro to the rail. The gathering of townsfolk parted to let them mount the stoop.

"The bank was robbed by a couple of hombres late this afternoon just before it was due to close," the deputy explained. "They shot Sam Peterson, the bank teller, killed him stone dead and frightened the life out of a couple of ladies who were in the general store across the street. Jed Kent had to give one some brandy and Martha his wife gave the other smelling salts. I was over at the undertaker's and came running when I heard all the shooting. I came out of the alley by the store in time to see Sherriff Lennox exchanging bullets with the robbers as they were trying to ride out. I saw him get hit. Blood spurted from his head and he staggered and then fell flat. I fired off a couple of shots at the robbers, but they were out of range by then. But I think the sheriff hit one before he went down, there was blood on the ground. Then the sheriff got up and he pointed to our horses. He managed to run to his and was just about to mount when he keeled over. And he's been out cold ever since."

"What about a posse?"

"After we got the sheriff back here me and half a dozen men went after them, but the light was failing fast and we lost their tracks. I'm planning to see if I can pick up their trail at first light."

The door of the office opened and a woman stood wringing her hands. It was Marilyn Whitaker, the schoolteacher, the sheriff's fiancé.

"Thank the lord you've come, Doctor Farris. He's . . . He's . . . barely breathing."

She spun round and led the way through the office and past the three empty cells. "He's in his room at the back."

Sheriff Dan Lennox was an imposing man of about forty with a black mustache, but as he lay on his bed with a makeshift bandage round his head he was a sorry sight.

"I've had to change his bandages four times, Doctor Farris," Marilyn said. "His wound won't stop bleeding."

"Has he vomited?"

"Once, a few hours ago."

"Has his breathing changed a lot?" Wes asked as he pulled a wooden chair closer to the bed and sat down. He picked up the sheriff's wrist and felt for a pulse.

"It's been getting shallower and shallower," Marilyn replied.

Opening his bag Wes pulled out his stethoscope and examined the unconscious man's chest.

"His breathing is shallow, but his lungs are clear and his heart is regular, albeit the rate is slow."

Swiftly he examined the sheriff to make sure there were no other wounds. "Well, let me have a look at his head wound," he said as he unwound the bandage to reveal a long wound running along the sheriff's right temple above his ear. "There's a definite furrow all the way along. The bullet ploughed its way along the bone."

"Another inch and he'd be dead, I guess," Deputy Clem suggested.

Wes grunted assent and continued to examine his patient. He lifted both arms and let them drop, noting how the left fell like a dead weight onto the bed, while the right dropped at a slower rate. Then he pulled back the covers and did the same with both legs, again with the left limb falling fast.

"That's not good," he mused.

Marilyn gasped and Clem cursed silently.

Shifting his attention to the Sheriff's face Wes raised both eyelids and looked at the unconscious man's eyes.

"Dash it! The pupils are different sizes. His right one is really constricted. It's as I thought, this isn't just a crease wound with concussion, he's had a hemorrhage inside his skull and his left side is paralyzed. That's why his breathing is affected." Replacing the bandage over the still oozing wound he gently felt the underlying bones.

He turned and looked over his shoulder at them. "Get me a basin of boiled water. His temporal bone has been depressed and I need to fix it."

"How . . . How can you do that, Doctor?" Marilyn asked, tremulously.

"I'm going to have to open his head and let the blood out." He looked beyond Clem and saw that there were several townsfolk hovering inside the corridor by the cells. "Tell those people to leave us alone. I have to operate on the sheriff right away."

While Clem went to usher the onlookers out and lock the office door Marilyn went to get boiling water. As they did so Wes cleared a small table and brought it close so that he could lay his things out for the impromptu operation. From his bag he took out his spirit burner and the bottle with string round it that he had been given by Finlay MacPherson. Topping the burner up from it he lit the wick and then took out a case containing a variety of surgical instruments, which had been well used over the years. One by one he heated them over the spirit burner, placing them in a zinc basin he had placed on the table.

Using scissors to cut hair from an area of the sheriff's scalp around the wound, he then picked up a small scalpel.

"How to you know where the bleed is?" Marilyn asked.

"I am not absolutely sure, but the pupil of his eye is constricted on this side, so I strongly suspect it is this side of his brain that is affected."

He made an elliptical incision, then worked quickly to lift a flap of the scalp.

He used a fresh flannel that Marilyn had found to wipe blood away and handed it to her. "If you can bring yourself to do it, just dab any blood vessels that ooze. I have to see what I am doing and my hands are going to be occupied."

The schoolteacher bit her lip, but nodded emphatically. Wes knew that she would be a woman of strong resolve.

Selecting a small ivory handled hand drill with a winding arm he placed the cutting edge against the bone and began to turn the arm to work the drill. The rasping sound made Marilyn and Clem wince, but gradually the drill bored a hole in Dan Lennox's skull.

"I'm almost through, so I have to be careful now. I don't want to go through into his brain."

And then there was a sudden spurt of blood. "Thank the Lord!" Wes breathed. "I was right, there is a collection of blood there."

Then working with a forceps and a probe, he made the hole slightly larger so that the blood oozed out to collect in another small zinc bowl he placed in readiness. He waited until no more came out then he replaced the scalp flap.

"This little operation is called trephination and it has been done for centuries when people have had head injuries from falls or battle wounds. Sometimes it would work and sometimes it wouldn't. Now we just have to wait and hope. If he comes round all right, then I'll stitch his scalp back tomorrow."

"What do we do now, Doc?" Clem asked.

"We watch and we pray."

"We all will," agreed Marilyn as she squeezed the sheriff's hand tight.

To everyone's amazement, Dan Lennox stirred two minutes later. About three minutes after that his eyes fluttered open and he tried to sit up. Wes held him down, pleased to see that he was using both arms, the cause of the paralysis having been removed.

"Easy, Sheriff. You have had a bad head wound and you need to lie still."

Dan nodded. Then he was aware of Marilyn squeezing his hand and he managed a smile. "Well, whatever happened to my head, I reckon it was worth it."

Marilyn bent down and kissed his lips, which deepened his smile.

"I think I've gone to heaven. Just . . . just feel so tired. I need . . . need to sleep."

And Wes nodded. "Sleep will be good, just as long as he doesn't vomit again. Hopefully there will be no more hemorrhage and he'll be out of danger by the morning."

"Well thank goodness," sighed Marilyn. "I don't think he realized how close he actually was to waking up in heaven."

Clem shook his head. "I guess when you've been so close to death you forget about things. He seems to have plumb forgotten that he was chasing bank robbers when he got shot. And that Sam Peterson was killed by those devils."

It was after midnight before Wes finally got back to his own home. After fixing himself a snack, washed down by a black coffee laced with some of Finlay's peatreek whiskey he literally slumped into his bed and fell into a deep sleep.

Sometime in the middle of the night he heard an insistent banging on his door. Shrugging off sleep he swung his legs out of bed, pulled on his pants and boots and went through his office and adjoining waiting room to open the door.

"Hold your horses, I'm coming," he called as he slid the bolt and opened the door.

To his surprise the door was shoved open and a gun barrel glinted in the moonlight.

"Don't make a sound," an unfamiliar voice snapped as the gun barrel was lowered and pushed against his chest. "Lead the way to get your doctoring things. You're coming with me. I got a hurt partner that needs a doctor."

Wes had the fleeting impression of a tall, lean man with red hair and a prominent Adam's apple and cruel eyes. He felt his pulse quicken, but held his nerve. His long medical experience had taught him never to exhibit doubt in his abilities or personal anxiety or fear.

"By hurt, do you mean an accident, or a knife or gunshot wound?"

"Bullet wound," came the short reply.

"I'll need my bag and some dressings. I'll need to light a lamp."

"Let's get them, but remember there's a gun in your back ready for any sudden moves. But there'll be no light."

Grabbing his bag and fumbling in the dark for some bandages, Wes picked up his hat and coat and found himself ushered to the door with the hard metal gun barrel in his back.

"It'll take some time to get my buggy."

"No buggy. I brung a horse for you."

They rode in silence except for the odd barked command from the red haired ruffian. They soon headed off the dimly illuminated trail and started crossing Twisted T country. Eventually they approached an old line cabin.

"You took your time, Grogan," a pained voice snarled as Wes was shoved through the door into the cabin illuminated by a kerosene lamp. "Is this the Doc?"

Wes stood looking down at the man lying on a cot bed. A thickset man with a heavy dark stubble was lying on his side, pressing a blood-soaked blanket against his side.

"I'm Doctor Wes Farris and I don't work well under the threat of a gun."

"Well that's a crying shame," returned the man, "but I'm in need of your services, so you'll do as I say."

The gun barrel was again prodded into Wes's back. "So get on with it!"

Wes put his bag down and drew up a stool to sit on beside the bed. He signed for the wounded man to release the blanket so he could examine his injury.

"You've been shot in your lower back. The bullet went right through you at an angle. The entry was in the back just above your pelvis and the exit is in your side. Look's as if you were lucky and it missed your abdominal cavity altogether, just passed through the muscles."

"Does that mean my innards are OK, medicine man?"

"Yes, but if an infection sets in it could kill you."

"You can see how much I've bled. I feel as weak as a kitten. Can you patch me up? We need to travel as soon as possible."

Wes grunted assent. "You two robbed the Dirtville bank, didn't you? Killed the bank teller and wounded the sheriff."

"The lawman's only wounded?" the wounded man queried, ignoring the statement about Sam Peterson the bank teller being dead. "My aim must have been thrown after he shot me."

These vermin don't care that they killed a man, Wes thought. So its unlikely they'll worry too much about murdering a small town doctor either. He looked over his shoulder at the man called Grogan.

"I need to open my bag, I have spirit to clean his wound and I need to light my spirit lamp to heat my instruments."

154

Grogan nodded and gestured for him to open the bag. "But no tricks or I'll blow your head or your hand off. I don't much care which."

Wes heard the sound of a chair creaking as the man with the gun sat down behind him.

"It's going to hurt," Wes told the patient. "I've got rotgut whiskey if you want to numb the pain."

The bank robber nodded and Wes pulled out and handed him a bottle before taking out his instrument case, the spirit lamp and the other bottle. He filled the lamp from a bottle and struck a light.

The patient uncorked the bottle and took a hefty swig of the raw liquor. The noise of him sucking air through his teeth was testimony to its strength.

"Gimme some of that, too, Danvers," said Grogan, reaching for the bottle with one hand while again increasing the pressure of the gun barrel in Wes's back.

Grogan and Danvers, Wes thought. If he got through the night alive he reckoned that Deputy Clem would find the names useful.

He heated a scalpel, forceps and a cautery iron, placing them each in turn in a zinc basin.

"Better give him more whiskey," he suggested to Grogan, who handed the bottle back after downing a considerable amount and belching loudly.

Wes waited until the patient had drunk more of the liquor then poured some liquid from his bottle over the abdomen, eliciting a howl of pain as the outlaw arched his back.

"I'm going to cauterize the two bullet holes and then stitch the back wound closed," he explained. "I need to leave a way for pus to escape as the wound heals. Otherwise you'll get an abscess and that would as like as not poison your blood."

And as the outlaws passed the bottle back and forth between them, he heated the cautery iron until it glowed a dull red, then applied it to the wound on the outlaw's back. There was the sound and smell of singing flesh. He waited while the patient let forth a string of curses before treating the exit wound in similar fashion.

"Now I'm going to stitch this hole up," he said, producing a glass vial containing ready threaded catgut sutures. Deftly, using the forceps to wrap the sutures around to tie surgical knots, he pulled the muscle walls of the wound and the opposing skin edges together to form a neat suture line.

"What you reckon, Danvers?" Grogan said, his voice noticeably slurred. "Shall we tie him up once he's finished?"

The wounded robber grimaced and began to blink. "Maybe, but he —"

Suddenly, he raised a hand and rubbed his eyes. "Damn, this whiskey is strong. I . . . I can't see clearly."

Wes felt the barrel of Grogan's gun was abruptly removed from his back and he heard the chair creak as the outlaw behind him stood up and cursed. "Damn it, my sight's gone cloudy, too. What the — ?"

The Dirtville town doctor acted instantly. He picked up the cautery iron by its wooden handle and spun round to see Grogan swaying unsteadily as he rubbed his eyes. Knocking the gun hand aside he jumped up and shoved the still searing iron straight between the outlaw's eyes. Immediately, Grogan howled in agony as the cautery iron branded his flesh and he ratcheted back the hammer on his gun. But before he could pull the trigger Wes grabbed his wrist and drove a knee between his legs and as he doubled up, following it up with a punch to his jaw that send him crashing backwards against the wall.

"You dog!" Danvers cried, reaching for the peacemaker in the holster on the ground on the other side of the bed.

Wes grabbed the whiskey bottle by the

neck and drove it down on Danvers's head, the glass shattering and showering the outlaw with the remains of the liquor.

"You bastard, I can't see —" growled Grogan, "but I'm going to kill —"

Wes spun round again, grabbed the scalpel and quickly raising it up beyond his ear threw it straight at Grogan. It embedded in the robber's hand and he dropped the gun. Picking up the other bottle Wes threw its contents over the outlaw and then tossed the lit spirit burner at him. With a whooshing noise the spirit erupted in flames and he watched dispassionately as the outlaw screamed and danced desperately around the cabin, flapping his arms uselessly as he tried to put out the fire that engulfed him.

Wes picked up both of the outlaws' guns. These vermin killed Sam Peterson and damn near killed Sheriff Lennox, should I put this cur out of his misery or should I let the law decide if they should hang?

The Hippocratic oath he had taken when he qualified as a doctor made up his mind for him. He turned Grogan's Peacemaker round and pistol whipped him. As the outlaw fell unconscious, he used a blanket to douse the flames.

When he heard the sound of horses approaching he went to the door and opened it. He was surprised to see that the sun was rising as Deputy Clem Brooks and his posse came galloping towards him.

He was relieved that he had not taken the law into his own hands.

Wes treated Grogan's burns with a salve as the outlaw lay on the bunk in his cell, next to the one containing Danvers.

"You did a good job, Doc, for all of us," said Sheriff Dan Lennox, from his bed after Wes had stitched his scalp flap and bandaged his head again. "I have to say, I could get used to this laudanum you've given me for the pain."

Wes rinsed his hands in the basin on the table by the window. "I'll be checking on you every day, Dan. You just get your strength back and I'll tell you when you can get out of bed."

Marilyn pursed her lips and rubbed the sheriff's wrist. "I'll make sure of that, Doctor Farris. We don't want him undoing all of your good work."

Dan Lennox smiled resignedly. "I guess it's all up to you, Deputy Clem Brooks!"

Clem was standing with folded arms. "Well, we got the bank money back and thanks to the Doc we caught these murdering dogs that we've got locked up, ready to go to trial. But tell us, how exactly did you get the drop on them, Doc?"

Wes grinned. "Finlay MacPherson gave me a bottle of his peatreek and a bottle of foreshot. The peatreek is the good whisky, but the foreshot is the bad stuff that is first to come out of the whiskey still. It contains all the bad methyl alcohol. It affects the vision and can make you go blind. If you have enough it'll kill you. Finlay saves it all up for me to use as rubbing alcohol and for cleaning wounds and burning in my spirit burner. I must have had the foresight to leave both bottles in my bag. I just swapped the two over, so they drank the foreshot thinking it was ordinary whiskey, while I put the peatreek whiskey in my spirit burner. As I thought it started to affect their sight. They didn't have enough to blind them, but they had enough to cloud their vision and give me a chance."

And he recounted exactly what happened during the night.

"It's a good thing Deputy Clem and the posse came along," he said as he finished his tale, "otherwise I'd have had to tie them up and come back to Dirtville for help."

Clem Brooks nodded. "Your tracks were the freshest and we thought we were following the robbers. We had no trouble following the trail you and Grogan left, although we didn't expect to find you there having dealt with them."

Marilyn smiled. "You look really tired, Doctor."

Wes rubbed his stubbly chin. "That's because I've barely slept for more than a couple of hours the last two days." He pulled out his watch from his vest pocket and clicked his tongue. "But I better get going. I'll have a full morning of patients to see and then I have to do my rounds."

Dan Lennox started to snore.

Wes rubbed his eyes. "Lucky man!"

"Maybe you should have some sleep yourself, Doctor Farris," Marilyn suggested.

Wes closed his bag and picked it up. "I'm afraid I have patients to see." He particularly wanted to see how Finlay MacPherson was and to thank him for his peatreek whiskey and his foreshot, for without them he doubted whether he would still be alive.

"Maybe I'll sleep tonight the same as everyone else."

Clay More is the western pen name of Keith Souter, a physician, medical writer and journalist and novelist. He has written around fifty books, some of which have been translated into over a dozen languages. He is a member of the Western Writers of

America and is a past Vice President of Western Fictioneers. A prolific short story writer, he has won prizes, including a Fish Award. With his other hat on, he is a qualified physician and his book *The Doctor's Bag — Medicine and Surgery of Yesteryear,* published by Sundown Press, is regarded as a useful resource book for writers.

THE GUNSMITH OF ELK CREEK
BIG JIM WILLIAMS

"Hey, Cody," yelled a friend from across the street, "there's a man lookin' for you. Says he's an old friend."

"What's he look like?" replied Cody James, leaving the town's café after supper.

"Wears snakeskin boots, cowhide vest and a derby. Got a gravelly voice and a face full of hair. Two men with him staying at the hotel."

Dammit! was all Cody could think. *Gotta be the Welcher Gang:* Wes Welcher, *One-Ear Cash* Gibbons and *Shorty* Stubbs. *How in the hell did they find me?*

Cody had lived quietly in Elk Creek in New Mexico Territory for over three years as a gunsmith, a business that took all of his money and a bank loan to buy. He stood just over six feet, had long brown hair, trimmed mustache and sideburns under a battered white Stetson. He wore regular glasses, a plaid shirt, cowboy boots, a brown vest and trousers.

A reverse-draw .44 pistol rested on Cody's left hip. He hurried toward the small building at the end of the street, his shop and living quarters shared with an elusive yellow cat and Wolf, a big dog that welcomed head-pats and food scraps. The building was away from others since it housed gunpowder.

The cat came with the store. Wolf had been a stray when Cody, needing a friend, rode into Elk Creek.

The CLOSED sign swayed in the window as Cody locked the front door behind him. It was getting dark. He lighted a lamp; then blew it out. He rubbed his eyes, placed his cocked pistol and double-barreled shotgun within easy reach. Ammunition and multiple weapons filled his shop. *Dammit! Don't wanna go down this path again. Thought I'd left Welcher and his gang behind.*

When Cody arrived in Northern New Mexico's big pine country, he liked the small town at the end of the stage run and especially Clara, who was 5 feet, 8 inches tall. She came with sparkling eyes, auburn hair, a slim figure and a ready smile for Cody. There was also a protective sister and two big brothers whose eyes said, "Look, but don't touch." Her little brother, Blake, considered Cody his hero after Cody gave him a pony for his sixth birthday.

After prison Cody had done cowboying, bartending, lumberjacking and wearing a badge, but they had little appeal. However, Elk Creek's gunsmith shop was for sale. He bought it from a man, tired of hot summers, who longed to return to cool Maine. Cody's father and grandfather had been gunsmiths and engravers, trades he had learned at their knees.

Old grudges and conflicts die hard. Wes Welcher had found Cody, intentionally or by accident. Or was he in Elk Creek to rob the bank? Either way meant trouble.

Cody had ridden with the Welcher Gang in cattle rustling, stage holdups, bank robberies, including one that wounded a bank manager. He had gone to prison after naming Welcher, One-Ear Cash Gibbons and Shorty Stubbs as accomplices. All three had promised to kill him.

Hate carries bad memories and deep scars.

Life was good in Elk Creek. Cody's only interests were his business and Clara, who, with her sister, ran the café where he ate most meals. Thoughts of marriage had crossed his mind, but he wasn't sure he was ready, although Clara would make a loving wife and mother. She was eighteen. He was twenty-five.

Pounding on the front door shattered his thoughts. "Hey, Cody," yelled a gravelly voice. "Open up. Know you're in there. Wanna talk. Didn't know you lived in this one-horse town."

The pounding continued until a second voice whispered, "Come on, Wes. We'll get him later."

"Let's eat," said a third man. "I'm hungry. Hear Cody's sweet on that young filly at the cafe."

Cody recognized the other voices: One-Ear Cash Gibbons and Shorty Stubbs.

Cash was a tall, stoop-shouldered man with bushy eyebrows, a whiskey-veined nose, broad tobacco-stained mustache and pistols on both hips. His left ear gone when a teamster's knife removed it during a fight over a woman. A facial scar came with the chopped ear. The attacker didn't get the $2 mattress queen, because Cash took his attacker's knife and whacked off the man's ears before he killed him.

Shorty lived up to his name. He was 5 feet, 4 inches, had squinty eyes and a pock-marked face. An old pistol of unknown make and caliber rested on his right hip by a sheathed knife. He liked to strut in fancy, high-heeled snake boots that lifted him about two inches.

The three outlaws were there when Cody, unarmed, stepped out of the bank at noon the next day after making anther loan payment.

"Been a long time looking for you, Cody." Welcher brushed his beard, and spit toward Cody's boots, Cash and Shorty at his side. "Had hoped one of your cellmates had gutted you, the only way to handle squealers."

"I did five years in prison with an iron bunk and thin, moldy mattress," admitted Cody. "Hot and humid in the summer, cold, clammy and windy in the winter with a barred window overlooking a brick wall. The rats were awful, the food worse. I've had all the trouble I need in life. I'm living a peaceful life in Elk Creek."

"Bet that cute gal in the café would drop you like a stack of dirty dishes if she knew you were an ex-convict."

"She knows, Welcher," said Cody. "Everybody knows, including the Sheriff, how someone young does stupid things, but can grow up. You should try it. Give up your guns so you can stop looking over your shoulder for lawmen and bounty hunters."

"Robbing banks pays good," grinned

Welcher, "and beats chasings cows for thirty and grub a month . . . or gun smithin'."

Cash reached for his cross draw pistol when Cody tried to go around him.

"Put that away!" ordered Welcher. "That'll get us hung."

Cody smiled, and then whistled.

A growl came from the bank's shadows as Wolf streaked to Cody's side and bared his teeth.

"Jesus!" Cash stumbled backward. "Where'd he come from?"

"He's mine." Cody patted the dog. "He's half wolf. If I told him to rip out your liver, he'd do it!"

Welcher stepped back. "Cody, squealers and snitches don't slide free. We got plans for you . . . big plans you ain't gonna like."

"I get the first shot," said Cash.

"Right after me." Shorty's right hand on his sidearm.

"Ain't nobody doing nothing . . . now," huffed Welcher. His eyes burned into Cody's. "We'll kill you and your damned dog when you don't see us coming. So forget about sleeping."

"They came in the café yesterday," declared Clara. "Said they knew you."

"Rode with 'em in the old days," explained

Cody. "Told you about it."

"They sat at a corner table." She nervously touched Cody's hand. "Kept leering at me. Got mad when I said we didn't sell whiskey." She wiped her eyes. "Cody, they scare me."

That night Cody squatted on the floor in his shop, Wolf at his side. The faithful animal protected the store when Cody was away. It was amazing how Wolf's growls kept the store free of after-hour thieves, although the dog was afraid of mice.

The shop's yellow cat preferred sleeping and hiding to making public appearances. It did occasionally capture a mouse or rat to justify its existence. However, it usually ignored Cody's, "Here, Kitty," commands, considered mere suggestions to the feline.

Large boxes now blocked the shop's entrance and rear door; loaded pistols, rifles and shotguns by Cody's side, along with food, water and blankets for the night. He crouched in the dark interior expecting Welcher.

He was dozing after midnight when the front window was shattered. Glass shards ripped the curtains and flew across the floor. It woke Cody from a lovely dream with Clara's soft voice and tender words.

Wolf growled. The hair along his backbone suddenly stiff like bristles on a wire brush. Footsteps pounded the plank sidewalk before the front door's glass disintegrated and a hand reached through an unlocked the door.

"Attack!" commanded Cody.

Wolf leaped toward the door, sinking his long teeth into a left hand that quickly vanished, leaving behind a bloody glove, screams and cuss words.

Cody fired two pistol rounds through the broken door.

"Jesus!" screamed someone outside.

A man's silhouette appeared in the shattered front window. Cody switched to his double barrel shotgun and released one round through the wide opening.

Wolf spun, jumped and growled as someone kicked open the back door. Cody twisted behind a crate and triggered his scattergun's second barrel as the intruder returned two wild shots.

Wolf tore at the man's trousers as the intruder dragged the animal outside the building before the cloth ripped away. Wolf relinquished his hold, and, with a mouth full of cloth, returned to Cody.

A lighted lantern was heaved through the front window. It struck the floor, instantly scattered tentacles of flaming kerosene, and spread like rushing water across the floor, up the walls, and toward display cases, ammunition, Cody's workbench and living quarters in back. The building became an inferno in seconds.

Gunfire stopped outside as a gravelly voice yelled, "Let's get the hell out of here!" More pounding footsteps and shouting followed as riders and horses vanished into the smoky night.

Boxes of ammunition began firing as Cody and Wolf stumbled through smoke and flames toward the rear door, the cat two lengths ahead. Cody circled toward the street as the expanding fire began destroying his business and home.

Many men were soon tossing buckets of water from troughs and the town's two wells onto the spreading flames. Choking black smoke and red-hot embers billowed skyward.

"Stay back," warned Cody as more ammunition exploded. He slumped against a wall several stores away, coughed and tried to clear his lungs, Wolf at his side.

Clara, in robe and slippers, was suddenly there. She hugged and kissed Cody, her eyes filled with tears.

"Who did this?" questioned the Sheriff, a

gun belt around his robe, nightcap on his uncombed gray hair, boots on his large feet.

"The Welcher gang," coughed Cody. "Wolf bit one and ripped the pants of another." He displayed the piece of torn trouser while watching his shop burn. "It was Wes Welcher, One-Ear Cash Gibbons and Shorty Stubbs."

"Can you prove it?"

"Know 'em. I rode with 'em. If you see a man with an injured left hand and another with torn trousers, lock 'em up."

The gang was gone when the Sheriff visited the hotel.

"Said something a day or two ago about maybe camping at Hidden Springs," said the desk clerk.

"Dang it," grumbled the lawman. "That's in the next county . . . out of my jurisdiction."

The Sheriff, a fellow bachelor, frequently asked Cody to join him for dinner. His cook always prepared an excellent meal, but the Sheriff always placed his wooden false teeth in the middle of the table, which stifled Cody's eating. He couldn't avoid looking at the choppers, so by the third meal he casually placed his hat over them, an action that saved his appetite and the Sheriff ignored.

■ ■ ■ ■

It was late afternoon the next day when Cody found Welcher's Hidden Springs' camp and watched from two hundred yards in a cluster of trees, sage, and brush with Wolf by his side. It would be easy to kill them with his rifle, if he wished. But he preferred taking them back to the Sheriff.

Two men were sprawled on blankets by a small fire. One was Welcher, the other, Shorty Stubbs, his left hand bandaged. *Maybe Cash Gibbons is gone,* thought Cody, yet three horses nibbled green grass near the spring.

Wolf softly growled when Cash came around the edge of a bluff. Part of his left pant leg was missing. He was carrying two rabbits. "Brought good eats," he announced, stepping over a stream.

"About time," responded Welcher. "I'm hungry. I'll eat your rabbits, but would rather have 'em cooked by that good looking waitress Cody's stuck on."

"Wouldn't mind marrying up with her myself," grinned Cash, dropping his kills by Shorty's boots. "Like 'em young and good looking. And I ain't talking about rabbits."

"I ain't skinning these." Shorty lifted his

bandaged hand. He kicked the carcasses over to Welcher. "Wish I could have killed Cody's damned dog!"

"Cash, you shot 'em, you skin 'em," ordered Welcher. "I ain't doing it."

"Ah, hell." Gibbons pulled his knife from his waist.

Wolf softly growled again as Cody aimed his long gun. "Not yet," he said, patting the eager animal. "You'll get your chance. And maybe you'll be eating those two rabbits before the day's over."

The dog wagged its tail.

Shorty placed the skinned rabbits over the fire where they soon sizzled and dripped their juices into the coals. The aroma made Cody hungry as he and Wolf tried to satisfy their hunger with jerky.

Cody waited until the outlaws were stuffing their faces before he sneaked behind them, Wolf at his side, ready to attack.

"That rabbit sure smells good," said Cody, his rifle pointed at the gang leader's back. "Anyone touch anything other than the meat they're holding and they're dead."

Three jaws stopped chewing.

"Dammit!" muttered Welcher, slowly lifted his arms. The others followed.

"I'm taking you three back to Elk Creek . . . dead or alive . . . unless you think you can outrun a .44," spit Cody. "Try if you feel lucky."

He made them drop their food and toss their weapons into the spring.

"Can't. My hand's dog bit," whined Shorty.

Wolf growled and advanced.

"Keep him away," pleaded Shorty, quickly using his injured hand to add his pistol to the water.

"Stand up . . . slowly," ordered Cody. "This rifle has a hair trigger that needs fixing, but someone burned down my shop so I can't do it. You boys wouldn't know anything about that, would you?"

They didn't answer.

"Didn't think so. Guess it was someone else."

Wolf quickly ate their food, including seizing the second rabbit sizzling over the fire.

"Wolf's also good at chewing hands and ripping trousers," added Cody.

More silence from the outlaws.

"Shorty," asked Cody, "how'd you injure your hand?"

"What . . . ?"

"Your hand?"

Shorty hesitated. "Snagged it on . . . cactus."

"You could get rabies if that's a dog bite,"

warned Cody. "You'll go mad, froth at the mouth, stagger around on all fours and bay at the moon. They say the pain's awful. Takes a long time to die. Feel like your guts on fire. We'll have to shoot you. If it's only a cactus scratch, nothing to worry about. But . . . if it's a dog bite you should start feeling *real* sick . . . soon."

Shorty turned pale.

Wolf remained in the attack mode. Saliva dripped from his bared fangs.

The day had turned to night.

Cody tied the outlaws' hands behind their backs, got them on their horses and strung the animals together. "The Sheriff said he wants to meet you fellers. Has a nice cold cell ready for you."

"He can't arrest us," raged Welcher. "We ain't in his county."

"Ask him about that when your trial's over and they lock you up," smiled Cody. "I'm sure the Sheriff would wanna know. He wouldn't wanna be unfair."

"Cody," said Welcher, "I got money."

Cody ignored him.

"Plenty of dough," continued the outlaw. "Give you $10,000 if you let us go."

"Where's is it?" asked the gunsmith.

"Buried it a couple of miles from here. Can show you."

"Welcher, you really got $10,000?" questioned Shorty.

"Shut up!" snarled Welcher.

"Bull!" huffed Cody. "If you really had $10,000 you wouldn't be in Elk Creek. You'd be off chasing women, drinking and gambling like you always do."

Still hours from town, it began to rain and quickly turned heavy. Lightning flashed in the east. Cody pulled on his yellow rain slicker.

"Untie us," pleaded Shorty. "Give us our slickers. We're gonna get soaked."

"When Hell freezes and men wear bustles," replied Cody.

Wolf trotted alongside as Cody moved the drenched lawbreakers from one rushing wash or creek to another in the sprawling land.

"Free our hands," yelled Welcher. "This water's rising. We could fall off and drown."

"That would be terrible," scoffed Cody. "Almost as bad as someone burning down my gun shop."

Again, no response from Welcher.

Lightning cracked the black night as thunder rolled across the endless miles and more flashes danced on distant peaks like deranged beasts. At the next crossing the water was higher, swifter running, and reached the horses' underbellies.

Cody lead the string of reluctant horses into the tumbling creek and across toward higher ground, but the rope leading to Welcher' horse snapped, releasing him and his companions. Welcher and his mount slid back and flopped on their sides in the waist-high current, the outlaw's derby lost in the mix of horses and humans. The man, coughing and spitting water, hands still bound behind his back, struggled to stand in the rushing force. He slipped as he tried to climb and get a foothold in the muddy bank. He cursed, again lost footing and was sucked under the surging water.

Cody jumped in to pull Welcher to safety, but was dragged under the tangle of horses, ropes and captives in the raging stream. He gripped the rope from Shorty's panicked horse and was yanked up onto the bank alongside Welcher. Cash remained in the saddle as his mount pulled him and Shorty to higher ground.

Cody knelt and gasped for air.

Welcher — hands now freed — staggered to Cody's horse, pulled the rifle from the saddle holster and pointed it at the ex-outlaw. "This just ain't your day, Cody."

Cody, on all fours, coughed water and continued to catch his breath. He rubbed mud and sand from his eyes.

Welcher cut the ropes binding his two sidekicks.

"Shoot him!" demanded Cash, rubbing his freed wrists.

"May just do that." Welcher slammed the rifle's butt against Cody's head. It drew blood.

"I . . . I almost . . . drowned," choked Shorty, the bandage on his hand gone. He re-wrapped the dog bite with his bandana. "Where's that damned dog? I'm gonna kill him!" His eyes searched the wet dark.

Wolf was gone.

"Run off," said Welcher, his body shaking.

"Hate dogs, especially that big mutt," spit Shorty.

"Anyone see . . . my derby?" coughed Welcher. "Ten dollars if you . . . find it. Paid good money for it."

"The hell with your derby," snapped Shorty. His chin string had saved his wide-brimmed hat that flopped on his head in another wave of cold rain. "Gotta . . . build us a . . . a fire." His body also shook, arms crossed seeking warmth. Water gurgled as he stomped his boots. "I'm . . . freezing."

"Shorty, if you've got some dry wood . . . and matches up your wet sleeves . . . we might do it," spat Welcher. "Or maybe you can rub some sticks together . . . if you can find any dry wood in this God-forsaken country."

Cody hated helping, but his hands and feet were numb. His head bled and hurt where Welcher hit him with his own rifle. "There's an old adobe . . . near here. Half its . . . roof's gone. Ain't much . . . but better than freezing out in the open."

They stumbled south for two miles, the outlaws riding, Cody walking. Welcher kicked Cody's back as the gunsmith led the way, a rope around his neck, his hands tied behind his back. He stumbled and fell several times over unseen rocks, Welcher's horse nearly stomping his legs.

"Cody," shouted Welcher, "you sure there's an old adobe out here?"

Lightning released some light as more rain slashed their soaked bodies.

"About a hundred yards . . . beyond those big boulders," replied the gunsmith.

They huddled in a corner under what little remained of the adobe's sagging roof. The small building smelled of animal droppings and decay. After several attempts, Welcher made a small fire in a corner, using Lucifer matches kept in a small glass tube in his jacket, and ripping dry wood from the shelter's old doors, window frames and limbs from its partially collapsed roof.

"Keep an eye out for that damned dog!" warned Welcher, hovering over the fire. "Probably waiting to rip out our throats. Kill it if you see it."

Cody thought he saw Wolf watching from behind the adobe, but wasn't sure. The dog would wait for the attack command.

"Cody, did you come here with your café lady?" asked Welcher.

He didn't answer until Welcher kicked his boots.

"Yeah, for picnics . . . a couple of times."

"You sweet on her?"

Cody didn't answer.

"She's one good-looking woman," declared Welcher, still shaking.

"She can put her high-button shoes under my bunk anytime," agreed Shorty. He sat on the ground pouring water from his boots. *Didn't know Shorty had enough sense to do that,* thought Cody, *without instructions on the bottom of the heels.* "Don't talk about her like that," he warned. "We may get married."

Shorty laughed and hit Cody's face with a boot, "If you live long enough."

If I live through this, thought Cody, *I will ask Clara to marry me.*

"So ol' Cody may get hogtied, branded, and saddle broke," chuckled Welcher, hands still over the fledgling fire. "Not like the old days when you chased anything that crawled."

I paid for those regrettable times in prison, thought Cody. He squatted against a crumbling wall, kept from the fire, unfeeling arms around knees tucked under his teeth-chattering chin. He too remained wet and cold.

Welcher slid a small coffee pot into the flames.

"We got coffee?" asked a surprised Cash.

"Lost the grounds in the creek," confirmed Welcher, "but drinking hot water is better than nothing."

Shorty stared at the fire, then glared at Cody. "Let's kill him," he demanded. He pulled his long knife. It glinted in the firelight. "Hate snitches." He swept the long blade under Cody's chin. "Don't like you breathing my air. Never liked you when we rode together. You always thought you was better than us."

Welcher grabbed Shorty's wrist. "Might need him."

"What for?"

Welcher nodded toward town. "Maybe a bargaining chip if the Sheriff shows."

"I say kill him and ride on." Shorty waved his knife. "Ain't nothing we need in Elk Creek."

"You're forgetting the bank."

"What about the $10,000 you buried out here?" Cash stretched his wet socks over the wispy flames.

Welcher huffed. "Grow up. Cody's right. If we really had $10,000 why'd we mess with Elk Creek's one-horse bank? Cody's café gal has probably got more money. Didn't know Cody lived here. Thought the law had snapped his neck years ago."

"I'll make him dead," grunted Shorty, his blade again under the gunsmith's chin, "after I cut off his nose. Never liked it breathing my air."

"NO!" Welcher knocked the knife away.

"What'd you do that for?"

"We may need him, like I said."

Cody's mind raced. *How do I get out of this . . . alive? One whistle and Wolf will attack, but could we survive?*

More cold wind and rain attacked the men and rotting building.

"Feels like it might snow," complained Cash, still shaking.

Welcher poured steaming water into a tin cup, took several sips and smiled. "That's better," he said.

"Let me have some." Shorty's hands were unsteady.

"After me," said Cash, snatching the cup from Welcher and downing several swallows. He handed the empty tin to Shorty, who cursed and refilled it while Cash laughed.

The outlaws shared the pot, and then refilled it with rainwater gushing off the roof.

Cody's hands and feet, now tied, had lost all feeling. The outlaws ate some soggy food from their saddlebags, but laughed when Cody eyed their stash.

"We don't waste food on squealers," confirmed Shorty, crunching dry corn.

"Especially," laughed Welcher, "when maybe I'll let Shorty cut you another mouth below that blabbering one you couldn't keep shut at your trial."

The hours passed and all Cody could think of was escape, and putting his cold, stiff arms around a warm and loving Clara. Getting back to her kept him trying to free his hands and feet. The ropes were looser behind his back. The outlaws were snoring, the fire only smoldering coals in the sheltered corner. Out of the dark, Cody saw Wolf's darting body and probing eyes. The dog crept closer, crouched, and waited behind a crumbling wall.

Welcher shifted his body, started to wake and returned to snoring, wrapped in a damp blanket, Cody's rifle across his lap.

I'll have Wolf attack . . . then I'll grab my rifle. Cody eventually freed his hands and slowly unwound his arms and legs as life slowly knifed back into his cramped muscles. He gritted his teeth, and didn't move until the pain passed, then twisted onto his knees. He nodded to Wolf and yelled *Attack!* and lunged for his long gun.

A sleepy Welcher, unable to comprehend what was happening, screamed when Wolf knocked him over, tore at his throat, and then attacked Shorty and Cash.

Cody jumped on his own horse, freed the others into a run, and yelled, "Wolf . . . come," as a pistol shot winged past his head. Three hundred yards away he leaped from his horse and rolled behind a protective barrier of rock and sand, Wolf at his side. "Good boy," he said, hugging the panting dog.

He released three rounds into the dark adobe. Someone groaned and fell.

"Dammit! He's shot Cash!" yelled Welcher.

"Is he dead?" questioned Shorty.

"Ain't moving. Got a big bullet hole where he don't need one."

"Should have let me kill Cody when I had the chance."

Wisps of smoke rose from the dying coals as Cody's next round scattered debris between the two survivors.

"Get down or we'll be next," yelled Shorty.

"His damned dog bit me, too." Blood covered Welcher's hand and dripped from his neck. "Hope I don't get rabies . . . froth at the mouth . . . and start baying at the moon."

"Look what he did to my hand." Skin dangled from under Shorty's loose bandage.

Cody, flat behind the sandy knob, searched for movement in the adobe. The rain had stopped. Faint daylight stretched across the east. He saw someone move and triggered a round that resulted in cuss words and a hole in the adobe's wall.

Shorty ripped the pistol from Cash's dead hand and returned a wild round.

"Dammit! Don't waste ammo!" ordered Welcher. "Could be here all day without horses. Gonna need every round."

The magazine in Cody's rifle was almost full.

Shorty, clutching the pistol — the outlaws' only weapon — rolled over a wall and scurried out of sight. All others weapons had been lost in the creek.

The desert remained silent for a long time until Welcher shouted, "Hey, Cody. Let's deal . . . so we can all live . . . and get the hell out of here."

More light edged the east.

Cody, hesitated, and then yelled back, "I'm listening." He carefully peeked from concealment, knowing it could be a trick.

"Let us get our horses back and we'll ride out of your life . . . forever," offered Welcher. "No one else has to die."

Cody hesitated before asking, "Is Cash dead?"

"Like a politician's promises!" replied Welcher.

Cody searched behind him. No one was there. *However, if One-Ear Cash is alive, he could be sneaking up behind me. But if someone's gonna use a knife it would more likely be Shorty!* "That ain't no deal, Welcher," shouted Cody. "You destroyed my business . . . everything I've worked for. You tried to kill me. No way you're riding out of here. Either surrender or go back to Elk Creek dangling dead across a horse and saddle; your choice. The same for Shorty."

Wolf sniffed the air, growled, and twisted behind them, the hair along his backbone again straight up.

Cody rolled over and searched the sprawling country marred by rocks, boulders, chaparral, brush and sage.

More teeth were revealed as the big dog growled.

"What's out there, boy?" whispered Cody into Wolf's ears. He searched behind. Then saw something: a man with a pistol in his right hand, his left hand bandaged.

Shorty Stubbs!

The outlaw darted from one hiding place to another, but remained within Cody's vision.

"Hey, Cody," yelled Welcher. "Take my offer. Then you can get back to that good-looking gal in Elk Creek you're sweet on. No sense us getting killed over all this."

Buying time, Cody responded with, "I'm . . . I'm thinking on it, Welcher."

Stubbs crept closer.

Cody dog-walked to his left behind some cactus. It gave him a perfect view of Shorty while Wolf circled to the right toward their approaching prey.

Stubbs crawled closer, the pistol in his sweaty palm.

A few more feet, thought Cody, *and I'll make sure Shorty joins Cash in the same grave.* He quietly moved ten feet to his left and sighted his long gun toward Shorty as the outlaw slid into a sandy wash, then raised his head and realized Cody had moved.

Wolf was now twenty feet from the outlaw.

Raise up one more time, Shorty, thought Cody, *and you'll be the main meat dish, minus potatoes, carrots, onions and gravy, at a buzzard's banquet.*

Shorty poked his pistol over the edge of the wash and fired.

The round hit Cody's arm below his left shoulder. He grimaced, and rolled onto his right side. "Dammit!" he muttered, angry he had let Shorty get the upper hand. He clutched the painful wound and squirmed into the wet sand. He ripped his bandana from his neck and wrapped the wound, tugging one end with his teeth. The flow of blood slowly stopped.

Cody awkwardly lifted his rifle with his right hand and sighted on the wash. He leaned back and waited until Shorty raised his head and shoulders like an inquisitive gobbler at a Thanksgiving turkey shoot.

Now it's my turn! Cody's shot tore through Shorty chest. The sound echoed across New Mexico Territory as Wolf snarled and jumped on the dying man, who fired, hitting Wolf. The dog yelped and fell.

Cody jumped into the wash, the unmoving Shorty on his back, Wolf across the outlaw's bleeding body.

I think they're both dead! thought, Cody.

Wolf whimpered and licked his bleeding right leg. Cody dropped to his knees, cradled the dog in his arms and wrapped the wound with Shorty's bandana. "You're gonna be all right, Wolf," assured the gunsmith, hoping he was right. With tears in his eyes, he gently stroked the dog. "We'll get you to the vet in town. He'll fix you up. Wolf, you're gonna be all right," he repeated."

Wolf whimpered and licked Cody's hand.

The sun, now fully crested, brought daylight over a wet landscape.

Hope my horse went back to Elk Creek, thought Cody. *If so, that should bring a posse.*

Cody stuffed Stubbs' pistol in his own holster, his sidearm lost at the swollen creek. Holding Wolf, he stayed low in the wash and turned back toward Welcher.

Several times the outlaw tried to escape, but each time Cody fired his rifle, Welcher fled back to the protective ruin. "And stay there," yelled Cody.

It would be another two hours before a posse approached from Elk Creek.

"Cody, you all right?" questioned the Sheriff, reining in his horse.

Cody said he was, but Wolf needed a vet.

"Your lathered horse came back to town," said the Sheriff. "Tracked it back here."

Cody pointed toward Welcher slumped in the adobe. "Sheriff, hate saying it, but you're out of your jurisdiction . . . you're a mile or two into the next county. You're not law, here."

"By, dogies," winked the Sheriff, "I think your right, Cody. That could be a problem at Welcher's trial. I'll apologize . . . after we hang him!"

Shorty Stubbs and Cash Gibbons did share the same unmarked desert grave. Welcher rode back to town, head down, hands cuffed behind his back.

"You can't arrest me," he kept saying, "I ain't in your county."

The Sheriff solved the problem by temporally moving the markers of the county line. The Sheriff in the next county didn't object.

"That's what we call justice in New Mexico," said Elk Creek's Sheriff.

The jury didn't hang Welcher, but sent him to prison for twenty years.

A teary Clara gave Cody a big welcome-home kiss and hug. Then she looked him in his eyes and demand, "When are you gonna ask me?"

"Ask you what?" quizzed Cody, knowing the answer, his arm in a sling.

"Cody James, you know exactly what I mean."

"No, I . . . ?" He played the game.

"To get married," she demanded.

"How about now," laughed Cody, returning her kiss.

The vet took care of Wolf's leg, the limp gone in several weeks. Wolf was soon back playing ball with Blake, Clara's little brother, and chasing Cody's cat that returned from the livery stable with a litter of kittens.

"I always wondered if I had a male or female cat keeping my shop clear of mice," said Cody.

Most everyone in Elk Creek attended the wedding. Blake carried the wedding rings on a soft pillow, each step down the church aisle guarded by Wolf and the bride's two brothers. Cody's best man was the Sheriff who gave a nice speech during the big barbecue-reception. Then, when everyone began eating, removed his false teeth and placed them on the table in front of the bride and groom. Clara gasped, paled and turned away. Within seconds Cody's hat covered the choppers.

The unfazed Sheriff continued gumming

his food.

The townspeople had a variation of a *barn raising* and rebuilt Cody's shop on its former site, while the bank extended its loan to help re-start the business. A $500 DEAD OR ALIVE reward for the capture of the Welcher Gang also helped.

Welcher had years to enjoy the same prison cell Cody had occupied, shared with a cellmate that refused to ever take a bath.

The cell was stuffy and damp in the winter, and stuffy and hot in the summer with one barred window overlooking a brick wall. To add to Welcher's misery, he couldn't avoid seeing Cody's name scratched in deep letters in the small cell's stonewall. There was also a steel bunk, thin mattress, and enough mice, rats, bedbugs and cockroaches to make sure Welcher wouldn't get bored.

It would be a long twenty years.

Big Jim Williams' initial novel, *A Desperate Cattle Drive,* won the Western Fictioneers' 2014 Peacemaker Award for Best First Novel. His latest novels on Amazon Books are, *Border Justice; Texas Justice; Silverhorn: Texas Ranger; Eye For An Eye,* and the short story collection, *Tales of The Frontier.* He's a member of the

Western Fictioneers, and Western Writers of America. He loves dogs, naps, friends, old movies, the Old West, beer, laughing, writing, and avoiding restaurant checks. He also writes radio plays, and home for money.

French Cooking and Fibs
Susan Murrie Macdonald

March 21, 1878
Micah Carlisle sipped his bourbon. The saloon was dingy and dirty. He'd never permit such squalor in his place, but the Kentucky bourbon was first-rate stuff. Even if he did have some doubts as to the hygiene of his glass. It was good to get away from his sanctimonious colleagues for a few days of serious card-playing, without being expected to play knight-errant. "Not very many customers tonight," he observed. The gambler was dark-haired and handsome, though not tall. Neither slender nor stocky, he was medium of build as well of height. His black hair, green eyes, and fair complexion bespoke an Irish ancestor.

"Maybe you scared them off," joked a man drinking beer.

The bartender shook his head. "Dance tonight. Half the town is dosey-doing." Micah thought a moment. There were few men in the saloon, and none of them rich enough to play for the stakes he preferred. Since it would be a waste of his time to try to strike up a penny-ante poker game, he might as well invite himself to the dance for some gentle exercise and female companionship. He glanced down at his attire: black linen trousers and jacket, red silk brocade vest, and a white linen shirt. When playing cards with strangers, it was always best to look as though he could afford to lose and pay his debts. He was definitely gussied up sufficiently for a dance, indeed, probably overdressed for a cow town square dance.

After several reels, square dances, and one waltz with a local belle completely devoid of grace, Micah took his trod-upon toes outside. He lit up a cheroot. A few moments later, a carrot-haired girl in a blue plaid dress came out.

"Evening," Micah greeted her politely. "I hope my cigar won't bother you."

"Oh, no, not at all. I just came out for a breath of air. It's so dreadfully warm in there," she said. Nonetheless, she made sure she was upwind of his cigar.

"It is," he agreed.

She strolled along the side of the building. Suddenly, she tripped and fell.

Micah threw his cigar to the ground and

hurried to help her up. "Are you all right?"

"Yes, I think so."

"Get your hands off my cousin!"

Both turned to see three men behind them. An ox of man was bellowing at them. With a sense of dismay, Micah recognized him as Carl Henshaw, a man he'd been warned by the barkeeper to avoid.

"Carl, I fell. This gentleman helped me up," she explained, keeping her voice calm and quiet.

"Don't you lie to me, Rina. I saw him with his paws all over you," Carl accused.

"Sir, I resent your insinuations," Micah replied.

"That's my cousin you're insulting with your attentions." Carl pulled his gun out.

"Round here we know how to deal with folk who don't know how to treat decent women," added one of the other men. He drew out a gun hidden beneath his jacket.

"What you want us to do, Carl, shoot him or string him up?" asked the third.

"Gentlemen, there's no need to be hasty." Micah thought of the derringer tucked up his sleeve. He hesitated to use it when he was outnumbered three to one, and two of them already had their six-guns out. His derringer held only two bullets.

"Carl, he didn't do anything. I just stumbled. He helped me up. That's all that happened." Rina explained in the slow, patient tone one would use to a not-too-bright child.

"That proves you two had an ass-ig-ee-na-shun," Carl declared. "If he didn't mean anything to you, you wouldn't care if we shot him or not."

Micah just stared at Carl Henshaw and his sidekicks, dumbfounded by his 'logic.'

"I recognize him," the third man said.

"Oh? Who is he, Jake?"

"Cardsharp. Been in town a few days, cheating honest people out of their money," Jake Barnes said.

"I did not cheat!"

"Can't trust a cardsharp," Carl said. "Can't trust him with cards or women."

"He compromised you, Rina. He's gotta pay," the second man said.

"Daniel Henshaw, are you deaf or just stupid? I told you, nothing happened."

"Don't you try to protect him," Carl scolded. "Nobody messes with a Henshaw and gets away with it."

"Nobody," Daniel repeated.

"He compromised you, Miss Rina. If he won't do the honorable thing, then he's gotta pay the price," Jake explained, now treating *her* like a dull child.

"Do the honorable thing?" Daniel repeated.

"Make an honest woman out of her." When Daniel and Carl still didn't seem to get it, Jake said, "Marry her."

The two Henshaws looked at each other, mulling over this possibility. New ideas, Micah thought uncharitably, seemed to be something the Henshaws had difficulty with.

"What do you think Gram would say about that?" Carl asked.

At the mention of Gram, Rina stopped protesting. She looked up at Micah speculatively. The gambler was reminded of the time he'd seen a rancher examining a prize bull, trying to decide if one he-cow was worth a year's pay for one of his ranch hands.

"Gentlemen, this is all just a misunderstanding," Micah said.

"Put your guns away. I'll marry him," Rina offered.

"Miss, we haven't even been introduced," Micah protested.

"I couldn't stand to have your death on my conscience. They're not joking. They've killed before, for less reason."

Carl stuck his gun inches away from Micah's face. "Which'll it be? You gonna see the parson for your wedding or your funeral?"

Gulping, Micah chose. "Wedding."

"I'll go fetch him," Jake volunteered. Carl and Daniel Henshaw kept their guns trained on Micah. The gambler kept waiting for them to relax their guard, so he would have a chance to escape, or to fight back, but they gave him no opportunity.

Two minutes later, Jake came back with a scrawny middle-aged man with thinning hair. He was dressed in unrelieved black.

"Rina Henshaw, I'm surprised at you. I thought you had better sense than to get involved with such a rogue."

"There's been a dreadful misunderstanding, Reverend. I did not —" Micah began.

"There certainly was a mistake, if you trifled with Miss Henshaw," the parson interrupted him.

"I did not trifle with the lady. I merely —"

"Hush afore we shoot you," Daniel ordered.

Micah hushed. Seeing no other options, he let them escort him to the church. His mind was racing, trying to find a way out of this mess. This was the sort of situation he'd expect his friend Michael Van Horn to get himself into. Without Van and Wilson and the others to back him up, outnumbered, outgunned . . . As a professional gambler, years of experience had taught him when to play and when to fold. Compliance seemed his best course of action, for the moment.

As soon as they reached the church, the parson started the ceremony immediately. He did not bother with a prayer-book, but recited the vows from memory. Neither the Henshaws nor Jake put their guns away. Although Micah's experience with weddings was limited to attending two or three of his mother's, it seemed to him the parson was leaving things out. Wasn't there supposed to be a bit about 'if any know why this man and this woman should not be joined, speak now or forever hold your peace?'

"For richer, for poorer, in sickness and in health, as long as ye both shall live?"

"I do," said Micah grudgingly, not bothering to hide his reluctance and distaste.

"The ring, please."

Daniel and Carl looked at each other. Biting back a sigh, Micah pulled a gold signet ring, inset with black onyx, from his pinky and placed it on her finger. "With this ring . . ." he recited mechanically after the parson.

"I now pronounce you man and wife. You may kiss the bride."

Rina looked up at him expectantly, almost

eagerly. He gave her a quick peck on the cheek. He ignored the look of disappointment in her eyes at not getting a more serious wedding buss.

"Now that we're married, can you holster the guns?" he asked, not concealing the sarcasm in his voice. From what he'd seen of the Henshaws, they were too dim-witted to catch the sarcasm.

Daniel and Jake looked to Carl for guidance. He nodded and holstered his gun. The other two did likewise.

The parson held out his hand. "An honorarium is customary at this point."

"A what?" Carl asked.

"He wants to be paid." Micah dug into his pocket and handed the man a silver dollar. "May I go now?"

"Just a minute, just a minute. You need to sign the parish register first. Mr. Henshaw, you'll need to sign as witness."

Micah scrawled his name quickly and sloppily, remembering his mother's advice that if they can't read your signature, they can't prove it's you. Rina, Carl, and Daniel Henshaw signed after him.

Rina grabbed Micah's arm. "If you excuse us, my husband and I have some things to discuss."

"We certainly do, madam."

Micah led her to his hotel. The night clerk stared at them, bug-eyed.

"Miss Henshaw!"

"Mrs. Carlisle," she corrected him primly. The clerk stared as she walked up the stairs, her hand resting on Micah's arm.

"You realize now that you've been seen accompanying me to my hotel room, you're well and truly compromised," Micah warned her.

"Doesn't matter now. We're married."

'I did not compromise you half an hour ago."

"No, but my cousins think you did."

"At their ages, they should know where babies come from. You do know, don't you?" Micah asked, suddenly frightened that he was tied not only to a virgin, but an ignorant virgin.

"I have a vague notion, but I'm sure you can show me later."

"No, thank you, madam. That will make it impossible to have this annulled."

"Annulled?"

"As quickly as possible, madam, as quickly as possible."

"Forgive me for being vain enough to think that matrimony with me was preferable to being shot," she replied sharply.

Micah took a deep breath. He looked his

wife over: a plain girl, no, woman, she was older than he'd guessed at first, with carroty hair and hazel eyes. Her scrawny frame was too thin to inspire lustful dreams. "I appreciate your rescue; I don't mean to seem like an ingrate. But surely you can't wish to be tied to a total stranger?"

"Mr. Carlisle, it's late. The stagecoach leaves town at 7:00 AM, and I think it would be a very good idea for us to be on it. Contrary to what Carl and Daniel think, Gram will not approve of our marriage. I want to be as far away as possible when she finds out. Perhaps we should get some rest?"

By Micah's standards, the night was still young, and he was not in the least tired. However, he was not a morning person. The notion of waking at 7:00 was distasteful enough. Being alert and active at that hour . . . he shuddered. Rest might be a good idea. Perhaps he would wake in the morning and find out this was all a nightmare.

"You may have the bed, madam. I'll sleep in the chair."

"Even if you didn't want to claim your — your husbandly prerogatives," Rina blushed over the euphemism, "there's still enough room for two."

Micah had no intentions of letting anything get in the way of an annulment. "No, thank you, ma'am." Micah sat in the chair next to the chest of drawers and starting laying out a game of solitaire. He couldn't help noticing her reflection in the mirror as she removed her dress and slipped into the bed in her petticoat.

"If you change your mind, Mr. Carlisle . . ."

Micah shook his head. It wasn't often he turned down a willing woman, but under the circumstances, no. "Sleep well."

"Mr. Carlisle?"

Micah murmured something incoherent.

"Mr. Carlisle, you need to wake up. I brought you some breakfast and coffee."

He forced his eyes open. "For the coffee, at least, I thank you." He saw his bride standing over him, wearing the same dress she had last night. "It wasn't a bad dream."

"I didn't know what you wanted for breakfast, Mr. Carlisle. I got you some toast and eggs," she said.

"I rarely partake of food this early, madam. Coffee will be sufficient." He stood and stretched. "Do we really need to take the first stage? Isn't there a later one?"

"Yes, but by then Gram will have found out what Carl did. I want to be well on the road before she notices I'm missing."

"Just what will your esteemed matriarch do when she learns what happened?"

"I don't esteem the old bat. I'm scared of her, just like everyone else in the county. But in an hour or two we'll be out of her reach, and hopefully she'll be vexed enough with Carl and Daniel that she won't bother coming after us," Rina said.

"What is it about your relatives that so terrifies everyone?"

"Gram owns half the county. She may be getting on in years, but she runs her ranch — and everyone else's affairs — with an iron hand. And Carl and Daniel — you saw what they're like. No one dares say no to them, or any of their brothers."

"Are the Henshaws entirely sane?" Micah wasn't sure, but he had a vague notion that a marriage could be annulled on the grounds of insanity.

She shook her head. "Why do you think everyone's so scared of them?"

"Would you be so kind as to turn your back? I'd like to change clothes."

"Dress quickly," she urged. "The stage will be leaving in a few minutes."

He obeyed, and swiftly packed everything into his carpetbag. They made the stage just in time.

"We appear to have the stage to ourselves," he observed.

"So nice for newlyweds to have a bit of privacy," she agreed.

Micah didn't want to touch that with a ten-foot-pole. "Is your grandmother opposed to gamblers in general, or just to the fact your idiot cousin thinks you were compromised?"

"Gram doesn't want to lose an unpaid abigail and amanuensis. She's done everything she can to stop any boy from courting me since I turned sixteen. If it was one of the ranch hands, then Henshaws don't marry the hired help. If it was someone else, she found another excuse. Her mind is still as sharp as a tack, but her hands are crippled by <u>arthritis</u> and her eyes aren't what they used to be. She made me her 'little helper' when I was a girl, after my mother died. Now that I'm grown, she doesn't want to let go. Anyone else would need to be paid, you see, nor would she want to trust a stranger with family secrets."

"Sounds like a lovely woman." Micah glanced out the window. "I can see why you'd be willing to marry a total stranger to escape."

"Mr. Carlisle, you don't hold yourself in sufficient esteem. You're a fine, handsome gentleman. Any woman would be proud to be your bride."

The gambler sighed. His bride seemed much less eager to escape the bonds of matrimony than he was.

"Mr. Carlisle, when we reach the next stop, would you oblige me by purchasing me a few things? I didn't dare return home for anything, and I haven't so much as a hairbrush, let alone a change of clothes."

"And I suppose that's my responsibility now?"

"With all my worldly goods I thee endow," she quoted.

"Very well, I suppose I can afford it."

She nodded. "You do look like you have more than two pennies to rub against each other, Mr. Carlisle."

"Under the circumstances, perhaps you should call me Micah, Rina."

"Marina, if you don't mind."

"I beg your pardon?"

"My name is Marina. The Henshaws shortened it when I married into the family. They couldn't manage anything with that many syllables," she sneered.

"Aren't you a Henshaw?"

"Heaven be thanked, no! My mother married Carl's uncle when I was ten. I was a Sheffield by birth and I'm a Carlisle by marriage, and I will never be Rina Henshaw again. Marina Carlisle, or Mrs. Micah Carlisle." She snuggled comfortably against him. "That has such a nice sound to it: Mrs. Micah Carlisle."

"Don't get used to it. I'll be seeing the judge about an annulment as soon as we reach Santa Ysabel." The reason he had taken this busman's holiday when he did was because Judge and Mrs. Carroll were due in town to visit Nellie and Todd, their daughter-in-law and grandson. Staying out of the judge's way had seemed a good idea at the time. He sighed. He'd never expected to be in a position where he'd be asking Judge Carroll for a favor.

Two hours later, they reached the next town. "Go buy yourself such falderals and furbelows as you need. I'll be in the restaurant, having brunch."

"Thank you, Micah." She tucked the money he handed her into her pocket. "I promise to be as frugal as possible."

"You can't possibly be any more extravagant than your mother-in-law," he muttered. He shuddered to think what Esther Carlisle would think of this situation.

It was a full two hours before Marina reappeared, wearing a yellow calico dress and carrying a carpetbag of her own. "I am sorry to keep you waiting, Mr. Car— Micah. But the dress had to be altered."

"The stage left an hour and a half ago."

"I know." She grinned mischievously, looking more like a girl than a matron. "And if Gram sends Carl or the others after us, they'll be following that stage west. There's a northbound stage we can take after lunch, and then change as necessary. They won't expect that."

"And where did you pick up the gift for intrigue, Marina?"

"Reading penny-dreadful romances aloud to Gram."

Once on the afternoon stage, Mrs. Carlisle plagued her husband with a hundred questions: his saloon in Santa Ysabel, his plans and ambitions, his friends whom were frequently deputized to assist the young sheriff, his views on politics, what he had done in the war, whether or not she could have a cat, everything.

"Are you aware, madam, that in the eyes of the law, if I take a stick to you it is no one's business but my own?" an exasperated Micah snapped.

"Yes, Mr. Carlisle," she replied meekly — so meekly that Micah regretted his harsh words. "But better a battered bride than an old maid. Besides," she added more confidently, "you would never lay a hand on a woman."

"Are you so sure of that?"

"You're too much of a gentleman. It just isn't in your nature to hurt a woman."

Micah scowled, but said nothing. His mother had brought him up to be a gentleman. It was easier to fleece a mark if he was polite about it. Then he thought a moment not about what she'd said, but how she'd said it. She had emphasized the pronoun.

"Who hurt you, Marina?" he asked gently.

For the first time in hours, she was quiet.

"Was it Carl?"

She said nothing.

"You're safe from them now, Marina." He patted her hand awkwardly. Dealing with womenfolk was usually easier for him than this. "And you may certainly have a cat if you like. Once the marriage is annulled, you'll be your own mistress. Safe from the Henshaws, and free to choose your own path. You can marry whom you want, or find a job, do anything you want."

"I'm quite satisfied with the husband Providence gave me, Micah. I know you can keep me safe. And I'll take good care of you, truly I will. I'm a good cook."

"There's more to matrimony than cuisine."

"Well, yes, but I'm sure you can teach me that." She smiled up at him shyly. "Carl said I was an old maid, but I'm young enough and strong enough to give you children. Lots of children."

"Unnecessary. I am not paternal by nature."

"You may change your mind in nine months."

Micah shuddered.

The stagecoach drew to a halt. "Santa Ysabel," the driver called.

Micah clambered out, then helped Marina out. He took her carpetbag in one hand and his in the other. "Let's find you a room at the hotel."

"No, Micah. No more hotels. We're home now," she said quietly, but firmly.

"Micah, hey there! Welcome home." A tall, red-haired man with a thick mustache greeted him warmly. "Who's your friend?" He touched his hat.

"Mrs. Carlisle, may I present my associate, Mr. Van Horn? Van, my wife."

"Your what?"

"How do you do, Mr. Van Horn?"

"I need to see the judge right away. Where is he?"

"Over at Nellie's," Michael Van Horn replied, still stunned by Micah's introduction.

Micah led his wife to the general store. "Mrs. Carroll, may I speak to your father-in-law?"

"What is it, Mr. Carlisle?" Judge Andrew Carroll stepped into the store. He frowned; he and the gambler were not friends.

"I need your assistance on a legal matter."

The judge raised one gray eyebrow.

"Actually, I need a favor. May we speak in private?"

"Certainly. Nellie, you won't mind if we go back to the storeroom, will you?" the middle-aged man asked his daughter-in-law.

"Of course not." The blonde tried not to stare at the strange woman with Micah. But when he didn't introduce her, she stepped forward and held out her hand. "I'm Nellie Carroll, owner of Carroll's Emporium."

"Marina Carlisle. Mrs. Micah Carlisle," the redhead clarified as she shook hands.

Andrew and Nellie Carroll were both taken back at that announcement.

"That's what I need to talk to you about." Micah gestured to the judge to precede him. Marina started to follow after them. "In private, I said."

"This affects both of us, Mr. Carlisle."

"Why is it when it's something you want, you're quite capable of remembering 'with all my worldly goods I thee endow,' but when it's something I want, you seem to forget 'love, honor, and obey'?" She looked up at him without saying anything. Sighing, Micah gestured for her to follow them back to the storeroom.

"Two days ago, I was the guest of honor at a shotgun wedding. I need your assistance in acquiring an annulment."

"I see," Judge Carroll lied. He turned to Marina. "And do you desire to have this marriage annulled?"

"Certainly not. I admit my cousin was hasty in forcing Mr. Carlisle to marry me, but what's done is done. That which God hath joined together, let no man put asunder," she quoted sanctimoniously.

"There appears to be a difference of opinion here. Why don't you tell me what happened?" the judge asked.

"We were attending a dance. I stepped outside for a cigar. Miss Henshaw —"

"Mrs. Carlisle," she corrected him.

"— came out for a breath of air. Her cousin regarded this coincidence as proof of an assignation. She tripped in the dark. I helped her to her feet. When her cousin saw me holding her, he insisted I'd compromised her virtue. His first reaction was to shoot me, but he eventually decided honor would be satisfied if I married the wench."

"You agreed to it," Marina reminded him.

"I had a gun in my face at the time," he pointed out. "And three guns trained on me during the entire ceremony. Doesn't that invalidate the wedding? Isn't there something in the law about vows given under duress not being binding?"

"Shotgun weddings are an informal, but recognized tradition," the judge replied.

"Well, can't the marriage be annulled since it hasn't been consummated?"

The judge looked up at him in surprise. "Mrs. Carlisle, I don't mean to embarrass you, but is what he says true? Has he taken you to the marriage bed yet?"

"Not yet," she admitted reluctantly, "but we've traveled together for two days and three nights as husband and wife. If that doesn't compromise me, I don't know what does. No one is going to believe that nothing happened."

"Especially with your reputation," the judge added.

"Separate hotel rooms," growled Micah, who'd been forced to pay for double accommodations.

"Not the first night," she reminded him.

"I slept in the chair!"

The judge had to force himself not to laugh. "The lady appears willing to honor the contract, Mr. Carlisle. Marriage to a good woman could well be the making of you."

"Judge, you know I'm no fit husband for any decent woman," Micah admitted, realizing he was throwing away any chance at Nellie Carroll if the judge bought this argument. "Miss H— Marina had a bad family situation. I can't blame her for seizing any opportunity to escape, but doesn't mean she should spend the rest of her life tied to me. I'm willing to make a financial settlement for," he thought quickly, "say six months, until she can marry a man of her own choice, or get a job and support herself."

"Mrs. Carlisle?" Judge Carroll asked. He tried to hide his amusement. If Micah Carlisle was willing to pay cash money to be rid of his wife, he was really desperate.

"I told you, I'm not willing to have your death on my conscience. If the Henshaws hear you cast me off, they'll consider that an insult to the family. They'll hunt you down and kill you."

Micah bit his lip. There was a certain logic to her argument.

"Henshaws? Is that the family that owns nearly a third of Franklin County?" When Micah and Marina both nodded, the judge continued, "I've heard reports of them — none of them good."

"Then your reports are accurate," Micah said sourly. "Sir, since you blackma— persuaded me to become a part-time deputy, I have run every little errand you have asked of Mr. Wilson and the rest of us without complaint." *Without too many complaints,* he thought to himself. "Some of them at great risk to life and limb. Surely you owe me a favor."

"I need to speak to Mrs. Carlisle privately. Would you excuse us, please?" It was an order, not a request. Micah had no choice but to obey. Once he was gone, the judge asked gently, "Were the two of you forced to marry against your will?"

Marina nodded.

"Micah is a professional gambler and a saloon owner . . . not the best possible husband for a decent woman. However, he is willing to release you. Men outnumber women three or four to one in this territory. You could probably find another husband — one of your own choice — within a month, if you wanted to."

"Reformed rakes make the best husbands." All the lurid novelettes she'd read aloud to Gram Henshaw had said so.

"Do you really think you could reform him?"

"Mr. Carlisle has been a perfect gentleman since I met him, so he can't possibly be as black as you're trying to paint him. And if he were, you wouldn't have deputized him as a peacekeeper," she pointed out. "Besides, I traveled with him without a chaperone across half the territory. Whether it's true or not, people will assume I'm a scarlet woman."

The judge thought over what she said. As rare as women were in the west, most men wouldn't mind an indiscretion or two in a lady's past. It was grief and love for his son that kept Nellie a widow, not lack of opportunity. "Are you sure you really want to keep him? You could easily do better than Micah. An annulment now wouldn't be difficult, but if you waited, a legal separation would be much more difficult."

"Your Honor, didn't your mother ever tell you that a bird in the hand is worth two in the bush? Could I really do that much better? I admit a rancher or a shopkeeper would be more respectable, but at least he's not a horse thief. He's a handsome man, and well-spoken. I could do worse. Much worse." She thought of her step-cousins, and was grateful for her escape.

"Are you sure, Mrs. Carlisle?"

"Quite sure," she said firmly.

The judge led her back to the front of the newspaper office, where Micah was attempting to sidestep Nellie's interrogation. "Let me not to the marriage of true minds admit impediments," the judge quoted.

Micah looked at him in horror.

"I am not going to grant you an annulment, nor will any other judge in the territory," the judge informed him.

"What about divorce?"

Judge Carroll ignored him. "Mrs. Carlisle, may my wife and I treat you and your husband to dinner tonight to welcome you to town?"

"I'd be delighted, if it's all right with Mr. Carlisle." She looked up at Micah.

Micah knew the penalties for upsetting the judge. "Certainly."

"We'll meet you at Joseph's restaurant at 6:30, if that's convenient."

"We'd be delighted," Micah echoed his wife. His tone belied his words. "Come, madam, let's get you settled at the hotel."

"No, Mr. Carlisle. Not at the hotel."

Micah grabbed the carpetbags and led the way out of the emporium, not willing to have a marital dispute in front of witnesses. "I live at the saloon — hardly a suitable setting for a lady."

"A wife's place is with her husband."

With an air of martyrdom, Micah led the way to the saloon. When they got there, his six colleagues were waiting.

"I've never been in a saloon before," Marina said as she stepped through the batwing doors.

"Nor will you again. Henceforth you'll use the outside door to the upstairs," Micah informed her sternly.

"Hey, Micah. Heard you got somebody special for us to meet," Rob Baxter teased.

"Is it true? Did you get married?" Billy Buchanan asked.

"Where's your manners, Billy? Say howdy-do to the lady," Isaiah instructed the boy. He touched his hat politely. The others did likewise.

"Gentlemen, may I present Mrs. Carlisle?" Micah introduced her reluctantly.

"This must be Sheriff Buchanan."

"Yes, ma'am," Billy replied, surprised.

"And you must be Rev. Sanders," she said to the tall man wearing the Cherokee amulet.

"Just a deacon. Be honored if you just called me Isaiah, ma'am."

"And you're Mr. Wilson?"

"Yes'm. Donald Wilson," the tall blond man replied.

"I've already met Mr. Van Horn, so you must be Mr. Fontaine," she said to the Negro cook. He nodded. "Mr. Carlisle told me all about you."

"Don't you go believing half of what Micah said, ma'am," Rob warned her. As the unofficial chamber of commerce of Santa Ysabel, the six businessowners were deputized as needed to assist the young sheriff, who'd only gotten the badge because no one else wanted it.

She nodded at the livery stable owner. "And Mr. Baxter."

Baxter nodded back to her, but said nothing.

"It's a pleasure to meet your friends, Mr. Carlisle." She smiled at the seven.

"Mrs. Carlisle is tired from our trip. She needs to go upstairs and rest," Micah informed his colleagues. And his wife.

"I confess I would like to wash up after so long on the road. I trust I'll be seeing you gentlemen again soon?"

"We'll be counting the minutes," Deacon Isaiah replied.

221

"This way." Micah led her upstairs.

"He talks almost as pretty as you do, Micah," Marina said.

"If you'll agree to the annulment, you'd be free for him to court you," Micah whispered. "You charmed all of them, and any one of them would make a better husband than I would."

"You don't value yourself highly enough, Mr. Carlisle."

As he took her to an empty room next to his own, Micah reflected that she was one of the few people who thought so. "It's a little dusty."

"I'll soon put it to rights," she promised. "But where do you —"

"Until I completely give up hopes of an annulment or a divorce, Mrs. Carlisle, separate quarters."

"Judge Carroll seemed quite determined," she reminded him.

"Yes, he did." He looked over his bride. Scrawny, red-haired, she was not at all his type. But unless he could think of something, she would be his companion for the next thirty or forty years. Eventually, propinquity would lead to a consummated marriage . . . which would make an annulment impossible. "Stay here and get settled. I'll be back in a bit."

"Yes, dear."

Micah tried not to flinch at the endearment.

When Micah got downstairs, he called Buck over to the bar. "Van, let me buy you a drink. I need to talk to you."

"Micah treating? He's got something up his sleeve," Donald Wilson warned.

Van accepted the whisky. He drank half of it before asking, "What is it?"

"You have a certain knack with the ladies."

The redhead nodded and took another sip of whisky.

"I'll pay you $200 to seduce my wife."

Van Horn spit out his whisky. "What?"

"I'll pay you $200 to seduce my wife," Micah repeated.

"I've had men threaten me for not leaving their wives alone, but never offer to pay me to go after 'em."

"Three hundred dollars."

"Why?" Van Horn wondered.

"The judge won't annul the marriage. But if she commits adultery, then I'll have grounds for divorcing her, or else she'll divorce me because she wants out."

Van laughed in his face. "You've only been gone a week. You can't have been married more'n a few days, and already you want a divorce?"

"Annulment, divorce, whatever it takes to regain my freedom."

"Why on Earth did you marry her, then?"

"Her next of kin thought I compromised her," Micah admitted.

"Hey, Don, come over here. You gotta hear this," Van called.

Micah poured himself another shot of whisky.

"Mr. and Mrs. Carlisle, how nice to see you," the judge greeted them at the restaurant door. "You've met my wife, haven't you, Micah? My dear, may I introduce Mrs. Carlisle?"

As the two ladies greeted each other, the judge drew Micah aside. "I've been hearing some disquieting rumors from the saloon."

"You should never listen to barroom gossip, sir."

"If you don't treat that lady properly, you'll answer to me. Understand?"

"Yes, sir."

"That which God hath joined together, let no man put asunder," Judge Carroll quoted. "Shall we go join the ladies?"

After a somewhat strained dinner, Micah walked Marina back to the saloon, leading her up the outer stairs to the top floor. "I don't want you going through the saloon. Always use the outside stairs."

"Yes, Micah."

"If you want a husband to sit and read to you in the evenings while you knit, you'll be sadly disappointed. I have a business to run and evenings are my busy time."

"Yes, Micah. I understand."

"Don't bother waiting up for me."

"Good night, Micah," she said as he left her at her doorway.

Feeling guilty, he stopped at the head of the stairs and said, "Good night, Marina."

Downstairs, Micah helped himself to a whisky. He'd been thinking and thinking, and he still couldn't find a way out of this mess. Judge Carroll had made it quite clear that he could not only expect to maintain his marital status, but that he was to be downright uxorious. He poured another whisky. Maybe the alcohol would help him think.

What was he going to do with a wife? Especially a respectable maiden lady? The last time he'd bedded a virgin he'd been seventeen. He had long since learned to prefer the company of professional ladies, who regarded the situation as a matter of friendly commerce, or willing wives and widows who knew the rules the game was

225

played by. He poured another whisky. Perhaps some Dutch courage.

Two hours later, Isaiah Sanders carried Micah's unconscious body upstairs.

Marina poked her head out the door. "Micah?"

"He had a little bit too much, ma'am," Isaiah explained unnecessarily.

"I see. Bring him in here."

Isaiah hesitated. He knew perfectly well that Micah's room was the next door over. Then he shrugged and followed her directions.

"Just lay him on the bed. I'll take care of him."

"Yes, ma'am." Isaiah politely averted his eyes away from her, dressed only in a flannel nightgown. Her bedroom had been scoured clean since that afternoon. A handful of wildflowers sat in a glass of water on the table, next to her sewing. "You sure you don't want any help getting his boots off?"

"I'll manage. Thank you, Mr. Sanders."

"Good night, Mrs. Carlisle."

Micah awoke the next morning, stark naked and in a strange bed. Disoriented, he sat up, and instantly regretted his action.

"Drink this," a vaguely familiar voice

urged him.

There was a cup at his lip. He drank, then pushed it away. "That's horrible. Coffee. I need coffee."

"After you drink this."

His green eyes focused enough to see Rina bending over him. "What is it?"

"Something my cousins and stepbrothers swore by when they were hung over. You'd probably be happier not knowing what's in it," she advised. "Force it down."

He took the cup and gulped the foul mess. "That's terrible."

"Yes, but it works. Would you like some coffee now?"

"Please." He looked around and realized he was in her bedroom. "Where are my clothes?" he asked suspiciously.

"Already washed and hanging on the line. I brought a change of clothes for you from the other room."

"Would you mind leaving the room for a minute, or at least turning around whilst I don fresh attire?"

"After last night, is such modesty necessary?" she asked.

"Last night? Did we . . ."

She nodded mendaciously.

Micah groaned. So much for an annulment. "Would you be kind enough to get

227

me a cup of coffee? Better yet, just bring the pot."

"Of course, Micah. I take it you don't want any breakfast yet?"

He shook his head. "I doubt I could keep it down. Perhaps later, thank you."

"I can have flapjacks ready as soon as you want," she offered.

"I don't suppose you could manage omelets?" he asked wistfully.

"Of course, Micah, if you prefer."

He looked up at her, for the first time with a spark of interest in his eyes. "Coffee now, please, and omelets in about an hour."

"Yes, Micah." She hurried to obey him, knowing all he really wanted was some privacy to get dressed. She smiled as she went down to the kitchen. Her fib should save a lot of argument tonight. She hadn't lived with the Henshaws for thirteen years without learning how to get her way. And if it took French cooking and fibs to keep the man Providence had given her, then those were the tools she would use. Anything — even being married to a handsome stranger — was better than going back to the Henshaws.

And if the two of them didn't live happily ever after, it wouldn't be for lack of trying on her part.

Susan Murrie Macdonald is a stroke survivor and a freelance wordsmith. She has sold roughly 20 stories, mostly science fiction and fantasy, including the Darrell Award nominated "As Prophesied of Old" in the best-selling *Alternative Truths*. She is an ex-schoolmarm and a staff writer for Krypton Radio's website. Her only other western stories are in the e-book *Knee-High Drummon and the Durango Kid*. She was a volunteer at the Mid-South Renaissance Faire and is the author of *R is for Renaissance Faire*.

INCIDENT AT MISSION DE SAN MIGUEL
JAMES J. GRIFFIN

It was a peaceful afternoon in the town of Thunder Gulch, New Mexico Territory. The sun was approaching the western horizon, signs of dusk already appearing in the canyons to the east. Townsfolk were going about their final shopping and visiting, before returning home. There was no sign of trouble about to shatter the idyllic scene, until gunfire erupted from inside the First Territorial Bank of Thunder Gulch. Five masked men backed out of the bank. Each held a money-stuffed canvas bag in one hand, a six-shooter in the other. Another masked man on horseback, leading five other mounts, galloped from the alley behind the bank. As they mounted, one of the bank tellers appeared in the doorway. He got off one shot from the small revolver he held. The bullet barely grazed one of the robbers' shirtsleeves. Their return fire cut him down, leaving him sprawled lifeless on the boardwalk. They spurred their horses to race out of town.

Deputy Don Hargrove came out of the marshal's office. He lifted the rifle he carried to his shoulder, took aim at the fleeing outlaws, and fired. One of the bank robbers sagged in his saddle, but clung to his horse's mane. Leaning over the animal's neck, he kept going. One of his partners turned in the saddle and sent two quick bullets at the deputy. The first missed, but the second caught Hargrove square in the middle of his belly. He dropped his rifle, grabbed his bullet punctured gut, and jackknifed to the road.

Marshal Tom Brandon had been in the middle of getting a haircut and shave when the robbers struck. He ripped off the apron covering him, jumped out of the chair, and ran outside. The robbers were already past the edge of town. Brandon looked toward the group gathered around his downed deputy. One of them looked up at Brandon and shook his head. The marshal nodded his understanding. He shouted to two other men. All three went to the livery stable, got their horses, and took off in pursuit of the gang.

"Lanny, looks like the marshal got a posse together," Mason Wilson said to Lanny

Roberts, the gang's leader. "Doesn't seem like much of one, though. Looks to be only three men all told."

"I told you Brandon wouldn't give up without a chase, jurisdiction be damned," Roberts answered. "We'll be rid of him soon enough."

Still at a gallop, the gang turned to the west. They rode until they came to a shallow draw, which contained enough moisture in its soil to support a screen of brush. They turned parallel to the draw, rode for another quarter mile, then dropped down into the draw. They dismounted, pulled out their rifles, and bellied down under the brush, watching as the marshal and his deputies drew nearer. Half-blinded by the setting sun, the posse men didn't see the ambush until it was too late.

"Now!" Roberts ordered. A volley of gunfire burst from the brush. Two of the approaching men were shot out of their saddles. The third slumped, but managed to stay mounted. He turned his horse to retreat. A bullet in the back finished him off. He toppled to the dirt.

"Watkins, Quinn, grab those horses," Roberts ordered. "We don't want 'em heading back to town, and lettin' folks know the posse's all dead. Besides, we might need an extra mount, if one of ours goes lame. Soon as you've got 'em we'll head for the hideout."

Two hours later, just after full dark, the gang's destination loomed in the distance, The light of the rising full moon bathed the abandoned Spanish Mission de San Miguel in an otherworldly cold white, making it appear much like a ghost ship, drifting on a calm sea. Twenty minutes later, the outlaws rode up to the crumbling adobe church.

"Morris, Devens, help get Hank inside. We've got to see how bad he's hurt," Roberts ordered. "The rest of you unsaddle the horses and turn 'em into the corral. Feed and water 'em. Soon as that's done, we can eat."

Art Devens and Joe Morris dismounted. They lifted the wounded Hank Lundy off his horse. Roberts opened the mission's front door, so Lundy could be carried inside. He was placed on one of the front pews, near the altar.

"You hang on, Hank," Roberts ordered. "We'll rest here for a couple of nights. You're gonna be all right. When we leave, we're takin' all the gold pieces with us."

Despite being abandoned for so many years, the church's altar was still adorned with gold candlesticks. The gold tabernacle in the center of the altar was still in its place. Over the altar hung a large crucifix.

"I dunno," Lundy answered. "Bullet went in awful deep. It hurts every time I breathe."

"Soon as the rest of the boys come inside, I'll see what Moe can do for you," Roberts said. He scratched a lucifer to life on the altar to light a candle. It immediately went out. It took five more matches before one was able to light the wick.

"Damn strange," Roberts muttered. A groan echoed through the church.

"What the hell?" Roberts cursed. The groan echoed again.

"Mebbe you shouldn't cuss in a church," Morris said.

"This place ain't been a church for a hundred years or more," Roberts answered. "Don't tell me you're startin' to believe in all that sky pilot preachin' talk. I stopped lettin' my ma take me to church soon as I was too big for her to drag me there."

"I'm just sayin' why take chances?" Morris said.

"This place does give me the willies," Devens said. "That statue over there's watchin' me. I can feel its eyes on me, every move I make."

"You're both plumb loco," Roberts said.

"This is just an old building, like many others we've used for hide outs. Watch."

He pulled out his six-gun and shot the plaster saint in the shoulder. Bits of the statue flew into the air. Immediately, water began running from its eyes. A red streak ran down its side from the bullet hole.

"Look! It's cryin'!" Devens exclaimed.

"It is not. That's just moisture that got loose when I shot at it. The red is rust in the water."

The other three men hurried inside.

"We heard a shot," Moe Quinn said.

"Art was getting' spooked by one of the statues, so I shot it," Roberts said. "Bust up a couple of chairs for firewood. We can build a fire in that basin. After we eat, we'll count the cash we took today."

He indicated the church's baptismal font.

"I'll take care of it," Quinn said. He took a chair from alongside the altar and smashed it to bits. He stacked the wood in the font. The flames had just taken hold when a strong breeze swept through the church, blowing out the flames.

"I'm likin' it here less and less," Wilson said. He attempted to light the wood again. Three more times, wind blew through the old mission and extinguished the flames.

"Now I really don't like it here," Wilson

repeated.

"Would you rather be outside facin' a passel of lawmen's guns?" Roberts asked. "Let me get that fire goin'."

He struck a match and touched it to a splintered piece of wood. This time, the flame quickly took hold, building to a good sized blaze.

"You see? There's no ghosts in this place. No one here but us."

Roberts had no sooner finished speaking when a stream of water gushed from the font. It filled the bowl, dousing the flames.

"We'd better get out of here," Devens said.

"And go where, exactly?" Roberts answered. "Besides, Hank ain't in any shape to travel. If we try'n move him, we'll kill him."

He dug around in the soaked wood.

"See here?" He indicated a hole in the bottom of the font. "This here basin is spring fed. It must've clogged up with dirt over the years. The heat from the fire busted the clog loose. That's all it is. You're all lettin' your imaginations get the best of you. There's no one here but us."

The single candle Roberts had lit extinguished itself. At the same moment, all the other candles in the mission, including those suspended from the ceiling, came to life. Despite the fact the mission's bell had long since fallen from the tower and shattered, the peal of a bell split the night air.

"Then who are those?" Lundy cried. He pointed to a column of brown robed men, who wore ropes for belts, and sandals on their feet. They were singing a Gregorian chant as they neared the altar.

They broke into two rows, and filled the second pew on each side of the aisle. One of them approached the altar.

"Have you men come to pray with us?" he asked no one of the outlaws in particular.

"Not hardly," Roberts answered, with a snort. "I don't know where you men came from, but we're usin' this place. So just get."

"I'm afraid we can't do that," the padre replied. "This is our church. It's time for our evening Mass."

"I'll show you what it's time for," Roberts shouted. He pointed his gun at the padre's chest and fired. The man stood, unperturbed.

"What the devil? I know I hit him, plumb center," Roberts said.

"There is no place for Satan in God's house," the padre said. "However, the Lord is always ready to forgive those who repent of their sins. Are you willing to turn away from the devil, and renounce your wicked ways?"

"No!" Roberts answered. "None of us are. But we'll leave."

He turned toward the back of the sacristy. A line of black robed nuns blocked the exit.

"I'm afraid that isn't possible," the padre said. "You will either repent, and ask God's forgiveness, or you will perish here tonight, and face the eternal fires of Gehenna."

"Look, Jesus is alive on the cross," Quinn screamed.

Indeed, blood was running from the nail holes in Christ's hands and feet, the welts on His back, and down his face from the crown of thorns He wore. His eyes were filled with a deep sadness.

"I'll repent," the dying Lundy cried. "I know I'm dying. I've done so many wicked deeds, I'm paying for my sins now. Jesus, forgive me. Please forgive me."

"Your sins are forgiven, my son."

"I ask Your forgiveness, too, Jesus," Devens pleaded. "I'm sorry for all the hurt I've caused, and the wrong I've done."

"You have it, my child."

"I don't know what's goin' on here, but I know one thing for certain," Roberts shouted. "Jesus Christ never rose from the dead. There's no such place as Heaven, or

Hell. That's all a bunch of hooey. And statues sure as Hell don't come to life, and men and women don't appear out of nowhere. This is all one big trick, from the law, to fool us into turnin' ourselves in, so we can be hung."

"You have disobeyed God's laws," the padre said. "You have one last chance to repent."

"I'll show you how we repent," Roberts screamed. He emptied his gun into the corpus hanging from the crucifix. Except for Lundy and Devens, his partners did the same.

The padre shook his head in sorrow.

"Satan has claimed your souls."

As Roberts, Wilson, Morris, and Quine reloaded their guns, he turned to face the altar. The other friars, and the nuns, joined him as he prayed.

"Saint Michael, the Archangel, defend us in battle; be our defense against the wickedness and snares of the devil. May God rebuke him, we humbly pray; and do you, O Prince of the heavenly host, by the power of God, thrust into hell Satan and the other evil spirits who prowl about the world seeking the ruin of souls. Amen.

"Most Sacred Heart of Jesus, have Mercy on us.

"Most Sacred Heat of Jesus, have mercy on us.

"Most Sacred Heart of Jesus, have mercy on us."

The unrepentant men had fired every bullet they owned into the assembled friars, and the row of nuns, to no effect. As the last words of the prayer faded, Wilson looked at one of the stained glass windows. He screamed in abject terror.

"Lanny, take a gander at that. This sure as hell *is* for real."

The stained glass image of St. Michael the Archangel had come to life. The leader of the multitudes of angels in Heaven was soaring toward the outlaws, his sword of the Lord's vengeance grasped in his right hand.

Lundy's and Devens's souls had already left their bodies, which lay in repose as if peacefully sleeping. Roberts and his remaining partners turned and ran for the door. Morris and Quinn dropped in their tracks, dying of sheer fright. Wilson made it as far as the door before the avenging Michael smote him across the back, the sword sinking deep into his flesh. With the next stroke of his sword, the Archangel severed Roberts's head from his body. Roberts's momentum carried him into the courtyard, where he dropped.

St. Michael returned to his place in the window. Jesus's corpus returned to its previous state. The statue of St. Joseph Roberts had shot was restored. The water in the font stopped flowing. As the candles went out, one by one, the spirits of the friars and nuns faded into the dark. The only sound at the ancient Mission de San Miguel was the cooing of two mourning doves, as they settled back in their nest.

Late the next afternoon, Ronald Banks, the sheriff of Sandoval County, and a posse of six deputies rode up to the Mission de San Miguel. The bodies of Lanny Roberts, Mason Wilson, Joe Morris, and Moe Quinn were lined up in a neat row, just outside the mission's courtyard. In the cemetery, mounds of fresh dirt indicated two new graves. The outlaws' horses, and those they had stolen from the slain Thunder Gulch posse, were scattered around the church, grazing, or dosing in the sun.

"Sheriff, what in the blue blazes happened here?" Tommy Heath, the youngest deputy, asked.

"I'd say we found the Roberts gang," Banks answered. "The other two members must be in those new graves."

"But who killed them? They look like they saw Beelzebub himself before they died,"

Heath pressed.

"More likely it was the fear of God," Banks said. "You're new to these parts, so I'd better explain. For almost two centuries, San Miguel was a peaceful place. The Apaches who lived here had been converted by the Spanish padres that brought the Word to the new world. They had become farmers, raising their own crops and sheep. Then, about a hundred years ago, a band of renegade whites attacked the mission. Killed everyone here, the padres, the nuns, old men, women, and children. It was a massacre. Legend has it one of the Apaches was a medicine man. Before he died, he put a curse on this place. Said anyone who trespassed here, or disturbed the dead from their rest, would face the wrath of God. These men ain't the first ones to try'n defy the curse. This is what happens to those who do. Rumor has it St. Michael himself extracts God's punishment from those who defile this old church."

"But, those new graves?"

"Part of the curse supposedly offers salvation, and a Christian burial, to anyone who repents here, before they die. I'd reckon two of the gang did just that. They'll be in those graves."

"But that's . . . impossible," Heath said.

When he did, thunder rumbled over the mission, from a cloudless blue sky.

"You want to chance rilin' the Lord, son?" Banks asked.

"No, Sheriff. I reckon I don't."

"Smart boy. Let's collect these bodies, and leave this place in peace."

James J. Griffin, while a native New Englander, has been a student of the frontier West from a very young age, and has been an avid horseman all of his life. Jim writes traditional Westerns with strong heroes highly reminiscent of the pulp westerns of yesterday, the heroes and villains are clearly separated with few shades of gray. While Jim writes fiction, he strives to be as accurate as possible within the realm of fiction by travelling extensively out West. Visit Jim online at jamesjgriffin.net.

SPECIAL OCCASIONS
J. L. GUIN

July 1878

As darkness began to shroud the men and a quarter moon rising in the eastern sky, John (Jude) Manning brought his horse to a halt prompting the mounted man on either side of him to pull their reins as well. Manning pointed a finger toward a flare of flickering light in the distance. "Who do you suppose that is?"

Bart Knolls, sitting on a sorrel to his left rolled a shoulder, "Who knows Jude, you wouldn't figure it would be anybody on the run, with a value on his head, to allow that fire to tell us where they are."

Henry Riggins on Manning's right flared a hand toward the light, "Most likely some traveling pilgrims made their camp for the night."

Manning considered both men's guesses then said, "Well, I guess it don't really matter, but I hope it is a pilgrim's camp. I figure we ought to ride over there real friendly like and see. Who knows, whoever has that fire going might be fixing supper and we ain't et since this morning."

Whomever was there did not matter to the three men now staring at the distant flickering fire. All three cared only for what they could gain from the travelers for themselves. Each man was slovenly in his appearance, speech and actions and lived violent lives. If asked, they would profess to be bounty hunters on the trail of some miscreant for the bounty offered on his head. In actuality all three men were no accounts, thieves, liars, cheaters and killers. They held no respect for anyone or anything; their only objective being to obtain money, or goods to exchange later for money, any way they could, then spending the booty at their leisure. In the past, they actually had brought in the bodies of various wanted men to law offices, in various locations, for the bounties offered but brought in dead bodies only, never bothering to bring a man in alive.

They used the guise of being bounty hunters in order to roam around the frontier west in search of unwary travelers who possessed any sort of material goods. Once travelers or a lone traveler were located, the three would shadow from a distance long enough to make sure they could close in, usually after dark, and do as they pleased without outside interference. It did not matter what the unfortunate traveler had brought along. Money, horses, weapons and food topped the list but whatever the person or persons owned would be taken, which included the traveler's life. Killing off the intended victims was simply a matter of logic conceived shortsightedly in the belief that anything done out of sight was out of mind. If there were no witnesses left to voice a complaint then no one would have knowledge of any wrong doing.

At the campfire were three men who worked for the Circle C ranch which was located next to the Colorado River and near Big Springs, in northwestern, Texas. They were the cook and two drovers whom, along with the boss plus six other drovers, had driven the Circle C's herd of longhorn cattle to market in Denver. The drive to Denver had been, for the most part uneventful, other than the usual problems keeping the herd together and steadily moving north. River crossings were always challenging and they inevitably lost a few head. It took 74 days to travel the roughly 550 miles of range land before arriving to the loading pens in

Denver but they had made the trip in Cunningham's estimated time of travel.

After the delivery was complete and Circle C owner William Cunningham had been paid for the herd. He passed the word for all the men to come to his hotel and he would pay them. He sat at a table in a room at the Excelsior Hotel in Denver. The rancher had ridden right along with the drovers, having ramrodded the drive. As each man stepped forward, Cunningham acknowledged him by name, he paid the man his wages in cash then gave him a handshake in appreciation for his service. Six of the drovers had hired on for the drive only, and were now free to go elsewhere to seek future employment. Only three men, fifty year old Chester (Chet) Olsen, long-time cook for the Circle C, along with steady riders and drovers for the ranch, 28 year old Larry (Lars) Larsen, a five year veteran, and 19 year old Lonnie Beck, a two year rider for the Circle C were paid their wages then assigned to return the chuck wagon and several worthwhile horses back to the Circle C. Cunningham himself would take the train to Kansas City to visit his oldest daughter for a time before returning to the ranch.

Chet Olsen, Larry Larsen and Lonnie

Beck spent the night in Denver. The next morning, after having breakfast, the two drovers headed to the livery then busied hitching up the mules to the chuck wagon and saddling their own mounts while Chet went to a nearby mercantile to purchase enough supplies to sustain the men for the return trip.

They'd been traveling for 12 days at a steady comfortable pace for the team of four mules pulling the chuck wagon, making roughly 25 miles a day. They were now in the northeast corner of New Mexico near the Canadian River north of Tucumcari. When the sun was ready to dip behind the Western horizon, Chet figured it was time to make camp for the night so he brought the chuck wagon to a halt. Larry and Lonnie busied unhitching the mules and unsaddling their horses, giving all of them, including the four other Circle C horses a bait of oats to munch on while they inspected hooves and gave each animal a quick wipe down with a wadded burlap bag. Chet got a fire going then busied making coffee and began cooking a supper for himself and his two cohorts.

"That stew smells mighty good, Chet," Lonnie Beck said as he lounged near the fire. Nineteen year old Lonnie Beck was lean of frame, weighing 140 pounds and stood five foot ten. He had sandy hair, hazel eyes and a ruddy complexion.

"It's about ready Lonnie, bout five more minutes or so the biscuits will be ready then we can eat." Fifty year old, cook Chet Olsen said as he stirred the pot of venison stew he'd made from a small deer Lonnie had shot earlier in the day. Olsen was a small bent man, standing five foot six and weighing around 130 pounds. He wore a short brimmed gray slouch hat over his thinning brown hair and an inch long beard, both of which were streaked with gray. The man had a gruff voice which gave others the opinion that he was perpetually grouchy, though that was not so. Actually the old cook was kind and understanding, having been living and working on ranches his entire life. All the drovers were younger men, who were used to taking orders and out of respect for Chet's age and knowledge, always did as he asked.

Chet let the large spoon rest in the pot then said, "I figure we'll be back to the ranch in ten days, maybe late next week."

"You in a hurry to get back, Chet?" Larry Larsen grinned when he asked. Twenty eight year old Larry Larsen was not a big man either. He stood five feet ten, weighed around 160 pounds. He had brown hair and a stubble of a beard. He usually shaved clean once a week. Larry had a perpetual wad of tobacco in his mouth which bulged his right cheek. He began riding for the Circle C five years ago after he had sold his own small neighboring spread to William Cunningham. It was a good arrangement for Larsen as his spread was failing and would have been repossessed by the bank had not Cunningham came to his rescue. He was quite happy to ride for the Circle C and was loyal to the ranch.

Chet Olsen nodded his head up and down, "Yeah, I'd like to get back to my kitchen and I miss my bunk. Driving these mules all day, living out of the back of the wagon and sleeping on the hard ground is getting mighty tiresome for this old man."

"Looks like we got company coming," Lonnie Beck suddenly said to alert the others of the three riders he saw in the darkening distance riding slowly toward the flickering campfire fire.

Chet Olsen eyed the approaching riders then stepped close to his double barreled shotgun leaning against the wagon bed. Larry Larsen reached a hand to his holstered six-gun on his side and undid the keeper thong, just in case. Lonnie Beck likewise unloosened the keeper on his .45 colt that was belted for a right handed cross draw across his middle.

"Hello, the camp," Lead rider, John Manning called out then said, "We're friendly travelers. We saw your fire and was hoping you might have a spot of coffee, maybe some food to spare. We're a might hungry but we can pay." Two of the riders stopped their mounts twenty feet away as Manning allow his mount to step forward slowly.

The old cook, Chet Olsen spoke up, "Come on in stranger. I know what it's like to be hungry. We got enough cooked up that we can share with you and your companions."

Manning dismounted, dropped his reins to the ground then turned and waved his arm in a signal for his two fellow travelers to come forward.

When all three men stood in the firelight, Manning spoke up, "I'm John," he then turned and pointed to the other two men whom had stepped to stand on his left, "Bart and Henry. We sure appreciate your hospitality." Manning was a big man, standing six feet tall and looked to weigh close to two hundred pounds. Bart Knolls stood at five foot eight and barreled shaped with a protruding belly. Henry Riggins stood five foot ten and was skinny as a rail. All three men's clothing were rumpled and dirty. It looked as if they hadn't changed their outfits for days, possibly weeks.

Chet acknowledged their names then nodded, "I'm Chet, he's Lars and he's Lonnie," he pointed out each man and used their first names only as the intruders had done. He was wary of the shabby looking three. They each had a long gun hanging from their saddles and at least one handgun snug in a holster strapped to their waists. There wasn't anything unusual about that, most travelers were armed in like manner. What made the old cook edgy was that all three men had the hard restless look of men who used their guns for a living. Chet glanced to his own companions, Larry Larsen and Lonnie Beck, catching a hint of a concerned look in their eyes as well. He then pointed to the back of the chuck wagon, "Cups over there, men, help yourselves. Be but few minutes before the biscuits are done."

The three new arrivals stepped over to the chuckwagon, took a cup in hand then stepped to the coffee pot sitting on a flat rock next to the campfire. Each man filled his cup and began sipping the strong brew it held.

They stood off to one side facing the

seated Lonnie Beck and Larry Larsen.

"Looks like you boys are part of a herd gather beings you got a chuck wagon and all?" Manning questioned.

The man was curious, so Chet Olsen, having nothing to hide answered, "We work for the Circle C ranch down by Big Springs, Texas. We delivered a herd to Denver and now making our way back to the ranch. He took a breath then didn't mind asking, "How about you men? What are you doing out here in the middle of nowhere?"

Manning shrugged a shoulder, "Oh, we're bounty hunters looking for some men needing to be caught up with."

Chet nodded his understanding, "Reckon that's a might risky job." He said while figuring that all three men bore the look of men on the run themselves. He was growing increasingly remorseful for not having told the visitors to keep on riding. Chet dished up a plate of food and took it over and handed it to Lonnie Beck who looked up in surprise because Chet had never done that before. Previously, Chet cooked and others were expected to help themselves. When Lonnie looked into Chet's eyes, the man rolled his eyes as a cautionary warning.

He then dished up another plate of stew

and a biscuit and handed it to Larry Larsen giving the man the same eye roll. Chet then began dishing up his own plate and called out to the others, "Foods on," then flared a hand toward the stew pot then stepped back as the three visitors crowded forward.

When everyone was sitting on the ground silently shoveling food into their mouths Lonnie spoke up, "Mighty larruping stew, Chet."

Chet in an attempt to lighten the mood said jovially, "Hell, Lonnie, I've never figured that you had a bad meal in your lifetime."

Lonnie nodded, "You're right about that, Chet. The only thing I ever had trouble with was the getting fed to start with and then getting enough. All I know is that you always make some mighty fine dishes. The only time I had as good was when I lived at home before my folks passed on from the fever. Afterwards, I rode our mule down to Texas looking for work, heard they were hiring at the Circle C, and sure enough, Mister Cunningham put me to work knowing I didn't know squat about herding cattle. He said, they'd teach me and I've been here ever since. The Circle C is my family now," he declared.

Chet laughed, "I know that since you been

at the Circle C, you never seemed to be filled up." Lonnie nodded again.

John Manning smiled then asked snidely, "Where are you from boy?"

Lonnie, in his youth knew that some men liked to use that tone of voice in order to prove that they were superior but he didn't like for anyone to call him boy, when they knew his name.

"Why I was born and raised near Arkadelphia, Arkansas. My folks had a little place there. My ma made up some fine dishes from some of the coons, possums, rabbits and squirrels me and dad hunted down and brought in."

"You ate coons and possums?" Manning chuckled.

"You bet," Lonnie was quick to answer. "We ate a lot of game. Baked coon or possum and sweet potatoes together with some greens from the garden, when we had them, made for some of finest meals I ever ate. It was a welcome change from just having beans, taters and cornbread. Then on Sunday mornings, we usually had squirrel brains and scrambled eggs to go with our flapjacks."

Manning chuffed a laugh then he began to get down to business, "I see that you have a big pistol in a holster across your middle.

You any good with that thing?"

Lonnie shrugged a shoulder, "I can usually hit what I'm aiming at."

Manning snorted then said, "Aiming and shooting is one thing but a man in my line of work has to be able to draw and shoot in a heartbeat; ain't no time for aiming. You suppose you could do that?"

"I reckon, if I had to but don't know if I could hit anything," was Lonnie's terse reply. He stood, walked over and put his dirty dish on the wagon tailgate then stepped to take a wad of sage brush in hand and pitch it onto the fire, which immediately flared up.

"Damn!" Manning said as he stepped back from the flames, "You trying to burn us up?"

Manning had been toying with the young man to see how far he could push.

Manning did not know that Lonnie Beck had lied when he said he didn't know if he could hit anything he was shooting at. Actually, Lonnie was very fast on the draw and very accurate in his shooting, in fact he was the best shot of all the Circle C riders. When Bill Cunningham had hired Lonnie, he had handed him the holstered .45 colt that the young man now wore around his middle. "A friend of mine gave me that gun when he retired, said for me to pass it on to someone who could put it to good use. I think you could be that someone. I encourage you to practice shooting that weapon, at least once a week, don't worry about the cost of bullets, I'll give you one box a week or until you get so's you can hit what you're pointing the thing at. My old friend, a gunfighter in his younger years, said whenever he pulled his six-gun he pointed the muzzle at the largest part of the object, usually a man, and pulled the trigger. He said aiming the weapon was a waste of time when you don't have the time to take aim unless you become proficient enough to hit what you are pointing the gun at. It always worked for him and he never lost a gunfight. Don't get the idea that I want you to be a gun fighter; nothing is further from the truth but you ought to know how to use a good six-gun and feel comfortable with carrying it around. Who knows, it might come in handy someday."

Lonnie took Cunningham's advice and practiced shooting without aiming at least once a week. He also practiced daily, just drawing the six-gun and cocking it. Drawing the six-gun was no problem but it had taken a lot of practice and concentration before he was able to make the bullet go where he wanted. The result, some four months later, was that he became very fast on the draw and could knock a can or bottle set on a fence post at 20 paces with only one bullet without aiming.

Manning had been toying with a very dangerous young man but didn't know it. He did however, switch his inquiries to the oldster Chet Olsen. "Bet your outfit got good money for that herd eh?"

Chet nodded, "That's what the boss man said. Told all of us he was paid Sixteen dollars a head. He paid us all off then left town on the train."

"And took the money with him, I suppose," Manning pried.

"Yep, he sure did," Chet replied.

"How much you boys get paid?" Manning asked.

Chet felt the heat going up his collar. How much they earned was nobody's business but he let the fool question slide and gave a standard answer. "Ain't no secret, all the hands at the Circle C make a dollar a day, food, a warm place to sleep and a horse to ride."

"You got a bottle in your wagon there, Mister cook?" Manning jeered.

Chet winched then said, "I keep one for snake bites or for a toast on special occasions but that's all the bottle is for. None of the Circle C hands imbibe liquor out on the trail; boss's orders."

It was Bart Knolls that ended the question and answer game. He pitched his cup and now empty plate to the ground then pulled his six-gun as he stood, "Why don't you dig out that bottle of hooch and show us the money you got paid so's we can put it to good use." He pointed the gun at Chet. "Stay away from that scatter gun and just put the bottle and the money on the tailgate."

When Knolls stood, Henry Riggins pulled his six-gun as he stood and pointed it at the still seated Larry Larsen, "Don't touch that six-gun on your hip or I'll plug ya. Just dig out your money."

Lonnie Beck was standing off to the left of Chet and Larry Larsen.

John Manning was grinning as he leered at Lonnie, "Well, looks like my boys have you boys covered. Now you, mister coon eater, just reach your thumb and fore finger to the handle of that six-gun you're packing and pinch the handle then bring it out real slow like and drop it on the ground. That way I don't have to pull my six-gun and kill you, cause I don't pull my weapon except when I am ready to put it to good use."

Lonnie nodded, the hair on the back of his neck was bristling and his heart was thudding in his chest. He began to edge his hand toward the handle of his six-gun. He'd never killed a man before, fact was, he'd never even shot at anything other than targets or game for their hides or for food. He knew, however, that if he did not do something, these men would kill Chet and Larry and himself and leave them lying here for buzzard bait. He was not about to let that happen. He willed himself to calm down as best he could so that he could concentrate. He knew that he would feel no remorse by shooting these men and he not only figured but believed that he could put a bullet into each of the three before they could react. He had no choice but to do something. Killing them wouldn't mean any more to him than shooting a skunk or a snake.

"Careful now," Manning advised as he leaned forward with his own hand around the handle of his holstered six-gun.

Lonnie Beck did as told with thumb and forefinger stretched out to touch the handle of his six-gun then as a grinning Manning watched closely, Lonnie hesitated for one heartbeat then jammed his hand onto the .45 colt and extracted it.

Bam! Bam! Bam! John Manning had gotten his six-gun clear of his holster but failed to raise it when, all of sudden, everything went black. He fell straight back with a bullet to his forehead.

Bart Knolls was knocked sideways with a bullet through his left arm that went on further to puncture his heart. When the bullet struck him, his arm and the six-gun lowered from pointing at Chet. Reflexively he pulled the trigger as he fell to the ground, blasting up dirt near his own right boot.

Henry Riggins stood wide eyed, while shaking his head side to side. His lips moved but no sound came from his mouth. He began swaying from side to side as his right arm and six-gun, still extended toward Larry Larsen began to lower to his side, then the gun dropped to the ground as the man fell to his left. He'd been hit under his right arm, the bullet raking the top of both lungs and nipping his heart as well. The whole shooting episode had lasted but mere seconds and all three men were down, and dead or dying.

Lonnie stepped to stare at each body until he was satisfied that all three were down and would not rise.

"I never seen the likes of it!" Chet exclaimed, clapped a hand to Lonnie's back then said, "That was mighty fine shooting, son! Thank you for saving us, Lonnie. I don't doubt those bastards would have killed all of us before the night was over."

Larry Larsen stood and extended a hand to Lonnie, "For a while there, I thought we were all goners, Lonnie. I knew you were a good shot but I had no idea you could do what you did. You must have nerves of steel. That was some damn fine shooting and I am grateful."

Chet walked over to each of the downed men and nudged each body with a booted foot. "All that vermin is done for," he said.

"What are we going to do with them?" Larry Larsen asked.

Chet began, "For now, were going to strip them of their hardware and use a rope and one of their horses to drag them away from camp. I don't want to smell em' all night. In the morning, we'll search the bodies and their saddlebags for any valuables, which I doubt, but we might somehow learn their names, case some lawman ever asks. I believe we ought to turn those horses loose. From what I can see all three are just plug sorrels and ain't worth keeping."

"Are we going to bury them?" Larry Larsen asked.

Chet wagged his head, side to side,

"Nope!" He said emphatically then added, "they don't deserve it. We'll leave them where they lay after we've dragged them away from our camp. As far as I'm concerned they're nothing but buzzard bait and critter food." He then stepped to the back of the wagon and opened a compartment and extracted an unlabeled bottle of whiskey. He pulled the cork out with his teeth then handed the bottle to Lonnie. "Let's have a drink, men. This here is a special occasion."

J.L. (Jerry) Guin is a veteran of the U.S. Navy and a retired wholesale lumber trader. Jerry's first western fiction short story was published by Western Digest in 1995. Since then, his writing has been exclusively western fiction. Jerry has penned over 48 western fiction short stories, six of those were presented in the Western Fictioneers Wolf Creek series many others have appeared in anthologies such as *The Traditional West, Outlaws and Lawmen, Best of the West, The Untamed West* and many others. He has written 15 western fiction novels, the most recent being *Reluctant Partners,* released August 2020.

Joe the Bartender Saves the Day

BEN GOHEEN

It was a dusky dark Tuesday evening in the 1888 Arizona town of Black Ridge when Joe Tapper first laid eyes on the tall stranger. The sun had disappeared behind the far-away hills, leaving a purple-hued sky that never failed to stir something inside him. He had even named his establishment The Sunset Saloon in homage to that vision. A noticeable coolness in the air tagged along behind the dropping of the sun as Joe settled in for the evening.

Joe watched as the stranger, wind-burnt and weary-looking, slapped the dust off his trousers with a dingy tan hat, then walked up to the bar. He guessed the sandy-haired stranger to be around twenty-five years old at most, dressed in a red, sweat-stained flannel shirt and tattered black denims. He set a Winchester rifle on the bar while he inspected his looks in the gilt-framed mirror attached to the back wall.

An out of work cow puncher probably, Joe thought, or maybe just a fiddle-footed drifter trying to find his way in an ever-changing world. Having spent forty of his sixty years behind a bar, Joe had seen all kinds come and go.

"Evening," Joe said as he wiped the dark oak bar with a hand towel. "What'll you have?"

"Whatever you have handy will do nicely," the stranger said as he turned to scan the room where half a dozen men sat around the poker tables.

"Things always this quiet around here?"

"Mostly. Black Ridge is a peaceful little town aside from an occasional rowdy Saturday night after payday at the ranches and mines. But we give 'em a chance to burn off their hoo-rah without causing too big of a fuss."

Joe stuck his hand over the bar and said, "The name is Joe. I'm chief cook, barkeep, and owner of this here joint." He placed a glass and a bottle on the bar. "First one is on the house."

"That's mighty kind of you, Joe. You can call me Wesley."

Wesley downed the drink, wiped a hand across his mouth, and asked, "Your town marshal is a man named Jeffords, right?"

"Yep. Chalk Jeffords."

"Chalk. Now there's an odd name if I ever heard one."

"Well, it fits Jeffords well enough since he is a mite different from most men."

"How so?"

"Chalk is slow to act, slow to talk, but when he does, a man oughta pay attention. I've seen him back down a crowd of hard-nosed miners with nothing more than his cold-eyed stare. He's getting on in years now, but he's still a man not to trifle with once he gets his hackles stirred."

"He's not one of those lawmen who likes to shoot first and talk later, is he?"

"Naw. Chalk has the patience of Job. But once he has had enough, watch out. That's when he can turn into a real bad-tempered cougar."

Wesley scratched at his stubble. "Is there a hotel in town where I can clean up a bit and get a room for the night?"

"Gracie's Boarding House is across the street. I expect she can fix you up."

"By the way," Wesley said. "Where does Jeffords live?"

Joe hesitated for a few seconds, then asked, "Why are you asking? Is it curiosity, or do you have something else on your mind?"

Wesley picked up his Winchester and said, "Well Joe, let's just say I've got some important business to take up with the marshal."

Esther Jeffords stepped out on the rear porch and shouted, "Chalk! Supper's on the table."

"I'm coming." Chalk propped the hayfork in the corner of the shed, slapped Rattler on the rump, and headed for the house. Along the way, he stopped at the well where he drew a bucket of water and poured it over his head. After he shook off the excess water like a shaggy dog, he dried his salt and pepper hair with a towel Esther had laid out for him.

Chalk pulled out a chair at the kitchen table and sat down across from his nineteen-year-old daughter, Jenny. Every time he looked at her, he got a lump in his throat. Jenny was so much like Esther when she was that age. Both were petite women who wore their long dark hair pulled back and tied with a ribbon. They had matching sparkling green eyes that carried a hint of humor, and both were as pretty as a morning sunrise.

"That's a mighty pretty dress I see over on the settee. Is it new?"

"Kind of new. Mom and I have been stitching on it all week."

"You got a special occasion coming up?"

"A girl needs to be ready in case one wanders by."

The three of them made small talk over their meal, then Chalk brought up a subject that had been on his mind ever since Jenny had returned from Denver a month ago. "Jenny, since you've been back from boarding school, you seem to be preoccupied. At times you seem to disappear into a world of your own. Like me and your mom are not even here. Is there something going on we need to know about?"

Jenny smiled and reached across the table for her father's hand. "Nothing that won't work itself out in time, Dad. It's something I can handle on my own. You and mom don't need to worry about me."

"Jenny," Esther said. "It's part of our job to worry about you. Did the big city life in Denver spoil you? Is that it? Would you prefer to live your life in a city rather than live in this harsh, barren country?"

"Believe me, Mom, I will work everything out — and soon."

With that said, Jenny excused herself and went to her room.

Chalk and Esther talked for a few more

minutes, then there was a knock on their front door. Chalk pushed away from the table and strolled through the parlor to the door. When he opened it, he found Joe Tapper standing there.

"Come in, Joe."

"No, no. Let's talk out here, Chalk."

Chalk stepped out on the porch and said, "You've got a worried expression on your face. Is something wrong down at the saloon?"

"No, it's not that. It's just that a grungy looking stranger came in a little while ago carrying a Winchester. He said something that worried me — something I think you oughta know."

Chalk nodded for Joe to continue. "Go on, Joe, tell me."

"Well, he said he had some important business to take up with you."

"Hmm," Chalk said. "What do you think he meant?"

"I don't know, but he is spending the night at Gracie's if you want to ask him."

"Thanks for letting me know."

Chalk watched the barkeep walk away while he thought about what he had heard. Was this stranger someone from his past out to settle an old account, or was Joe's vivid imagination running amuck again?

Well, he figured whatever the stranger wanted would wait until tomorrow.

Joe was mopping the floors of the Sunset Saloon the following morning when he heard a banging on the window. He glanced at the clock behind the bar. 9:08 a.m. He eased over to the grimy window, peeked out, and saw the man called Wesley standing on the boardwalk. Joe set the mop aside and unlocked the door. He was surprised at the change he saw in Wesley. Not only had he shaved off his stubble, but he'd had his shaggy hair trimmed, and had donned clean clothes.

"Not open yet," Joe said. "Come back later."

"I can't wait until later."

Joe stepped aside and ushered him in. "Alright, come on in."

"One drink is all I want. Just one to settle my nerves before I go see Jeffords. I have to take care of my business now and get back to my men before dark."

"Get back to your men? What do you mean?"

"They are camped about ten miles south of here. They're waiting until I get my personal business with Jeffords taken care of before they ride in to celebrate with me."

He's got a gang waiting for him.

Joe stared at the young man, unsure of what to do, or what to say. While he did not resemble the grungy stranger who had stumbled into the Sunset Saloon the previous day, his talk was still worrisome for sure — maybe more so now that he learned Wesley had a gang backing him up. And they were going to celebrate when Wesley was finished with the marshal.

"Wesley, I don't know you from Adam, but you should go back to where you came from. If you have it in your mind to tangle with Chalk Jeffords, you'd be making a big mistake."

Wesley shook his head. "A man has to do what a man has to do regardless of how it might turn out. What's more, I have to do my business with him face to face. There's no other way."

Joe let out a loud sigh as he pushed a bottle toward him. "Help yourself."

"One drink is all I need. I have to be clearheaded and sober for what I have in front of me."

Joe complied with Wesley's wishes, then hurried out the back door of the Sunset Saloon.

"I don't know what Wesley has in mind, but

it bothers me to think he might be up to no good where Chalk is concerned," Joe said.

"Chalk can take care of hisself," Sam Kirk replied. "He ain't never needed our help before."

"But this varmint said he has a gang waiting for him a few miles from here just waiting for him to take care of Jeffords before they ride in. Besides, we all know how Chalk has slowed down over the past few years. And what's worse, Wesley might be aiming to sneak around and ambush him with that Winchester he carries."

Joe had gathered Sam Kirk from the harness shop, Louie Rymer, the town banker, and Mayor Arwood Callahan, the town's only lawyer, to fill them in on his suspicions.

"That part about him having a gang bothers me," the banker said. "The payroll for Red Butte mine is due in here tomorrow afternoon. That could be what they are after."

"It'd be a plum haul, that's fer sure, if Joe here is right," Sam said. "But we all know how he can turn a cat into a catamount, too."

"Are you sure about all this, Joe?" Mayor Callahan asked.

Joe held up his right hand. "I'm telling you straight what I heard and saw."

They swapped thoughts and ideas for a few minutes, then the mayor asked, "Where is he now, Joe? I think we need to go get him, truss him up, and ride him outta town on a rail just to be safe."

"But what about his gang?" Louie asked. "If we anger him, he might come back with his whole gang, steal the payroll, and burn this place to the ground for us interfering."

They all sat quietly and thought about their predicament for several minutes. Finally, the mayor stood and said, "We can't just sit here and do nothing. I'm going to get my rifle. We've fought Indians, border bandits, and every kind of varmint God put on this earth. We can surely handle one man, or even his gang if it comes to that. We owe it to Chalk to help him after all he's done for us."

"I left Wesley in the saloon," Joe said, "But he might already be headed for Jeffords house by now."

"Get your guns and we'll meet at the end of the street. If he's already at Chalk's place, we'll surround him and give Chalk all the support we can muster."

"You men go ahead," Joe said. "I'm going to try to get to Chalk's house before Wesley does and warn him."

■ ■ ■ ■

Chalk and Jenny were up early tending to their chores. Both had wandered over to the shed where Chalk had Rattler saddled and ready for the day. Jenny sat on an upturned bucket and watched her father go through his methodical routine.

"How old is Rattler?" she asked.

"Don't know. I never asked him."

"Funny, funny," she said. "You've had him as long as I can remember."

"I plan to retire him in a couple of years, if he lasts that long — or if I last that long."

"Oh, Dad, both of you are indestructible and you know it."

Chalk checked the cinch one last time and had a foot in the stirrup when Joe Tapper ran through the shed's rear doorway. He dropped to his knees in front of Chalk gasping for breath.

"For Heaven's sake, Joe, slow down."

"He's coming after you, Chalk," Joe said. "He's on his way."

"Who's on his way?" Jenny asked.

Joe waved his hands, still trying to catch his full breath. "A killer named Wesley, that's who."

"A killer named Wesley!" Jenny shouted.

She looked from her father to Joe. "What's he talking about? A killer . . ."

At about that same time, there was a shout from the rear of the Jeffords' house. It was Esther. "Chalk! There's a man on the front porch who needs to talk to you."

"That's gotta be him," Joe said. "That's Wesley. Be careful, Chalk."

Jenny started for the front of the shed, but Chalk grabbed her arm and pulled her back. "Whoa, girl. You stay here."

"But, Dad!"

"Do as I say."

Chalk tugged at his gun belt until it was comfortable, then stepped out of the shed into the morning sunlight. He blinked several times as the sun was blinding in its intensity. He eased himself to the left until the sun was no longer shining directly in his eyes. Wesley had moved off the porch and stood twenty yards from him, his arms hanging loosely at his hips.

"I'm Jeffords. What do you want?"

Wesley strode slowly toward him.

Chalk held up his hand. "That's close enough. Now, tell me what this is all about?"

"Mr. Jeffords, we need to . . ."

Suddenly, Mayor Callahan and two others rushed out of the bushes, their guns at the ready. "We've got him surrounded, Chalk.

He's not going to cause us any trouble now."

Chalk glanced around and spotted Sam and Louie, as well as Arwood Callahan, all armed to the teeth. The mayor ran over to Chalk and said, "He has a gang a few miles from here just waiting to steal the mine payroll after he takes care of you."

"After he takes care of me?" Chalk asked as he pointed toward Wesley. "What's he gonna do, throw a flowerpot at me? He's not even carrying a gun."

Callahan glared at Joe Tapper as he said, "Dang it, Joe. Is this another one of your exaggerations?"

Joe ducked behind the banker and tried to hide.

Jenny ran up to Wesley and grabbed his hand. "Dad, you have to listen to Wes."

Chalk glanced at Jenny, then at Wesley. What in Hades was going on here? He nodded at Wesley and said, "Talk."

"I came to Black Ridge to ask you for Jenny's hand in marriage. That's all. Jenny and I met in Denver and fell in love. I promised her I would be here soon to ask for your permission. I was scared to death to face you, but we both wanted it that way. So, I built up my courage and here I am. So, I'm asking for your permission here and now."

"Wha . . . what about this gang you talked about?" Joe asked.

"It's called a crew, Joe, not a gang. I'm a mining engineer. My crew of surveyors, geologists, and I have been exploring this area for signs of copper deposits. The crew is waiting at our camp until I get Mr. Jeffords permission to marry Jenny. If I do, they're coming to Black Ridge to celebrate with us."

Chalk saw the gleam in Jenny's eyes as she held on to Wesley's arm. He now understood why she had been acting differently the past few weeks.

"Go get your mom, Jenny," he said.

With Esther, Jenny, and Wesley standing in front of him, and the good citizens of Black Ridge cowering in embarrassment behind him, Chalk held out his hand and said. "Son, you have my permission with all my blessings."

Wesley had a wide grin spread across his face as he grabbed Chalk's hand. "Thank you, Sir." He then grabbed Jenny around the waist and swung her round and round.

Chalk turned to Joe Tapper and said, "After this fiasco, Joe, I think the drinks for this celebration should be on the house, don't you?"

"I surely do," Joe said. "I surely so."

Ben Goheen is a former secondary-school teacher, and human resources manager in the chemical industry. Ben's novels of the Old West, written under the name Ben Tyler, are *Echoes of Massacre Canyon,* winner of the 2016 Peacemaker Award as Best First Western, and his follow-up novel, *Mabry's Challenge.* A third western novel entitled *The Cowboy and the Scallywag* is due to hit the shelves within the next few months.

Blood Money
BARBARA SHEPHERD

Charcoal clouds crept in, dueling for position in a starless sky. Hunkered down near a stand of pines with my black gelding and pack mule, I adjusted the blood-soaked bandannas tied around my head. I knew better than to pass out. So tired I had to fight sleep, I willed myself to concentrate — on anything. The snow of '69 came to mind.

Winter stung like a bullwhip that year, ripping autumn leaves from the trees, covering the valley with ice thick enough for skating. But play had no place for us Tollett boys.

Cattle needed tending and protection from wolves, hungry to put on weight before heavy snows forced little critters underground. Horseshoes clattered on frozen streambeds as Jasper and I herded cattle into a box canyon for the night.

Dawn revealed a blanket of white, rippling as the cows milled and mooed, slow and soft, the snow on their hides an insulator for the cold. Before noon, a silent breeze sneaked in from the west, gifting us with the glimmer of a sun, streaking through a sky so gray it melded into the rocky horizon.

Later, the tease of warmth vanished when an arctic wind exhaled, whirling the snow into funnels, blowing it from the cow's backs, forcing tumbleweeds into an ugly race. We rounded up the cows and herded them down to their southern pasture, earlier this winter than any other. That was the last year Jasper and I herded cattle together, the last time we headed home to the same house, and the last civil words we spoke to one another.

So different from here and now. Parched landscape in this forsaken country should welcome rain. By morn, I'll likely see a flood in that little arroyo down there. Mountain air and a hideout were what I needed, but my animals deserved a rest first.

Before we hunkered down, I filled my canteen and looped the grain bags over Star and Zack's ears to let them eat before they drank what little water was left in the streambed. Once we got up in these trees, I loosened the animals' cinches. Zack gave a soft whimper before the old mule closed his eyes and slept.

I rubbed the star on the gelding's forehead. "Sorry you have to stay saddled, Star. Those bounty hunters may find us even though I swept the trail clean back there. No need to take chances."

He nickered like he understood every word.

"Once we get this rain, you and the saddle will get washed clean from all this blood. Lucky for me, their bullet only grazed my noggin." I winced from the pain. "A head wound always makes you bleed like a stuck hog." I stroked Star's rump and left him ground tied before I hobbled Zack for the night. "Once we know we've given these bounty hunters the slip, we'll head north into the timber."

I settled into a small, rocky crevice and unfolded the wanted poster I always carried. "The photo looks like me, Star. Last name's Tollett. No wonder bounty hunters keep my trail hot. Only problem for them, I'm not the one they're looking for. Nowhere does it say Jefferson Tollett. Everything on this poster belongs to Jasper. Remember him?"

Star gave his head a couple of big nods.

"Yep. My twin." It got too dark to read the wanted poster, so I folded it and put it away. I had the charges against him memorized anyway. "I miss Ma but am grateful she passed on before Jasper turned bad."

He was so good with cattle and horses I thought he'd make a great Texas cattle baron someday. But something twisted inside him, and he coupled that mean streak with his skill with a gun. Our paths only crossed twice since then.

I'm not searching for him now, and I don't know which one of us will shoot if and when we meet. I hope I don't have to make that decision. A man shouldn't have to face his brother in a gunfight.

Covering up as best I could didn't block out the cold. Funny how hot the desert can be during the day, yet it turns cold soon after the sun sets. A small fire would have felt like heaven, but I didn't dare. The bounty hunters could be closer than I thought, and since they started chasing me, I wasn't sure whether they had hunted me or slipped up on me while tracking Jasper. I chewed hardtack and jerky, washed down with spring water from my old canteen. How I missed my coffee.

Always alert, I listened but heard nothing out of the ordinary. Until later, when the first raindrops fell. So much louder out here on rocks and trees, rain did not patter. Each drop slapped dry leaves and crashed against hard stone.

Zack jerked awake and brayed. Star shivered but remained quiet. Both stayed put while the raindrops increased in size.

When the clouds burst open, the rain spewed forth like in the stories from the Bible. Thunder cracked, louder and louder, while a sky full of crooked lightning continued to put on a show. I'd heard of people seeing great white thunderclouds in the open desert and rain afterwards, but I was not prepared for such a wild thunderstorm. I thought we'd be safe since it would be difficult for anyone to travel in the middle of rain as heavy as this. Doubted they could see a foot in front of them.

A couple hours later, rain still poured from a sky I could no longer see. The sound of rushing water proved me right — the arroyo was flooding. Star, Zack, and I were wet, cold, and bent over — beat down by heavy rain.

C-r-rack!

I hadn't heard thunder in a while, and surprised, I almost yelled out. Good thing I didn't.

Gunshots peppered the soggy air — in front of me and from behind. I managed to roll over and lie on my stomach, hoping to see better. I pulled my gun, so wet and slick, hard to hold onto.

Wedged into the middle of a gun battle was a crazy place for a man to be. My animals reacted, giving away our location but then, the shooting stopped. For no reason, the rain switched to a trickle.

Lightning flashed again, illuminating a figure striding toward me. He holstered his weapon, and I did the same. "They're down," he said.

I looked behind me to see the bounty hunters lying in the mud. Even in the darkness, I could make out an old, grizzled guy draped over a smooth rock. The youngster beside him should have been courting a sweet girl in school instead of chasing outlaws. Same bounty hunters who shot me earlier.

When the man walking toward me got close enough, I recognized him. He studied me for a moment. "Jefferson! What you doin' way up here, brother?"

"Ranch got too big for me. Sold it. Headed up here to see the northern mountains. Maybe buy a little spread or pan for gold. Until bounty hunters mistook me for you, Jasper."

"Sorry 'bout that, Jefferson." He tapped his forehead. "You hurt bad?"

"No, but who knows how the next skirmish will end. You're my brother, my twin, my blood. Why'd you have to put me in danger like this?"

He shrugged.

My temper wanted to take over. "I didn't know if you were up ahead or they just spotted me and figured I was you. I'm tired of having to explain there's two of us."

"Ma was the only one who could tell us apart," Jasper said. "How is she?"

"She's gone, Jasper. She was never sick. Doc and I figured she died of a broken heart after worrying about how bad you turned out. Why'd you have to do that to her?"

He didn't answer. Instead, he stumbled and sat down on a rocky outcropping.

The black clouds parted enough for the moon to peek through, giving me enough light to see the bloody vest Jasper wore. "How bad is it?"

He ignored my question. "Hate for it to end this way," he said, his hand itching to draw his pistol.

I saw determination in his eyes, that look of steel some talk about, that point of no return. He would draw, and he was far faster than I ever could be. No matter how angry he had made me over the years, I never wanted to shoot my own brother. Could I?

He gave me no choice. I reached for my gun, but he cleared leather and shot before

I could aim. My body lurched forward.

Just then, the grizzled bounty hunter fell beside me, staring up at the night sky. The man had summoned enough strength for one last shot. He must have moved like a cat. I never heard him come up behind me. A dark stain on the ground in front of me grew bigger. My brother had shot him but not before the old guy pumped a bullet into my back.

Jasper crawled over to me but paused to pick up something on the way. "Lucky for you," he said. "He missed your spine and got you in the shoulder. This bullet went straight through you. Stop the bleedin' and bandage up. You'll live." He ripped my drenched coat and shirt off of me, balled them up, and helped me stop the flow of blood. My blood, ignoring his wound.

I tried to help him, but he shook his head. I felt weak and had to fight to keep from passing out.

He stared at me for a moment. "You thought I'd shoot you, didn't you?"

"I saw that steely look, Jasper. You were going to draw. No one could've stopped you."

"You're right. But I was savin' your life." He poked me in the chest with his finger. "You were drawin' on me, Jefferson. Your own brother."

"Didn't think I had a choice. Jasper, I'm sorry."

"Don't worry. You never practiced enough to have a quick draw." He laughed but then choked up and collapsed in front of me. I cradled his body and watched his eyes turn glassy.

He struggled to get enough air to speak. "Haul my carcass into the nearest town, will you? Give me a real burial. Keep the horses and the bounty money." He coughed up an awful amount of blood. "Will I get to see Ma, do you think?"

"Not sure, Jasper. You've broken a lot of commandments."

"But I never killed anyone. Not before tonight, and this was self-defense."

"Guess you can argue that at the pearly gates."

"Yep. If nothin' else, maybe Saint Peter will let me peek through one of the gates and see Ma, happy as a lark and not a care in the world."

"Maybe so." My tears melded into the last raindrops on my face.

His body shook as he struggled to breathe, and then he was gone. My brother, my twin, hoped his soul headed to heaven.

My body and soul had more work to do.

If I planned to live much longer, my new mission required destroying every wanted poster for a Tollett that ever existed.

The thunder gave one last bark, so loud the ground shook like I was in the middle of an earthquake. And then, the storm subsided. Dark clouds skated away, taking the rain with them, and let hundreds of stars shine like diamonds. I'll take those. I don't need to pan for gold.

Barbara Shepherd is an award-winning writer, poet, and artist. Published books include: Historical novel set in 1830s Texas — *River Bend,* children's picture book — *The Potbelly Pig Promise,* cookbook — *Vittles and Vignettes,* and poetry chapbook — *Patchwork Skin.* Her work also appears in magazines, literary journals, and many anthologies and cookbooks. A young adult novel is due out in 2021. Visit her online at barbarashepherd.com.

The Miner and the Greenhorn
Charlie Steel

A warm wind blew in the dry desert. The sun set and the sky darkened. The velvet black revealed bright stars, and along the horizon, a full moon was rising. Brody Simpson, three days without water, was losing his vision. Soon his brain would overheat, and he would die. Using the very last of his strength, he stepped forward and fell to his knees. His vision now badly blurred, he crawled towards an incline, hoping to come to water. Slipping on the edge of a precipice he could no longer see, his body slid head forward down a rock, went over a cliff, and fell through the air. When he landed on the pile of loose mining debris, the young man was unconscious.

"What in tarnation!" exclaimed Rufus out loud, his aged, rough voice unused to speech.

Dust rose up from the powdery heap below, and the old miner held a lantern and looked down to see what had just interrupted his placing of gold particles into his leather bag.

"Whatever fell from above sure don't sound like rock," growled the old man.

The object was lying on top of the detritus.

Maybe it's a bighorn sheep that fell off the cliff from above, he thought. *Happens sometimes. Even an animal as graceful and as sure as them four-legged creatures are, they can lose footing. It don't happen often, but it's possible.*

Rufus walked into the entrance of his cave, and removing a rock, hid his precious bag of gold in a crevice, and replaced the stone. Thinking about the fallen object, the old man was building up curiosity and gumption enough to climb down and take a look. Tired of beans, totally out of supplies, the thought of fresh meat finally motivated the miner to move his aching body down the steep hill and dig in the dirt. The old man was on his knees when he discovered the object was not a bighorn sheep, but a man.

"Of all the darn luck," rasped Rufus, speaking again out loud for the third time in weeks of complete silence.

Turning the body over, he saw the face of the stranger was covered in dust, and it was impossible to tell whether he was young or old. The powdered dirt clinging to the man's face made the fellow look like a pale dead ghost. Rufus shivered at the image, reminded of his own nearing mortality.

"Dead!" gasped Rufus, and this time the exclamation hurt his throat.

Trying to rise, Rufus accidentally leaned on the dead man's chest. Rufus felt heat from the man's body. Pushing on the chest made the stranger groan. Holding the lantern up, the miner saw a puff of air that rose from the stranger's lips in a miniature cloud of dust.

"Alive!" gasped Rufus.

Rising as best he could, the old man climbed back up the hill, and went to his canteen — pulling the stopper, he took a drink. Pondering on what to do, Rufus stood there, swishing water in his dry mouth, before swallowing.

Why in all the gosh darn luck did this have to happen to me? thought the miner. *One thing I hate worse than people is a claim jumper!*

Thinking on it some more, Rufus realized this was no claim jumper but some stranger who had lost his horse and was wandering around looking for a spring. *Looks like another dumb greenhorn come to the desert to die of heat and thirst.*

Rufus pondered on the sudden situation. The decision was up to him. Let the stranger lie there and die, or give him precious water and try to bring him back to life. It would take a lot of effort to save that prostate form.

Why did he have to fall down here? He'll drink up all my water, and if he lives, probably be all sorts of trouble, thought Rufus irritably. *He'll et my food, talk me to death, and when he realizes this is a gold claim, slit my throat and steal my dust.*

Rufus sat down on his favorite perch, a nearly square rock in front of the cave entrance. An old blanket kept his bony butt from touching solid rock. The miner looked up at the stars so bright in the black sky. He could see part of the Milky Way, and for a moment he forgot himself and stared at the spectacular scene above him. The full moon rose higher and, along with the stars, created light and deep shadow — bright enough that the miner turned down the wick on his lantern.

After a good half hour of furious self-argument, it was curiosity that finally motivated the old man to get up and return to the prostate form below. The old man climbed down and taking his canteen, he removed the stopper and very carefully dribbled drops onto the unconscious man's lips. The stranger groaned and stuck out a dried-up tongue. Rufus poured more water into the open mouth. The man swallowed and then began to choke. Grabbing the dirt-covered shirt front of the stranger, Rufus lifted up the torso to a sitting position, and the coughing stopped.

With gnarled old hands, the miner plugged the canteen, slung the strap over his shoulders, and bent down. Gritting his teeth, with all the strength his aching muscles gave him, he lifted the man and began to drag the body backwards up the hill. The boot heels of the unconscious fellow scraped the hard ground as Rufus continued to pull. When he came to the cave entrance, the old man dragged him inside.

Panting, Rufus grimaced in disgust, rubbed his wrinkled hands, and felt the fatigue of his body. Age was doing what sixty-one years of hard work could not, stealing strength, turning his steel-like body and muscles into a weakness he could not overcome. How unfair it was to grow old and more feeble day by day.

From the dim light of the lantern at the cave entrance, Rufus studied the dusty face of the stranger. Not liking the ghastly image, the oldster found an empty flour sack, picked it up, and bent down and rubbed roughly, clearing away the dirt. It was then the miner saw that his unwelcome guest was a young man.

"Just a kid," whispered Rufus, his voice echoing in the hollow of the cave. "A young whippersnapper!"

Wetting the flour sack with water from the canteen, Rufus rubbed more dust off the young man's face. Then he folded the cloth, lay it on the lad's forehead, and applied more water. Again he poured precious liquid into the man's mouth. The stranger swallowed and coughed. Rufus roughly grabbed the shirt front and lifted until the coughing stopped. He left him lying on the hard ground of the cave.

"I'll go easy with the water," whispered Rufus out loud. "See to whether you live or die before I go wasting more. Besides, too much would probably kill you."

Rufus, more gently now, felt the man's forehead. He realized he was hot to the touch.

"Perhaps the coolness of the cave will help ya, Sonny."

Changing his mind, Rufus gave the struggling lad more water. When the stranger swallowed that time, he did not cough. In a gesture of kindness, the old man poured water onto the lad's fevered and sunburned face.

"Well," said Rufus. "That ought to kill ya or cure ya."

The miner rose, and ignoring the young man, he began going about the makings of his dinner. He lit a fire outside and hung a pot of beans over it. When it heated, he took a spoon, dished a portion onto a tin plate, and sat on his rock. He sat and chewed and looked over the landscape from his favorite perch.

Under the bright moon and stars, he could see the land before him. Endless miles swept away into undulating hills, buttes, and valleys. Most of the ground nearby was barren rock. Further down, the lower prairie was a wide vista of grass, intermingled with shadows of pinion and cedar. Rufus never got tired of the night, or of observing the star-laden sky. This was a special evening as the Hunter's Moon, along with the bright stars, gave off a light nearly as bright as dawn.

While he chewed his beans, he unconsciously smiled. It softened his brown, wrinkled face and made him look younger.

After a few minutes of quiet reflection, Rufus finished the beans and walked over to his cleaning pit. He used a rag and sand to scrub spoon and plate clean. He never wasted water. Going to the pan, the beans were hard and probably had seen their last use. Still, he couldn't afford to waste them. He'd add water in the morning and try to chew them down.

It had been a long time since he had gone for supplies, and he was out of everything, including coffee. It was the new vein of gold that kept him there. He dare not leave it until it played out or proved up. Here was his life's last work, and, at his age, he would do no more prospecting. A solitary miner, a man who spent a lifetime looking for gold, his days were numbered. He would die as he had lived, completely alone.

The stranger was a complication. For a week now, he had worked the mine with the feeling that someone was watching. Going back to the seat next to the cave, he relaxed. The sudden feeling of eyes upon him came once more. It was a tangible and creepy feeling, and he knew his sixth sense was not wrong. Getting up, Rufus went in the cave and rummaged around and found the old Walker Colt. It was a massive piece of iron, loaded, and unfired for many a year. By rights, he should fire it, clean it, and reload, but the thought of breaking the stillness and silence of the night was a task he could not bear to perform. Perhaps the stranger who lies in the cave mumbling in fevered delirium was one of those claim jumpers. Rufus pondered a bit and then doubted the lad was anything but a dumb greenhorn. Just another foolish easterner come West and taken by the desert.

The old man went into the cave and picked up the empty canteen. Taking a torch and lighting it with nearly the last of his sulfur matches, he went back into the darkness. Following the rough and crooked walls he had dug with his own horny hands, Rufus came to a large crack in the ceiling. Here was a bucket, and he heard plainly along with his ragged breathing, the plop, plop of the loud drip of water. Shoving the torch into a hole in the wall, and finding the funnel on a rock shelf, he set down the canteen. He picked up the bucket, and using the funnel, poured water into the canteen. It was a well-practiced routine, and none of the precious liquid was wasted.

When the process was done, the old man carried the canteen back to the entrance. The torch was stuck in a mound of soft dirt and went out. Standing above the groaning and fevered stranger, Rufus removed the stopper and again dripped water into the young man's mouth. Except for a little coughing, he drank the liquid down. Perhaps, in time, the fellow would recover. Only time would tell.

Rufus gazed at the stranger. His color did look a bit better. Right now he was mumbling something. The old man leaned down to hear better.

"It's alright, Ma. Pa is just mad . . . I'll show him . . . I'll . . ."

The lad continued to mumble, but those few phrases were all Rufus could make out.

He hung up the canteen and went back outside. The stars and moon were unbelievably bright. Even after a lifetime of living out in the open, they still took his breath away. The old man hurt in every joint of his body, and sleep would be hard to come by. It would be a long night.

In the last few months, he had dug out and crushed a good amount of gold — more than he had found in some time. The vein was no wider than a lead pencil and only a few inches deep, but maybe it would increase. Rufus was excited. Then, once again, the feeling that eyes were upon him, overwhelmed him in a suffocating embrace. Rufus was bothered. He got up and went for his ancient pistol. He stuck it in his belt and vowed to carry around the cumbersome thing, if for no other reason than the comfort it gave him.

Rufus leaned down and turned up the wick of the lantern. Picking up a sweat-stained, dog-eared Bible, the miner read from a chapter in the Old Testament.

Hard to figure how a man like Solomon, with God's gift of wisdom, could squander so much, thought Rufus. *Bet if I was him, I wouldn't of done what he done. Why a leader like that would . . .*

"Alright, Mister! Put your hands up!"

Rufus couldn't believe it. And he growled with disgust at the man's voice. It came from behind a jumble of rocks next to the cave. The only way that feller could have sneaked in without being heard was when he was back getting water.

Of all the gosh darn luck! thought Rufus.

Rufus dived off the rock and for the entrance of the cave. A rifle blasted, and a bullet hit the miner in the leg with a loud whump. That didn't stop the old man, and he continued crawling forward, ignoring the sudden pain and flow of hot blood. Another blast of weapons, this time several rifles fired, and a second bullet hit Rufus in the side. Boot heels sounded on hard ground, and three men came running to the cave entrance. One thumped the old man on the back of the head with the barrel of a rifle.

The miner, knocked silly for a moment, lay still. When he came to, he found his hands tied in front of him, and he was sitting up against a wall of rock outside the mine entrance. The old Walker Colt was missing from his belt.

"Sloan," ordered the leader. "Tie up them wounds. We don't want the old fool to bleed to death before he tells us where the gold's hid."

There were three dirty, bearded men who stood outside in the light of moon and stars. Each one of them looked like the scavengers they were. Their clothes were tattered and patched, and each wore a stained, dirty, and dilapidated sombrero. The one called Sloan knelt down, took hold of Rufus's shirt, and pulled hard. It began to rip. Using both hands, Sloan roughly pulled the shirt off the old man, while the other two thieves laughed. They watched their partner began to rip the cloth into strips to use as bandages. Sloan knelt, examined the leg wound, and bound it tightly. The bullet groove in the side, was near the waist, and above the old man's belt. Sloan wadded up a piece of the shirt, stuck it under the belt, and then jerked it tight.

"That ought to fix em," commented Sloan, rising to his feet.

"Alright, that's enough nursing. Now, old man, tell us where the gold is."

Rufus stared up at his captors. A dark expression of hate engulfed the gold miner's face.

"Why you skunks! I wouldn't give you lazy, thieving buzzards a blasted thing!"

The leader, a carbine in hand, came close and kicked at the wounded leg with his foot.

"Before this day is out, old man, you'll be howling out everything we ask."

"Try me!" shouted Rufus angrily.

The leader leaned his rifle against a rock and then pulled a dirty knife from a scabbard on his belt. Coming close, the crook bent down over the old man and placed the tip of the blade against the miner's hairy chest. The thief made a quick slashing cut, and blood welled up in a long line and began to flow.

"Ahhhhhh," Rufus gasped in sudden pain.

"Now tell me you ain't going to talk!" shouted the dirty leader, holding the crimson-stained knife.

The two thieves behind joined in loud laughter.

Inside the cave, Brody Simpson, unconscious a few moments before, was suddenly thrust awake by the painful blow of the heavy Walker Colt. One of the gold thieves had removed the revolver from the old man and tossed it inside the cave. It landed with heavy force on Brody's chest. It was the hard blow that shocked the young man awake.

Thirsty and groggy beyond belief, the lad had no idea where he was or what was going on. Rising to a sitting position, his right hand touched a hanging canteen. He pulled on it, and it fell on his chest. Brody unstoppered the lid, raised the vessel to his lips, and took a drink. His head ached terribly, and he felt weak. Brody took another drink, trying to focus his eyesight in the dim light of the cave. He also tried to understand where he was, and what the angry voices outside the cave entrance were saying.

"Cut him again!" shouted the other man of the trio.

"Don't kill him, Rocky," said Sloan. "Not afore we find the gold."

"Shut up, Sloan!" shouted the leader. "I'll just carve on him some until he starts blabbing like a baby!"

The two other thieves laughed hysterically, and then came a deep-throated groan of pain from the old man.

Brody Simpson listened intently. He took another drink from the canteen, and it seemed to clear his senses. His head ached horribly, and the blood pounded in his ears. He lifted the canteen and poured water liberally over his head and face. That seemed to revive him more. The men outside were laughing and talking loudly. It didn't take long for Brody to understand what was going on. This was a gold mine, and there were three men out there torturing the owner.

Probably the same person who had dragged me in here and saved my life, he thought.

"Old man," said Rocky. "Are you going to talk or not? I can keep this up all day and night."

"Go to blazes!" gasped Rufus, as Rocky, made another gashing cut on the bare bony shoulder of the old man.

"Ahhhhhh."

Brody, inside the cave, continued to listen. Picking up the pistol, he examined it in the dim lantern light. The revolver was an ancient and heavy thing. There was rust on it, and it looked like it hadn't been fired in years.

Surely the old man has a better weapon than this. Perhaps a rifle?

Brody tried to come to his knees, and the sudden movement made him dizzy. For a moment, his vision went blurry. Pausing, the dizziness subsided. He continued to force himself to move. On his knees, he crawled towards what looked like a backpack against the wall of the mine. Coming near, he saw an old rifle — a single shot Sharps — leaning against stone. Gradually, the lad struggled to his feet. There came more dizziness and a severe flash of pain in his head. When it subsided, Brody picked up the rifle.

"Alright, old man!" shouted Rocky. "Tell us where the gold is!"

"Never!" gasped Rufus.

"Why you old fool! Talk or get more of the same!"

"Ahhhhhh," groaned Rufas.

Brody bent down and picked up the heavy pistol. This he shoved into the waistband of his belt. There was only one shot in the rifle — once fired, the pistol was the only weapon left to rely on.

"I swear, old man!" yelled Rocky. "I'm going to cut your gizzard out! Now talk!"

"Ahhhhhh," came another long gasp from the man being tortured.

Waiting no longer, Brody, still weak on his feet, swayed toward the mine entrance and then walked out into the light of the Hunter's Moon.

"Stop it!" whispered Brody Simpson.

The sound of the rifle hammer being cocked was heard clearly in the night air.

Brody aimed at the outlaw with the knife.

"Where in Hades did you come from?" asked the leader.

"Never mind that," answered Brody weakly. "Put your hands up."

Sloan and the other two outlaws laughed and then began to pull their pistols.

"Shoot!" shouted Rufus. "Shoot you fool kid. Before it's too late!"

Brody had never in his life aimed a loaded weapon at another person. Sloan had his pistol up and cocked when, in a thundering voice, Rufus shouted once more.

"SHOOT!"

Holding the rifle loosely at waist level, Brody shifted his aim and pulled the trigger. The firing pin hit the cap and the rifle blasted. The heavy .52 caliber bullet struck Sloan in the middle, and he flew backwards in a splatter of crimson. Brody's rifle jumped from his hands and clattered to the ground. The discharge knocked the young man sideways, and he fell to one knee. A bullet from the other outlaw went over Brody's head. Rocky, the leader, dropped his knife and grabbed for his pistol. Rufus jumped to his knees and dove for the legs of the leader and drove him backwards.

While Rufus was reaching for the knife, he shouted once more at the young man.

"For God's sake, shoot that polecat!"

The third outlaw fired another shot, and this took a groove of flesh from Brody's left shoulder. Still on one knee, the lad reached down and pulled the Walker Colt from his belt. The other outlaw shot and struck Brody in his right leg. It knocked him backwards. Brody, using both hands, awkwardly cocked the heavy revolver.

Rufus, fumbling with tied hands, finally managed to pick up the fallen knife. He rushed forward, came to the fallen leader who was reaching for his pistol. The old man, blood flowing from his many wounds, raised the knife, and with both hands, plunged it deep into the chest of the gold thief.

The last outlaw turned his pistol towards the old man when Brody, lying backwards, finally managed to fire the Colt. There was a delayed snap of the cap and then a loud explosion. Copious amounts of black powder rose around the ancient pistol, and the .44 caliber ball struck the third thief in the head. The outlaw collapsed with a dull thud and a large puff of dust. The fight was over.

"Well, Sonny," exclaimed Rufus. "It's about dang time!"

Charlie Steel is a novelist and internationally published author of short stories. Steel credits the catalyst for his numerous books and hundreds of short stories to be the result of being a voracious reader, along with having worked at many varied and assorted occupations. Steel's work has been recognized and reviewed by various publications and organizations including Publisher's Weekly, Western Fictioneers, and Western Writers of America. Steel holds five degrees including a PhD.

Be sure to visit Charlie online at: amazon.com/author/charliesteel

A Little Night Action
J.E.S. HAYS

Devon Day and the Sweetwater Kid were on the way back from a very successful banking transaction — that is, Chance Knight and his partner Kye Devon were headed to the Inter-Ocean Hotel in Denver. Dev and Sweet had, with their usual panache, vanished like the puff of smoke from a gunshot after the robbery.

The only problem, in Chance's opinion, was that there was no train service to Nevadaville. Thus, to reach the bank, they'd been forced to utilize this inferior mode of travel — and after most of a day, the stagecoach was starting to wear on Chance. Not to mention the condition of his rear end on the hard seat. Their driver seemed to go out of his way to hit every hole in what passed for a road in the benighted wilderness.

As they stopped in yet another mountain hamlet, he took the opportunity to stretch his legs, leaving his snoring partner inside the stage with their unremarkable canvas bag as his pillow. Maybe a cup of coffee would settle Chance's stomach. He stepped up to the door of the tiny cafe next to the stage stop, just in time to open it for the Classy Lady inside.

He put on a Suave Face and gave her a little bow as he held the door for her. Fine shoes, the latest fashion in skirts (emerald green velvet with gold trim), topped with a sensible traveling hat over expensively-coiffured auburn locks. The Lady was Classy all right.

Chance had never met a woman who wasn't lovely. Sometimes you had to look a bit harder, but they all had that certain something. This Lady though . . . big green eyes, flawless complexion, a delicate chin and a mouth that needed kissing often. He felt a genuine smile stretch his own lips.

"Good afternoon, ma'am," he murmured as she passed. She smiled down at him, but said nothing.

Chance noted with interest that she headed for the very door though which he'd exited. Was their little party to be enlarged by one? One such would certainly make the time pass more quickly.

He slipped into the cafe for that coffee, then returned to the station in time to see the stationmaster help the Classy Lady aboard. Maybe Chance could forget his aching behind and rest his eyes on some true scenery.

The Lady smiled again as he climbed into his seat, resting his feet on the ubiquitous mailbags such coaches were always packed with. Her own feet were daintily perched upon another bag, her skirts covering all but the toes of her patent leather shoes. Chance elbowed Kye, who gave a snort and jerked awake, one hand on the handle of his pistol.

"Chance Knight, at your service," Chance told the Lady, "and this is my partner, Mr. Kye Devon."

At a discreet nudge, Kye gave the Lady a brief nod and a smile, but ruined the latter with a prodigious yawn.

The Lady nodded graciously in return. "I am Miss Althea Hathaway."

She turned to the portly salesman at her side, who grudgingly introduced himself as Smithers, then turned his attention pointedly to the novel he'd been reading since they left Nevadaville. He kept one arm on the samples case at his side, as usual. Smithers took up most of the seat, so Miss Hathaway was squeezed into her portion of the coach without opportunity to stretch out as

Kye and Chance were doing.

Kye yawned again, and as the stage jerked to a start, rested his head back upon the canvas bag which held a good bit of their take. The remainder of the loot was hidden in the secret compartments of the bags they'd stowed atop the coach. They'd have stashed all of it there, but the compartments had proven too small for the job, something Chance would rectify at their earliest convenience back in Denver.

With Kye dozing and the salesman absorbed in his book, Chance cast his eye upon the Lady. She showed no signs of either napping or reading, and turned from her perusal of the scenery out the coach window to return his smile.

"Are you and your partner traveling all the way to Denver?" she asked.

Chance saw no (real) reason to lie and admitted the fact. "We've been seeing to our holdings in Nevadaville."

A twinkle appeared in the bright green eyes. "You seem a bit young to have 'holdings,' sir. Did your fathers send you all the way out here?"

That smarted, but it was nothing Chance hadn't encountered, considering he'd yet to hit his growth spurt and Kye's so-called mustache still looked like something Granny

Matilda might grow. He put on a Mature Face and a Charming Smile.

"We're not as young as you might think. We make quite a bit of money from mining."

This was completely true, as the mine owners tended to stash their profits in banks.

Chance leaned back in his seat, trying for as much nonchalance as possible when one was jolted about like a puppet controlled by a madman. "How the old mountains drip with sunset," he quoted, thanking old Turley for recommending that book of poetry.

"I see you are a well-read gentleman. And yes, the sunset is lovely today. We should see an equally attractive sunrise, should any of us remain awake that long. I am most glad the weather is supposed to be clear for our journey."

A glance out the window did show a clear sky, with only puffy clouds reflecting the crimson light from the western mountains. The rocks shone bright red themselves, with the snowcapped peaks towering above the coach. He supposed nature did have its appeals, if you liked that sort of thing.

Miss Hathaway proved an able and interesting conversationalist, and as the sun dipped behind the mountains, she and

Chance moved from poetry to literature and then on to that new Gilbert play, *The Gentleman in Black.* Almost before Chance knew it, the sun had fully set and they spoke only by the shaky light of the lanterns attached at the front of the coach.

The coach made one more stop, picking up a rail-thin traveling pastor who squeezed in beside Chance, promptly dropped his chin to his chest and began snoring.

The moon rose over the peaks, shedding its dim light along the roadway behind them. Chance was just opening his mouth to reply to Miss Hathaway's latest comment when he spotted movement along that roadway. Could someone be riding along behind them? At this hour?

The hairs on Chance's nape tingled.

"What is the matter, Mr. Knight?" Miss Hathaway peered out the window, evidently seeing only the dark roadway.

"It may be nothing," he murmured, elbowing his partner to an upright position again. "But someone is following us."

"At this hour?" Kye echoed Chance's sentiments as he pulled the pistol from its holster. He twisted to stare ahead of them, then returned his attention to the road behind. "Looks like three men, riding easy. They're not trying to catch up with us."

"Perhaps they are merely riding to their homes from the last town," Miss Hathaway ventured. She made as if to lean from the window for a view, but Chance reached forward to place a warning hand on her arm.

"Let's not show them we're aware of their presence," he said, pulling his own pistol. "If they are innocent, the most we'll lose is a little sleep."

Kye shot him a sour glare.

"We should be coming up on a station soon," Chance said, having read the schedule while waiting for the stage to depart. "If they're after something we're carrying, they'd do well to hit us before then."

"Maybe they're waiting for us to hit the middle of nowhere," Kye muttered, daring another peek through the window.

"Or," Chance said as the coach slowed for an incline, "they're waiting for a spot we can't get out of easily."

He readied his pistol, seeing his partner from the corner of his eye doing the same. Miss Hathaway's green eyes were huge in the dim light. She shrank towards her rotund seatmate, who'd looked up from his novel at last.

"Why are you two — ?"

As if in answer, a gunshot sounded behind the coach. Chance couldn't hear any signs that it struck anything.

"This is a hold —" a deep voice began, but was interrupted by the boom of Kye's Colt. The voice gave a grunt and broke off.

"Never flap your mouth unless you want someone to know exactly where you are," Kye murmured, his teeth flashing in the moonlight as he grinned at his partner.

Chance thought of firing as well, but as Kye put it, he had trouble hitting the broadside of a barn at noon, so he had little hope of hitting a moving target in the darkness.

For moving the men were. Hoofbeats sounded on the dirt road, headed away from the coach. Chance reached out to slap his partner's back in congratulations, but paused at the roar of the shotgun from above their heads.

"They're headed for the cut-off," the driver yelled. He chirruped to the mules, who quickened the pace just a bit.

"I think I hit one of 'em," the shotgun rider yelled back. "He slumped over anyhows."

"Folks," the driver yelled, "there may be more of those galoots ahead of us, and those three are headed for a shortcut through the mountains. If they join up with the rest of their gang before we get to the station —"

"We're in a heap of trouble," Chance finished for the man. He stuck his head out the window and looked upward. "What in blazes are we carrying?"

"Blamed if I know! Any of you fellows beat the local cowboys out of their paychecks or anything?"

Chance sat back with a sigh. He had been teaching the Nevadaville locals not to draw to an inside straight. He hadn't won that much though — just a few hundred dollars. Of course, what was now peanuts to the two of them would be a hefty paycheck for a cowboy.

"You did!" Smithers shouted, pointing a chubby forefinger at Chance's chest. Chance swatted the finger away. There had to be a way to outthink those cowboys.

"This is all your fault," Smithers said, thumping his novel against the palm of his hand to punctuate his sentence. "We ought to toss the two of you right —"

His voice trailed off as the end of Kye's gun barrel rotated towards the end of his nose.

"You're the biggest," Kye said softly. "Stands to reason we'd go faster if you walked to the station instead of rode."

"Gentlemen," Chance interrupted. "We may need every hand if those fellows bring along their friends. How many pistols do we have?"

Smithers swallowed hard, his face the color of his starched collar. He gingerly pulled a lady's derringer from the pocket of his jacket. Chance looked at the pastor, whose eyes widened. He held up both hands, palms upward.

"For cryin' out loud." Chance opened the carpet bag just enough to get his hand inside and pulled out the spare pistol, an old Remington Army they'd won in that poker game. Ordinarily, Chance didn't deal in weaponry, but he'd disliked the sneering rancher who'd put the gun on the table.

Handing the revolver to Smithers, he pulled out the box of ammunition he'd purchased and shoved that into the salesman's lap. "Try not to waste it," he warned.

Kye leaned forward to speak even more softly. "That means you don't fire unless you can see what you're aiming at."

Smithers nodded quickly, sweat beaded on his broad forehead. He loaded the pistol and held that and the box of ammo in his lap.

Chance traded places with the pastor, putting the unarmed man in the safer spot and putting himself where he could shoot from the window without the pastor in his way.

He glanced at Miss Hathaway, who, though pale with fear, had made no sound.

"Smithers, hand the lady your pepper pot," he commanded, nodding to Miss Hathaway. "She may need it if they get past the four of us."

The coach slowed again as they reached the top of a ridge, then the shotgun boomed again. Gunfire erupted ahead of them as the driver yelled to his mules, slapping the reins loudly.

"Hi, Rusty!" he bellowed as the coach picked up speed. "Dusty, move on now! C'mon, you lop-eared sons of bitches, run!"

The four animals took off, jerking the coach to a rolling gallop down the steep roadway. Chance took one look out the window, saw moonlight sparkling on the river far, far below them, and averted his eyes. His stomach was bad enough as it was. He peered ahead instead, spotting four dark shapes on the roadway.

The shotgun roared once more, and Chance heard loud cursing from the quartet. Faced with a hurtling stagecoach barreling down upon them, they spurred their horses up the side of the hill. One animal lost its balance, rolling back toward the roadway. There was a scream and the coach gave a great jolt, then steadied down once more.

"Three down," Kye muttered, glancing back up the road. "Them others is coming after us, though."

His pistol barked twice. "Can't see enough to hit nothing," he yelled, pulling his head back inside.

From overhead, the shotgun boomed again and again. The coach swayed and bounced until Chance was certain they were going over the side of the mountain.

"Hi! Hi!" the driver bellowed. "G'up mules!"

Chance held onto the strap with his right hand, aiming his pistol out the window and trying not to look at the blurred rocks and trees rushing past. The seat was swaying so badly he knew it'd be a miracle if he hit anything, even if the bandits rode directly alongside the coach. At least the road was too narrow for such a trick, though that narrowness worked at Chance's nerves something fierce. He spotted the river glinting below them again, and turned his gaze on the lovely Miss Hathaway.

She was clutching her strap as well, her lips tight against clenched teeth. When she spotted his gaze however, she gave him a brave smile. What a woman.

Smithers had stuffed the ammo box into his coat pocket and was hanging onto his strap, his pistol dangling in his right fist, his face going greenish. The pastor was praying softly. Or Chance assumed it was praying. He couldn't make out the words but they sounded totally sincere.

"Nearly there, folks," the driver shouted suddenly. "Everybody hang on."

The coach whipped into a tight curve, nearly going over onto its side. The wheels on Chance's side left the ground and the floor plan of the Nevadaville Bank & Trust flashed before his eyes.

With a thump, the wheels hit the ground again, and they raced across a relatively flat patch of roadway. Thank God they hadn't dumped the hefty salesman back there. Chance's weight wouldn't have pulled the stage back down alone.

The coach jerked hard. The driver yelled "Whoa, team!" and slammed his foot against the brake. Chance was tossed backwards, banging his head against the back of the seat and bringing tears to his eyes. Smithers lost his grip on the strap and flew into the air. Chance had time for half of a "Tarnation" before the portly man slammed into his midsection.

The air left Chance's lungs with a whoosh,

and he thought he heard something crack — hopefully the wooden seat. For a long moment, he couldn't breathe, couldn't get his lungs to suck air inside. He slapped at Smithers' broad back, shoved at the mass lying atop his lap.

Smithers scrambled to his knees just as the coach jerked again. This time he collided with Chance's chin. Chance's head bounced off the side of the coach. He would have slid to the floorboards except for the two-hundred-plus pounds of weight on his legs.

"Everybody out!" the driver bellowed as the coach gave another huge jolt, this time in the opposite direction.

Smithers flew back toward his own seat, grunting as his back struck the edge. He lay there for a moment without moving. Chance would have worried the man had broken something, but he was too worried that something was inside Chance's own chest. He tried once more to take a breath. Fortunately, this time he was successful.

There was no stabbing pain as he sucked air into his lungs, so Smithers hadn't broken any ribs at least. His head sure was throbbing, though. Chance kicked his feet free from the man's weight and scrambled out behind the pastor and Kye, who'd already pulled Miss Hathaway from the coach and set her on the path to the station's door. Chance headed for the squat stone building, then hesitated as his partner didn't follow.

"C'mon," Kye said with some disgust, closing his free fist over the collar of Smithers' jacket.

The man managed to haul himself to his feet and exit the stage, though he staggered into the station dead last, just in front of the shotgun rider, who slammed the door behind them. The driver pulled the stage around the station's far side, then darted for the door.

"What in blazes?" came a man's voice behind them. Chance turned to see the presumed station owner at an inner door, possibly leading to the kitchen, for he held a coffeepot in one hand and a stack of tin cups in the other. "Have you two lost your minds coming down the hillside like that?"

"Outlaws," the shotgun rider said shortly from a front window, where he was peering into the moonlit yard. "We ain't sure what they're after."

Smithers dropped heavily to a seat at the bench against the right-hand wall. He raised a hand to point. "They're after those two. They cheated in a poker game!"

Kye sighed and reached for Smithers' lapels. "Don't sit in front of the blasted window. And we don't cheat. My partner's just got a knack for card games."

Chance considered explaining how little he'd actually won, but the thought of letting Smithers — not to mention the driver, shotgun rider and station owner — know how much his wallet now held left a sour taste in his mouth, so he kept it shut. Besides, his head already throbbed without Smithers' ranting. Chance picked a spot at the window Kye had just removed Smithers from in front of.

Kye shot him a glare and jerked a thumb to the right. Chance moved over to give his partner the best spot at the window, facing the side yard, toward the mountain. Chance got a good look at the road they'd come down and nearly said a few choice words himself. That thin ribbon looked barely wide enough for a stagecoach at all, and the incline . . . .

It was a wonder they'd made it to the bottom of that hill without going over into the river.

Hoofbeats sounded on the roadway, and Chance ducked down to spy through the window. Kye took up a position to the left of the opening, with barely one eye peering from behind the wall.

Six horses skidded to a halt at the edge of the yard. Even with the moonlight, Chance could barely make out the dark shapes against the lighter rocks of the hillside.

"All right," a deep voice yelled from the darkness. It sounded familiar. Chance shot his partner a glance. Kye shrugged.

"Hard to hit anything in this light," he muttered.

The voice continued. "We ain't meaning to hurt nobody. We just want what's rightfully ours. You know exactly what we're talking about here."

"We ain't got nothing that belongs to you," the driver yelled back. "You fellows are breaking the law interfering with the stage."

"We ain't the ones broke both of Wagner's legs, old man."

"Your pal shouldn't have been trying to rob the stage, son. I wasn't aiming to hit him."

"Ain't robbing the stage, are we?" called another voice. "Just taking back what belongs to us."

Chance leaned toward his partner. "I swear," he whispered, "I don't remember either of their voices at all. You think they're the cowboys from our game — or is this whole thing some sort of mistake?"

Kye gave him a keen glance. "If you don't remember them, they weren't at the game. What in tarnation is going on here?"

"I don't remember anyone named Wagner, either." Chance bit at his lip, trying to ramp his aching brain to full speed. He'd assumed it was his poker skills that had gotten them into this mess, but what if he'd been mistaken?

Before he could come up with an idea, a shot came through the front window, smashing the pane and ricocheting from the stone floor to clang against the pot-bellied stove in the far corner. The station owner tipped the long wooden table over. There was a flurry of movement as everyone else — including Smithers, who let fly a word his mother would have washed his mouth out for — dropped to the floor and crawled to a hiding place behind it. Miss Hathaway gave a muffled yelp as Smithers ran over her toes.

The driver returned fire from one front window, his old Winchester rifle nearly deafening inside the room. The roar of the shotgun joined the fire. Kye peered carefully, then let off two shots, one after the other. Chance saw a dark shape drop from one of the shadowy horses.

The rest of the horses scattered, some going up the hillside behind the station, the others to the right and left along the river. Gunfire followed their paths, some bullets striking the house and others the windowpanes. The pastor's voice grew louder, his prayers more fervent.

"They'll try to get behind the house," Chance told the station owner. "Is your door locked?"

The man peered from the back room. "Doubt they can get down here, but it's locked. Windows are too small to climb through, too. Think they'd try to set fire to the roof?"

"Hopefully they won't think of it," Chance muttered. The stone house wouldn't burn, but the smoke might drive them out where they'd be easy to pick off.

"I think we ought to turn the two of you out," Smithers said without moving from behind the table. "Give them what they're looking for and they'll leave us alone. Stands to reason."

Chance had his mouth open for a retort, but Miss Hathaway was faster. "There will be no more of such talk, sir. If those hoodlums did lose money in a poker game, it's their own fault for betting."

"The lady has a point," the driver said, crossing towards the back room. "It ain't like nobody made 'em bet their paychecks."

"If we give the money back, then —"

"Do be quiet, Mr. Smithers," Miss Hathaway said firmly. "By rights, you should be at a window with your pistol, protecting the pastor and myself."

Smithers blustered a bit at this, but had no recourse except to follow the lady's orders.

A voice from outside bellowed. "There's no way out, folks. You may as well hand over our money and we'll be on our way."

"That ain't the way it works," the shotgun rider yelled back. "When we don't make it to Floyd Hill, they'll come looking for us. All we got to do is sit tight."

As Chance had figured, this didn't deter the bandits. "We got all night before anybody rides out after you. Just toss the money out front and we'll be on our way."

"Shooting at folks is no way to get your money back," the driver called. "If you fellows ride off now, we'll forget any of this ever happened. You hit someone, you're getting yourself a free trip to jail."

In reply, a bullet cracked through the broken pane in the front window. This one landed in the fire, scattering cinders, and the shotgun rider, with a muffled oath, hurried to beat out the smoldering rag rug in front of the hearth.

Chance took a glance out the window, his pistol at the ready. He couldn't see anything on the dark slope next to the house, but near the river he thought he spotted a crouched shape close to a rounded boulder. He squeezed off a shot the way Kye always taught him, then ducked back behind the wall.

Kye shook his head. "You aiming to murder that poor ol' log, partner? Why don't you save your bullets 'til they come a bit closer?"

"Fine. Don't blame me when they come in the front door."

"That log ain't moving, kid."

Chance let him have one right on the biceps. On his off arm, of course, but a nice hard wallop that had Kye frowning and rubbing the sting out of his muscle.

Just as Chance pulled his arm back, there was a crack at the window. He felt a tug at his shirtsleeve and let out a word his mother would have been surprised he knew. That was a new silk shirt, damn it all.

Kye reared up suddenly, letting fly with a roll of shots that sounded like thunder. "You want something?" he bellowed. "Come in and get it."

From the undergrowth on the slope came

a strangled shriek. The brush thrashed wildly for a moment or so, then went silent.

"Rafe?" someone called from behind the station. The station owner and stage driver both opened fire, the rifles booming. A haze of gun smoke drifted across the room.

"Damn it, boys," cried a voice from the river. "I didn't sign up for this."

Gravel crunched and Chance spotted a crouched figure dashing for the trees. He took aim. Kye put a hand on his arm.

"Let 'em go, kid. How bad're you hit?"

Chance looked at his partner in surprise. "I'm not —"

Something wet trickled down his elbow and dripped to the floor with a splash. Startled, Chance glanced down at the red puddle forming at his feet. He holstered his pistol and clapped a hand to the tear in his shirt. His fingers came away red.

Only then did he become aware of the throbbing in his upper arm. It felt like a hive of bees had stung that arm, leaving a trail of venom that passed from one side clear to the other. He'd be hard pressed to decide which was worse — the pounding in his noggin or the sting of the bullet's track.

"You done gone white, kid," Kye said, grabbing Chance's good arm and slinging it over his shoulder. "Best to sit down and let

Miss Hathaway tend to you."

The Classy Lady gave Chance a wide-eyed look that told him she'd never dressed a wound in her life. "I hope you don't expect me to begin ripping up my petticoats," she murmured, scooting to one side so Chance could lower himself to the floor beside her.

"It's just a —" Chance tried.

Kye pulled out his knife and ripped the sleeve from Chance's brand new shirt. Damn, the man ought to know better. "Bullet's still inside, kid," he muttered, studying both sides of the arm. "I can see it just under the skin here."

"Can't you cut it out then?" Miss Hathaway suggested, pulling an ivory fan from her reticule and fluttering it before her face.

"They're coming back!" the driver shouted. "Man the windows."

Kye gave Chance a panicked look, glanced once at the window they'd been covering. Chance shoved him away.

"It'll keep, old man. Just make sure they don't get inside."

"I'll take care of him," Miss Hathaway promised. She fanned Chance's face as well, which felt awfully nice. A bead of sweat trickled down Chance's forehead and into his right eye. He made the mistake of trying to shake it out, which set his head to throbbing with new sincerity.

The station owner appeared at the kitchen door brandishing a filleting blade. "We'd best get that bullet out, young fellow, before a fever can set in."

Chance tried to struggle to his feet, but a wave of dizziness returned him to a seated position. "Are you kidding? Did you even sterilize that thing?"

"Did I what?"

"Ster— did you run it through a flame? Douse it in alcohol?" At the driver's blank expression, he sucked in a disbelieving breath. "Do you even know where that knife has been?"

"Sure thing, young fellow. I keep it safe and sound in the drawer next to the stove."

Chance glanced down at the puddle now forming between his backside and the larger one belonging to Smithers at his right side. "For Pete's sake, at least rinse it off with some whiskey. And wash your blasted hands, too."

"What for? I ain't been to the outhouse lately."

Chance thumped his head back against the bottom of the overturned table, regretting the move instantly. He gritted his teeth — damned if Miss Hathaway would hear a groan of agony wrung from his lips — and tried to keep an even tone. "My pa's a doctor and he says clean hands means a clean wound. Plus you need a clean knife."

"This un's clean enough."

Miss Hathaway gave a discreet cough. "Perhaps you should humor Mr. Knight and pour some whiskey over your hands and the blade. I shall be happy to purchase the liquor from you."

The station owner looked at her as if she and Chance had just escaped a locked ward, but he shrugged and pulled a bottle of what probably wasn't actual whiskey from a cabinet behind the table. Chance could only hope it had enough alcohol in it to make a difference.

In the background, he was aware of the roar of the shotgun, the flatter bang of the rifle, and the pow-pow-pow of Kye's revolver. The scent of gunpowder wafted through the room. The odd bullet whizzed past the table. One lodged in the mantel. Another toppled a silver candlestick from the cabinet the station owner had just moved away from. He reached up and righted the stick before the candle could set fire to the cloth runner.

"Here, young fellow," the station owner said, scooting close and brandishing his dripping blade. "Let's get that out of your arm."

Miss Hathaway slipped one of her own arms about Chance's shoulder at that moment, and he'd have probably allowed the station owner to operate on his head as well as the arm.

"Rest your head on my shoulder," she murmured into his ear. Chance felt goosebumps break out along his neck at the warmth of her breath. If he'd not been in so much pain, he'd have taken far more advantage of their closeness. As it was, he merely followed her suggestion, extending his arm to the station owner.

He could see the bullet himself now. It did lie just beneath the skin on the inside of his arm. Should be easy to cut out. He had only to bear a few moments of extreme pain . . . .

He'd be damned if he allowed Miss Hathaway to hear a peep out of his lips.

"Bite down on this," the Lady said softly, pressing something soft to Chance's mouth. He glanced down to see it was a folded handkerchief. A flowery scent wafted to his nose and he nearly smiled. What red-blooded male wouldn't appreciate being held in a lovely woman's arms, smelling her perfume and feeling the heat of her body next to his?

The station owner sliced his blade across Chance's skin and he quickly bit down on the handkerchief. Damnation, that nearly eclipsed the throbbing of both injuries put together. The tip of the blade slid beneath his skin, digging about for the bullet. Chance's vision darkened. Black spots sparkled at the edges of his sight. His head swam.

When he could see again, he was looking up at the wide green eyes of Miss Althea Hathaway, whose brow was furrowed.

"You have the most horrendous knot on the side of your head," she murmured. "You passed out. Mr. Trevors says it was blood loss but I wonder if the knot may have had something to do with it."

"I might have a concussion," Chance whispered, trying not to react in any other fashion to her sweet breath on his face, her fingers gently brushing the damp curls from his forehead.

"You're such a brave young man. Just lie still while Mr. Trevors finishes tying off the bandage."

A sharp stab of pain let Chance know the station owner was still there. He'd applied a pad made from the remnants of Chance's own shirt sleeve and was tying it off with strips of what looked like an old sheet. Chance hoped he'd at least turned the sleeve inside-out before applying the dusty material to the wound.

"There you go, young fellow," he said heartily, patting Chance's arm and sending a wave of pain up through his jawline to collide with the throbbing in his head. "I put in a few stitches. You're good as new."

Hardly that. He felt as if he'd been trampled on by the four mules — and sat on by Smithers again. And he doubted Trevors had sterilized the needle and thread.

Chance gritted his teeth against the groan that wanted to slip out, then struggled to sit upright. Miss Hathaway tightened her grip on his good shoulder.

"Lie still, please. I don't want you passing out again. Here, drink some of this."

She held a tin cup to his lips. It was the pseudo-whiskey from Trevors' bottle. The fumes curled Chance's nostril hairs. He took a sip and shuddered at the taste. Did he detect a hint of rattlesnake?

Trevors let out a whoop. "That'll put hair on your chest. Take a good gulp there."

Another bullet whipped past his head and he ducked back down behind the table again.

Chance looked up at Miss Hathaway. "I

don't suppose there's any bourbon? Or even a halfway-decent bordeaux?"

She chuckled and ran her fingers gently through his curls. Ladies — they couldn't keep their hands off the blasted ringlets, which was why Chance didn't shave the things off completely.

"I fear that Mr. Trevors keeps a limited cellar," Miss Hathaway said. "But you need to replace the blood you've lost."

She raised the cup to his lips again and he shuddered. "Coffee?" he tried again.

Trevors slapped a hand to his forehead. "I plumb forgot. I had a pot fresh made when you folks got here. Let me pass that around."

He rose to a crouch and scurried into the kitchen, to return with the coffeepot and a handful of tin cups.

"Sugar?" Chance asked, eying the tarry fluid askance.

Trevors pulled a sugar bowl from the cabinet behind them and Chance added three cubes to his cup. He sipped with a wince — tasted like it'd been cooking for days — but met Miss Hathaway's worried eyes and kept sipping. Trevors managed to smuggle cups to the men at the windows without getting hit, then returned to the kitchen.

"How're you holding up," Chance heard him ask the driver.

"I think they've about had enough," came the reply, quickly followed by a bang from the man's rifle.

"We got one more of 'em," the shotgun rider chimed in from the front window. "I reckon the other two ought to pull out any—"

Hoofbeats sounded on the roadway outside the station, moving fast. The driver took one more shot with his scattergun, then turned with a grin. "That'll learn 'em. They won't bother us again."

Kye's big clodhoppers thudded across the floor and Chance looked up to see him peering over the table, that line between his brows that said he was about to worry himself into an ulcer. "How is it, kid?"

"I'm fine, old man. Just a scratch like I tried to tell you."

Miss Hathaway was busy fashioning the rest of Trevors' old sheet into a sling for Chance's arm. Once she'd gotten that tied on properly, Chance took Kye's extended hand and got back on his feet. He was loath to leave the lovely Miss Hathaway's lap, but a man had to do what a man had to do. And they had to get to Floyd Hill in time to catch the next train to Denver.

The rest of the coach ride was uneventful, if you call several more hours of bouncing about on a hard seat uneventful. Chance was about ready to slice his own head off to stop the ache. His arm throbbed. The two wounds didn't even have the decency to keep time with one another.

Smithers and the pastor disembarked and vanished into the town. Chance was heartened to see Miss Hathaway headed for the railway station, as he and Kye were. He quickly tossed her smaller bag onto the trolley they're hired for their own satchels and offered the Lady his good arm.

"Such manners," she said with a smile that reached her eyes. "I've become quite fond of you, young Mr. Knight."

"Then I hope you only become more fond as we travel to Denver together. Perhaps we could play some bridge to pass the time?"

She laughed and handed the ticket master the price of a first-class ticket. "I'm afraid I have little skill at bridge. Perhaps we can find another game to enjoy, once we're on our way."

Chance could think of one game he'd enjoy, even with a bum wing and busted head. But a gentleman would never even entertain such thoughts. He gave her a Charming Smile and replied, "Perhaps I can teach you a card game or two."

"I do believe I'd enjoy that, Mr. Knight."

Chance handed over the money for their tickets then, also first-class of course. He was lucky his good left arm hadn't been hit by that bullet. He'd have the devil's own time working with only his right. He helped Miss Hathaway to her seat, then he and Kye sat opposite.

As the train pulled from the station, Chance slipped his deck of cards from his pocket. "What would you like to learn to play, Miss Hathaway?"

Was that a twinkle in the green eyes? "I have always wondered about poker."

Chance had to keep a tight hold on his Face so his surprise didn't show. He supposed a woman might indeed wonder about the game, wonder what men did all night in a saloon — well, aside from the obvious.

"I think Kye and I should be able to teach you the rudiments within a few hands," he told the Lady.

Miss Hathaway proved a quick study, and within three or four hands, actually managed to pull together three eights, beating Chance's two pair.

"Would you like to make this a little more interesting?" she asked, raising an eyebrow and reaching for her reticule.

Chance's nape tingled again. Maybe he hadn't taught the Lady anything she didn't already know. He glanced at Kye, who shrugged and dug into his pocket for a handful of coins.

"Penny ante?" Chance suggested.

Miss Hathaway chuckled. "I'm sure you can afford a bit more than that, as can I."

Chance studied the Classy Lady. Her green eyes were definitely twinkling. A smile lurked at the corner of that kissable mouth. She pulled a handful of paper bills from her reticule. "I'm feeling lucky, gentlemen," she said.

"Those cowboys," Chance said, reaching for his wallet, "they were after you, weren't they?"

Miss Hathaway laughed delightedly. "None of them could believe a mere woman could be good at poker."

"I shall not make the same mistake, ma'am." As the train rolled on toward Denver, the morning sun streaming in through the windows, Chance dealt the next hand.

J.E.S. Hays is the author of the Devon Day and the Sweetwater Kid stories and their anthology *Down the Owlhoot Trail* (2013). She's also contributed to the Western Fictioneers books *Luck of the Draw II,* Hunter's Moon, and *The Untamed West.* She loves traveling, especially in the American Southwest, where she can see where her stories have been set.

The Midnight Train
JEFFREY J. MARIOTTE

Noah Redfern buttoned his corduroy jacket and looked at the bouquet of roses in his fist, hoping the cool air of encroaching autumn wasn't too much for them. *Bouquet* might have been too grand a word, he decided. He'd only been able to get five with enough stem attached to make them easily portable, and he'd tried to fluff it out with leaves. The thorns poked his hands, and he wished he'd thought to bring some gloves. He hadn't expected the night to get so chilly, after how warm the days had been.

The train station at his back would have blocked the wind, had it been blowing out of the north, but instead it came from the east, following the seemingly endless rails, perhaps all the way back to Kansas City. Blowing Madelyn toward him, he hoped.

Across the tracks, daylight would've revealed miles and miles of empty prairie. It wasn't as flat as it looked; rolling hills in the distance blocked the view of his farm. If he stood on the roof of his house, though, he could see the gas lights of the depot, glowing through the long nights. His own home, his own farm; things he had never dreamed possible, until two years ago when he'd headed west, determined to forge a new life. He glanced at the roses again. Perhaps not much of a bouquet, but he'd grown and picked them himself. They would, he believed, help Madelyn see that she'd made the right choice.

If she showed at all.

Noah heard boots scrape against the platform, and a voice asked, "Those for me?"

He turned to see three men standing behind him. They looked like rough types, but they were smiling, and one of them — presumably the one who'd spoken — held out an open hand, as if he expected Noah to place the flowers in it. He was a head taller than Noah, with broad shoulders and a barrel chest. He wore a black hat, a red shirt with a vest over it, canvas pants tucked into boots, and a pistol at his hip. He looked like he hadn't shaved in several days but had not yet decided to grow a beard. A scar at the outer corner of his left eye almost looked like a teardrop.

"They're for my girl," Noah said.

"Aww, ain't that sweet. They're for his girl. Why didn't we think of that?"

The other men chuckled at that.

"Are you here to meet a girl, too?" Noah asked.

The men roared. The eyes of the big fellow in the red shirt really did fill with moisture, and spittle flecked his whiskers.

The smallest of the three, rail-thin and with a nose that looked like it would off-balance him unless he tied some weights to his back, answered him. He was younger than the others, close to Noah's age. His bowler hat looked like it had been stomped on and dragged around a barnyard for a spell. "We're here to meet a friend. If you called him a girl to his face, those might be your last words."

"That's enough, Hank," the big man said.

"He don't mean us no harm," Hank said. His breathing was loud, almost a wheeze. "Do you, mister?"

"Of course not," Noah answered. "Just passing the time is all." He glanced at the clock on the wall of the depot. "Got another twenty minutes to go."

Just less than, really. Although local folks called it the midnight train, its posted arrival time was 11:58 P.M. It only stopped here on the rare occasions that it carried passengers bound for this specific destination; otherwise it barreled through, slowing only enough for the fireman to snatch train orders off the hoop. The depot had been brand new when Noah arrived two years earlier; weather had faded the paint a bit, but it was still the town's most impressive structure.

"I reckon we'll wait together, then," the man called Hank said.

"Looks that way," Noah agreed. To be neighborly, he added, "I'm Noah Redfern."

"Noah like the ark?" the third man asked. He was about Noah's height, but muscular, with a bull neck and an aggressive stance. His black hat was pulled low, its brim shading the upper half of his face, but his mouth carried a sneer that appeared to be permanent fixture.

"Like the feller who built it," Hank shot back. "The ark weren't named Noah."

"That's what I meant," the other said. "I remember enough damn Sunday-school lessons to know that."

"Yes," Noah said quickly. The two men seemed antagonistic toward one another, and the mood there on the platform had suddenly turned tense. "Like the man who built the ark. My folks loved animals, and they thought Noah was the most heroic figure in the Bible because he saved them all."

Leave it to his parents to name him after somebody that everyone else thought was crazy. And then to treat him, most of his life, like they thought *he* was crazy. The fact that he'd felt the call of the west — ultimately deciding that only going there would keep him sane, even though, or especially because, it meant leaving his home and family — only convinced them that they'd been right all along.

"Well, it's a pleasure to make your acquaintance," the big man said, drawing Noah out of his reverie. "Even if it's only for twenty minutes or thereabouts." He glanced at his companions, who seemed to cool down at his intercession. Noah got the impression that this was a regular occurrence among the three. "I'm . . . Tom," the man added. "These here are Dick and Harry." He nodded toward each in turn.

The one he called Harry, Noah already knew was Hank. The names were fake, then, which meant the men had something to hide. He had figured them for rough customers from the start, but now he began to worry. Were they outlaws, here to rob the train when it slowed or stopped? Could

Madelyn be in danger?

Not likely, he decided. He'd tried to tell himself that she was coming, but the truth was, he knew she probably wouldn't. He hadn't had a letter in weeks. In her last letter, she'd tried to be encouraging, but she had told him that if she could ever get away, she would arrive by the end of the month. If he didn't see her by then, he was to stop writing and leave her be.

He had thought she would write again when she had made firm plans, but no more news had come, and today was the last day of the month. For the past three weeks, he had made the trip into town three times a day, to meet the trains at 10:40, 3:50, and midnight, and had gone home disappointed each time.

At least this trip would be the end of it. He had brought flowers, and had a blanket rolled up under the wagon's bench to put over her for the chilly trip back to the farm, but he had a growing feeling that he wouldn't need either.

And now there would be three spectators to his humiliation.

"Where's your girl comin' from?" Hank asked.

"Kansas City," Noah said. In the letter he'd sent along with ticket money, he'd detailed the arrangements she would need. She could board the Atchison, Topeka and Santa Fe right there at the Union Depot. She would have to change trains at Florence, and again at La Junta, but that was all.

Nothing too complicated about it. But she would be a woman traveling alone — he hadn't been able to get away from the farm long enough to go back there and accompany her, and anyway, it had taken him more than a year of scraping and sacrifice to save up that much. He was barely more than skin and bones now, having sold most of what he grew rather than eating it himself. Once she arrived — if she did — he could spend less time on upkeep, and she could help with some of the lighter chores, and the farm would provide for them both. But it was hard to manage on his own.

"Our friend got on at Trinidad," Hank offered.

"I said that's enough." The big man, the one who called himself Tom, glared at Hank. "Can't you ever quit your yappin'?"

"Sorry," Hank said. He glanced at the big man once, then turned away from him, eyes on the toes of his worn boots. Unlike the other two, Hank didn't wear spurs, and his clothing didn't quite fit. Noah wondered if he had acquired his garb second-hand, or if he'd lost a fair amount of weight recently. Given the condition, though, patched in places and frayed in others, he suspected it was a combination of both. He knew how it felt, having had to cinch up his own belt a few notches lately.

Noah eyed the clock again. Twelve minutes to go. The more he studied on the three sharing the platform with him, the less he liked it. They were trouble, he decided. Up to something, even if he didn't know what.

Even at this hour, there was an operator in his office, inside the depot. Noah wondered if he should share his suspicions with him. But what could he do, if Noah were right? He was a meek little fellow, pudgy and bespectacled, with soft hands and a voice that he couldn't raise above a whisper due to whatever had scarred his throat.

But this was the county seat, and the sheriff's office was only a couple of minutes away. Surely there'd be a deputy inside. He could walk over there, explain his concerns, and be back well before the train arrived.

He cleared his throat. "I'm awful dry," he announced. "I'll be back directly."

"No hurry," the one called Dick said. "Your girl shows before you get back, we'll keep her entertained."

The others laughed at that. Whatever these men were planning, it had put them in good spirits.

Lowell Street was mostly dark, though lights still blazed inside Beaulah's, and raucous laughter punctuated the piano music spilling out into the road. Noah saw light in the sheriff's office as well, so he picked up his pace. When he reached it, the front door was locked, but he tapped on the glass. A deputy sat at a desk inside, half-dozing, but he looked up at Noah's knock, rose, and came to the door.

"What can I do for you, mister?" he asked. "Out late, aren't you?"

"I'm waiting for my girl, coming on the midnight train," Noah said, showing the roses as if to offer proof. "But there's three men there. They look like bad types to me. They're all wearing revolvers, and they gave me phony names, called themselves Tom, Dick, and Harry, even though one of them's named Hank. They say they're waiting for a friend."

"Could be they are," the deputy suggested.

"I thought maybe you would come and take a look."

"I can't leave here," the deputy said.

"Why not?"

The deputy glanced over his shoulder. Noah knew there were some cells on the other side of the back wall, though he couldn't see them from here.

"I had to double up two men in a cell," he said. "They don't much like each other, and I don't want to have a fight on my hands. But I got to keep one cell empty. That train you're waitin' on is carrying Mo Bramley."

Noah had heard the name, but he couldn't remember the context. Hearing it troubled him, for some reason he couldn't pin down. "Who's that again?"

"Feller killed Sheriff Tompkins," the deputy said. Then Noah remembered. An outlaw had gunned the sheriff down right here on Lowell, three weeks earlier, after an altercation in Beulah's. "He was arrested up in Denver. Federal marshals are bringin' him back here to stand trial. They took the late train because it's usually pretty empty."

"Well, that's it, then!" Noah said. He had studied the railroad timetables until they were memorized. Hank had said their "friend" boarded in Trinidad, which was the southern terminus of the Denver line. To get here by rail, he'd have to change trains there. "Those men are waiting for Bramley! They'll likely kill the marshals and set him free!"

"Like as not they'll try," the deputy said. "But those marshals are tough as boot leather. And until Brawley is delivered to this office, he's their responsibility, not mine."

"So you'll just sit here, knowing that men are laying in wait for them?"

"I don't know anything of the sort. I only know you *think* that, based on some hunch you had about three men you've never laid eyes on before. Meanwhile, I don't want the marshals showing up here and finding a dead man in one of my cells. I can't arrest those fellers because you don't like the way they look, and even if I could, I got no place to keep them."

"My Madelyn might be on that train," Noah said. "I don't want her stepping off it into a gunfight."

"Might be?" The deputy's gaze traveled to the wilting roses Noah carried, and his lips curled into something like a smirk. "Look, mister. You can go back and wait for her, or you can keep away from the depot. Don't matter to me either way. My orders are to wait here until the marshals bring in Bramley, then keep him caged until the circuit judge shows up."

"So you can't take five minutes, go over and see if you recognize the men."

"That's the size of it."

Frustration clenched Noah's guts like a vise, but there was nothing to be gained by arguing. If Madelyn didn't see him out the train window when she arrived, she might just stay on board and never write to him again.

After all, she had a husband back in Kansas City.

She had refused to go west with Noah, but implored him to write when he settled and hinted that she would join him at the time. While he was gone, though, some other jasper had caught her eye, or she'd caught his. Either way, he had courted her, and he had money to spare. Her parents had been thrilled that Noah — who they'd never liked — was gone, and somebody they considered a far more desirable suitor had taken an interest in her.

The letter she had written him explaining that she'd married had been blotched with what Noah could only surmise were teardrops.

Letters since then carried tales of her husband's casual cruelty. Noah had insisted that she leave him, come west and be with the man she truly loved, and who would only be good to her. Madelyn had replied that she knew the marriage was a mistake, but she had taken vows not easily broken.

Hurrying back to the depot, he eyed the flowers still clutched in his fist with disgust. He was a damn fool, that's what he was. She wasn't coming. Not tonight, not ever. He might just as well get in his wagon and head back to the farm he would keep working, alone, until the end of his days.

He reached the buckboard, almost climbed up onto the bench, then stopped himself.

Less than ten more minutes. He was already a fool; he could be a fool for another short while. In ten minutes' time, he would know for sure that she wasn't coming, and he could get on with things instead of living in a dream world, hoping for something that would never come to pass.

Besides, maybe he'd get a look at a famous outlaw.

He patted Nellie's muzzle, where she liked it, and returned to the platform. Tom, Dick, and Hank were still there, chuckling over something he'd missed. He realized he was more anxious now than he had been before he'd left. Maybe he shouldn't have returned, after all.

On the other hand, if Madelyn wasn't coming, there might be worse things than being killed in a shootout.

Tom spotted him first. "Better?" he asked. "We thought maybe you wasn't coming back."

"Busy at Beulah's," Noah said. "Had to wait to get the barkeep's attention."

"Gets that way," Dick said. "Especially on payday for the ranches."

You would know, Noah thought. But he said only, "I mostly stay down on the farm." These men were lying to him, so he figured lying back couldn't hurt. Besides, up until he had started coming to town three times a day, that had been true.

He was suddenly struck by how pathetic he was. The farm had been struggling, he had been shorting himself of sustenance, but three times a day he had left it to make the thirty-minute trip each way, then stood around waiting for the train. More than three hours out of every day that he should have been working or sleeping. All of it for nothing. He was worse than the original Noah. At least that one had been right. The rains had ultimately come, the ark had held fast, the creatures of the earth had been saved.

Again, he thought about the wagon and the mule waiting for him in the darkness on the other side of the depot. Nellie wouldn't mind getting home a few minutes earlier than usual. She certainly wouldn't mind not making this journey every day for nothing.

He started to turn, to walk away, but then he saw the train's headlight in the distance.

"There it is," Hank said.

"Not long now," Tom added.

"This friend of yours," Noah said. "He traveling alone?"

"He's got some company with him," Hank said.

"Sounds like a regular gathering, then."

"Something like that." Hank wore a worried look. The other two men, Noah thought, were plain mean. Like Madelyn's husband, he guessed, cruel just for the sake of cruelty. He had a hunch that Hank had fallen in with them, but perhaps not by choice. Nothing about him — not the way he carried himself, not the way he kept reaching out, conversationally — struck Noah as anything like his companions.

"I'm sure you'll be glad to see him. I don't really think Madelyn's coming on this one, but since it's almost here, I'll wait with you all, just in case."

"He'll be glad to see us," Hank said.

Tom took a sudden step toward them, his spurs jingling. "Hank, I told you before. Shut it."

Noah saw tension in Tom's face; his jaw

was tight, a vein in his temple throbbed like a blue worm. The big man was ready for trouble.

When the train arrived, he decided, he would step to the side of the depot, out of the way of any bullets that might fly. Madelyn — if she came at all — would certainly have sense to remain where she was until the shooting stopped.

He wished the sheriff's deputy had come back with him, or better yet, rounded up a posse to take these men before Mo Bramley ever showed.

But then, he had wished a lot of things in his life. Very few of those wishes had come true.

He could hear the train now, the chug of its locomotive pulling its burden down the steel rails. Smoke billowed from its stack, gray blotting out the stars until it rose beyond the glow of the headlight. As it drew ever nearer its whistle sounded, shrill and insistent. The rails hummed.

Now Noah was as tense as Tom, or more so. He could hear the blood rushing in his ears. His fist clenched on the rose stems until the thorns dug through his flesh, but he couldn't relax his hand. His insides felt like ice. The train slowed, pulled into the station. The smell of hot metal stung his nostrils.

The depot door flew open, splashing more light onto the platform. Noah turned abruptly and saw the operator step outside, just as round and soft as he remembered, with some papers in his hand.

The other three men were gone.

No, not gone, he realized. They had melted into the shadows, but he could see them there, could even hear Hank's wheezing breath.

Then all he could hear were the locomotive's brakes squealing, the deafening hiss of steam. He studied the windows but didn't see Madelyn. He did see other forms, unrecognizable through smoke and steam, moving around inside.

The locomotive had stopped past where he stood on the platform, its engine still chugging gently. Behind it were a number of cars, most of them dark, but the two in front had lights on. The door was between him and the other men. He started toward it.

So did they.

When they neared one another, Hank took an additional step toward him.

"You best stay back," he said. "You don't know what —"

Noah cut him off, his words surprising him even as they escaped his lips. "No, you don't know what you're involved in. You still got time to do something different with your life. I know you're not like them."

"You don't know me," Hank said.

"I know what I see." Noah stepped closer, put one hand against Hank's chest, lowered his voice. "Run. They'll be busy for a spell."

"You think so?"

"Don't think about it, just go."

Hank swiveled his head to see where his partners were. In that instant, Noah snaked an arm out and snatched Hank's revolver from its holster. Hank either didn't notice or didn't care; he took off at a sprint for the darkness of the depot's far side.

"Hank!" A desperate shout from Tom, followed by, "We'll deal with you later, you damn coward!"

The train car door opened. Tom and Dick had guns in their hands, all their attention on the doorway. Noah still held Hank's pistol. He knew how to use a gun, though except for killing snakes and coyotes and the occasional rabbit stealing crops, he rarely did. He wasn't even sure why he had taken it.

The station operator, he realized, had ducked back inside. Probably smart.

Then he heard a new voice. "You men, drop those irons!"

The deputy. He stepped onto the platform, a shotgun in his hands.

Tom spun toward him and fired twice. The shotgun's blast was louder, but the round that struck the deputy's collarbone threw off his aim.

"Shoot, damn you!" the deputy cried.

Seconds elapsed before Noah realized the lawman was talking to him. He turned the gun around in his hand.

At the same time, gunfire erupted from inside the train. A muzzle flash brightened the doorway for an instant and, something shattered a window.

Tom fired at the deputy once more, dropping him in his tracks. Without pausing, he whirled around and kept firing at the train.

Noah saw Dick look at him, seeming to realize that he was now holding a pistol. As if deciding the marshals on the train posed the bigger threat, he trained his fire on them instead.

Noah had never shot a man. Even in his imaginings, the only man he'd ever wanted to shoot dead was the one Madelyn had married. He tried to pretend that Dick was that man, and raised the revolver in trembling hands.

He yanked the trigger. The gun bucked; the shot flew wild.

He tried to steady his hands, to get a better grip despite palms slick with sweat. He knew better than to jerk the trigger. This time he squeezed it.

He missed again. But Dick, deciding he was a problem after all, spun toward him.

Before he could fire, though, another flash flared inside the train, and Dick made a noise, threw his arms out, and pitched forward. Yet another shot came from inside, and Dick lay still.

Tom snatched up the gun that Dick had dropped. With a pistol in each hand, he fired at the train, at Noah, and back at the train.

Then the depot operator stepped out of his door again, holding a shotgun with the barrel sawed short. He squeezed one trigger, then the next. The first blast knocked Tom off his feet, and the second one sprayed what looked like jelly across the platform.

The operator turned to Noah. "You all right?" His voice sounded as hoarse as Noah remembered, like whatever had left his throat scarred had just happened the day before.

"F-fine," Noah managed. "Shaken up is all. Never been in anything like that before."

"First time's the worst." He touched his

ruined throat. "Don't ever get easy, though."

A man stepped down from the train car, a revolver in his hand and a badge on his chest: a circle with a star inside it. "That all of them?" he asked.

"There was one more," Noah said. "But he didn't want to stay."

"Wise choice," the marshal said.

The only wise one on the platform, Noah thought, but he kept it to himself.

Another man stepped down, this one with his hands behind his back. He looked angry, resentful, and enough like Tom to be his brother. He probably was, Noah realized. The man, who had to be Mo Bramley, looked at the fallen outlaw. "You bastards," he said. "You killed a good man."

"Other way around," the second marshal said. He descended the steps right behind Bramley, holding onto the handcuffs and carrying a pistol of his own. "You killed a good man, and you're here to pay for it."

"There's no one at the sheriff's office to meet you," Noah said. He pointed toward the fallen deputy. "He came here, instead. Said there's some guys doubled up in a cell that might get into a fight."

"We're not going anywhere until tomorrow, then," the first marshal said. "Reckon we'll camp out there until someone shows up we can turn this killer over to."

By this time, the engineer, the fireman, and a conductor had all emerged from the train and were talking to the station operator, eyeballing the carnage at the same time. Noah realized his left fist was still wrapped tight around the roses, and he opened his hand, letting them spill to the platform. A line of bloody gashes marked where the thorns had been.

He looked for someone to give Hank's pistol to, but everybody who hadn't been shot was talking to somebody else. People were starting to trickle in from town; drinkers from Beulah's, he guessed, who had heard the commotion. He just held the gun at his side, then let it drop. It landed on the roses, spun in a quarter-circle, then stopped.

He hoped all the noise hadn't disturbed Nellie too much. He turned and started toward the wagon, and home.

"Were those roses for me?" a voice behind him asked.

Not quite the same question Tom had asked, what seemed like a day earlier, but close.

This voice, though, was high-pitched. Feminine.

He turned, almost afraid to look.

Madelyn hurried toward him, struggling

with an overstuffed carpetbag.

Noah stepped toward her, stopped with one foot on the roses, his toe bumping the pistol, and held out his arms. She dropped the bag and hurried into them, and he drew her close, held her, feeling the pounding of her heart in her breast and inhaling the scent of her hair. "You came," he said. "You're really here."

"Of course I am, silly," she said. "I told you I'd be here by the end of the month, didn't I?"

"You said maybe."

"A girl can't sound too desperate, Noah. You know that."

"I guess I don't know much of anything about anything," he said. He glanced at the clock on the depot wall. "But I know one thing for sure. You're five minutes late."

She tilted her head up, pressed her lips against his. When she broke the kiss, she said, "What's five minutes, at the start of forever?"

He started to answer, then decided against it. Nothing he said could make any difference now, anyway. Instead, he wriggled free of her grasp, picked up her bag, then took her arm. "Come on," he said. "It's late. And Nellie's been waiting to meet you for a long time."

"Nellie? Who's Nellie?"

"You'll see."

"That was so exciting, wasn't it?" she said. "A real wild west gunfight. You must see those all the time. Mr. Bramley was very polite with me, and the marshals were nice, too."

Together, arm in arm, they stepped off the platform and out of the light. With the midnight train chugging and the music of her voice and the rush of his pulse in his ears, Noah led her toward the wagon.

After the storm, the original Noah had promised, there would be life.

Noah thought that perhaps that guy made sense, after all.

He put her bag in the buckboard's bed, helped her onto the bench, unrolled the blanket and tucked it around her. Then he climbed up beside her, took the reins.

When they passed beyond the town's gentle glow, Madelyn looked at the sky and gave a soft gasp. "So many stars!"

Noah just smiled and thought, she's going to like it here.

And so am I.

Warm now despite the chill, he drove into the velvet night and the start of forever.

Jeffrey J. Mariotte is the author of dozens

of novels and short stories and hundreds of comics and graphic novels, most of which take place in the historical or contemporary West. Work in the Western genre includes the Peacemaker and Spur Award-finalist novella "Byrd's Luck," weird-Western novel *Thunder Moon Rising*, comic-book series *Desperadoes* and *Graveslinger* (with Shannon Eric Denton), and short fiction in anthologies such as *Lost Trails, Ghost Towns, Westward Weird,* and *Straight Outta Deadwood*. Visit him online for the latest at facebook.com/JeffreyJMariotte.

Cybil

EDWARD MASSEY

Helena Grange, resolute and righteous, burst through the door of the county jail in the cold, gray dusk of the October evening.

"Sheriff Simms, do you know what your daughter is doing?" she said. Her greeting reached him before he could enjoy his expectations of an evening with Ebby or put the key in the lock.

"Evening, Mrs. Grange," said Sheriff Simms, and he touched his hat.

"Don't avoid the subject," she said.

He nodded and stood away from the door he held in hopes of closing it.

"Sorry, I can't offer you a cup of coffee."

"Sheriff! You know I do not drink coffee."

"Yes'm," he said. He spread the ashes to cool the fire in the cast-iron stove. After pouring the cold coffee in the bucket and dumping the grounds from the little metal basket, he turned to her.

"Now, Mrs. Grange, it was kind of you to

come down here before supper to ask about my daughter. She got married and lives in the big city."

"You know very well that is not what I am talking about. Thea is a good girl. A smart girl. You know I am talking about the other one."

"Cybil? Well, she is up at home doing her school work," he said.

"I am talking about when she is at school; about what she is doing when she is not under your roof." Mrs. Grange waited, expecting a response, and when she got none, added, "About what she did today at school."

"Why don't you just tell me," the sheriff said.

Mrs. Grange amused him some. She'd take off on some crusade about what the kids were doing wrong, but he was too much the sheriff to play the guessing game with anyone.

"I find it hard to bring myself to repeat what she did. I would not even touch the subject; but an upstanding citizen has to recognize that what she is doing is immoral. It has to be stopped."

"Immoral, huh?" He put the coffee pot on the stove, ready to boil the coffee tomorrow as hot as Mrs. Grange. "That bad, huh?"

"Now don't you take this lightly," she said. "I warn you, just because this brazen little girl is your daughter."

"No'm," he said. "I don't get many warnings, you know. When I do, I don't take 'em lightly. Just what did Cybil do?"

She seemed to stand even straighter and folded her arms across her well-tethered breasts, "She showed my LaGrange her panties."

Sheriff Simms was not so damn sure that a young boy, even one named LaGrange Grange, had been shown Cybil's panties. Most young boys, even ones named LaGrange Grange, would steal a look for themselves.

"Say again?"

"You heard me," said Mrs. Grange. "For a nickel."

"For a nickel?"

"That's right, Sheriff. Your Cybil showed my LaGrange her panties for a nickel."

"Uh, did he give her the nickel?"

"My land, Sheriff, how do you think I found out about it," said Mrs. Grange. "You got boys. No fourteen-year-old boy is going to tell his ma a pretty little girl showed him her panties."

"Cybil is a pretty little girl." That truth offered no help. Normally a flood of talk, at that moment, Mrs. Grange stood there looking at him. Sheriff Simms said, "Evidently he did tell you just that."

"Not directly," she said. "He came asking for another nickel."

"Uh?" He could hear Mrs. Grange ready to tell a worse story. He figured it was not the time to smile. "Mrs. Grange, are you telling me your son plans to purchase a second look at my daughter's panties tomorrow?"

"I should say not. He came asking for another nickel and so I asked him what he done with the last one. I'm pretty good at getting to the truth. At first, he said he just spent it. I asked on what. He said, just spent it. That made me suspicion him. So I asked him on what again. He said he just gave it to Cybil. I said what fer. He said, just did. And I said what fer. About that time he started to cry. At least the boy is not shameless. Not like your daughter."

"I'm not so sure a thirteen-year-old should be ashamed just 'cause she's pretty. Is that it?"

"You aren't are you? Well, I asked him why he used his nickel to pay her when he knew he shouldn't. And you know what he said?"

"No, Mrs. Grange, what did he say?"

"He said he did it because everybody else

in school was doing it."

Simms felt sure and certain the way to deal with that information was to say the least. In fact, say nothing.

"Well, what yer going to do about it?" asked Mrs. Grange.

"First thing I'm going to do, Mrs. Grange, is give you back your nickel," said the sheriff. He reached in his pocket and got out a nickel. "Then, I'll take care of it. You have my word, Mrs. Grange, my Cybil won't be doing that anymore."

Sheriff Simms disliked giving Mrs. Grange that measure of satisfaction. It would only feed her obsessive need to be the conscience of all the young kids in their small town. He had to say that to get Mrs. Grange out of his office, if ever he was to get to supper. And he had to say it because he couldn't let it go unfixed. Even as he said it, he knew Cybil would not be doing that anymore but God knows what she would be doing.

After supper, he took his younger daughter out to the chicken coop. The chicken coop had been the site of many thrashings. He took great care not to strike his children out of anger. He warmed their fannies with the belt only after he explained why. When his first daughter, Thea, slipped out of childhood, he began to doubt that form of punishment. With Cybil developed into a long legged thirteen-year-old beauty, he was not about to turn her over his knee and warm her fanny. Still the chicken coop was the place of judgment.

"Do you know why we're here?" he asked.

" 'Cause you're gonna' thrash me," she said.

"Yes, but why?" he said. "Stand up straight and look at me."

She rose up off the feed bin. She did not look like the siren of the schoolyard dressed in her older brother's bib overalls and wearing his red hunting shirt.

"Did I do something wrong?"

"You tell me."

"Did somebody complain about me?"

"Yes."

"Why?"

"Jesus, girl," he had to yell at her to keep from laughing. She was a piece. "You tell me."

"Didn't do nothing wrong. Don't know why anybody'd complain."

She was very good at this game. He doubted her guilty of so many indiscretions and outrages that she had no idea which one brought the complaint. A sheriff's daughter lived the straight and narrow as her way of life. She simply couldn't find any of her behavior worthy of prompting a complaint.

"Mrs. Grange came to see me today."

She looked at him. Said nothing.

"What did you do in afternoon recess today?"

She looked at him. Said nothing.

"You better answer me girl."

"Don't know what to answer."

"Figgers."

He worked the boxes with the hens. She watched him. The two said nothing.

"Did you show LaGrange your panties?" he asked.

"Not just him, Pa."

"That don't make it better." The sheriff had six children and all the rest of them were damn serious. Where did she come from? Maybe Troy, the brother next to her, was a bit of a rogue too. Where did they come from? "And another thing. Did you ask him to pay money?"

"Sure did. That was the deal."

"Do you know what that is?" Her age and her physical development confused him. She was straight out a woman made even more dangerous to herself by the dew of morning on her looks. The children in his county were children for a long time and being thirteen up there in the mountains meant knowing how the animals bear young every year but it did not mean knowing much about the ways of men in the world.

"Business?" she said hesitantly.

"Well, some call it that," he said. He still could not decide what her answers hid or told. She had learned well from her Pa. "Some call it prostitution."

"What's that, Pa?"

"Don't play with me, Cybil. I'm in no mood. You sell your body like that and you'll be in my jail." He paused, and then added. "Worse. You'll be out on your ear."

"I wasn't selling my body, Pa," she said. Now she was standing straight up. No slouch and no whispers. "I never let nobody touch me, and I don't aim to. I was letting them boys look at my panties for a nickel."

"Why?"

"Because they're always trying to look at my panties. They ask me to stand on ladders and walk upstairs and they drop things on the floor and I know what they're doing. I just got tired of it. Goddammit, Pa. They want to see my panties so much, I figured I'd make a nickel."

"Jesus, girl."

He said no more. She made too much sense. He had to punish her but he sure had no idea what to do. He thought about it in silence so long she interrupted him.

"We finished, Pa?" she asked. "It's getting late. Can I go to bed?"

"Not yet, girl, you've got to be punished." Her desire to leave the chicken coop inspired him.

"You'll clean out the coop for a month and care for the chickens."

The perfect punishment. When Helena Grange stood at his door first thing in the morning demanding to know what he had done about his daughter, he planned to tell her that he had sentenced Cybil to get up early and clean up the chicken shit all around her.

Mountains and pioneer heritage gave **Edward Massey** the willingness to set out on his own and try. Good people and great institutions molded him. These influences bear total responsibility for his progress and none for his setbacks. With four published novels, *Cybil* is his seventh short story to be published. Please visit edwardmasseybooks.com.

Hanging Tree Bounty
Benjamin Thomas

Charlene pushed her ceramic plate back, wiped her chin on her sleeve, and looked down at the remains of the fine frontier meal she and her grandfather had just polished off. Fried mountain turkey with cranberry jelly, fresh savory mushrooms, and hot rolls with melted butter. It was too much, really, and not at all what they were accustomed to from the nearby mining camps in the Rocky Mountain foothills. How would she sleep on such a meal? And Pops had even finished off a slice of fruit pie although he'd been hard pressed to identify what fruit exactly had been baked into it. He'd since paid their bill, both for food and their hotel stay over the past ten days and then retreated to their room upstairs to begin preparing for the early morning departure. A celebration of sorts, it had been. Successfully collecting on one bounty even while a jewel thief had slipped through their trap.

Such was life these days for the odd pair of bounty hunters. At eighteen years of age, Charlene realized she'd been following around her scholarly grandfather for close to three years now. They'd generally met with a fair amount of success but had run into some failures as well, not to mention a bit of danger. No matter. This was the life for her. Most gals would be for marriage and a couple of youngins by now, but Charlene preferred the freedom of the trail and the adventure of the unknown right around the corner.

"Pardon me, miss." The baritone drawl of a southerner interrupted her reverie, yanking her back to the present. "I wanted to stop by and introduce myself."

The polite voice belonged to a handsome man in his early thirties, dressed in a spotless gray waistcoat, wool trousers, and matching vest as well as a wide elaborate cravat prominently displayed. Charlene couldn't help but notice the mule ear pockets and the gold chain draping out of the right-side watch pocket. No mere prospector, this. The well-trimmed sideburns and chin whiskers spoke to the same conclusion.

"Well, sir, I was just about to leave. My

meal, as you can see, is complete." She smiled at the empty plate before turning her chin up to gaze at him. Her eyes met his brilliant brown ones. Her smile deepened. "But . . . I suppose I can spare a few moments. "She gestured at the empty chair across from her. "Please."

"Thank you, miss." Once seated, the man allowed his eyes to linger on hers for a moment more than necessary before saying, "My name is Edward Owlswick." He smiled this time, displaying a set of teeth whiter than any she'd seen for donkey's years. A pair of striking dimples invaded his cheeks as he said, "And you, my dear, are Miss Charlene Gordon, a key member of the 'Leland Gordon Medicine Show'. I saw you both in action a couple of months ago up in the mining camps. It was magnificent."

Charlene wasn't sure how to take this. Was he truly inspired as he appeared to be or was he perhaps a disgruntled customer of their charade, in pursuit of a refund? The medicine show was a tool they had used several times as part of their bounty-hunting practice, allowing them to close in on a target. She settled for, "Thank you, Mr. Owlswick. I will pass on your compliments to my grandfather."

"Very kind of you miss. It's all a fiction, of

course, but you carry it off well. Snake-oil salesmen, the both of you." He held up a firm hand, preventing her defense. "Apologies for my impertinence. You see, that is exactly what I am looking for. I wish to hire you and your grandfather. A little job, but one I'm sure will be to your liking."

"Well, sir. That's certainly provocative." His looks and charm overcame any pushiness. She let her head fall to the side a little, indicating he should continue.

"Allow me some explanation. You see, I am a lawyer by trade. As of late, I have been retained by the family of Mrs. R. B. Bradford. Perhaps you've heard of her?"

"I don't believe so, no."

"Ah. Well, then. Mrs. Bradford and her husband, Major Bradford, were the ones gunned down in cold blood during the recent Claim-Jumper's War."

Charlene kept her expression neutral, an effect she'd learned usually prompted further clarification. Mr. Owlswick obliged by offering a summary of what she'd already known. Denver City was hardly more than a babe as far as towns went but the nearby gold fields were spurring rapid growth. A city government had been organized with John C. Moore elected as Mayor during the closing days of 1859. This, however, did not prevent occasional outbreaks of lawlessness, and an affair known as the Claim-Jumper's War marked the following month. Some enterprising citizens "jumped" a portion of the town site, and the resulting conflict between them and the town company lasted five days, ending in bloodshed. Fortunately, the better class of law-abiding citizens interfered and arranged a compromise, preventing further loss of life. But not in time to save Major Bradford and his wife.

"Colonel Dick Whitsitt, Secretary of the town company, had a rifle leveled at his head during the controversy as well, but was saved by the interference of friends." Here Owlswick paused to ensure his listener was absorbing it all.

"Go on, Mr. Owlswick," she said and sat up a little straighter in her chair. "You tell an absorbing story. But what does this have to do with my grandfather and our Medicine Show?"

"Just this," he said, eyebrows narrowing over those delightful features. "Major Bradford was shot at three times and killed by a negro. Wayne Cade is his name. The Major was no doubt the target but one of the bullets strayed and hit his wife in the neck, killing her too. Horrible, it was. But you see, while Cade is well known as a drunkard and a brawler, he is also the owner of a silver mine in the area. It is thought that he remains in hiding somewhere nearby, not wanting to give up rights to the mine. Mrs. Bradford's parents want justice and I intend to see that they get it."

"And you seek our help? Can I assume a bounty has been placed on this Wayne Cade? I must inform you, sir, that my grandfather and I are not in the habit of sharing bounties. Further, it would seem you would be better served with a posse of lawmen than an odd pair of medicine show performers."

The dimples reappeared in his cheeks while the warmth of his eyes held hers. "The issue, Miss Gordon, lies in finding the man. He is holed up somewhere and, I believe, we must coax him out into the open before we can capture him. And I hasten to add that the recovery of the bounty would be entirely yours. I am, I can assure you, already well compensated by the family."

"But surely . . ."

"There's more." He stretched an arm across the table, resting it just short of her hand. "This Cade fellow . . . he had a wife, you see, that died about six months ago. A white gal. Not a favorite around town I can tell you, for marrying a negro. Anyway, since her death, Cade seems to have lost his way. He's become a wild, carousing sort, even more so than before. He's not in full command of his faculties. He's even been known to "talk" to his dead wife, calling out to her when in his cups at the saloons. Unpredictable behavior to be sure. And now, he's even shot two people to death. While that seems to have driven him into hiding, I fear if he is not brought to justice, there will be more bloodshed. Perhaps much more."

Charlene couldn't help but be caught up in her companion's earnestness. He seemed a little younger than she had at first surmised. A bit closer to her own age although undoubtedly a man experienced in the ways of the world. She looked down at his open hand and noticed a pale brown smudge on his wrist where the sleeve had ridden up. A birthmark. At last, a physical flaw in the otherwise perfect exterior.

"Sir, forgive me. I am having trouble placing your accent. The deep south, I suspect. Is it Alabama?"

Owlswick smiled, showing a full set of straight white teeth. "South Carolina, in truth. But I can assure you, my dear, my sentiments are not with the slaveholders of my region. I find it a peculiar institution and chose several years ago to depart the warmer climes and move out here to pursue my career as a man of justice. Bring the law to the wilds, as it were."

For a moment, Charlene was lost in his words. He spoke with such eloquence. The sounds of the dining room faded. His eyes held hers and she felt herself falling.

The silence swelled until he eventually continued, "I've come to you because of what I saw at the medicine show," he said. Your grandfather and yourself . . . the showmanship . . . the way you control the crowds. You have them eating out of your hand. I'm certain," he said, leaning back in his chair once again, "you can bring that same show here, and in some way, lure Cade out of hiding."

Leland Gordon wished for better light in the hotel room as he sifted through a pile of correspondence trying to decide which of them he would need readily at hand for the trip south. Would have been better to have done this during daylight hours. He had high hopes for the Pikes Peak region and the little town of Colorado City that had been founded at the confluence of Fountain and Camp Creeks just a few months ago and he was anxious to get on the road and seek out opportunities there.

But his focus waivered from the letters as he listened to his granddaughter's report of her encounter with Mr. Owlswick. Finally, he looked up from the papers and gave his full attention to her. An opportunity, it appeared, might be awaiting them right here.

"That's quite a bounty," he said at the end of her narration. "No doubt augmented by Mrs. Bradford's family. Lord knows Denver City alone, wouldn't post so much for a mere shooting." He dropped the letters on the desk and rubbed a hand across the bristly grey hairs on his chin, starting to warm to the idea. "I do recall seeing a wanted poster for this Cade fellow yesterday at the marshal's office. I ignored it, naturally. No dollar amount listed and no drawing of his likeness. It might be difficult to identify the man. I've noticed a lot of negroes hereabouts. Freedmen or escaped slaves looking for opportunities I'd wager."

"You think it's all right to delay our departure to take this on?" Charlene sat on her bed, still feeling giddy from her conversation downstairs. "You're always goin' on about what a bird in the hand is worth. We've just come off that job where we lost Slippery John. It's left a bitter taste in my mouth and frankly, I was looking forward to putting this town behind us."

"I know, I know," Leland said. "But why go looking for a job when one is staring us in the face right now? Maybe we can take this one on, hopefully catch us a killer, and be well staked for the trip south in about a week or so. From your description of this Mr. Owlswick I don't suppose you would mind a delay either."

Charlene felt her blush and tried to hide it by coming to her feet and pacing across the limited floor space. She was determined to turn the conversation back to the job and away from the handsome Mr. Owlswick.

"I confess I'm struggling to think of a way to use the medicine show though," she said. "How's that going to coax Cade from his hiding spot?"

"Ahh, Charlie, my dear. That's just it. I don't want to use that tactic at all. The medicine show should remain 'legitimate', at least as far as that's possible, anyway. No need to risk it being labeled a fraud when we could go a different route altogether."

Charlene stopped her pacing. "What route?"

"You said Mr. Owlswick mentioned Cade talking to his dead wife, I believe. Aloud. He's clearly a believer in the supernatural, the arcane, the ability to pierce the veil between our world and the next."

"Either that or he's simply a drunk or belongs in an asylum."

"Hmmm . . . quite right. Doesn't really matter, I suppose. I think he might jump at the chance to actually speak with her though. To converse and have her respond to him." Leland's eyes sparkled with a tinge of mischief.

"You want to hold a séance?"

"Seems like something we could pull off. I can rig some contraptions to convince the skeptical — strange noises, ghostly apparitions — that sort of thing."

"And I suppose you want me to play the medium?" Charlene asked, already knowing the answer.

"You'd be splendid, my dear." This was the only part of his idea that he wasn't sure would go over well but one glance at her face told him the plan excited her.

"Assuming I agree to all this," she said, "I have to say I don't like the idea of duping innocent folk out of their money. The medicine show is one thing but at least they get actual products that do some good, even if it's not quite what is promised. But to take their money for a completely made-up thing is like . . . a lie."

"Don't worry, honey. We'll run the shows for free. We can encourage donations afterwards for people who feel they got what they came for. Sometimes, after all, people just need closure and talking with a departed loved one may bring them peace they wouldn't otherwise have. That's worth more than you might think. But still, we'll earn our money from Mr. Owlswick's engagement of our services. The rest is just gravy."

"Good. Let's see . . . we'll need to put a lot of effort towards publicity. Have to make certain Cade hears of it and decides to come or else it's all for naught."

"Agreed. We can print up some advertisements and post them around town and make sure word gets to the mining camps. We might have to hold more than one session so word of our successes will spread."

"I imagine Mr. Owlswick has connections hereabout and would be willing to help spread the word. I'll ask him in the morning. He . . . er . . . asked me to join him for breakfast." Eyes dropping to her lap she added. "He's anxious, you see. To hear if we will take the job."

Leland nodded once but said nothing in response.

A full week passed. Young Owlswick had proven enthusiastic and more than up to the task of rapidly building publicity. When told his order for signs would not be ready for ten days, he used some inside knowledge involving the printer's private life, thus receiving the final stack of completed posters and accompanying flyers in a single day. He also hired a group of boys to hand out pamphlets across the town and up in the mining camps. They had decided on 'Lady Beaulieu' for Charlene's stage name since she could affect a slight French accent with no trouble and she wouldn't have to alter her skin tone to match the Romany persona Leland had suggested.

Daily, Leland disguised himself with fancy coat, britches, and top hat and escorted the beautiful Lady Beaulieu about town. Not wanting to be recognized from his Tonic and Elixir Medicine Show, he made sure to blacken his hair and beard with shoe polish. His natural thick Scottish brogue also entered his speech. The medium herself only had one costume but used it to full effect during these outings, causing a spectacle with her long scarlet dress and its plunging neckline where several gaudy necklaces rested. She also wore a wig sporting long luxuriant black hair held back by a headband featuring a prominent fake emerald in the center. A matching green cape completed the exotic look. They would stop briefly in busy spots and be seen supping at various eateries in full view of curious onlookers.

Publicity may, in fact, have been too good. A free show was a rarity in gold country. Five seances had to be scheduled, forcing Leland to establish a policy of no more than one per day to allow Lady Beaulieu a chance to rest and regain her spiritual strength. Of greater importance was the time required for Leland to reset all the gadgets and machinery to carry off the various illusions as well as gather pertinent personal facts on the guests. To aid in this effort, they accepted no repeat customers due to the ectoplasmic currents needing to be reset with the cycle of the moon. Clients would, of course, be welcome to come again in April.

Owlswick called in a favor from a wealthy client named Jacob Bannister, who allowed the use of several rooms in his Wazee Street residence which he had presumptuously named "Washington House". Most of the town's residents knew of Washington House and its location just one block north of the Hanging Tree which stood at the intersection of San Luis and Wazee. It was also not too far from the Platte River with a clear view of Indian Village on the opposite banks of the picturesque Cherry Creek. All these factors, Leland felt, lent an air of mystique to the proceedings.

"Full house tonight," Leland said, peeking through a tiny gap in the curtain. He was dressed as a down-on-his-luck old miner with a crumpled hat and dusty boots. "Seventeen clients out there awaiting the spiritual wisdom and dulcet tones of Lady Beaulieu."

"The biggest yet," Charlene said into a mirror, putting the final touches of color to her lips. "Any sign of our bounty this time?"

"No indication from Owlswick, I'm afraid. We must resign ourselves to the fact that this séance idea just isn't going to pull him out of hiding."

"I suppose so. I'm glad this is our last one though. It's too much work for what Ed is paying us. The medicine show does so much better. If it weren't for the donations, we'd probably be losing money." One last look over in the mirror and then Charlene stood up straight. "Ready when you are, Pops."

He nodded at her, left the room by a side door, rounded the house, entered again through the front door. He paused only to brush the snowflakes off his coat, along with a fair amount of dirt. When had it started to snow? And when had his granddaughter begun calling Owlswick, Ed? Scowling, he tried to put it out of his mind. He made sure to stoop as he shuffled along, completing his illusion of a crusty old miner.

Making his way into the front parlor where the séance would take place, he checked the large oblong table. They'd moved it in from the dining room before the first seance session five days ago. The overlarge white linen tablecloth was thankfully draped and hanging to the floor on all sides. That had been a problem on their second show. This time, all appeared to be in order, so he began to mingle with the other guests. He adapted to his role as a hopeful believer as if he were putting on a favorite pair of shoes. Even so, he couldn't resist sneaking in a couple of quick glances up towards the ceiling and around the room to ensure his various contraptions including sound, lights, and smoke effects were in place and adequately concealed.

A single paraffin oil lamp hung suspended near the center of the ceiling, giving the room a soft, pleasant glow. The sun had set outside and the shadow in the corners seemed to grow darker as the light slowly diminished. This was the first of Leland's contraptions, involving an opaque shade attached to a timing mechanism. It unfolded so slowly it was unnoticeable but had the effect of dimming the amount of light at floor level.

Just when it was getting difficult to see, a muted gong sounded from somewhere nearby, resulting in a sudden stop to conversation. All eyes turned to the wide curtain at the end of the room where Charlene had appeared out of the shadows. She stood in full Lady Beaulieu regalia, complete with long black-haired wig and swept back cape revealing her slender tanned arms bare to the shoulders. She held a single lit candle by its base. The flame flickering slightly, casting eerie shadows across her cascading scarlet dress and causing the metals in the necklaces to sparkle. A whispered voice from one of the participants teased, "Nothing up her sleeves . . .". Keeping her expression neutral she advanced to the edge of the table, placed the candle in a holder, let go, and watched as it slid by itself across the surface to the exact center. Leland smiled to himself knowing Owlswick had successfully performed his only bit of the show, lying underneath the table and dragging a large magnet along the underside, pulling the metal candle holder along with it.

Charlene took her place at the head of the

table and said in her softest French-accented voice, "Please, everyone. Sit." They complied with her wishes, Leland finding himself sitting between a large woman who smelled of goat cheese and a young dandy wearing a monocle. Owlswick, per the script, had taken advantage of the scooting chair noises and crawled through Leland's legs to escape his under-the-table activity, disappearing through a door directly behind him.

Lady Beaulieu spoke her opening lines, encouraging the participants to remain quiet. Only if they were spoken to by herself or directly by a visiting spirit could they respond. She then reviewed her relationship as an acolyte and student of Daniel Douglas Home, the great clairvoyant and trance medium. They would already know this from the posters around town, but it was worth reiterating. Per Leland's instructions, she wasted no words on what they should expect. Let the suspense build. Charlene instructed all participants to hold hands and not to break the circle under any circumstances while she was in active communication with a spirit. To do so would cause extreme harm to herself, as the medium. She alone would not be part of the circle, but rather the conduit between the circle and the other side of the veil. She looked so sweet and innocent with her pretty face, furrowed eyes and slim bare arms. Anybody would be hard pressed to go against her wishes and risk her health.

"Now then," she began, looking at Leland who would act as her shill and get the séance rolling. "Mr. Deetz, is it?" I understand you wish to contact your deceased wife. Six months in the grave, I believe. Her name is Rebecca, is it not? But in private, you call her Petals because of her soft and beautiful skin."

"Why yes, ma'am. But how'd you know all that? I never told no one 'bout Petals. Ask her if she'll wait for me on the other side."

Charlene reminded them not to break the circle and then closed her eyes. She began to sway her head from side to side, slow at first and then faster and faster. She hummed a steady tone but then as her pace picked up, she inserted gaps in her humming, as if interrupted. After a couple of minutes of this, she abruptly stopped and opened her eyes wide. A faint smell of peaches could be detected. Leland was pleased with this effect using powdered peach-scented soap in a tiny puff-bag he had pre-placed at the foot of his chair where he could step on it at the appropriate time.

"Rebeccaaaa Deeeeeetz . . ." Charlene called. "Hoooow do you answer your husband's questionnn . . . ?"

Spirit rapping consisted of the medium reciting the alphabet aloud and listening for some sort of sound from the beyond. The sound is heard at the appropriate letter in the alphabet, spelling out an answer. This was a tiresome process so Charlene was always glad to get this act out of the way early.

She recited the alphabet up to the letter 'N' and then cracked her big toe. The sharp popping sound seemed to emanate from the center of the table and was clearly audible. She started again at 'A' until she came to the letter 'O' when they all heard another popping sound. Her grandfather usually complained about her cracking her joints and often grumbled she would someday come to regret having done it so much in her youth. But he was happy to make use of her skill now.

"Mr. Deetz, your wife has answered, 'No'. She will not wait for you."

"Well, ask her why?"

Charlene played it out, tediously spelling out the reply with her cracking of big toes, "A..M..E..L..I..A". Charlene looked over at

Leland once again, "Does that answer your question, sir?"

Leland's eyes lit up in glee. "Indeed it do, m'lady. Indeed it do. She means it's fine for me to take up with this little lass I met t'other day. Amelia. A purty young thing and now I know I have Petals' blessin'." With a big grin plastered across his face, he took both of his neighbor's hands and thrust them together, allowing him to leave the circle. "I'll be headin' out now. Got what I came fer." He came near to dancing a jig as he left the room and went out the front door.

Darkness enveloped him outside like a blanket thrown over his head. He didn't see Owlswick until he had almost smacked into him. "He's here," the excited lawyer said in his thick Carolina drawl. "Cade. I didn't spot him before but I could see him clearly once I got back to the side room behind the curtain."

"Which one?"

"The one right next to your granddaughter. On her immediate left. He's grown a bit of a beard and keeps his hat down low but it's him all right."

"Good. I'll signal Charlene. You go on in and get ready to help nab him once she gets him to confess. This might just pay off after all."

Before following, Leland turned and hooked a length of wire to the door handle and then looped it around a lever at the top of the transom. This, in turn connected to a liquid-filled bucket painted black to blend in with the night. There, that should do it. The back hallway was well blocked so this was the only way Cade would know of to escape the house.

Once back inside the house Leland removed his disguise with relish. All the stooping when he walked was giving him muscle cramps in his back. Peeping through the tiny gap in the curtain, he could see Lady Beaulieu already engaged in the second act of their séance show. Now she used a spirit trumpet, which was really nothing more than a long cone-shaped work of papier-mâché painted in wavy lines of green and yellow.

Timing was everything in this show and he had arrived just in time. His part in this act was crucial. Charlene had selected a woman this time, a petite young lady dressed in simple clothing and a bonnet. Their research had revealed that she wanted to address her deceased father about an inheritance. Charlene had already heard the question and was in the middle of her head-swinging/humming ritual, clutching the spirit trumpet to her bosom.

Without warning, she flung her arms wide, freeing the spirit trumpet to float in mid-air and rise toward the ceiling. Leland winced when the thread dragged over a rough spot in his pulley system, causing the trumpet to shimmy once during its slow rise. Even so, it achieved its intended effect if he could judge by the slight gasps from around the table. Tying off the thread on a boat tie behind the curtain, he remained confident that the dim candlelight wouldn't reflect off the dull brown thread and give away the trick. The trumpet came to a smooth stop, broad end pointed down toward the assembly as if ready to speak from the heavens.

"Lady Beaulieu . . . Lady Beaulieu . . .". The deep masculine voice seemed to issue from the trumpet rather than the end of a rubber speaking tube that stretched from Leland's lips to a spot near the top of the ceiling. "Lady Beaulieu . . ." he said through his end once again.

"Calvin Baxter, father of Molly Baxter. Hear the plea of your daughter." Charlene stated, keeping her slender arms wide, palms up toward the ceiling. "Molly wishes to know where you hid your gold. It is her rightful inheritance after all."

Leland improvised a response, knowing Charlene would recognize a change in the script and understand he was trying to communicate something to her. "Lady Beaulieu . . . 'tis a hidden cache. Hidden for good cause. Here be claim-jumpers. Molly beware. Search your heart and there the treasure be. Lady Beaulieu . . . to the left one step. There your quarry be . . . bounty enough for all."

Leland peeked through the curtain's gap again and saw Charlene nod once. "We understand, Calvin Baxter. Molly must search her heart for her true inheritance and this will lead her to the gold."

Good. Charlene had picked up on his clues and was ready to proceed to the next act and chase Wayne Cade out into the open. Looking over at Owlswick, he noted the man's cool demeanor. He seemed in his element, confidant. A good lawyer, no doubt. A good match for Charlene? A way to get her out of this wild bounty-hunting life and into a more normal and respectable one? She could do worse than a young up-and-coming attorney.

"The spirits are restless," Charlene said to her audience as she stood up. She gazed around at the participants at the table although it was hard to make out their faces in the dim candlelight. "We've had two successful contacts so far but I sense further contacts may not be forthcoming." She let a few murmurs of dissatisfaction resonate before cutting them off. "This sometimes happens when one or more of the séance participants is hiding something. There are no secrets on the other side of the veil but the spirits can sense secrets among the living." More grumbles. Somebody cleared their throat. Mustn't let them become too disgruntled.

"But do not worry, I have encountered this before." A second candle appeared in her hand, seemingly from nowhere. Unlike the pure whiteness of the first candle, this one was of a reddish hue. Leaning forward to light the new candle from the old, she paused, letting her necklaces swing forward, catching the light. Once the new candle was lit, everything would have to be perfectly timed. She had practiced the forthcoming maneuvers with Leland over and over until they had it right every time. But only three times with a live audience and one of those had just barely succeeded. No help for it. She switched the two candles and lit the new one, placing it in the holder in the center of the table.

It sizzled a little at first but soon settled down to a nice steady flame. The scent of cinnamon wafted among the gathering.

"Cinnamon soothes the spirits. I can already sense they are calmer. If we are lucky, they may be responsive to our requests for contact." She sat down at her place once again and immediately looked at the man at her left. Cade.

"You, sir. Your aura is the strongest in the room and most likely to pierce the veil and establish contact." Cade looked nervous and ready to bolt for the door. Need to calm him, she thought. Don't use his name or he will flee. Have to get him to admit to who he is and seek forgiveness for his crime. That won't be easy.

"Sir, I know you have experience in speaking with your wife. Though she passed over several months ago you and she can still communicate. Even without a medium such as myself present. Perhaps it would ease your mind and soul if you could speak directly with her and not merely hear her voice. I believe, considering the strength of your aura, that I can coax her spirit to our side of the veil so you can not only speak with her but see her with your own eyes. We will attempt it here, now."

Cade's eyes were as wide as saucers above his gaping mouth.

Charlene pressed on, knowing time was running out for this phase. "All I need you to do is focus your thoughts on her. Concentrate. Put all your energy into picturing her in your mind. Say nothing aloud as that will break the pathway through the veil. Your companions here at the table will support you through their hand contact, ensuring the circle remains strong and the energies remain pure. We will know it has started working when the candle goes out. Do not be alarmed as that is simply a signal from beyond. It means a pathway from that world to ours is beginning to form." Charlene's eyes moved from one person to the next as she spoke, ensuring their rapt attention. "This won't take long but it is important that everybody in the circle look up to the heavens and think only of strengthening the pathway. If everybody lends their mental strength, and the circle of hands is not broken, then the pathway will become complete. You will know it is so when the candle re-lights. Then sir, at that exact moment, you must shout out your wife's name. If any of these steps are not followed to the letter, then the pathway will not be fully formed and no visitation will occur."

Cade had been listening, jaw now closed and set, eyes boring into hers, a look of confidence permeating his face. He nodded.

She returned the nod and said, "Begin now."

Cade closed his eyes, squeezing them tight as he concentrated. Charlene began her head swinging motion once again but altered it somewhat, looking straight up periodically as if seeking divine guidance. Any second now. Just have to keep it up . . .

Suddenly, the candle went out leaving the room in complete darkness. One of Leland's stunts, of course. It was a trick wick that was timed to go out after a set period which had now expired. Inside the wax was a bit of magnesium, shielded from oxygen and cooled by liquid paraffin. Once the flame went out it was just a matter of time before the ember ignited the magnesium dust. Leland had constructed the wick with enough distance between the magnesium and the still-burning ember to last about a minute. Charlene would only have that long before the magnesium dust would relight the paraffin vapor, bringing the candle flame back to life.

Ducking behind the curtain, she yanked off her black wig and stripped off her red dress, letting it fall to the floor even as Leland lowered a large diaphanous gown over her shoulders. It dropped into place in an instant, designed with speed in mind. No arms to worry about, just a neck hole with an attached hood that draped over her entire head, hiding her flaming red hair and most of her face. Charlene divested herself of all necklaces and bracelets while Leland began pump-spraying a clear sticky substance all over the gown. Where it landed, it began to glow with a phosphorescence. Leland's spray-on concoction included oil of phosphorous, a substance he had also added to the bucket currently perched above the outside of the front door.

Taking a deep breath, Charlene composed herself as she awaited the candle coming back to life and Cade's shout out for his dead wife. Leland kept spraying, filling any gaps that he missed on the first pass. He did pause to wink at her and whisper, "This is it, Charlie. Don't forget to turn on your specter voice when you talk."

And then, just as expected, Charlene saw the candle reignite. She stepped through in all her glowing glory before anybody's eyes could adjust.

At that exact same time came the shout from Cade, "Major Rufus Bradford!"

Silence reigned throughout the room. Nobody so much as breathed. Charlene stood like a statue just in front of the curtain, hood pulled low across her face. That hid her mortified expression from those in the room but inside she was fighting down panic. Cade was supposed to call for his wife. How could she now be Major Bradford when she was dressed as a woman?

No help for it. Time for improvisation.

"Mister Cade, is it?" Charlene dropped her voice a full octave and added a little warble to the vowels. She'd practiced this "specter" voice a lot over the past week, preparing for this scenario. For what it was supposed to be, that is. "The Major is not willing to speak with you so he sent me in his stead. I am Cornelia, his wife." She was guessing at the name but figured Cade wouldn't know it either.

"But," Cade said, "I need to speak with Major Bradford! He can prove that I didn't shoot him. It was the man who was standing next to me that done it. I'm sure your husband saw him, even if nobody else did." Cade's voice held a warble of its own.

"Mr. Cade." Charlene moved forward a single step, keeping the hood pulled low and allowing the candle to light her features from the underside. She knew this would

405

serve to enhance the eeriness. "I did not cross the veil to hear you try and blame your terrible deeds on another. You seem to forget that I was also struck that fateful day. By a bullet from your gun. Best if you admit your guilt and confess before man and God. As for my husband, you will be lucky if he does not hunt you down and haunt you."

Cade was furious. "I'm innocent, I tell ye. It's the Knights who's behind the whole thing. I'm innocent!"

Charlene almost forgot to lower her voice but caught it just in time. "The Knights?"

Another guest chimed in, the dandy that had been sitting next to Leland at the beginning. "You mean the Knights of the Golden Circle? I've heard they're trying to get a chapter started around here."

An older swarthy woman added, "Oh yes. I've heard that too. Trying to raise money for their ridiculous cause. It started with that George Bickley character, you know. He's the founder. My husband knows all about it. He says they have this goal where they hope to form a slave-holding empire that works like the East India Company. Something about annexing Mexico, the Caribbean Islands, and Central America, I think, into the US and calling it The Golden Circle. Hogwash, if you ask me."

Cade, sensing at least part of the group was on his side piled on. "It's my partner that shot the Major." He paused but then added an afterthought, "And yourself."

"Your partner?"

"In my silver mine. He put up some seed money back when I was desperate to expand. I needed more money to buy the bigger tools, you see. Hire a couple strong backs. I had to give up ten percent but I figured it was worth it." Cade peered around the dimly lit room, frantic for people to believe him. He was breathing hard like he'd just finished a race. Charlene could see his knuckles had turned white where they gripped the hands of the poor guests on both sides of him. "And now that I've tapped a rich new vein, he wants it all! He's trying to blame me for the shooting so he can get his hands on my silver and use it for the Knights. Don't you see?"

Charlene paused to think. Could it be true? Had Cade been set-up?

"Mr. Cade," she resumed, "I will need to speak with my husband but I suspect he knows no more than I do of any partner of yours. Your blathering has no proof behind it and I rather think your attempts to contact my husband are but a way to cast your own guilt elsewhere."

"But I *do* have proof! Here, look at my wrists!" He dropped his neighbor's hands and shoved up his sleeves. "See? No marks! The man who shot Major Bradford had a tattoo on his wrist. Three letters. 'KGC'. Major Bradford had to have seen it as plain as I did when the man's sleeves rode up a little. When he stretched his arm out to shoot."

Cade was desperate. But whether that desperation grew from a guilty conscience or a frame up, she couldn't be sure.

Uncertain what to say next, Charlene stalled a moment by letting out a long sigh. "I grow tired. I must retreat to the other side and rest. But I will speak to my husband about this."

A series of tiny pops sounded from overhead. Leland had remotely set-off a string of minuscule firecrackers near the ceiling, made from one of his chemical concoctions. He had been waiting for Charlene's cue that she was about to leave. As the startled séance participants looked up toward the ceiling, Charlene reached a hand out from under her glowing gown and pinched out the candle, bringing the room back to utter blackness. Then she darted back behind the curtain.

■ ■ ■ ■

Leland met her and began the quick-change process of turning her back into Lady Beaulieu. "Not sure what to make of that," he said.

"Well, it sure wasn't a confession." She'd started to escape the phosphorescent gown knowing Leland waited on her to lift her arms to receive the scarlet dress over her head.

Her eye caught Owlswick's nearby.

A single drop of sweat ran down the side of his face. Odd, considering the cold February weather. He hadn't needed to exert himself so why the sweat? His eyes flitted from the curtain, to Charlene, and back to the curtain.

"Wait a minute . . ." she began. "You have a mark on your wrist . . ."

Leland paused, saw the direction of her gaze, and turned to face the lawyer. He saw the same drop of sweat, the furtive glances. The man was poised to run.

And then it all made sense. The territory of Colorado had many southern sympathizers and a great potential to "go South" as it was said. Many thought strong feelings from both sides had fueled the so-called "Claim-

Jumper's War". An assassination of a pro-Union leader like Major Bradford would serve to bring the matter to a boil. Couple that with a chance to take over a rich silver mine and use it to fund a new chapter of the KGC and you had a recipe for tipping the balance.

Owlswick had brought this case to them. His smooth southern charm belied his deviousness. Leland could see it clearly now. Cade would be an easy mark for a smooth-talking lawyer. Not hard to suspect such a rough-edged man in a shooting. A man arrested and hanged, even if innocent, would clear the way. The fact that Cade was a negro was all the better for a KGC operative.

The tattoo would be the proof. Charlene thought she'd seen a birthmark, but it could have been a tattoo. Leland stared at Owlswick, hesitant to accuse but reading the panic rising in the man. Why so nervous if not guilty?

Owlswick could take no more. He scurried for the door but Charlene, now free of her glowing gown and dressed only in her skimpy undergarments, moved to block the exit. Leland raised his clenched fists, prepared to put the boxing experience from his youth to work once again.

But Owlswick was younger, faster, and desperate. One blow from a meaty fist was enough to pound through Leland's defense and smash his jaw. Leland collapsed, bouncing off a wooden chair before landing on the floor. The lawyer, astonished at his successful punch, looked up at Charlene, saw her look of horror rapidly turning to anger, and decided to try a different route to escape. He smiled at her and said, "Ah, my dear. What could have been . . .". His eyes took in her abundant amount of visible skin, his leer growing in intensity. Blowing her a kiss, he scooted through the curtain without a backward glance.

"I'm fine, Charlie," Leland managed to blurt through the pain of a smashed lip. A trickle of blood fell and she could see more blood surrounding his teeth. "Don't let him get away!"

From the other side of the curtain, they heard Wayne Cade cry out, "That's him! The one that done shot Major Bradford!"

Cade's pronouncement had caused a ruckus in the main room if the sounds coming from there were any indication. Somebody knocked a chair into the curtain allowing a brief glimpse of the tumult; there would be no rescuing the show now. But no matter. It had served its purpose and brought their quarry into the open.

The real quarry.

But there was no sign of Owlswick. He must have run from the scene. The only way out was the front door.

Charlene clenched her jaw and started to throw on the red dress, intent on chasing after Owlswick. But there was no time. She settled for throwing the green cape about her shoulders then charged barefoot through the side door and around the side of the house. Stopping short, she saw the bucket lying empty on its side near the front door, a glowing puddle of phosphorescent paint having spilled from it. Shining footprints angled away toward the street, clear evidence that Owlswick had at least stepped in the substance as he'd made his escape.

Charlene's loose cloth drawers only reached to mid-thigh and her short sleeveless cloth undershirt didn't reach past her ribs. But the cold night air didn't faze her as she scampered after the footprints. Her thoughts swiveled between catching up to the culprit that had punched her grandfather and feeling conned by a handsome smooth talker. That wasn't fair. To con others was one thing but to be conned was something else.

The ground was partly covered from the

light snow but the glowing footprints shown through like beacons as she approached Ferry Street. Her heavy makeup was still in place and was beginning to sweat into her eyes. By the time she reached the corner of Wazee, the prints began to peter out and she could barely tell when they abruptly turned south.

Ahead she thought she could see a whitish blob angle off the street. The glowing substance on his feet might have worn off but not from the rest of his clothes where it had spilled. Had he realized he was glowing and needed to hide?

When she arrived at the spot, she turned left into an alley next to the post office. And there he was. The stylish lawyer hunched over behind a pile of garbage sacks trying frantically to scrub the shimmering slime off his shoulders.

He glanced up at Charlene, shook his head once and said, "Come here. Help me get this off."

She could see the stylized 'KGC' tattoo on his wrist as he flapped about. "You fiddle headed bottom-feeder!" Charlene spat. "You set up an innocent man to take the fall for your murders!"

"Innocent! Cade is not innocent. He needs to be taught his place and if he is punished to further the cause of freedom, then so be it."

"Freedom? Is that what you think you're about? Seems more like you want to take freedom away!"

Owlswick scoffed at her, maintaining his superior attitude. Other people were starting to appear now, forming a small crowd. Some, Charlene identified from the séance. But without her long black wig and Lady Beaulieu outfit, she doubted any of them would recognize her.

Owlswick started to peel off his jacket having given up on trying to brush it off. Charlene saw her chance.

Just as he had the jacket down around his elbows, she charged, ramming her shoulder hard into his flat stomach. His breadbasket as Leland was want to say. They both toppled to the ground but he had freed an arm and used it now to grab her cape and force her face into his chest. Some of the phosphorescent paint got in her hair but that was the least of her worries.

His grip was strong as he squeezed. Charlene felt herself getting dizzy and knew she had to act soon. No hope that any of the onlookers would step in and help. She'd have to do this on her own.

Balling a fist she thought of his duplicity

and used that power to ram it into Owlswick's crotch. She heard groans coming from some men in the crowd even as Owlswick grunted. But he maintained his grip on her cape so she relaxed, twirled, and managed to stand up, freeing herself from the garment. She punched him once in the jaw and then swirled around on one leg, bringing the full power of the other to his face in a fierce roundhouse kick. Her heel slammed into the bridge of his nose bringing a fountain of blood spewing forth and knocking him back into the sacks of garbage.

Charlene stood back, waiting for him to climb back to his feet when she would kick him again. She knew she had to stay out of his reach and away from his superior strength.

One hand covering his nose, Owlswick started to rise to his feet, taking his time to try and regain a little dignity. Pushing aside a stained burlap sack that reeked of spoiled cabbage he suddenly grabbed it and flung it at Charlene. She managed to dodge to the side but it was sufficient for him to dash the other way, back toward Wazee street. Charlene recovered in an instant and ran after him.

Speeding down the street she knew they were near the edge of town and edging closer to the banks of the Platte river. If she couldn't catch him by then he might well escape. But she also figured she was in better shape and could keep up with him for now.

Ahead, she saw him slip on a patch of snow. Not much, but enough to stagger his gait. She dove at his ankles not seeing a large tree looming in the darkness right in the middle of the street until she was already airborne. They came down in a tumble, arms and legs tangled like a couple of mating spiders.

Charlene grabbed him around the waist to keep him from getting to his feet again, only to realize he wasn't moving at all. He had gone limp in her arms, his chin lolling on his chest.

"That's enough honey. I think you got him." It was Leland smiling down at her through blood-stained teeth, trying to catch his breath. Cade stood next to him smiling in relief. "I can get the handcuffs on him now. Between you and the tree, he's been knocked senseless."

She peered up at the odd-looking tree that grew in the middle of the street noting its thick twisting branches sticking straight out and then arching up out of sight into the night like the devil's pitchfork. She began to relax. Taking a deep breath, she disentangled herself, climbed to her feet, and realized how cold the night air was and just how few clothes she was wearing.

"Well, Pops, you know after I let Slippery John slither through my fingers, I wasn't about to let this fish wiggle off the line."

Leland frowned at her. "Don't you worry, we'll meet up with Slippery John somewhere down the road and you'll get a second chance. But for now, let's revel in this victory, shall we?"

She grinned back at him.

"That's the Hanging Tree," said a skinny young man wearing a white shirt and black suspenders. "The one he crashed in to. Seems appropriate somehow. Maybe we could just cut to the chase and string him up right now."

Leland shook his head. "No. We worked too hard for this, even if we were chasing the wrong man. He'll stand trial." He leaned down and whispered to his granddaughter, "And I suspect we can still get a substantial reward."

Another bystander spoke up. It was the portly older woman from the séance who had told of the KGC. How had she managed to run here so fast? "I never thought I'd see a grown man in our town brought to justice by a soiled dove, but it seems so. Them ladies of the evening can sure fight like cornered cats."

Leland draped his long coat over his granddaughter's shoulders, wiped some of the thick makeup off her eyelids, beamed at her and just said, "That's my Charlie."

Benjamin Thomas is a retired US Air Force Medical Service Corps officer, having enjoyed medical assignments all over the US and in several hospital administrator positions in Germany and The Netherlands. Benjamin is the author of several short stories in a variety of genres as well as a science fiction time travel novel. Besides reading, writing, and reviewing, Benjamin is an active paperback hunter, as evidenced by several rooms of his house devoted to them.

NIGHT TRAIL
G. WAYNE TILMAN

The red Wells Fargo stage sped along the straight portions of the Santa Fe Trail and hurled around curves, George Blaine expertly getting the most out of the six-horse team and the Abbot-Downing Concord coach. He ran the horses hard, knowing a fresh team waited at the next station. He was one of Wells Fargo's best stage drivers. And, shotgun guard, Cimarron Kincaid, was legendary. His shotgun, and sometimes his Colt, ended robberies, often before they started. Most recently out of Trinidad, Colorado, Blaine and Kincaid were on a long run. It went from Santa Fe all the way to Independence, Missouri.

As the stage sped around a curve in the road passengers sliding sideways on the hard, flat seats, Blaine saw a freshly cut tree dragged across, blocking his path. He could not avoid it and several of his horses stumbled as they tried to plow through it. The stage wheels hit the five inch diameter log with its branches still attached. The Concord cleared it, but the jolt threw Kincaid soaring through the air. The stage teetered and fell over on its side. The horses, some already injured, were broken loose from the stage, though still harnessed together.

George Blaine hit the side of the road hard. Even though he was dazed, he reached for his Smith & Wesson Schofield revolver. A rifle bullet ended his draw before he cleared leather.

Kincaid landed badly, breaking his leg and one arm. It did not matter. Another rifle spoke and his form twitched.

Six masked men moved forward. Two were the riflemen, four had revolvers drawn and at the ready.

Scared and injured passengers were trying to crawl out of the coach. But, they had to exit by the skyward-facing side door, since the Concord laid on its side. Several stage robbers clambered up to assist. Not because they were decent humans. They were anything but decent.

They just intended to rob the passengers. As the three male passengers, a woman and one child were lifted out, other robbers tore the strong box, the drummer's case and passengers' luggage from where they were secured at the rear of the coach, under a canvas tarp.

A shot rang out as the leader of the gang, Bill Pierce, destroyed the strong box's padlock. It was standard Wells Fargo issue: an iron-strapped wooden box painted green and big enough to hold a Stetson without wrinkling it. It had a hasp with a now-destroyed padlock. He threw open the lid with the alacrity of a starving man digging into a plate of food. His sidekick, Henry Olson, watched greedily. Green money and shiny gold coins filled it.

The four others began to frisk and question the passengers. One drummer sold cheap revolvers to general merchandise stores. His valise of wares was welcomed by the robbers.

The other drummer sold various elixirs, the bottles of which claimed to cure about everything, including maladies the listed name of which had no medical provenance. He was a snake oil salesman.

One of the four robbers pistol whipped him. "Which one of these has alcohol? And, a lot of it?" he asked. "All of them. That's why people like them, you fool!" the drummer said through broken teeth. The next pistol blow to the side of his head collapsed him with a probable concussion. None of his miracle elixirs could provide relief for the blow. Or, much else.

The traveler provided a gold pocket watch and a thick wallet with bills and gold coins. They relieved him of an English bull dog revolver. It was quite effective for a hideaway, but they were unaware of how difficult it would be to find the next six cartridges here in the American West.

Then came the woman. One man grabbed her inappropriately and was struck in the jaw by another. Even among thieves, women were generally treated with respect. Time would tell in this situation.

The woman, twenty-nine year old Jenny Bonner, was a comely redhead. Her beauty was now hidden by abject fear. Her fear was not for herself, but for her son, Tommy. Jenny was tough and had handled the death of her husband in an accident, loss of their ranch, and the near loss of Tommy due to pneumonia six months before. But, now her sole concern was her son. If the boy were to be hurt or killed, she just could not survive the anguish.

"You men! Unharness the horses standing there broken loose from the stage. Shoot the injured ones and pick two good ones to take with us." Shots rang out again as the men put the wounded animals out of their misery. Pierce and Olson checked the two Wells Fargo men. The driver was down for the count. They were not too sure about the shotgun guard, so Olson shot him again. Kincaid's Greener shotgun was broken in half in the fall, and Olson kicked it to the side of the road.

"The woman and boy are going with us. They may have some money value beyond just keeping a posse from opening up on us," Pierce ordered.

Then, Pierce made a good decision, despite his lifelong history of bad ones. He realized the woman and boy could not ride one of the stage horses bareback. At least not very fast.

"Utter! Put the woman and the boy on your horse. You ride one of the stage horses and lead one more. We can sell them," Pierce ordered.

Jenny Bonner was helped up on Utter's horse, with Tommy behind her. She knew her ankles and calves were drawing too much attention for the day and time. Pierce signaled to ride and the six men, one woman and one boy galloped off. They left two bodies, two shaken men and one unconscious one. Wrecking a coach and killing two men constituted a botched robbery by anybody's definition. Pierce knew this. He also knew he would have the law on his trail. Worse, he would have Wells Fargo after him with a vengeance. And, Wells Fargo did not give up.

It was late afternoon in Trinidad, Colorado. Wells Fargo agent in charge, Homer Withrow looked forward to getting home to his wife. More specifically, he looked forward to getting home to the meal he knew she was preparing. It had been a busy day and he skipped the sack lunch he brought to work. His stomach growled like a mountain lion fighting for a piece of a downed elk. Nobody was close enough to hear it though. The telegraph operator was across the building at his own workspace. The cashier was doing the night money count in the vault and the new detective was doing . . . well, Withrow did not know exactly what he was doing.

He was a tall and quiet man, sent personally by Chief Detective James B. Hume. Withrow reckoned, along with many folks, Hume was equal in stature to Allan B. Pinkerton as a detective. He had been Wells Fargo's chief detective for going on twelve years. And he, or his men, always got their man.

Those facts being known to Withrow, he

figured the new man was probably going to be pretty good. Only time would tell.

Withrow, in his dark uniform with the standup collar and Wells Fargo badge, was an imposing figure of officialdom. And, he was a highly respected manager within the spreading Wells Fargo network of freighting, stages, pony express and train express services. If it had to do with valuables or people to be delivered somewhere safely and on time, Withrow's well-run company was the best.

He heard a message coming in from forty feet away. Withrow watched as the telegraph operator began to receive and write the text of a message. Withrow saw the worried look on the operator's face. It prompted the Trinidad manager to unlock a drawer in his desk and remove a hardback, black book. It had gold embossed writing on the cover which read Wells Fargo Money-Transfer Cipher Book. He knew the ciphers or word exchange codes by heart. But, he would still need the book. The codes were determined by how many words there were in the telegram. And, Withrow did not know how many words — yet.

The gravity of the situation was further shown by the speed at which the operator cleared the space and handed the superintendent the message.

"Good heavens!" Withrow thought, it was not in code at all. He took it and nodded at the operator in thanks. Out of the corner of his eye, he saw the detective rise and start his way.

As he read, he knew the new detective's time to shine had come. He turned to Detective John Pope as he arrived beside him.

"Pope, this is from Hume. The number 780 stage on the Santa Fe Trail has been robbed. It left from here in Trinidad this morning and was hit somewhere in the Hole in the Rocks and Timpas area. It was before the home station in Bent's Fort," Withrow said, referring to the bigger station with a kitchen and food for passengers.

"The driver and the shotgun guard were both shot to death. The passengers were robbed but the men were not seriously harmed. However, Hume advises a young mother and her boy were taken. He wants you to go up there and get enough information then get on the trail after the robbers. Mainly, try to recover the mother and boy safely. There were six murderous miscreants who did this. I will be getting a detailed account of the items taken from the passengers and the waybill about the money in the strongbox. That will give me sufficient idea about our automatic reimbursement for customer losses. The strong box had money being transferred to a bank in Independence, Missouri. The amount was noted as five thousand fifty dollars, mixed paper and gold." Pope wrote all of this down in a leather-bound notebook, using a pencil sharpened by his Barlow pocket knife.

The telegraph operator brought another message over. It said a freighter picked up the male victims and took them ten miles north to Timpas.

"So, this was on the Santa Fe Trail Mountain Branch through Colorado, not the Cimarron Cutoff that connects Santa Fe with Cimarron, Kansas? I'm still trying to get the hang of the geography here," Pope said.

"Yes, exactly! I have already, or will shortly, put together everything I need for my part in compensating victims, including the bank, and getting a stage back on the run. Hopefully this one is not damaged too badly. Do you need a draft or cash to begin your search for the robbers?" Withrow asked.

"Thank you, I believe I am okay as to travel needs. I will grab my saddle bags, bedroll and long gun from my rental cottage and get on the way," Pope said.

"Detective, the second telegram says the alert about the robbery came from an Oteros County deputy after a freighter picked up the three male passengers and took them to Timpas. There is no information on which way the robbers went or how the woman and child are. Nobody has been back to the crime scene," Withrow said.

Pope walked over to the map of the Santa Fe trail with the mountain and Cimarron cutoffs and showing the rest of the way to Independence, Missouri. He reckoned he could get to the crime scene for a quick look in five hours. That would be around ten o'clock tonight. Then, he would follow whatever trail he could find for the woman and the boy. Tracks would be difficult on the well-worn trail, even with eight horses, assuming the woman and boy each had one. Or, they might be riding double. The robbers were likely to stop for the night. If he hit their trail, the camp was where he would get them. He always had a pair of iron nippers in his gear. But, not enough pairs to handcuff six men. Thoughts ran through his head, but he dismissed them to get home and saddle up and hit the trail.

With a salute, the detective left for his small cottage, where he strapped on his longer belt holster. His daily carry bird's head grip Merwin & Hulbert had a three and a half inch barrel. The finely machined revolver's barrel was changed to a seven inch one within seconds. Pope's gun belt had bullet loops with .44-40 cartridges surrounded its circumference. He traded his suit coat for a dark canvas jacket. It was wool-lined. Pope saddled his horse in the small stall behind the house and added his canteen, saddle bags and bedroll. He put his rifle scabbard on the saddle and added a lariat. A canteen of fresh water and bag of jerky, corn pone and biscuits from the local café were added to the usual stock of beans, flour, salt and coffee he kept in a saddle bag. The last thing he added was a small Dietz police lantern with a flash beam. He had used it as a detective with San Francisco Police Department. Pope kept it filled with whale oil and added a small metal container of the oil to a saddle bag.

A long black duster over the cantle of his saddle, and he was ready to ride.

Pope's horse was a fine trail animal. He was a buckskin Morgan, fifteen hands high. Pope had used him in pursuit of several groups of fugitives in his first Wells Fargo office, Denver. He had named him Jim, after his boss, James B. Hume, but had neglected to share the significance of the name to anyone.

Jim hit a solid canter and Pope let him determine his speed. They stopped for several breathers and water. It had become pitch dark an hour into the ride north from Trinidad.

At ten o'clock, Pope came upon the crime scene. He dismounted and energized the Dietz lantern, focusing the beam on the stage laying on its side, the dead horses. The tree had been moved, probably by subsequent travelers. He scanned the side of the road with the lantern until he found the driver and guard. Some traveler had kindly moved them off the edge of the road and onto the grass beyond. They even still had their guns. He removed his hat and looked at them in the lantern's light. The one nearest the shotgun had a close-up gunshot wound. Pope could tell from the powder burns surrounding it. He had one distance wound. The other man, clearly the driver, had a single wound. His jacket did not show powder burns, so he was shot from more than several feet away. He walked around with the lantern looking for the lockbox. He found it cast aside, open and empty.

The presence of the victims' guns told the

detective the robbers were in a hurry. Maybe they had panicked from causing the wreck. The road was full of horse prints from traffic. Pope checked the shoes of the dead horses. They were all shoed the same and he memorized the shoe characteristics. He would seek a group of horses with one or two shoed like these, probably toward the middle of the pack. Those would be the prints for the woman and boy. "Still a long shot . . ." Pope thought to himself.

The robbery had taken place between two and four o'clock, Pope figured. Trinidad had been notified just before five. If the freighter had discovered them and delivered the victims to Timpas, that would have taken a couple hours. The stage ride from Trinidad would have taken until two or three. "So," Pope asked himself, "which way would the robbers have gone?" They didn't back track west towards Hole in the Rock or Frost's way station. He had come along the trail through both. If the freighter picked up the victims quickly — and he had to in order for them to have gotten to Timpas before five, people in Timpas would have seen six men and their captives riding with someone riding bareback on horses as they were coming through. Nor did the freighter with the victims come upon them.

Pope did not remember any cut off trails between the crime scene and Timpas. He concluded unless they left the Santa Fe Trail and took a wide circle around Timpas, which was probable, they may have moved off the road to camp and split the money. He then discounted the early camp idea. They knew posse's might come from either or both directions and they did not want to be caught between two, camping just off the road.

So, Pope concluded circling Timpas and getting east of it before a hue and cry was made was the most logical. He knew criminals were not always logical. But, nobody had seen these riders with their notable hostages. This worked better than any other idea he had to act upon. Keeping the lantern lit, but away from Jim's side, Pope rode on. This time, he held Jim to a walk, searching for signs with the lantern's shaft of light along the way.

Jenny Bonner tried to remain stoic about her and Tommy's circumstances. But, it was difficult. She had seen these men kill two people and pistol-whip one. Each had looked leeringly at her ankles and calves as she rode. She worried what they might do, and worse, what her little boy might see.

Jenny knew there was little law enforcement between towns and suspected her chances of rescue were somewhere between slim and none. Her only option would be to escape with Tommy. Somehow. It was the "how" part of somehow that she did not have a clue about. Perhaps God would send her a sign. She had grown up going to church, but the yelling, exhorting preacher had turned her against organized religion. She reckoned if she read the Bible, treated everybody fairly and taught the same kindness to Tommy . . . . well, that would be enough.

Jenny pulled the Lord's Prayer out of her memory and silently mouthed it in the dark as they rode to who knows where.

Pierce had questioned Jenny during the ride. He was clearly trying to determine her value for ransom. She assured him she had no relatives and there was no value. Then, she realized she may be signing her own death warrant, and Tommy's.

"The folks with money are Wells Fargo," she began. "I bet they'd pay to get Tommy and me back safe and sound."

Pierce bought the logic of her words without response and nothing further was said about the matter. Or, anything else.

They made a wide circle off the main

road. Avoiding a town, she suspected. After another two hours, the leader, Pierce, signaled a stop. The men made camp and gathered wood for a campfire. They must feel pretty confident about not having a posse on their trail, she thought sadly.

A fire was built and two of the gang prepared traditional camp fare of coffee, beans and bacon. Jenny and Tommy gulped the hot coffee. The rider had taken his canteen and nobody had offered water along the way. They were parched.

The night had gotten colder as time progressed. Jenny wore a travel dress and a coat, Tommy wore pants, shirt and coat. But, their outfits were not sufficient for the dropping temperatures. After eating, one of the men tossed her a blanket and she and Tommy wrapped up in it on the cold ground as far away from the group as they would allow. She finally edged to a tree, which was a bit warmer than damp ground.

One man demanded his part of the take. He said he wanted to ride back towards the rough country around Hole in the Rock to lay low for a couple of weeks. Pierce, without counting, gave him an amount likely less than his due and sent him on his way. The leader figured if anyone was following, an unlikely prospect, the out of work puncher, Smith, would delay them and not be able to add anything of benefit to a lawdog or posse.

In addition to being cold, mother and son were stiff and sore. Neither had ridden for a while, and the long ride had been grueling.

Huddled up, they settled in for a cold, miserable night.

Pope rode through the night. He doused the Dietz lantern to save oil. He was pretty sure he was on the right trail anyway. A few miles outside where he guessed Timpas would be, he spotted horse tracks veering off to the left. He dismounted to study the tracks under the light of the Dietz. Sure enough, there were two sets of the tracks he determined to be from the stage team.

Pope let out a sigh of relief. His logic had proven correct. They were circling around Timpas to not be seen with obvious hostages. He reckoned they would stop for the night, if for no other reason, to warm up. He had already donned his duster and was still cold. He wore gloves, but the doeskin gloves where thin enough to not impede his draw. So, they did not offer much in the way of warmth.

Pope wondered about the woman and kid. Were they freezing? How were they being treated. He really needed to rescue them quickly. One against six. It would take creative thinking.

Or, a lot of shooting. A whole lot.

Pope remounted Jim and sped from a walk to a canter. He blew the cold, crisp air out of his nose to better allow odors to come in. Campfire. Cigarette smoke. Close enough, he could maybe even detect the smell of man or horse. He did not want to ride on top of them. He just wanted to figure out where they were so he could formulate a plan to rescue the woman and child safely. If he could get them to Timpas or Bent's Fort, he could double back on the gang and recover the stolen money and make an arrest or two.

He rode on, having no idea one of the robbers was galloping towards him.

Later, he guessed around two in the morning, Pope was cantering. He felt, then heard, the sound of a horse ahead. The sound was increasing. A horseman was coming and faster than a normal traveler.

Pope transferred the .44 from the holster into the covering duster's pocket. He slipped off Jim and left him, reins hanging down and stepped away to protect the horse if things got violent.

In the road, Pope raised his hand and

waved to the rider.

Ev Smith saw a man in dark clothes waving from the road ahead. The man did not seem to have a gun out and was wearing a derby hat. He looked like a traveler whose horse was lame or something. Smith's first thought was to rob him and add to the take from the stage, so he drew his Colt .38 Lightning and held it out of sight at his off side.

"Howdy, mister! Got a horse problem here. Can you give a hand?"

From ten feet, the detective saw the rider's revolver come up between his body and his horse's neck. The muzzle was swinging towards Pope.

Pope drew the Merwin & Hulbert .44 and fired twice. The man fell off his horse and hit the road head first. If the shots did not kill him instantly, the fall did. Pope reloaded before moving forward.

He checked the body. Two shots in the heart. One broken neck. The man did not have a wallet on his person or in his saddlebags. But, he had a letter from his brother addressed to "Hiram Smith, Santa Fe, New Mexico." Also in the saddle bag was a bandanna tied around five hundred dollars of paper and coin. Gold coin.

"Well," he thought, "I've recovered a tenth

of the take from the robbery. Now the hostages. I wish I could have interrogated him . . ."

Pope took the man's jacket in case the woman or kid could use it, his gun belt and the horse. There was no rifle.

He tied ten foot latigos to the reins and led the horse as he proceeded on his trip.

Behind, Hiram Smith lay propped up against a tree, with a note saying "Stage robber Hiram Smith, killed by Wells Fargo detective. Resisted arrest," tucked in his vest.

Not an hour later, Pope smelled wood smoke. It was ahead and off to the right. He thought he detected the distinctive aromas of coffee and bacon. Both made his empty stomach growl. Canteen water and jerky had been a poor excuse for dinner.

He stopped by a grove of trees and tied Smith's gelding to a branch. He knew Jim would stay until called with just his reins dropped to the ground.

Removing his Winchester, Pope began to stalk the unknown distance to the camp.

The fire was burning, though for heat not cooking. The bacon and coffee smell had come from a black frying pan and matching pot. The pan appeared empty but the grease still in it.

There were five men. Pope realized they had not posted a guard. Good for him and bad for them.

He saw the woman and head of the young boy as they laid against a tree, wrapped in a blanket. Both appeared to be asleep.

The wind had picked up and was blowing hard and cold. Sleet was beginning to come down. Or, blow sideways would have been more correct.

Pope circled around through the woods to a point just behind the tree where the hostages slept. Feeling on the ground, he found a small twig. He threw it softly at the woman. She brushed it off in her sleep.

He threw another. Bigger, it hit her on top of the head. This one woke her up and she looked around, vexed.

He moved his arm and flashed his badge at her. She saw it and smiled. Having her attention, he raised a finger to his lips to keep her silent and motioned her to come towards him.

She put her hand over Tommy's mouth and awakened him. She whispered in his ear. They crawled on all fours in Pope's direction. "Smart lady!" he thought.

When they got to him, he took one last look at the camp.

"This was too easy," he thought. Everyone was still asleep. The first thing he would have done after grub was post a guard. Yet, there they were. Snoring like hibernating grizzlies. Except, grizzlies were a lot smarter than these men.

Pope whispered in the woman's ear.

"I am Detective John Pope from Wells Fargo. I have come here for you and your son. Don't say a word and tell your son not to, either."

She nodded and they crawled another fifty feet, then stood and walked carefully to the two horses. Pope helped her up and lifted the half-asleep child on the back. He instinctively hugged his mother around the waist. Pope took both reins and led the two horses onto the road and pointed towards Timpas. He walked them west on the Old Santa Fe Trail for a mile, then mounted. After an interval of thirty minutes, he stepped it up to a canter.

He fell back and watched little Tommy. He was hanging on like a trooper.

"Son, how are you doing?" Pope asked.

"I'm not scared now! But, why didn't you shoot those men?" Tommy asked.

"Sometimes, it's better to quietly leave and go back another day. And, that's just what I'm going to do. I'm going to go back and surprise them and arrest them."

"What if they shoot, Mr. Pope?"

"I guess I'll have to shoot back faster and more accurately."

"I hope they don't hurt you!" Tommy said.

"Me, too, son. Me, too."

Jenny turned to Pope and gave him a radiant smile. Nobody had ever smiled at him like she just did. He smiled back automatically.

Whether she knew or not, she had just gotten through to a solitary, tough detective. He knew it and bargained she did, too.

The youngster saw the detective smile at his mother. Tommy smiled. He liked this tall man in black with his ivory-gripped silver revolver, and his funny hat. Detective Pope made him feel safe. Safe was something the boy had not felt for a while.

Pope maintained the pace all the way to Timpas.

It was almost dawn when they got to the small stage stop town. There was a deputy sheriff's office in town and they went there first. Once Jenny was questioned by the deputy and the Wells Fargo detective and signed a statement about the robbery, murders and their kidnapping, they got her and Tommy a room at the boarding house. It was the closest thing the town had to a hotel. The two lawmen awakened the Western Union operator and sent telegrams to the US Marshal and Wells Fargo Chief Detective Hume. The deputy put together a posse of three to recover Smith's body.

Pope went to the boarding house.

"I just wanted to check on you two and say goodbye. I am leaving to get the rest of the gang," he told Jenny at the door.

She insisted he come in to the meager room and sit in its only chair. She sat on the bed where Tommy slept soundly.

"Oh, Wells Fargo always reimburses customers who were robbed or whose trips were interrupted. I mean, you bought a ticket to Independence and all . . ." For some reason, the presence of the lovely redhead made the tough detective a bit tongue tied.

He took out his wallet and gave her fifty dollars in mixed bills and gold coins. He knew it was too much. He would only expense a small portion of it. But, he knew it was the right thing do. And, what he wanted to do.

Jenny Bonner was taken aback. Pope saw a tear appear in the corner of one eye.

"Detective Pope, that's 'way more than our two tickets. I cannot take all of this!" she said.

"No, you must Mrs. Bonner. I insist. I

would enjoy visiting more than you know, but I have to get on the trail."

"It's too dangerous! One man against five. You'll be killed!" she said, a tear forming.

"It's my job, Ma'am. And, I tend to work alone. I play the odds and am careful. I avoid taking chances as much as possible."

She grasped him and buried her now wet face in his vest, a strong woman whose emotions were finally breaking loose and allowing her to sob aloud.

"Thank you for rescuing Tommy and me! May God ride with you and guide your gun hand, Detective. And," she hesitated, then spit it out "may we meet again soon!"

Pope took one of his Wells Fargo cards from his pocket and pressed it into her hand. She held it against her breast.

"Let me know where you and Tommy land in your journey. I will come to see you. No matter where!" He hugged her closely for a second and stepped out of the door.

Jim had munched grass several times and had water so he should be ready for the trail. Pope filled his canteen from the town pump and picked up several ham sandwiches, some corn pones and a can of peaches at the café, which had just opened. Buying a small bag of feed as a treat for Jim, he turned the horse east and headed out of town.

The day was uneventful and, quite frankly, with his excellent night vision and the Dietz lantern almost nobody in the West had, he preferred tracking fugitives in the dark.

By midday, Pope decided on a day camp and found an area with a stand of cottonwoods well off the Santa Fe Trail. He pitched camp, fed and watered Jim. After putting a hobble on the horse, the detective settled into his bedroll and slept well into the night. During daylight, the derby hat blocked the sun from his eyes.

He awoke, perhaps at ten at night. Without a watch and without the sun or moon, he did not know exactly. What he did know was a thick coating of sleet had covered his bedroll and it was really cold.

He built a small fire, which was his favorite kind. Big fires were a waste of fuel and drew too much attention for a fugitive hunter. Within a half hour he was drinking hot, but not yet strong enough coffee and eating a ham sandwich. Pope buried the embers and the sleet insured the fire was out. He saddled and mounted Jim and they headed east again, Dietz lantern in hand but unlit. He knew he was not close enough, so there was no need to waste precious oil. This promised to be another long night trail.

Pope knew the fugitives would travel a full day to put distance between them and the scene of their crimes. Then, they would camp and sleep until dawn before starting off again. He wished he could have found out more about the leader from Smith. Jenny had not heard anything suggesting Pierce's ultimate destination. Other than forts, they could have been heading to Cimarron, which was the first town in the direction they were heading. Or, on to Dodge City, Diamond Spring, Council Grove, Kansas City or Independence.

Pope would bet on Dodge City, if he was a betting man. They would fit in there and could hide in plain sight. But, even if they were headed there, he wanted to catch them first.

He smelled, then saw the glow of a campfire ahead. As he had done when he rescued Jenny and Tommy, he left Jim in a grove and quietly walked in, this time rifle in hand.

He watched behind a tree. There were three men cooking and talking. None matched the forty-year old, lanky and bald description Jenny had given him on the ride back of Pierce.

Pope decided to chance it.

"Hello, the camp!" he yelled.

Men scrambled for their guns, surprised

in the middle of nowhere.

"Wells Fargo detective. Can I come into the light?"

The men held their guns, but not pointed.

Pope walked in, his 1873 Winchester in his left hand. His right was convenient to the butt of his holstered Merwin & Hulbert, unseen in the dark. His badge was now prominently pinned on the outside of his jacket.

One good thing about his job was Wells Fargo men were universally respected for their efficiency and honesty.

"Gentlemen, I'm looking for five fugitives. They robbed a stage, killed the driver and guard and kidnapped a woman and her boy. Thank God, the woman and boy are back safe now," Pope said.

"What do these fellers look like?" one man, obviously a cowpuncher, asked.

"The leader is a man called Pierce. He's tall, gangly and has a bald head. He's in his forties. I don't have anything on the other four," Pope replied.

"We seen a feller like him leading a bunch before dark," the man said.

"Where?" Pope asked.

"On the road near Bent's Fort. They was riding fast. Gonna wear out their horses that way," he added.

Pope did some quick figuring. If they were at Bent's Fort around time he left Timpas, they would be about twenty-five or thirty miles ahead, riding fast. But, if they met these riders coming west at dusk, they were probably getting ready to bed down soon.

"How soon after you saw them did you stop here for the night?" Pope asked.

"Pretty doggone soon, Detective."

These three men may be the solution to a dilemma Pope had worried about.

"I figure from what you say and what I know of their habits, the fugitives ought to be camped pretty close by. How would you three gentlemen like to make five dollars each for a half-night's work?"

"Might it involve gunplay?" another man asked.

"It might," Pope admitted.

"Make it six each and we're your posse."

Pope stopped and pretended to be thinking it over.

"You boys cut a hard bargain. But, I guess I will do it. Three each now and three when we capture or kill them. I'd rather capture them, unless we have to defend ourselves.

The men nodded and he counted off nine dollars from money folded in his vest pocket. No need to show strangers the wallet.

"Here's what I'd like to do. You," he said, pointing to the first man who spoke, "and I ride ahead to cut sign. The other two ride covering us about a hundred yards back. When we reckon we've found the camp up ahead, I will signal for everyone to stop. We will gather and decide how to hit them. That sound good?" he asked.

"You done this before? I mean, no offense Detective, but you look like an Eastern dandy with the hat and all."

"I have done this many times. And, I was a San Francisco detective for some years before Wells Fargo. We are expected to have a certain image. The hat is part of it."

"Okay, we'll saddle up and check our guns," the apparent leader of the riders said.

"My job is to take these men in custody if at all possible. We have witnesses so at least two will hang for murder. The rest will be tried for robbery, kidnapping and conspiracy to murder. I'd like to think they'd be miserable longer behind bars than for the short time it takes to die from gunshot."

The men nodded. What they would actually do when confronted with the robbers remained to be seen. But, Pope had said his piece. He retrieved Jim while the men saddled up.

They mounted and went two-by-two as

Pope had said.

Much like when he came upon the men in his posse, Pope saw a glow ahead and smelled wood smoke. He held up his hand in the universal sign to halt. The posse dismounted and all but Pope tied their horses to branches. Jim was trained and would stand, reins down until the cows came home.

They approached on foot, the crackling of frozen branches masked by the sound of sleet and wind.

When they saw the men sitting around the campfire, Pope spread his men in a semicircle to give a broader field of fire without shooting one another. Once they were set, he walked into view, rifle at the ready position, and announced "Wells Fargo! Throw up your hands!"

Pierce drew his revolver and Pope killed him with a shot from his Winchester. Unbidden, Pope's shot initiated a volley from the posse. The outlaws shot back until they realized they must be outnumbered by the multiple directions of incoming rounds. They threw their guns down and their hands up.

Pope yelled "Cease fire!" to his men and, to his relief, they complied immediately. In a gunfight where fifty shots or more were fired, the only one struck was the leader, Pierce.

Pope shook his head at this. It proved an aimed shot was always best and most riders could not hit the broad side of a barn.

The posse men moved in from their semicircle and took the stage robbers into custody. Having only one set of nippers, the rest were tied with latigos. All were checked for weapons and the stolen money recovered. It was complete. Only Smith's amount was missing. The greater part of the gang had not split the take yet.

Pope checked the downed man. He was deceased. Removing the hat off the corpse, Pope saw a bald head. He matched Pierce's description. When questioning the prisoners, all said Pierce had shot the driver and shotgun guard. Pope doubted that, but knew there was no way for him to determine a second shooter. Maybe a slick prosecutor would. But, he was taking them back to wild, rural Otero County. It was probably not the kind of place an outstanding prosecutor would call home, at least not in 1884.

"You men want to help me take these prisoners back to Timpas, I will continue paying you at the agreed rate of six dollars per day, plus I'll throw in a dollar bonus for each." All agreed. One or two dollars a day was average for posse men in those parts. This was a bonanza to out-of-work riders.

Pope and his posse men took turns standing guard for the rest of the night. The next morning, breakfast was a mishmash of whatever the riders, Pope and the fugitives had.

"At least the coffee is hot and good," Pope observed to nobody in particular.

The trip back to Timpas was uneventful. The prisoners were formally arrested by the sheriff's deputy and locked up. The posse men were paid in full. The recovered money was put on the next westbound Wells Fargo stage. Pope got a receipt before releasing the recovered funds.

Pope drafted a telegram to Chief Detective Hume which, once unencrypted, would read "Summary regarding Santa Fe stage robbery, murder and kidnapping. I recovered kidnap victims unharmed. All $5,050 recovered and on Stage 799 due to Trinidad office tomorrow. Had to shoot gang leader Pierce and member Smith due to resisting arrest. Both deceased. Other gang members in custody of Otero County, Colorado awaiting trial. Investigative books closed unless you have further. Det. J. Pope." As expected, the operator would put it in wire format with appropriate stops and brevity before keying it.

Before handing the draft of the telegram to the operator, Pope turned to the station master and the deputy.

"Are Mrs. Bonner and Tommy still here?" he asked.

"No, they got on the east bound stage early this morning. Ticket for Independence. She paid with a gold coin. I had to break it for change."

Pope set the telegraph form down and added. "PS: need two weeks emergency leave. JP"

He nodded to the three men standing there as he walked out the door and mounted Jim.

He would catch that darned stage if he had to chase it all the way to Missouri. He galloped off without looking back.

It was going to be another night trail. But, he pretty much knew this one would have a good ending.

G. Wayne Tilman is the direct descendent of a 1680 sheriff, one of the first in the New World. He has bachelors and masters degrees from a southern university. He was awarded the Certified Protection Professional (CPP) designation. It is the highest International board certification in security and law enforcement. He earned a US Coast Guard Master Captain's license (50 gross ton inspected vessels). Tilman has been a Marine, deputy sheriff, investigator, security contractor and FBI Unit Chief. Since retiring from the government, he has been a full-time writer and is the author of sixteen novels. Several have been Amazon Top Sellers.

Taking Bliss Home
TERRY ALEXANDER

Mr. Daugherty walked to the old freight wagon. He grabbed one of the spokes in the wheel and looked up at the gray-haired man on the spring seat. "Now Simms, the sheriff over at Lonesome Oak will be expecting you there about ten o'clock tonight."

The old man nodded. "I'd feel a lot more comfortable, if I was making this run in the daytime."

"Can't be helped. They found old man Bliss yesterday and his wife wants the body returned home for a Christian funeral and burial in the local cemetery." Daugherty moved his hands to his lapels. "Just keep the team moving. Don't stop for nothing."

"Wish the undertaker could have done something about the smell." Simms shook his head. "Can't say I'm looking forward to this trip. Don't see why Mrs. Bliss wouldn't bury her husband over here. He ain't gonna know the difference."

"She's paying good money to have his body delivered home." Daugherty nodded. "You'd best get started. Remember don't stop for anything and don't open that box."

"I won't." Simms popped the reins. The mules leaned into the collars and moved the wagon forward. "Get up there Jim. Come on Tom, get moving." The two mules pulled in concert. The iron rimmed wheels cut into the soft dirt. "Everybody knows that Bliss was sneaking over here to see Beth Cothern. Wasn't like it was a big secret." He popped the reins over the mules a second time.

Three people lined the streets of Redbud to see him off. Preacher McMahon clutched his bible close to his chest, whispering a few verses. Sheriff Bob Reynolds, and Mr. Daugherty, the local attorney stood a short distance away. Simms twisted his body and glanced back at Daugherty. The lawyer stood on the boardwalk. A fresh cigar glowed red in the night marking his position. Simms cursed himself silently for accepting the job. He could be at home with a full belly lying in his own bed, but he was sitting on an uncomfortable wooden seat, taking a week-old corpse twelve miles to be buried. Still the twenty-five dollars he was going to get paid for this job would wipe out his debt at the general store and leave him with some spending money.

He passed the last building. The stars and the weak moon cast scant illumination on the road ahead. Simms used his memory and kept the team and the wagon on the correct path. A white blob appeared next to the road about a hundred feet ahead. Simms knew someone was holding a small lantern aloft to get his attention.

"Can't be bandits. No one in their right mind would want to rob a corpse." He chucked the reins. "Come on, fella. Get in there."

The image gradually solidified into a white horse, with Beth Cothern sitting in the saddle. "Stop the wagon, Mr. Simms." She said as the vehicle drew near. "I'd like to spend some time with Henry."

Simms pulled the team to a halt. "I'm not supposed to stop, Miss Cothern. Mr. Daugherty told me to keep the team moving. I'm supposed to be in Lonesome Oak by ten."

"Let me ride with you in the wagon. I promise, I'll get off before we get to Lonesome Oak." The pain of loss tainted her voice. "It's important to me Mr. Simms. I want to say goodbye. You know I can't go to the funeral."

"Yeah, I know." Simms nodded. "Climb aboard. I figure you've got three hours to say your goodbyes."

"Thank you, Mr. Simms." She swung her leg over the saddle and stepped to the ground. "Come on, Jericho." She led the horse to the rear of the wagon and tied him to the tailgate. She walked back to the front of the wagon and climbed on the wagon wheel to reach the spring seat.

Simms got his first good look at Beth Cothern. She wore a brown shirt and skirt, with high-topped lace up shoes on her feet. A low-brimmed hat sat at an angle on her head. Her dark hair framed her oval face. Wrinkles around her eyes and mouth were beginning to tell her age. She reached out for Simms's hand as she stepped over the wagon seat, giving the old man a look at the calf of her leg.

The old teamster looked away. "Best get a good grip, Miss Cothern. We need to get started."

"Thank you for allowing me to accompany Henry on this journey, Mr. Simms, and please call me Beth," she said.

"Okay, Beth. Get a grip on that box." He popped the reins over the mules. They moved the wagon forward. Within seconds the sounds of subdued crying reached his ears.

"I told you to stop coming to Redbud," a whispered voice mumbled. "I begged you to stop, but you kept making the trip, once a month, regular as clockwork." She paused for a minute to control her shaky voice. "Just to see me."

Simms tried to screen out her words, but they stuck in his head like tar on a rooftop. A howl to his right sent chills up his spine. Wolves, they caught the scent of corruption and they were moving in for a bite to eat.

"Miss Beth, I hate to intrude, but maybe you should get up here with me. Those wolves might jump on the wagon." Simms shifted the old .45 in his coat pocket, getting the grip in a better position should he need the weapon.

"Do you think they'll attack us?"

"I don't think so, but I really don't want to take the chance. Get on up here. They should get discouraged and leave us along after a mile or two."

"What if they're starving? What will they do then?" She left the box and moved to the seat. Her hand settled on the old man's shoulder, as she climbed over the backboard and settled into the spring seat. "Can you get these mules to go any faster?"

"I could, but then one of them might step on something in the road and get hurt, and then we'd really be in a fix. Best to go slow and steady."

"Yes, you're right." She glanced off into the darkness beyond the road. "I loved Henry Bliss. He asked me to marry him once, many years ago and I told him no." She grew silent. "I wanted a rich man. I didn't want to settle for a man trying to build his ranch. I ended up with a low life husband that ran off with a younger woman and left me holding a big sack of bills."

"Here, take the reins." He passed the leather straps to Beth. "I want my hands free in case I have to use this." Simms lifted the pistol from his lap and cocked the hammer.

"All right." Beth nodded. "Do you think the wolves will attack Jericho?"

"If they go after him, he'll kick the dickens out of them." He shrugged. "I can get back there and snap off a shot or two at them."

"Henry bought Jericho for me. I don't want anything to happen to that horse."

"I understand." Simms glanced over into the brush along the road. He caught sight of movement, looked to be three maybe four wolves keeping pace with the wagon.

"After I told Henry no, he started seeing

Ila Happ. They were sparking for a year when she discovered she was with child." She paused a moment, as a low growl came from the darkness. "Henry married her to give his child a name, but he didn't love Ila. Their first child was conceived on a buggy seat. They named her Helen. Henry doted on that girl."

A young wolf ventured too close to the wagon. Simms moved the pistol quickly and snapped the trigger. The animal yelped and ran away into the darkness. A series of low growls and whimpers came from the brush. An animal howled in pain and agony. The unexpected sound produced a burst of speed from the mules. The horse shied to the side and pulled on the reins holding it to the wagon. The braided leather held it fast. The wagon hit a hole at the edge of the road, the box slid forward and nearly knocked Simms to the ground. He caught himself on the siderails and held on.

"They're eating that young one. The pack is hungry, and the scent of blood drove them mad. They're not going to nurse a wounded animal." He climbed over the seat and flopped down on the spring seat. He wiped his forehead with his sleeve and took the reins from Beth. "Here take this." He handed her the pistol. "Shoot if you have to, but I don't really think we'll have any more problems with those things tonight."

"Thank you, Mr. Simms." A long-held breath passed her pursed lips. "That could have been terrible."

"I'm glad I managed to hit that one. That'll keep the others busy and give us some time to get down the road." He stopped for a moment. "It's the odor that's making them act like that."

"I know. The smell of death always brings out the carrion eaters."

They grew quiet for a moment, that stretched into minutes. Simms broke the silence. "I hauled a piano out to Henry's place once. Seems like his wife took a notion to start playing."

"She did." Beth nodded. "I never heard her play myself. Some folks told me she was the worse piano player they had ever heard."

"I heard her play for just a few minutes, and I have to say she didn't impress me much."

The uncomfortable silence returned. Beth turned her head and glanced at the wooden crate. She reached out and touched the rough-cut wood. "You know life is peculiar. I never pictured my life the way it turned out. I always figured to have a husband and kids, maybe be a schoolteacher or something. I never thought I'd be riding in a freight wagon late at night with a man who's delivering a corpse."

The wagon hit a hole in the road, and something thumped in the crate.

"Damn it." Simms cursed. "That hole snuck up on me, hard to see everything."

"Stop for a moment, Mr. Simms." Beth reached out and took his hand. "I'm going home."

Simms pulled back on the reins. The wagon came to a stop. "What? I thought you was going to ride closer to Lonesome Oak?"

"I was, Mr. Simms, but I've changed my mind. I'm going home, I've got a bottle of whiskey that Henry left at my house and I believe I need a drink." She stepped over to the wagon wheel. "Come by for Sunday dinner, Mr. Simms. I'm cooking fried chicken and potatoes. I'll expect you there by one, and I might have a drink of whiskey left over." She hopped down to the ground.

"I'll be there, Beth." He nodded. "Just call me, Simms. Everybody else does."

"Don't you have a real first name?" Beth's hands settled on her hips.

"My given name is Lemuel. Nobody ever called me that though."

"Here, take your pistol. You might need it."

He shook his head. "Keep it, you might run into them wolves again." He rummaged through his coat and found some extra bullets and held them out to her. "I'll get it when I come over Sunday."

She took the bullets and walked back to Jericho then patted the animal's shoulder when she untied him. Her foot slid into the stirrup as she swung up into the saddle. "I'll see you Sunday." She turned and rode into the darkness.

Simms watched, as the gloom slowly absorbed the white blot. "Get up there, Tom, come on Jim." He popped the reins over the mules. He rode in silence for several minutes, his thoughts on Beth Cothern and fried chicken. His arrival on the banks of Dutchman's Creek surprised him. He scratched his whiskered jaw and aimed the wagon at the crossing. A second thump came from the crate.

Chill bumps ran the length of Simms arms, crossed to his spine and ran back to his waist. It sounded like Henry was trying to break out of the coffin inside the wooden crate. His thoughts went back to the long-standing relationship that Henry and Beth enjoyed. Maybe Henry wasn't ready for it to end. Simms pushed the nonsensible thought from his mind and concentrated on crossing the creek bed.

The thump came again, as he urged the mules up the short incline. Simms jumped at the noise. "Ain't no such things as haints. You leave me alone, Henry Bliss. I'm taking you home to Ila whether you like it or not."

The wagon emerged from the creek and the mules moved down the road. A light coating of dust clung to their legs. Simms glanced up at the thin clouds blotting out the moonlight. He passed a gnarled Blackjack tree and knew he was within three miles of Lonesome Oak. The mules sensed their nearness and picked up their pace. Simms gave them their head, knowing they'd be disappointed when they didn't go to the stables and get some of the sweet grass hay old Bishop kept on hand. Their destination lay five miles on the far side of town.

The front wheel dropped into another hole, the wagon lurched to the side, followed by a banging from the crate in the bed. "Simmer down, Henry. You keep bellyaching and I'll have your wife play the piano at your funeral."

The team topped a small rise and began the slow descent into Lonesome Oak. Simms picked out a single bullseye lantern and assumed the sheriff was waiting outside. He gently applied the brake, just enough to slow the wagon and not crowd the mules. "You're nearly home, Henry."

Simms pulled the team to a stop several minutes later. A pot-bellied man by the name of Kincaid came forward leading a chestnut gelding, Simms saw the star pinned to his chest. He tied the horse to the back of the wagon, in the same spot Beth had used earlier. "Bout time you got here. It's coming up on eleven." He tossed his jacket onto the wagon seat and climbed aboard. "Ila wanted us there by midnight. We'll be lucky if we make it by one."

"Had a little trouble with wolves back down the trail. They caught Henry's scent and wanted an easy meal." Simms popped the reins over the mules. "Get up there." The leather creaked as the animals leaned into the collars.

"Wolves, huh." Kincaid licked his lips. "Didn't figure on wolves following the wagon."

Simms shook his head. "Hadn't seen any for a few miles. I think they found an easier meal."

The sheriff nodded. He lifted the lantern and extinguished the flame. "Go straight out of town and take the first right. The

Bliss place is a little over four miles out. Ila is waiting on us."

"I was out at their place once. Hauled a piano out there for her." Simms popped the reins, and got the team moving again. "That road still as rough as ever?"

"Sure is. Can't get in much of a hurry. Take it real slow, and we'll be alright." The sheriff pulled his coat on. "Wish I was in bed right now, but I promised Ila I'd see you got Henry and the casket there safely."

"I made it this far. I imagine I could have found the ranch on my own."

Kincaid nodded. "Maybe so, but you might have got a gutload of pellets. Ila keeps Henry's shotgun loaded with double ought buckshot." He placed the lantern at his feet. "I was out there today. Henry had a real nice spread. Most men would give their eye teeth for a ranch like that."

"Sounds like it impressed you." Simms mumbled.

"Sure did. I can see myself, sitting on that front porch sipping coffee in the morning, giving orders to all the hands." The sheriff grinned.

"Looks like you got everything figgered out."

"Course I'll give her time to grieve over Henry, say about six months. Then I'll get my courtin' clothes on." Kincaid glanced over to the teamster. "I don't want to be a smalltime sheriff all my life."

The wagon hit a rough spot in the road and lurched to one side. Three solid thumps came from the coffin as the crate shifted position.

The sheriff jumped to one side, staring in wild-eyed fear at the crate. "What in the world was that?" His right hand circled his pistol grip.

"That's Henry. He doesn't want to go back to the ranch. He wanted to stay over in Redbud." Simms scratched at his hairy jaw to hide his grin. "He gave me the devil's own time getting him this far. He keeps trying to get out of that coffin. Good thing Crenshaw built it good, or he would have done escaped."

"That's bull, ain't no such thing as ghosts." Kincaid struggled with the words.

Bam, Bam, Bam. The thumping came from inside the crate, as the wagon hit another rough spot.

"Good God. Have mercy on me." The sheriff licked his lips. "Did he do that all the way over here?"

"I told you, Henry fought me the entire way. Told you he wanted to stay in Redbud."

"For my money, you could have left him

there." Kincaid reached for the lamp. The wagon hit another bump, the banging from inside the crate grew louder. "I can't take this." The sheriff grabbed the lantern and jumped from wagon. He bent at the knees and rolled on impact and stood up in one fluid motion. He pulled a match from his coat and lit the wick on the lantern. "Tell Miss Ila I had really important business to take care of in town, and I'll be out tomorrow for Henry's funeral." He untied the horse and swung up in the saddle

Simms grinned. "I'll pass that message along." He popped the reins, absently thinking of Sunday and a chicken dinner. "Proud you took a hand back there, Henry. We need to get you home. I expect Helen will be grieving for you."

He eased the mules along the trail, trying to find the landmarks in the dark. After nearly two hours he nearly missed the turnoff and had to encourage the mules to back up. "Come on, Boys. We're nearly there."

The mumble of voices came to his ears before he spied the single lantern. "Looks like they're waiting for us." He pulled the hat from his head and wiped the sweat away. "Mrs. Bliss, this is Simms. I've got your husband in the wagon."

"Bout time you got here." A rough high-pitched voice answered. "Where's Percy Kincaid. He's supposed to be riding with you, said he'd deliver Henry personal." An older woman stepped toward the wagon, she held the lamp in one hand and a shotgun in the other.

"Said he had some urgent business back in town." Simms pulled back on the reins. The tired mules came to a stop. "Sorry it took so long. Had some problems along the way."

A young woman stepped forward. "Thank you, Mr. Simms. I'm glad you brought my daddy home."

"I was glad to do it." Simms nodded. He stepped down from the wagon and patted the mules. "You boys earned a break. We'll rest fer a little bit fore we head back."

"Joe, get up there and get that crate open." Ila glanced at a heavyset man holding a crowbar and hammer. "I want to make sure Crenshaw followed my directions."

"Yes Ma'am." The old man climbed up into the wagon. The nails screeched as he pulled them from the wood. She passed him the lamp when he removed the lid. "Miss Ila. You need to look at this."

Ila grabbed the man's hand and climbed on the wagon wheel to the bed. She glanced inside the crate. "Crenshaw is a wool-headed idiot. Blasted handle is loose on one side." She turned her scorn to Simms. "I imagine this thing banged all the way here?"

"No Miss Ila, didn't bang at all. Them last bumps we hit must have done it." He hid a smile. "If it's okay with you, I'd like to rest the mules till daylight, then head back to Redbud."

"Put your mules in the holding pasture then go over to the bunkhouse. Get a little shut eye. You can eat breakfast with the hands in the morning."

"Thank you, kindly." Simms nodded. "Appreciate that. I need to get home, I've been thinking on buying me some new clothes and cleaning up some. I'm gonna have a chicken dinner on Sunday."

Terry Alexander lives on a small farm near Porum, Oklahoma. They have three children, fifteen grandchildren, and three great-grandchildren. Terry is a member of the Oklahoma Writers Federation, Ozark Writers League and Tahlequah Writers. He has been published in various anthologies by Airship 27, Pro Se Productions, Oghma Creative Media and Mooonstone books.

The employees of Thorndike Press hope you have enjoyed this Large Print book. All our Thorndike Large Print titles are designed for easy reading, and all our books are made to last. Other Thorndike Press Large Print books are available at your library, through selected bookstores, or directly from us.

For information about titles, please call:
(800) 223-1244

or visit our website at:
gale.com/thorndike